The Subtlest Soul

The Subtlest Soul

Virginia Cox

The Subtlest Soul

© 2013 Virginia Cox

Issicratea
ISBN 9780615778921

Cover art: Paul Greene
The design reproduces a bas-relief in the collection of the National Gallery of Art, Washington (School of Andrea Verrocchio, *Alexander the Great*)

CONTENTS

FOREWORD

*It is necessary for a ruler, if he wishes to survive, to learn
how to be not good, and to employ this skill or not employ it
as necessity demands.*

Machiavelli, *The Prince*

THE PERIOD OF ITALIAN HISTORY in which this novel
is set was an extremely dramatic one. The year 1494
saw the beginning of a series of wars ("The Wars of
Italy") that would continue sporadically until 1559 and saw
their fiercest phase between 1498 and 1512. The chief players in this conflict were the two greatest European powers of
the age, France and Spain, in a series of constantly shifting
alliances with the various states of Italy. All of these Italian
states had their own territorial ambitions and were prepared
to jeopardize the independence of the peninsula while pursuing their own shortsighted ends. Such is the conclusion of
Niccolò Machiavelli's *The Prince* (1513), the most penetrating
analysis of this phase of Italian history and one of the greatest
political works of all time.

The effects of the Italian Wars were far-reaching and
profound. In 1494, the Italian peninsula was occupied by
five major powers—Venice, Milan, Florence, the papacy,
and Naples—and a constellation of smaller ones, including
Ferrara, Mantua, Siena, and Urbino. Most of these states were
governed by single rulers holding the title of duke, marquis,
or, more generically, *signore* ("lord"), though a few cities were

republics, notably Venice, Florence, and Siena. A lesser republic was Fermo, the home town of this novel's protagonist. In the course of the Wars of Italy, two of the largest Italian states, Milan and Naples—the former encompassing most of northwest Italy; the latter, the whole of the south—fell to the French and the Spanish. They would remain in foreign hands until the nineteenth century.

This loss of independence was experienced as a profound trauma in Italy. Even though the peninsula had not been politically unified since the time of the Roman Empire, a strong cultural sense of Italian unity endured, and the subjection of major parts of Italy to "barbarians" from beyond the Alps was a harsh reality to endure. Machiavelli describes Italy in the final chapter of *The Prince* as "without leadership, without order, beaten, stripped, mutilated, ravaged, and subjected to every sort of ruin." Besides political humiliation, Machiavelli refers here also to the huge physical and human cost of the Wars. Artillery played a more significant part in these than in earlier European conflicts, and the numbers of casualties shocked contemporaries. If we also take into consideration the arrival of syphilis, which first appeared in Europe in 1494 during the French invasion of Naples, it is not difficult to see why many Italians of this time felt they were living in an apocalyptic age.

In the midst of all this devastation, some saw opportunities for themselves. At the time of this novel's action, the papacy was in the hands of Rodrigo Borgia, or Alexander VI: a descendant of a Catalan dynasty that had established itself in Italy when Alexander's uncle became pope in the 1450s. Many Renaissance popes were nepotistic and keen to use the vast resources of the papacy to expand their dynasties' secular power, but Alexander took these tendencies to new extremes, using his talented and notoriously ruthless son Cesare— something of a hero for Machiavelli—to establish a unified state that would remain to the Borgia dynasty after the pope's death. In doing so, Alexander and Cesare drew on the military support of the French king, Louis XII, and of various Italian condottieri, or mercenary captains. These were mainly either lords of small independent central Italian city-states such as Perugia, Città di Castello, and Urbino, or members of great, many-branched Roman baronial families such as the Orsini, powerful enough to threaten the pope's power in Rome.

The relationship between Borgia and these condottieri, several of whom could compete with him in the Machiavellian skill of being "not good," is central to the novel's political plot. Similarly central is the feud between Pope Alexander and Cardinal Giuliano della Rovere, like Alexander the nephew of a pope, and a man with an eye on the papacy himself. After losing out to Alexander in the papal election of 1492, della Rovere conducted an energetic campaign of defamation against him, and even went so far as to attempt to get Alexander deposed, urging Louis XII's predecessor, Charles VIII, to move against the pope while he was in Italy in 1494. Alexander succeeded in defusing the threat through negotiation with Charles, and by 1496 he and della Rovere had reached some kind of truce. It is during this period of uneasy détente between the two that the main action of the novel begins.

LIST OF HISTORICAL CHARACTERS

- Alexander VI, Pope. See Borgia, Rodrigo

- Baglioni, Giampaolo (b. 1470): mercenary captain; hereditary lord of Perugia

- Bibbiena, Bernardo. See Dovizi, Bernardo

- Borgia, Cesare (b. c. 1475): illegitimate son of Alexander VI; duke of Valentinois; cardinal, 1493-98; military leader from 1498

- Borgia, Rodrigo (b. 1431): nephew of Pope Calixtus III; elected pope in 1492

- Buonvicini da Pescia, Domenico: Dominican friar; follower of Girolamo Savonarola; executed with him in 1498

- Carvajal, Bernardino Lopez de (b. 1455): Spanish cardinal

- Coreglia, Michele da [Miguel de Corella]: henchman of Cesare Borgia

- d'Alviano, Bartolomeo (b. 1455): Umbrian condottiere; enemy of Cesare Borgia

- da Vinci, Leonardo (b. 1452): artist, inventor, engineer; in service of Cesare Borgia from c. 1502

- d'Amboise, Georges (b. 1460): French cardinal; papal candidate

- della Rovere, Felice (b. 1483): illegitimate daughter of Giuliano della Rovere and Lucrezia Normanni

- della Rovere, Galeotto Franciotti (b. 1471): nephew of Giuliano della Rovere

- della Rovere, Giuliano (b. 1443): nephew of Pope Sixtus IV; cardinal from 1471; opposed election of Pope Alexander VI in 1492

- della Rovere, Raffaele: illegitimate son of Giuliano della Rovere
- Domenico, Fra: see Buonvicini da Pescia, Domenico
- Doria, Andrea (b. 1466): Genoese soldier; later famous naval commander
- Dovizi, Bernardo (b. 1470): secretary to Cardinal Giovanni de' Medici; known as "Bibbiena" after his home town
- Euffreducci, Oliviero (b. 1473; portrayed in the novel as b. 1475): orphaned nephew of Giovanni Fogliani; mercenary captain
- Felice, Madonna: see della Rovere, Felice
- Fogliani, Giovanni (b. 1450): member of ruling oligarchy of Fermo; father of Nicolosa Fogliani; uncle of Oliviero Euffreducci
- Fogliani, Nicolosa: daughter of Giovanni Fogliani
- Galeotto, Cardinal: see della Rovere, Galeotto
- Giovanni, Cardinal: see Medici, Giovanni de'
- Giovanni, Messer: see Fogliani, Giovanni
- Girolamo, Fra: see Savonarola, Girolamo
- Giuliano, Cardinal: see della Rovere, Giuliano
- Guidobaldo, Duke: see da Montefeltro, Guidobaldo
- Giustiniano, Antonio (b. 1466): Venetian ambassador to Rome
- Liverotto: See Euffreducci, Oliviero
- Machiavelli, Niccolò (b. 1469): Florentine statesman and political theorist
- Manfredi, Astorre (1485-1502): lord of Faenza, deposed by Cesare Borgia in 1501
- Medici, Giovanni de' (b. 1475): son of Lorenzo de' Medici and Clarice Orsini; cardinal from 1489; exiled from Florence with his family in 1494

- Michelotto, Don: see Coreglia, Michele da
- Montanina, Madonna: see Ottoni, Montanina degli
- Montefeltro, Guidobaldo da (b. 1472): duke of Urbino
- Orsini, Francesco (b. 1465): mercenary captain; duke of Gravina; cousin of Paolo Orsini
- Orsini, Paolo: mercenary captain; cousin of Francesco Orsini
- Ottoni, Montanina degli: noblewoman from Matelica; wife of Giovanni Fogliani
- Petrucci, Pandolfo (b. c. 1450): ruler of Siena from c. 1500
- Roano, Cardinal: see d'Amboise, Georges
- Savonarola, Girolamo (1452-98): Dominican friar and prior of San Marco, Florence; attacked Pope Alexander VI; executed by Florentine republic
- Sforza, Ascanio (b. 1455): cardinal; papal candidate
- Sforza, Francesco (1401-66): mercenary captain; lord of Milan
- Sforza, Giovanni (b. 1466): lord of Pesaro; first husband of Lucrezia Borgia, daughter of Pope Alexander VI
- Soderini, Francesco (b. 1453): cleric and diplomat; bishop of Volterra from 1478; cardinal from 1503; brother of the statesman Piero Soderini
- Valentino, Duke: see Borgia, Cesare
- Varano, Giulio Cesare (b. 1434): lord of Camerino
- Vitelli, Paolo (1461-99): mercenary captain; brother of Vitellozzo Vitelli; executed by the Florentines on suspicion of treachery
- Vitelli, Vitellozzo (b. 1458): mercenary captain; lord of Città di Castello; brother of Paolo Vitelli

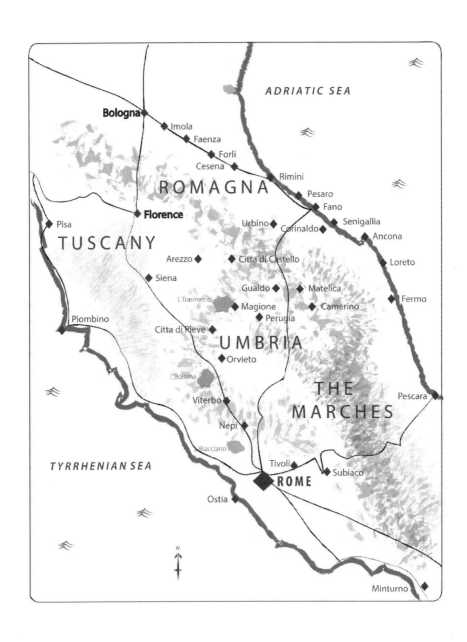

ADRIATIC SEA

Bologna ◆
◆ Imola
◆ Faenza
◆ Forlì
◆ Cesena
◆ Rimini
◆ Pesaro
◆ Fano

ROMAGNA

◆ **Florence**

◆ Pisa
Urbino ◆ ◆ Corinaldo
◆ Senigallia
◆ Ancona

TUSCANY

Arezzo ◆
◆ Citta di Castello
◆ Loreto

◆ Siena
Gualdo ◆ ◆ Matelica
◆ Fermo

L.Trasimeno
◆ Magione
◆ Camerino

Piombino ◆
◆ Perugia

Citta di Rieve ◆

UMBRIA

◆ Orvieto

L.Bolsena

THE
MARCHES

◆ Pescara

Viterbo ◆

Nepi ◆

Bracciano

TYRRHENIAN SEA

◆ Tivoli
◆ Subiaco

◆ **ROME**

Ostia ◆

N

Minturno ◆

BOOK ONE

I

There are times when a sickness seems to come upon the world and it vomits up monsters. Such was the age of the worst emperors, Suetonius tells us, and such was the time of my youth. There were many who foretold that the half-millennium of 1500 would bring the skies crashing around our heads and leave the dead earth swarming with demons. These prophets spoke falsely, but for those of us who lived then, it sometimes seemed we were seeing nothing less.

I SHOULD INTRODUCE MYSELF FIRST, as a man must if he hopes for a courteous audience. My name is Matteo da Fermo, and I was born in the noble city of Fermo, close to the Adriatic Sea, in May of the year 1482. I will speak of my father later. My mother was a tailor's wife—or a tailor's widow by the time I knew I was in the world. She was a woman of great beauty, one of the loveliest in our city, with hair the color of honey that fell almost to her waist. Men loitered across the street from our house hoping for a glimpse of her without her veil. She would send her maid to the window to report on what they were doing, and the two of them would laugh at these admirers until tears ran down their faces. Sometimes my mother would send me out, a boy of four or five, to tell them they were wasting their time and should leave her alone. The cleverest ones would equip themselves with candied figs to bribe me, and I would diligently report back the words that they told me. Just one moment, they begged—just one moment at the window, so they could die happy men.

I was in love with my mother just as much as these suitors, but I had an advantage over them, because she was in love with me too. "Will you look at this child?" she would say to her neighbors. "He has the face of an angel." She should have known, for it was the same face as hers.

My brother Corrado—or Dino, as we called him—did not look like us in the least, and I thought of him as our enemy. He was a big, dark, angry child, and my mother spoke to him in a sharp tone that she never used when speaking to me. Dino was two years my elder and seemed to me strong and fierce as a mastiff. He would stamp on my fingers or twist my arm behind my back, and my mother would beat him with a leather strap, and he would cry out foul words. She complained of him to Messer Giovanni, who was Dino's godfather and one of the leading men of Fermo. Messer Giovanni would rebuke Dino, and he would stand there sullenly, pretending to be sorry, his dangerous hands twitching at his sides.

Messer Giovanni was the only man allowed in our house. Sometimes he came alone, sometimes with his sour-faced wife, Madonna Dianora, who made my mother so nervous that she sat on the edge of her chair, her fingers tightly pleated in her lap. It was always an event when Messer Giovanni came. The room would fill with his tall, lordly presence, and my mother would produce a special glass beaker for him to take his wine in, a thing that lent him great mystery in my eyes.

Well, all this came to an end when I was six years old. I came back one day from playing in the square, and my mother was ill. She had been seized by a fever. She was sick all that day and the next, speaking words that made no sense and rolling her eyes in her head so you only saw the whites. I was so frightened when I saw her that I screamed and would not stop screaming. A neighbor had to take me to her house.

At the end of the second day of her illness, my mother died, and for another two days her body lay on her bed, as the people of the neighborhood paid their respects. She was laid out wearing a nightgown with her hair loose at her side, and the men who had lingered across the street thirsting for a sight of her were finally able to come in and get their fill. Messer Giovanni came late on the first day, towards evening. Everyone bowed as he entered the room.

The first night when my mother was lying dead in the house, I crept down from the room I shared with Dino and the maid so I could spend the night with her. She frightened me now with her stiffness and sunken eyes, but I did not want her be alone when she would so soon be lying under the earth in all that darkness. I crouched in the corner of the room, remembering how it had felt lying in that same bed in her warm arms, and the world seemed a new and cold and terrifying place.

The second night I went down again, but when I got to the door of her chamber, I found it slightly ajar. Light was coming from within, and a strange, muffled sound. I pulled the door open an inch or so further and looked in.

A man was lying on the bed next to my mother. I could tell from his clothes that it was Messer Giovanni. His face was buried in her hair, and I could see in the candlelight that he was holding her stiff body in his arms. The sound I could hear from outside was of him weeping. I had never seen a man weep before, only children and women. I wanted to rescue my mother from him, but I was too frightened to say a word. I tiptoed back to my bedchamber instead.

AFTER THAT, Dino and I grew up in Messer Giovanni's house, together with his daughter, and with his nephews, who were orphans like us. Dino was there because he was Messer

Giovanni's godson. I was there because I had nowhere else to go.

The new house seemed to me larger than I had ever imagined a dwelling could be, even the palaces of kings in the stories my mother told me. A pig might be roasting in the kitchen below, and from the upper rooms you would barely even catch the smell. To its front, the house faced the square, with graceful windows on its upper floors from which you could watch all the happenings of the day, good and wicked. Behind was a garden in which I often took refuge in my sorrowing early days at the house.

A strange thing happened when we moved to Messer Giovanni's house. Dino stopped being my enemy and began to be my defender. I remember exactly the moment when this occurred. On the first day Dino and I arrived, Messer Giovanni led us into the schoolroom as lessons were finishing and introduced us to the other children and told them to be kind to us. Then we went out into the garden, and Messer Giovanni's nephew Oliviero pointed at me and said, "That one looks like a girl."

"No he doesn't," Dino said, his chin jutting, and they kept that up for a while—yes he does, no he doesn't. Then Dino hit Oliviero so hard that blood sprang on his lip, and Oliviero hit him back and struck him to the ground. Oliviero would have been around twelve years old and Dino no more than eight, but he was a large boy for his age, with anger boiling inside him. This memory seems remarkable to me now when I think of it, knowing what this boy Oliviero would become.

SCHOOLING WAS the great new fact of our life at the big house, occupying every hour of the morning from just after dawn. We studied in an airy high room at the back of the house, away from the distractions of the street. There were seven of us in total in the schoolroom, besides the master: myself and Dino; Oliviero and his two brothers; a boy named Lorenzo, who was the son of a friend of Messer Giovanni's and became the dearest companion of my boyhood; and Messer Giovanni's daughter, Nicolosa. I stared at Nicolosa when we were first taken to the schoolroom, as I had never heard of a girl studying alongside boys, learning Latin. It was as if you had gone into a shop and seen a cat sitting there behind the counter, doing all a shopkeeper might do.

The master, Messer Domenico, was a remarkably ugly man. He looked like the gargoyles sculptors carve on the faces of churches to keep roving demons at bay. His ears were particularly startling: unbelievably long, with hair spouting from the middle and bulbous soft lobes. Sometimes I would amuse myself by trying to calculate how many of other people's ears could fit into one of his. Even Dino's were perhaps only half of the size, and Nicolosa's no more than a third or a quarter: miniature perfect things, half-hidden in her dark curls.

Nicolosa was the keenest of us all in her studies. She wanted fiercely to be the best of us, and she was. She could list many women who were famous for their learning, and she yearned to be numbered among them. She wanted popes and famous scholars to fawn over letters she had written, as had happened with these heroines of hers. Messer Giovanni indulged her, as any father might with a daughter like Nicolosa. You could see when he looked at her that he could not quite believe such a flawless creature had issued from his fallible loins. "Father," she would say in the manner of a miniature adult woman, "you have something on your collar." He would bend to let her remove it, enchanted by this solicitude. Nicolosa took after him more than she did after her mother, Madonna Dianora, a feeble and ailing woman who had failed her husband by producing no son.

I was the only one of Nicolosa's fellow students to offer her any competition. Latin came easily to me, and I liked it, but I studied mainly out of a spirit of rivalry and to win Nicolosa's attention, which I did. I still remember the look she gave me over her shoulder when I first answered a question to which she had not been able to respond. Nicolosa had the advantage over me that she could study after our lessons, when she was supposed to be attending to her needle and thread. I spent my afternoons in a field outside the city walls with the other boys, learning to be a man, which is to say swift and dangerous and strong.

These afternoon lessons were not ones that I excelled at, to my mortification. I could run well and leap well and ride well, but I did not love weapons, and in wrestling I rarely survived the first throw. Our fencing master once quipped that I was destined to be a deserter, as my best skills were all about running away.

Dino was my opposite in these studies. Latin was never going to enter his head. We would work together on our lessons in the evenings sometimes, huddled under a pile of bedstuffs and pelts in our room in the winter or perched up on the walls near our house in the summer, watching the swifts madly zigzagging above. Dino would listen intently and repeat back my words, but he might have repeated them a thousand times for all the good that it did him. By the morning, every last trace was gone.

It was very different with our afternoon labors. Fighting was what Dino had been born to do. He knew nothing of fear, and his body obeyed him like a well-trained dog does its master. I would watch his demonic swordplay and itch to have the same fluency, but I could no more follow him in this than he could follow me in my Latin. Only Oliviero was Dino's equal in fighting and he not the whole of the time.

CHILDHOOD IS TEDIOUS, because it is all about waiting. I shall not bore you with more of mine than you have already heard. If you are reading this, it is because you know that my life crossed with history. Perhaps you have even leafed forward to see whether you can detect famous names and deeds springing from the pages among the scratchings of my nib. *Pazienza!* They will come if you wait.

One day when I was around fifteen and strolling through town with my friend Lorenzo, I turned a corner and saw Dino coming towards us with a comely, fresh-faced young woman on his arm. The girl blushed when she saw us, but Dino just strolled past us with a careless smile, as if to say, "Well, and why not?" I saw, with a shock, that he was no longer my brother as I had always thought of him, a raw gangling boy, his wrists protruding from his outgrown sleeves. He was a tall, vigorous young man, with whom a girl might be happy to walk along, clasped together for the whole city to see. Anger no longer seethed within him, for he knew he would soon be able to do all the violence he wished and be lauded for it. Messer Giovanni had given him permission to join Oliviero, who was away studying the arts of war under the condottiere Paolo Vitelli, one of the most celebrated Italian generals of the day.

The young woman's name was Margherita. Dino married her before he left for Vitelli's army, and nine months later— or, to be honest, more like eight, or perhaps seven—she bore my absent brother his first son. By some strange conjunction of the stars, this birth coincided almost to the hour with a death in our household. The same morning when my nephew Giannetto came bawling into the world, Messer Giovanni's wife, Madonna Dianora, breathed her last.

THIS WAS THE beginning of great change for us. The poor lady was barely in the ground before the gossips began predicting

Messer Giovanni's remarriage. Most thought he would leap back into the marital saddle as soon as decency permitted, since he had a sniff now at the chance of a son. Indeed, the day after the term of his mourning was done, he signed a contract sealing his betrothal to an heiress from Matelica, who brought him the lordship of that town, together with castles and lands that made him the wealthiest man in Fermo by far.

We feted this noble marriage with three days of banquets and a horse race in the Piazza San Martino, which was won, to our jubilation, by a horse of our own, a chestnut colt Messer Giovanni had bred. The house was hung for the week of the wedding with garlands, so you might think you were strolling into a meadow when you came off the street. We of the household were decked out in new and lustrous apparel, made from silks and taffetas and velvets shipped down from Venice by the crateful. I had a new doublet for the occasion in green and white damask in which I fancied myself quite the young lord.

On the last evening of the festivities, Nicolosa and I danced for the gathered company, a dance we had been rehearsing for more than two weeks. It was one of those finicky, fashionable numbers, with no two steps alike, demanding some audacious leaps on my part. Nicolosa was dressed gaily, in cherry-colored silk, though I thought, left to herself, she would still be in black to mourn her dead mother. She looked beautiful and determined as we danced, measuring the beat with light steps while I whirled around her like an elegant madman, as the choreography required. When we had finished, I took her hand to bow to our audience and she smiled at me, a swift, wary smile, which I returned still more cautiously. It was a thrill to me to dance with her in public, but it also felt dangerous, as though the secret murmurings of my heart might be laid bare.

NICOLOSA! I MUST tell you of how things passed between us, or you will understand nothing of my history. For this I must return to my childhood a moment, even though I told you its telling was done.

Nicolosa and I were friends when we were children. When I had escaped from my afternoon lessons, I would go to her room and we would read together to practice our Latin. When we were younger, we would also sometimes play long elaborate games of Nicolosa's devising. She would be the duchess of Ferrara or Urbino. I was sometimes the duke, her husband, and sometimes an enemy she would defy with courageous long speeches from the city walls. Her maids watched us most of the time, exclaiming sentimentally about our beauty, but occasionally they would leave us alone, telling us to be good children. Mostly we were, though sometimes when I was the duke and Nicolosa the duchess, I would kiss her farewell as I was leaving for the wars.

By the time I was twelve, I had convinced myself that I would marry Nicolosa in reality when we were older. This was not likely, since I was a tailor's son and she the daughter of Messer Giovanni, but I had convinced myself vainly that Messer Giovanni's regard for me would outweigh these considerations of rank. He was proud of my looks and my progress in my studies, and he would take me with him when he went about the town on his business, dressed as nobly as if I were his own son. Sometimes I would even accompany him when he rode down to the coast to survey his orange groves, or out to his olive mill to supervise the first pressing of his oil. The peasants we met on these excursions fussed over me fondly, and Messer Giovanni smiled and ruffled my hair and expounded to me earnestly why his oil was the best of the whole region. I imagined when I was older I would ride to these places with Nicolosa and cut orange blossoms from the trees for her to place in her hair.

The reality of the thing became apparent one afternoon when Messer Giovanni found us alone in Nicolosa's chamber. We were reading a book together—Livy's *History*, if I remember right—and I had my arm around Nicolosa's shoulders. Messer Giovanni opened the door and stood staring at us in horror, as though he had seen his wife rutting with a dwarf, like the story in Ariosto. He said nothing for a while, simply because he was too angry to speak, his face becoming redder and redder. Then he strode over to us and grabbed me by my hair and the neck of my shirt and dragged me from the room and hit me about the head with some violence, so I was left with ink-colored bruises around both eyes for a week. The maids were sent packing that same day, without the pay that was owing to them, and Messer Giovanni told me if he ever caught me alone with Nicolosa again, he would hurl me from the window. This was not an idle threat. Everyone knew he had done this once to a servant boy who had stolen from him, smashing the boy's spine on the cobblestones below.

After that, I saw Nicolosa only in the schoolroom and at mealtimes and in dancing lessons, where we were supervised closely. She would sometimes smile her sweet smile at me when her father was not looking, but she had become careful, as also had I. Now that we could no longer be together, I found myself thinking back to our precious afternoons and being angry at myself for not having done some of the things to her that Messer Giovanni had feared would occur to me. It seemed a cruel waste that these dangerous illicit encounters of ours had been spent reading Livy or Virgil or laboring over the beginnings of our Greek.

My thoughts on this subject waxed more lurid as I became versed in the ways of the flesh. By the time I was fifteen, whenever I could scavenge a few *soldi*, I would have a tryst with Lena, who was the chief resource for these matters among the men of our household. Lena had a face horribly ravaged by a disease in her childhood and needed to save herself a good dowry to have a hope of a husband. Messer Giovanni paid her something to scrub the kitchen floor and scour pans, but she would have been slaving all her life before she could persuade a man to marry her if she had not supplemented her income in some way.

You might think it a sad induction into the pleasures of love to dally with a woman whose face caused people to cross themselves in pity when they saw her in the street. But Lena was a good-natured creature, with much patience for a boy's inexpert fumblings, and her body, by a cruel irony, under her ruined face, was as perfect as a woman's body could be. She would come to my chamber during the hot hours of the day, when people were sleeping, and I would make her undress in front of me, carefully keeping my eyes from her face. Before she arrived, I would lie there with my eyes shut, boiling with lust, imagining it was Nicolosa who was coming in secret to my room. I had become shy of Nicolosa as she grew into a woman. In my daydreams, I was anything but shy.

A FEW MONTHS after Messer Giovanni remarried, in the spring of 1499, an eminent guest graced our household, Cardinal Giuliano della Rovere. He was on his way to visit the shrine of Mary at Loreto, to fulfill a vow he had made when he was cured of the flux. The cardinal stayed with us for two days to rest on his journey and to renew an ancient acquaintance. He had been a friend of Messer Giovanni's brother when he was a youth studying at Perugia and had often come to Fermo to stay with the family. The connection endured even after

Cardinal Giuliano rose to high estate after the election of his uncle as pope.

The house was scoured from its rafters downwards to greet this honored guest, and the paneling polished until the whole place was fragrant with beeswax. All our fine garments from the wedding were shaken out from their chests, smelling of the lavender in which they were stored. Our cellars and larders groaned like the store cupboards of a fat abbot. You could not pass the kitchen door in the week before his arrival without seeing a brace of peasants heaving a barrel of wine over the threshold or a market boy staggering in with a gargantuan ham.

I was excited to see our guest, as a man whose life had meshed with history. I had heard many tales of him, as had everyone in Fermo; he was one of the chief men of our day. He was within a whisker of becoming pope in the '92 election, but he lost out to Cardinal Rodrigo Borgia, who had used his post as vice-chancellor of the Church to stock his coffers so he could bribe his way to the papal throne. Cardinal Giuliano railed against the new pope, calling him a man who thought nothing of bartering Christ's blood for his own profit and adding for good measure that Borgia was a whoremonger, a sodomite, a secret Jew, and generally unfitted to be pope. Nor did the cardinal limit himself to railing. He stormed up to France to persuade the French king to depose this disastrous new pontiff, who had named himself Alexander. Then the cardinal descended into Italy himself with the French army, riding elbow to elbow with the king.

I had formed a certain image of Cardinal Giuliano on the basis of these tales, and he did not disappoint my expectations. He was a tall, strong-jawed man in his fifties, who looked more like a soldier than a prelate. He also spoke like a soldier on occasion. The first morning he was with us, I heard him berating a servant who brought him his shaving water insufficiently heated and informing him that if he did it again he would have his testicles sliced off with his own razor and fed to the dogs. This threat came thundering through from the next room as I was reading from a book of saints' lives to Messer Giovanni's new wife, Madonna Montanina, a delicately bred woman. She looked at me startled and crossed herself, while I tried and failed to stifle a laugh.

To me, the cardinal was more civil. Messer Giovanni introduced us and boasted for a while about my intelligence, as I cast my eyes modestly to the floor.

"Let us see," the cardinal said; then he spoke to me rapidly in Latin to test me. Messer Giovanni had told him of my liking for history, and he asked me some questions about Sallust and Polybius, which I fortunately answered to his taste. "A talented boy," he said gravely. "As well as a fine-looking one. You should send him to me when he is through with his studies." This was clearly just politeness when I think back on it now, but it was enough to swell my head and set Messer Giovanni quivering with pride.

Cardinal Giuliano was much taken with Nicolosa, as well he might be. Messer Giovanni placed her beside him at dinner, and I watched them conversing together and felt proud that Fermo could offer a lady of such refinement. The townsfolk had sometimes laughed at Messer Giovanni for educating his daughter in Latin like a duchess, but you could see now that he had done so with good cause. Cardinal Giuliano's face softened when he spoke with Nicolosa, and when her father ordered her down from the table to show off her dancing, the cardinal did her the honor of escorting her to the floor. I heard him afterwards saying to Messer Giovanni that he only wished his own daughter were equally biddable. This was the famous Madonna Felice, of whom—God preserve me—I shall later have a great deal to say.

Poor young fool that I was, I little guessed that what I was witnessing during the visit of Cardinal Giuliano was the striking of a nuptial bargain. When our visitor left, Messer Giovanni summoned me to his study to inform me that Nicolosa was to be married to the cardinal's son. He looked at me searchingly as he said this, as if wishing to gauge my reaction. I listened in shock and stuttered out some words of felicitation, trying to stifle the wounded clamor of my heart.

After the dowry had been agreed on and the betrothal pledge signed, a portrait of the bridegroom arrived at the house, along with a length of brocade as a gift for the bride, so thickly encrusted with gold thread that from a distance you might have thought it solid gold. The portrait was hung in the great hall of the house, where I could not help but look at it when we were called to the table. I lost my appetite because of this, and took to wandering disconsolately in the olive groves below the walls, writing sonnets in my head in the manner of Petrarca, calling on nature to witness my woes.

I confided my feelings about Nicolosa only to one living soul, my friend Lorenzo. I had great love for this youth, who had been a companion of my studies since childhood and who would ride out with me now to hunt for hares in the hills and carouse with me in the taverns in town. Lorenzo was cynical in matters of love and liked to speak ill of women, but he listened with great patience to my amorous laments. I remember I even inflicted a few of my sonnets on him, one of which he set most dolorously for the lute.

Besides attending to my heart's sorrows, Lorenzo also regaled me with news of what Fermo was saying of Nicolosa's marriage. All were speaking of it, and none could agree on it. It had become the chief matter of the town. Some men, including Lorenzo's own father, praised Messer Giovanni's prudence in arranging this match. Cardinal Giuliano was a guileful and experienced man, and he had the favor of the king of France, having spent long years in that realm. If Pope Alexander were to be carried off tomorrow by the dropsy or a fever—or by the devil summoning him back to hell, if you were to believe certain rumors—then Messer Giovanni might find himself in the covetable position of sharing his bloodline with the next pope.

Others were less sanguine and said that the cardinal was a dangerous meddler, and that things would end ill for him and all who rallied to his banner. He had antagonized the pope with his attacks after the election, and Alexander was not a man to forget. The pope and the cardinal might appear to be reconciled now, but this was only because the king of France wished it, and both needed his friendship. Their peace could not last. You might as well throw a dog and a fox into a sack with a haunch of mutton and think them friends because they are quiet while they devour the meat.

THREE DAYS BEFORE Nicolosa's wedding, I was walking past her chamber when I heard her softly speak my name. I believed what Messer Giovanni had said about throwing me from the window, but nothing would stop me going to her if she called. I stood at her door with my heart beating hard, as if I were waiting for her to say, "Matteo, I must renounce this marriage. I can marry no man but you." Instead, she looked at me earnestly and asked for an opinion on the way she had dressed her hair.

I let myself gaze at her for a moment—at the fine dark arch of her eyebrows; at her eyes, evading mine; at the lovely curve of her lips. The sight of her so close was unbearable to me almost, when I thought how soon she would be in another man's hands. Nicolosa was looking intent, with an expression I knew well. I sensed the strength of her urge to success, just as when she was working on her studies. Her future husband was arriving the following day, and she wanted him to be dazzled and subdued by her beauty. She must be the loveliest bride in history, the equal of Guinevere and Helen. Every possible detail must be right.

Nicolosa's hair, which was plaited in a complicated way, looked wonderful to me, and I said so, without proffering further detail. She sighed and gave me a glance as if to say, "So much for the opinion of a man." I had no reason to stay after that. I felt I should unfurl some graceful augury for her happiness, but no words would come to my mouth. Nicolosa said nothing also, and we stood for a while in silence, I looking down at her intricate hair, which I noticed was strewn with threads of tiny pearls.

Eventually, she looked up at me and said, "Teo …"

"I know," I said bitterly. "I'm going. You don't need to tell me my place."

WELL, YOU ARE going to say that by the time Raffaele della Rovere entered the house, I was too prejudiced against him to be any kind of fair witness. That is obviously true, but you must also believe me when I say he was not an impressive figure of a man. His portrait was flattering, the one that had been leaching away my appetite at dinner. He had less of a chin than he had in that image and more of a nose. His eyes were small and too close together, and he had the simpering mouth of a fool. I felt sorry for Nicolosa, thinking of her anxiously burnishing her beauty to captivate this weasel of a man.

I sat next to Dino at the dinner following the wedding ceremony, along with his wife Margherita, who had decked herself out in some execrable costume in honor of the event. She was nervous at the big house and barely ate anything, afraid she would mishandle her fork. I too hardly ate, for my own reasons, and sat there morosely fashioning my bread into pellets. I had been thinking of feigning illness as an excuse for not attending, but Messer Giovanni had come himself to my room, leaving his swarms of guests below, fearful at the thought that I was suffering a sudden sickness of such gravity. I could not keep up my pretense in the face of his anxiety and assured him I was well enough to attend.

Dino had returned for the wedding in the entourage of Messer Giovanni's nephew Oliviero, who was seated on the high table with the bride and groom and the most dignified guests. I caught sight of Oliviero whenever my eyes strayed towards Nicolosa, as they could not help doing. Once or twice I met his eyes looking blearily back at me and quickly looked away. I did not like this man, who had always treated me with scorn, ever since my first arrival in this household, when he had mocked me for looking like a girl. He was around twenty-three or twenty-four years old at this time and had become a condottiere in his own right, having long since completed his training. He was a great hulking man now, quite the warrior, with a scar down the right side of his face like a badge of honor. Men had taken to calling him Liverotto, on account of his size, and that is what I will call him from now on.

At the time in the evening when the seating plans loosen, I was surprised to see Raffaele della Rovere come down from the high table to sit at our trestle. "For God's sake, man," I felt like saying. I could not imagine how he could bear to abandon his bride. He spoke first to a man on his left; then he leaned towards me and asked me in a wheedling tone how well I was enjoying the feast. As he spoke, he placed his hand on my left thigh, near my member, which unfortunately was erect at that moment, for reasons quite unconnected with him.

"Mmm," he murmured, bringing his head so close to mine that I could smell on his breath all the meats he had eaten in the course of the evening. I reached down and pulled his hand away, and he laughed at me sneeringly and turned back to the man on his other side.

Well, this was not such an extraordinary experience for me at the time. I was a handsome youth and delicate of feature, with a beauty I felt at this time only as a burden. Men had tried to make me their prey for almost as long as I could remember, although I had managed to keep them at bay. When I was perhaps twelve years old, Messer Giovanni told me that if anyone plagued me in this manner, I should tell him, and he would castrate the man to teach him a lesson. This was all very well, but I doubted this promise would extend to his expensively acquired new son-in-law.

Signor Raffaele remained at my side for perhaps ten more minutes, conversing randomly with the company and making further sporadic attempts on my virtue. Later in the evening, I watched him whispering in a corner with a serving boy, I imagine arranging some tryst. I looked up at Nicolosa at the top table, wreathed in candlelight, shimmering with pearls, looking like the brave and beautiful virgin martyrs her new stepmother loved to read about. A new sadness for her was beginning to weave itself together in my mind with the pity I felt for myself.

That night, I slept fitfully, tormenting myself with my thoughts. By the following morning, it was clear to me that I must leave Fermo. How could I possibly continue to live here, watching Nicolosa with this odious new spouse?

I tried a stringent tone with Dino the next morning.

"I'm coming with you, brother," I said. "I need a change."

"Coming with me? Fighting, you mean?" Dino replied. He looked understandably dismayed at the prospect.

"What else do you think?" I said, looking him in the eye.

There was a long pause; then Dino shrugged. I imagine he knew exactly why I wanted to leave Fermo.

"Very well, Teo," he said. "Come with me if you want. We'll see what kind of soldier you make."

IN THIS WAY I joined the army of Liverotto Euffreducci. I said nothing to Messer Giovanni, as I knew he would never have countenanced my departing. I did not even leave a note to let him know where I was going, as I thought he would write to Liverotto to order me back. I simply gathered my few possessions and left Fermo one day before dawn, scaling down from my window on a rope into the street below. I caught up with the army at a village ten miles to the north where Dino had told me they were encamped.

II

I DO NOT KNOW WHETHER you have ever engaged in soldiering, you who are reading these pages? If you have, you can imagine what a noisome life I found it in those early days, soft-bred youth that I was. Within a few months, my white hands were as calloused as a blacksmith's, and my head and heart were beginning to go the same way. I had slept on rough earth, shat in foul-smelling ditches, and heard the screams of men dying, their limbs torn apart by our guns. I had stood beside a man as he was smashed open by a cannonball, his bowels spilling obscenely from a rent in his side. I had wrenched rings off the fingers of corpses and near-corpses; ripped amulets from men's necks as they died, choking on their blood; smelled the vile stench of burning flesh from the buildings we torched, a smell that lingers in your nostrils for days.

My respect for Dino grew greatly when I began to fight at his side. He was a man of genius in his trade. If he had been of higher birth, he could have made a fine condottiere himself. He had the gift of command, and men followed him happily, emboldened by his entire lack of fear. He showed me no favors as his brother in public, but in the evening, in the quarters I shared with him, he would tutor me patiently, taking me through some wrestling move or sword thrust a score of times or more, until I had it precisely as he wished. He also spoke to me of strategy, an art that impassioned him. He had every major battle of the past century in his head to the last detail. This I found more congenial than the physical business of fighting. I caught his enthusiasm, and we would argue for hours about the conduct of some recent campaign.

I found my vocation in arms when we stormed our first besieged town, somewhere in the Casentino Valley. We pounded this place for four days with our artillery until there was a breach in the walls sufficient to make our attack. The siege ladders were brought to the walls under a hail of enemy fire, and, on an impulse, I volunteered to be first to climb one. I was light and swift and agile, and I was tired of being a second-rate soldier whom no one wanted to fight alongside. Dino looked at me narrow-eyed when I stepped forward, and I could tell he did not like it, but he could not stop me without spoiling his reputation for stern justice without favor. He beckoned a foot soldier to hand me a war hammer and pushed me toward the ladder, telling me to look sharp. He told me later he had thought at that moment he would next see his brother a corpse.

All went well for me in that scaling. I was like a man charmed. Stones and gunshot and arrows showered past me as I climbed, without any strikes other than a few glancing blows to my helmet and cuirass. As I vaulted down from the wall, a rock almost hit me, hurled by a defender at close quarters. I sensed it coming and ducked, rising to smash my assailant in the face with my hammer, so he staggered back screaming. By now, our men were swarming over the walls at my back, and the worst of the danger was past.

I was hailed as a hero after that first assault of the walls, and the men who had muttered about me before were suddenly gathering round to toast me with the wine we had plundered from the town's cellars. Their companionship warmed me, and some pleasure began to return to my life at this moment. I was beginning to accumulate some wealth also— not from the miserable stipend Liverotto offered, which in truth was rarely paid, but from the profits of looting and ransom. There was money to be made there, although most of my comrades squandered it instantly on gambling and whores. Dino, more prudent, had husbanded his takings and bought himself a small farm with an olive grove half an hour's ride from Fermo. He and I had ridden out to inspect this purchase one day when he was back for Nicolosa's wedding, Dino as excited as a child to sink his boots into loam he had earned through the sweat of his brow.

ONE EVENING WHEN I had been in the army a few months, I was resting in my quarters when a servant of Liverotto's came to fetch me. We had just stormed a town whose name now escapes me, although I well remember the labor it cost us in the taking: a grim, gray, flinty mountain stronghold, more fitting as a home for eagles than men. Dino had gone out to celebrate the capture with our comrades, but I felt sick and remained in our room.

I followed the feeble light of my escort's lantern towards Liverotto's lodgings, wondering what this summons foreboded. I had performed well that day on the walls and thought some reward might be due. It was some time in early spring, I remember, an unsettled, squally evening. The streets were slippery with mud and with the debris of the day's fighting. A few corpses were still lying around, picked clean of everything of value, the rats beginning to work on their faces. Sounds of revelry blasted out from two inns along the way, but otherwise the place was quite dead.

Eventually we reached a house with the air of a gentleman's dwelling, at the far end of the town. Armed men were posted at the doorway, and I was searched on my way in and my dagger removed.

Liverotto received me alone in a room at the front of the house with a handsome fire burning. A table stood in the center of the room, cluttered with maps and papers and the remains of a half-demolished shank of meat.

Liverotto greeted me affably when I entered the room and handed me a glass of wine.

"I thought we might celebrate."

I murmured something deferential and took a queasy sip of the wine. This proximity to our leader was disconcerting to me. I had never found it easy to look at him straight. His left eye was slightly askew, so you could not find a purchase. For the rest, he had a long, rough-hewn face, sallow from a recent illness, a crudely mended scar seaming one cheek.

Suddenly, as I was toying with my wine, Liverotto reached forward and took hold of the back of my neck and kissed me, trying to force his tongue between my teeth. I released myself, twisting my head away with all the strength I could summon, though his grip was like iron on my neck.

For a moment we stared at one other with loathing in our eyes; then he shrugged.

"As you will."

He called out, and three of his guards came into the room. He had them seize me and hold me over the table. I struggled at first, until one slammed my head down on the table, half dazing me. Another held a dagger against my cheek. Then Liverotto cut into my hose from behind and thrust himself into me. I cried out at first with the shock of it, then bit on my tongue until blood trickled into my mouth. The sickness I had felt earlier was welling up inside me as Liverotto did his business behind me, grunting like a hog. When the guards finally loosed their grip, I dragged myself from the table, sank to my knees, and vomited onto the ground.

After that, there was silence for a minute; then Liverotto spoke.

"Take him back."

One of the guards hauled me up by the shoulders. I wiped my mouth with the back of my hand. I was trembling and felt unsteady on my feet. I wanted to spit to clear my mouth of the taste of vomit, but I did not dare, in case Liverotto took offense.

"Keep your mouth shut about this," Liverotto said as I reached the door, escorted by his men, who were holding me like a criminal.

"I'm hardly going to boast of it, shitface," I wanted to say. Instead I nodded, my eyes on the ground.

I LAY AWAKE all that night, rigid with shame, trying to decide what to do. Dino came in late and I pretended to be asleep as he threw his clothes off and lay down at my side. My first thought was that I would tell him, and we would kill Liverotto to avenge me, but this was as much of a fantasy as my dreams that I would marry Nicolosa. To break through the cordon of guards Liverotto kept around himself was impossible, and he would be on the alert against both of us now that he had dishonored me in this way.

Aside from this, what could I do? I thought of returning to Fermo and resuming my life there, but the prospect was too bitter for me to stomach. I had built myself a dream since I left of returning home in honor, a man of means who had earned his wealth through the virile profession of soldiery. Instead, if I went back now, I would be returning a failed runaway, humbled into tolerating what I had left to avoid.

Looking back now, it seems strange to me that I did not simply depart for Rome or some other city and carve out a life for myself there. I had a good education and some experience in arms. Employment for such men never lacks. At this time, however, I would not have been capable of a venture of this kind. I was half a child still in my heart, even though I had been a few months in the army and learned how to curse and shed blood. I had always lived in Fermo. Even now, in Liverotto's army, I had my brother at my side and was fighting among men who spoke with my same accent and had been baptized in the same font as I had. I could not contemplate living in any other way. It was like asking a tree to abandon its roots.

So, in the event, I remained in the army and served Liverotto as his catamite when he wished it. I tell you this with shame. I would gladly have suppressed it, but you must know it if you are to understand my tale. My duties were occasional. Liverotto liked women also, and two or three of those who followed our camp were reserved for him. Most of the time they did well enough for him, but sometimes he lusted after darker meat, and then he would summon me to his quarters. It was never as violent as the first time. It did not need to be, since I was compliant to his desires, though I never feigned a liking for his caresses. After a while, he began to take a sentimental tone with me, plying me with gifts and looking deep into my sullen eyes, like a lover. He had itched to have me, he told me, since I was twelve or thirteen, cursing the fact that I was such a favorite with Messer Giovanni. It was just his ill luck that he had only come to enjoy me when I had almost grown into a man.

You may be wondering, if such things interest you, who it was that we were fighting all this time. The answer to this question is, frankly, that we hardly cared, as long as we had the opportunity for plunder. We fought first for the Florentines against the Pisans, alongside Liverotto's old mentor in warfare, Paolo Vitelli. Then the Florentines decided Paolo was a traitor and beheaded him, and we fought for the Pisans instead. After that, we fought briefly for Naples, but mostly for the Church.

Fighting for the Church meant for Pope Alexander and his son, Cesare Borgia, who were embarking then on their campaign to carve out an empire in the Romagna—a realm that would remain to the Borgias as their permanent seat of power when nature or poison put an end to Alexander's reign.

This task was easy enough on paper, since the Romagna was already the possession of the papacy. Alexander simply had to proclaim the vicariates of its various cities expired, which he promptly did in 1499. More difficult was physically to dislodge the men who had held these fiefs. These were not servants to be dismissed with a month's wages; they were proud lords with armies and treasuries, some of whose families had ruled these cities for centuries. Even with the gold of the papacy at Cesare's disposal and the arms of the French king, his father's ally, you might have predicted a campaign of at least a decade. Instead, he cut his path through his new dukedom with astonishing ease. He took Imola and Forlì in his first campaign in 1499; then, the following year, Pesaro, Cesena, Rimini—all proud cities. Men watched this in wonderment. It was like seeing some baleful comet burn a path through the sky, bringing destruction in its wake.

We joined with Duke Cesare's army for one campaign, in the winter of the second year of my service with Liverotto. I say "Duke Cesare," but I shall henceforth call him Valentino, which was the name by which we knew him at the time. In his early days, when his father had destined him to the Church, he was for a while archbishop of Valencia; and later, when he had defrocked himself, the king of France gave him the dukedom of Valence. For these two reasons, he was called Valentino, even though he had a liking for his given name also, so you would see his men march into battle with CAESAR emblazoned in great black letters on their backs.

At the time when we joined him, Valentino was camped outside Pesaro, trying to eject his former brother-in-law, Giovanni Sforza, the lord of that town. He was an unfortunate man, this Sforza. He had married Madonna Lucrezia, the pope's daughter, at a time when it seemed he might be useful to the family. Once it had become clear that he no longer served, he was forced publicly to declare himself impotent so the marriage could be annulled. This was in 1497, and here he was, three years later, more impotent than ever, excommunicated by his former father-in-law and with his former brother-in-law snarling like a wolf at his gate.

We were agog for a vision of Valentino, having heard so much of his legend. He did not disappoint in the flesh. We were on a slight incline, looking down, when he rode out to review his troops. It was early morning, and the sunlight was sharp and angled, still tinged with red-gold from the dawn. The duke was mounted on a white stallion, and when I say white, I mean white—the gleaming white they call *candidus* in Latin. His grooms must have been up all night washing the creature's coat and mane and tail until they shone. Valentino was dressed all in black, but his hat was decked with scarlet feathers, and two standard-bearers rode behind him carrying banners with his emblem of a red bull. His men were all dressed in identically colored livery, a great novelty in military discipline at this time. His army rippled across the plain, a blaze of crimson and yellow, like an emanation of its leader's valor, a thing beating with a single heart. What was anyone to do in the face of this splendor? Sforza capitulated by the end of the month.

One evening in the winter of 1501, Liverotto summoned me to his lodgings in a fortress we had captured—bloodlessly, in this instance, through the venerable expedient of bribing

the castellan. I went with an easy mind, for I was no longer
an object of lust to him by this time, having left the remnants
of my boyhood behind me. I had a more robust and manly air
to me now, and something of a beard, though I must confess
I was still hardly a Hercules. The following spring I would be
twenty years old.

Liverotto was discussing provisioning with his quartermaster when I entered. He was dressed in black, I recall, and
was shaven-headed, at his doctor's orders, to treat an infection
of the scalp. He looked fearsome in that guise, even seated at
a desk with account books strewn before him. He reminded
me of a pirate we saw hanged in the square outside our house
in Fermo one time, the first execution I ever saw.

Liverotto dismissed the quartermaster when I entered and
bade me sit. He told me he wished to send me on a mission to
Cesena, to deliver a letter to Duke Valentino and to report on
our progress and receive the duke's instructions. He needed an
envoy he could trust, and he also wished to cut a good figure
by sending an educated and mannerly man. I must be elegant,
also. Liverotto handed me a chit for his armorer, authorizing
me to sign out a sword of Damascus steel with a silver hilt. He
also gave me some garments to wear from his own wardrobe, a
cloak edged with lynx and a fine gray silk doublet. The doublet
I might keep, in lieu of two month's wages, for it would need
to be cut down to size.

I listened to our leader as he outlined the details of this
mission with a feeling of mounting excitement. This was an
opportunity for which any man in the camp would sell his
sister: a chance to place himself before the eyes of the duke.
I thanked Liverotto for the honor he was doing me, and he
gave me a strange, penetrating look, as if he were suddenly
not so sure he could trust me. He opened his mouth as if to
say something, then thought better of it and waved me away.

I REMEMBER THIS journey to Cesena in every particular, although I shall not trouble you with too much detail. This was the first time I had traveled any distance, other than at the sluggish pace of an army, and the first time I had men in my charge. Liverotto had accorded me an escort of six men for security and to lend me dignity with the duke when I arrived. One of these men, to my great pleasure, was my boyhood friend Lorenzo, who had followed me into Liverotto's service perhaps a year after my departure from Fermo. The others were mainly young men of the same noble status as his, condemned to the strange fate of serving at a tailor's son's orders. Whatever they thought of this in their hearts, they treated me outwardly with respect, and we rode in a spirit of comradeship, united by our youth.

Liverotto's secretary had divided the route into *giornate*, days of travel, and we took pleasure in beating his targets, clattering through wretched villages at dawn, throwing up clods of frozen earth in our wake. The peasants watched us pass with the defeated look of peasants everywhere, their women safely squirreled away. As we passed into the Romagna, there were gibbets on every road-fork, hung with corpses in various degrees of disintegration. Some of my companions took to tilting at these with their lances like quintains, though I soon put an end to this sport. This banquet of death was Duke Valentino pacifying his new lands, which had always been notorious for their banditry. At an inn where we stayed one night, our host spoke with great zeal of the improvement the duke's governance had brought to the region. "Animals" was what he said of the men on the gibbets. The ravens were welcome to this prey.

IT WAS A FILTHY day when we reached the outskirts of Cesena, pouring with rain mixed with thin, stinging snow. I had my party stop at an inn outside the town until the rain eased, so I could enter with my fine clothes unspoiled. We were escorted from the gates to the castle by some guards of Valentino's who were sent down to greet us, the first members of his legendary army I had seen at close hand. The city had an air of prosperity and bustle about it. It had surrendered to the duke without resistance, I remembered, wearied by the long feud between two of its families that had riven the place for years at the cost of much blood.

I was told I must wait until evening for my interview with the duke. I spent the afternoon in the fine chamber I had been allocated, nervously rehearsing what I would say and regarding myself in the mirror more than was seemly. Lorenzo kept me company, mocking me as I fussed over my sleeve ribbons and perfumed my linen. He amused himself also by improvising advice on court etiquette: I must be careful not to trip on a dwarf.

Eventually a steward came to fetch me and led me off through a series of corridors. In one of them, a page dressed in garish particolored hose was exercising a pair of greyhounds, throwing a ball for them to chase. They shot past us swift as creatures in a dream.

Shortly after the greyhounds, we reached a massive door with a guard standing sentry before it, and were ushered through into a long, high, echoing, wood-paneled chamber. The light was meager at the end where we entered, but a raised dais at the other was lit like a stage, with candles blazing over it by the dozen. There were braziers down there also, lining the walls, sending of sweet-scented wood smoke that drifted towards us down the room. A table stood on the dais, and a score or so courtiers were grouped around it in clusters, conversing and laughing—the men varying in age and appearance, the women, it seemed to me, all young and fair. A lutenist was playing for them, but I did not hear him at first, beneath their talk. Only as we approached and curious eyes began to notice us coming did the soft music creep on my ears.

When we reached the dais, the steward led me up there and escorted me to the end of the table, where the duke was seated. Silence had fallen on the company by now. I felt the weight of many eyes upon me and hoped I could keep myself from blushing like a girl.

The steward whispered in the duke's ear for a moment; then the duke turned and nodded to me.

"Welcome," he said. "I hear you come from my good friend Messer Oliviero Euffreducci."

I tried to make my bow in the graceful manner my old dancing master had taught me, masking the awe I felt at the duke's proximity. He was as imposing a figure near at hand as he had looked from a distance in Pesaro: handsome, erect, watchful, dark-haired and dark-skinned, wearing an expression of faint and tolerant disdain. He was dressed soberly and finely, in a doublet and cape of Genoa silk, dyed to that pure brilliant black they call *coracino*. He wore no ornament other than a silver clasp on his cape.

A strange little gibbering golden-haired monkey sat perched on the table beside the duke, secured by a silver chain he wore looped round his wrist. To my dismay, as I proffered Liverotto's letter, the beast snatched up the end of it with its long gray-black fingers and would not let go. Laughter started up around the table at the prospect of this curious tug-of-war. Then the duke came to my salvation, prying the paper from the creature's clutch with great gentleness and stifling his courtiers' titters with a glance.

A woman spoke from my left.

"What a beautiful young man! We must be grateful to this Euffreducci, whoever he is. Can we keep him?"

The duke smiled indulgently. "Let him alone, my sweet," he said. "He's an envoy, not a lapdog. I'm sure his master will be wanting him back."

I had turned to look at my admirer when she spoke. She was a woman of perhaps the duke's age, around twenty-five, with a singular face, from which it was difficult to take your eyes. She did not have the soft beauty of Nicolosa. Her face was all angles, but they were beautiful angles. The effect was sharp and intelligent and fine.

This woman was not going to give up her stirring. While the duke studied Liverotto's letter, she turned to a man who was standing beside her and nudged him, looking across at me and smiling. This was a remarkable-looking man, who had caught my attention as we were approaching the dais. He looked as you might imagine the wizards of romance. He was wearing a robe in a lurid purplish color and a white fur tippet round his neck, ending in what looked like two desiccated snakes' heads set in silver. His fine-featured face was surrounded by a great flowing mass of gray hair and a long beard that fell to his breast.

"Messer Leonardo," the lady said, "what do you think of this youth? Aren't you itching to paint him? He would do very well for a Saint Sebastian, don't you think?"

This meant I would be almost naked, with a forest of arrows sticking out of me. The thought of this image in a woman's mind made me blush.

The duke looked up distractedly from his reading. "Stop tormenting Messer Leonardo, *cara*. I've told you." He turned to me with a shrug. "I apologize. Try to ignore this madwoman if you can."

THE MADWOMAN CAUGHT up with me later as I was sitting by the fire with some of my escort, pondering the strangeness of my reception. She beckoned me aside mysteriously and led me into a small chamber, where she asked me many questions about my life.

This woman's name was Angelica, and, as I learned later, she was a Roman whore, or a courtesan, as it was beginning to become fashionable to call them. The duke had taken a fancy to her and kept her as his mistress, allowing her a freedom of speech other princes like to accord to their jesters. She was an extraordinary creature, frank and guileful in equal measure. She wanted to know the entire story of my life and wormed my secrets out of me with disconcerting ease.

"When did you say you left to join the army? Immediately after the wedding of Madonna Nicolosa?" She clasped her hands together in a pitying fashion at this revelation. "Poor Matteo. We must find you a girl to make you happy tonight."

She was as good as her word. Not long after I had retired to my chamber, Lucia opened the door with a shy smile, holding a candle. It was she who told me of Angelica's background and much more about the court besides. Lucia was a sweet-faced girl of perhaps sixteen. She told me she had grown up in a village near Rome, and she had something of the air of a country girl about her still. The duke had seen her as he rode through her village on a hunt and had taken her for his household there and then. The next morning, when I saw her in the daylight, I could understand the reason she had caught his eye. She had long straight hair of the darkest red, and skin pale as alabaster, a coloring you might see in one woman in a thousand. I have not seen it in such a pure form again.

That night, with Lucia in my arms and thoughts of Angelica in my head, I felt delighted to be back in the company of women. The crudeness of life in the army sickened me when I thought of it. I wanted to shed no more blood and to sleep no more on bare ground or on lice-ridden straw. I wanted fresh linen sheets and a girl in them—a girl like this, not some hard-faced army jade.

I resolved that, when I had delivered the duke's response, I would leave Liverotto's service and return to Fermo and continue with the studies I had interrupted. I had money from my soldiering to keep me for a while. Perhaps I would go to Perugia to study the law. It might be hateful to think of Nicolosa with her husband, but was this a reason to waste my life doing something alien to my nature? Everything was suddenly clear. I lay awake for a long time, basking in the faint scent of ambergris drifting up from Lucia's hair and planning the new course of my life.

ON MY SECOND morning at Cesena, I was lingering by a window, looking out at the land beyond the city walls, which was iced with hoar frost, when I heard a voice beside me.

"What do you see when you look at all this?"

It was the wizard from the previous evening, whose name I had since learned was Messer Leonardo da Vinci. I had heard much of this man, though it was hard to discover what exactly he was. Lucia told me he was an alchemist and a necromancer, though Angelica described him, more prosaically, as a painter, and a fine one. He was in Cesena working on plans for fortifications and siege engines for the duke.

I looked down on the scene I had been regarding, peasants going about their winter labors, at a loss as to how to answer this strange question.

"Five hundred years ago, a thousand years ago, we would have seen this same scene here, essentially unchanged." Messer Leonardo sounded indignant. "How do you think it will look in five hundred years' time? Things will be so changed we can barely encompass them with our mind. No, keep your head just as it was."

A board with a piece of paper tacked to it was resting on his right arm, and he was drawing me as he spoke, with rapid strokes of a pencil. We were silent for a while as he sketched, I attempting to examine him discreetly while keeping my head at the angle he wished. I was greatly intrigued by this curious man. It seemed entirely of a piece with what I had heard of him that he drew with his left hand and not the right, like a normal man. Lucia had recounted to me that morning how he would eat no animal flesh, in the manner of Pythagoras (I supply this erudite analogy, needless to say, not Lucia). She also told me he had notebooks in his lodgings filled with strange cryptic lettering that he summoned a spirit to write.

"Are you familiar with the phenomenon of a printed book, young man?" Messer Leonardo asked suddenly. I was taken aback by this question, wondering whether there was some trick in it, and could only nod in reply.

"Of course you are!" he continued. "You have never known a world without such a thing. I knew that world and so did my forefathers and yours, back to the time of Adam. Just think, I first cast my eyes on a book that had not been copied out by a man's hand when I was around the same age you are now."

He paused and scrutinized his sketch for a moment, his eyes flickering between the paper and my face. Then he continued, half-muttering, as if he were speaking to himself.

"It won't stop with printing, you know. Why are we still moving ourselves around like the ancients, no faster than the number of horses we can attach to a chariot? Why do we remain bound to the land like earthworms, leaving the air to the birds?"

His sketching fingers were flying across the page as he came out with this nonsense, seeming to operate quite independently from his volition. I wanted him to go on with his monologue, which I was gleefully storing in my mind to recount to Lorenzo. Instead he continued drawing in silence, once reaching out to turn my chin a fraction to the left.

Eventually he came to a close and said, "Here," handing me the drawing. Then he turned away abruptly, as if to escape my thanks, and vanished down the corridor in his odd purple garment, leaving a faint odor of musk in his wake.

Messer Leonardo's drawing was a thing of great beauty. I can see it very well in my memory: my young, shadowy, dreamy-eyed face. I do not have it now. I sold it to a connoisseur in Rome a few years after the time of this history. In truth, I could hardly bear to look at it, remembering the moment it was drawn.

III

I STAYED TWO DAYS WITH THE DUKE, and I must confess I was captivated by his court and by the man himself. He was virile and dashing and courteous and a man of keen intelligence and good judgment. Take most princes off their thrones and strip them of their pomp, and you would have a man you could pass on the street without notice. Not so with Valentino: you might have dressed him in the garb of a rag picker, and he would remain a fine figure of a man. He had an air of authority about him that reminded me a little of Cardinal Giuliano della Rovere, but he was less grave and liked to jest and to listen to Angelica teasing his courtiers. He was an excellent wrestler and a most elegant dancer—one of the best I have seen in my life, exempting professional dancing-masters. His only physical defect was the scarring he had suffered through a bout of the French disease, but he grew his beard carefully to cover the scars on his face and wore gloves to cover those on his hands.

I am sorry to disappoint you in this account of my embassy, if you were expecting something more lurid from a tale of the Borgias. I know the reputation this family has acquired by this day, and of course it was no different at the time. Everyone knew that Valentino had murdered his brother-in-law, Alfonso of Bisceglie, and many thought also his own brother, Juan, duke of Gandia. Some rumors portrayed him, shockingly, as the lover of his sister, Lucrezia, although few men of judgment gave heed to these tales. Much was spoken of the licentious tenor of life at his father's court, which reportedly rivaled Nero's in its orgiastic debauches. Men believed the pope and his son to be imps of Satan, capable of any excess.

The only sign I saw of this perversity on my first visit to the duke's court was an entertainment I witnessed on my second night there, which culminated in two male dwarves fornicating with a female. It was a curious little play in Latin, involving a rivalry between the two men over the woman. They first tried to kill each other; then they settled on sharing her and pulled up her skirts there and then. The women of the court watched this spectacle alongside the men, most of whom by the end were in paroxysms of laughter. I looked over at Angelica, who was sitting near the duke. She glanced back and discreetly rolled her eyes.

WHEN WE LEFT, the duke came to see us off at the drawbridge, a signal honor. It was a cold, clear day, and we stood there stamping our feet as we waited for him, our horses off to one side with the grooms. He finally strode out in a black, sable-trimmed mantle, followed by a gaggle of soldiers and whey-faced, shivering courtiers. The monkey accompanied them, carried by a servant, wrapped so thickly in furs that you could see only its face.

Valentino drew me aside and handed me his letter for Liverotto. We spoke of the weather and the journey for a moment; then he asked me a question.

"Do you know what was in your master's letter?"

When I told him I did not, he gave me a look I could not fathom and asked whether I was contented in Liverotto's service.

"Your Excellency, I was raised with him," I said.

"A diplomatic answer, Messer Ambassador," the duke replied, smiling. "Cain was raised with Abel, was he not? If you ever think to leave him, let me know."

I bowed low in reply, flattered, and was turning to go when Angelica shot out of the castle doors and ran over to embrace me. She was a late riser. Her long black hair was still loose about her shoulders, and she looked like a beautiful, gleaming-eyed witch.

"Matteo!" she said. "I hope my lord has done all he can to lure you away from your master?"

The duke drew her to him and kissed her on the lips, right there before my eyes. I felt a shiver of desire, watching. Then Valentino turned back to me with his inscrutable smile.

"Perhaps his master will take care of that himself."

ALONG WITH HIS missive to Liverotto, Duke Valentino had handed me another sealed note, which he said had been enclosed with the letter I brought him. It was addressed to me and was from Liverotto, written in his own hand. The note told me I was not to return where I had left Liverotto. He had business to settle in Fermo. I was to ride down the coast and meet him there instead.

The manner of the delivery of this instruction seemed odd to me, for why had Liverotto not told me this himself when I left the camp? There seemed some subterfuge here, but I could not fathom its purpose; the message seemed harmless enough. My heart quickened at the thought that I would soon be in Fermo, just when I had resolved to return to that city to live, abandoning the army. We were a hundred miles distant. With our horses well rested, it would not take us much more than two strenuous days.

OUR JOURNEY PASSED without incident. On the morning of the third day, I was riding along with Lorenzo conversing about the duke and his court and his women, when one of the other youths spurred up behind and said, "Fermo, have you seen?"

We both looked up and fell silent, for there was our city, glowing palely in the sunlight on its green hill. I felt the sight of it in my heart, almost before my eyes could encompass it. I had been absent from Fermo now for two and a half years, Lorenzo for perhaps eighteen months.

I have been remiss, by the way, in not describing my city to you, in case Fortune has never been kind enough to guide you there. Fermo stands on the crest of a hill some four miles from the Adriatic, the glitter of whose blue waters may be seen from its uppermost parts. The city, which is built in brick the color of peach and sand and almond, commands a wide vista. Below are fruit orchards, vineyards, olive groves; in the distance, the bleak slopes of the Sibillini Mountains, swathed in snow for three months of the year. No castle crowns our city, such as you might expect to see. A fortress stood there for a decade sixty years before the time of which I am writing, when the tyrant Francesco Sforza briefly held our city. When the people rose against him, they tore the place down, stone by stone—a story I heard a hundred times as a child. At the time I was raised there, the great buildings of Fermo were the palaces of the nobles, the houses of God, and the Palace of the Priors, where our elected government gathered to rule us. We were free men in a land of tyrants; this was our great boast, beholden only to a far-distant pope.

APPREHENSION WAS BEGINNING to grow in me as we began to wind up from the plain towards the city walls. It perturbed me a little to think of encountering Messer Giovanni for the first time after my discourteous departure from his household, although I had written him a contrite letter some months after I left and a congratulatory one a year later when Madonna Montanina bore him a son.

I had resolved not to think too much about meeting Nicolosa, but thoughts of her began to rush on me as I came nearer the ground she trod. She was a mother now, I knew, and twice over. Both her children were sons, so much had Fortune smiled on her marriage. I wanted to be pleased for her, but the thought of her sons conjured unwelcome imaginings of the coupling that had led to their conception. Two years after her wedding night, it still disturbed me to think of Nicolosa as the plaything of that dolt.

"God rot him," I said through my teeth. Lorenzo looked over at me and shook his head, smiling. He did not need to ask whom I meant.

IT WAS CLEAR that something was wrong as soon as we reached the city walls. The men at the gate were not the usual companionable jesting guards who had seen us through this threshold since our childhood. They were soldiers from Liverotto's army, our comrades in arms, who now looked at us, however, like strangers. I asked one of them what they were doing there. He looked back scornfully and did not reply. I explained why we were there and showed him Liverotto's note, and he went into the guardroom to consult with a superior. Eventually, we were allowed through, but we had to disarm. Nor could we ride on without an escort. We had to wait outside the gate while they summoned men down from the walls.

There were few people on the streets as we rode up through the town, even though it was late morning, and a market day, Tuesday. You would have expected the place to be crammed with peasants and chickens and shouting market folk, the smells of mule dung and roasting chestnuts in the air. Instead, it was empty and the few people we saw in the streets looked fearful, scuttling off like beetles, not raising their eyes when they saw us. Lorenzo called out a greeting to a priest he knew as we passed San Domenico, but the man ducked his head without speaking and vanished inside.

When we reached the piazza, our escort split our party. I was led off to the right, towards the Contrada Fiorenza, while my companions were taken left, towards Campolege, where Messer Giovanni's house was. The men I was with took me to Liverotto's family home, a place I had never been inside, though I had passed it many times. There were soldiers at the door there who searched me again before they would let me inside. I waited for a while in the courtyard, which was swarming with armed men; then a servant in livery came out and led me into the building. I noticed that this servant, too, was armed, as was everyone we passed in the corridors inside.

I was taken first to a small room with a basin of water and a towel, where I washed off the grime of the journey, then to a room upstairs that looked like a study, painted with scenes from Ovid in an old-fashioned style. After a moment, Liverotto came in, his huge frame filling the doorway as he entered, two armed guards and a secretary in his wake.

"Well? How did it go?" he asked. "Do you have anything for me from Valentino?"

I handed him the duke's letter, and he tore it open and cast his eye over it greedily. I watched him with a strange numb feeling, going back in my mind over what I had seen. Liverotto had somehow made himself master of the city. That was the only explanation that made sense. How he had done this it chilled me to think.

When Liverotto looked up, he was smiling.

"'A most civil young man.' That's what he says about you. I knew you would do me credit." He pointed to a chair. "Sit. Tell me, how was your journey? What kind of court has the duke put together up there?"

AFTER MY INTERVIEW with Liverotto, I was taken to the house of Messer Giovanni, where the rest of my entourage had been taken, as I later discovered. I had been allocated a room and a servant, a thin, ferret-faced man with a Roman accent, who I thought was almost certainly a spy. The house where I had spent my childhood had taken on the appearance of a barracks. The square outside where the church of Saint Zenone stood was full of soldiers and horses and chaos and shouting. Inside, the doors of the great rooms were all thrown open, and you could see guards invigilating while men in civilian clothes, presumably notaries, crawled around taking an inventory of the contents. Where was Messer Giovanni? Bound and bleeding in a dungeon somewhere? And Nicolosa? I tried asking my servant, but he shook his head and scurried from the room.

I HAD RESOLVED to go to Dino's house as soon as I could. I had seen one or two men from our company on the streets, and I hoped that meant Dino was in Fermo too. I had noticed, looking down from the window, that everyone entering the building was being questioned and searched, even tradesmen carrying provisions. I wondered whether I would have difficulty getting out, but in the event, they let me pass, after a guard had gone inside to ask permission. Two armed men escorted me through the streets to Dino's house, which lay near the Porta San Giuliano, and positioned themselves outside the door as I knocked.

A maid opened the door to me. I saw Margherita behind her, her face crumpled and her eyes red. Then Dino's arms were around me, holding me so tight he squeezed the breath out of me. He drew back and looked at me as though he could not quite believe what he was seeing.

"Thank God, Teo," he said. "I thought he'd got you as well."

We stood looking at each other, dazed, for a moment. Then I said, "What happened?"

Dino passed his hand over his face. He had dark circles beneath his eyes and looked haggard in a way I had not seen him look before.

"You haven't heard?"

"I just arrived here this morning."

Dino nodded and said, "I will tell you," but he did not speak for a long time afterwards. Margherita was sobbing behind him, and he turned around to look at her. Without a word, she retreated upstairs.

Eventually, Dino spoke, his eyes fixed on the floor.

"Liverotto left the camp to come here the day after you left for Cesena. He said he wished to visit Fermo to survey his inheritance and asked permission to bring fifty men with him as an escort, for his dignity. I was annoyed not to be chosen at the time." He frowned, as if remembering. "The rest I know from what I have been told. Messer Giovanni and all the leading men organized a welcome for him, and Liverotto invited them to a feast at his house the next evening. When they cleared the table after the meat, Liverotto started speaking of the pope and Valentino. Then he said this was all too delicate to speak of in public. He took them into a room behind the main hall. Messer Giovanni, Raffaele, all the notables— Bongiovanni, Paccaroni, Gualteroni ..."

He paused, as though he could not go on. A new and terrible thought came to me.

"He killed them."

Dino nodded. "First Messer Giovanni, then the others. Then he sent for the rest of us to secure the town."

I looked at him, trying to take in this horror. Suddenly I had a feeling there was more to come.

"Nicolosa," I said.

"Do you want to sit down?"

"Dino, tell me what's happened to her." I was shouting by now.

"They came for her the next day," he said. "She was mourning her father and husband, and she had her sons with her. Matteo, they killed them both. There, in front of her eyes. The younger one they had to tear from her arms."

IV

LIVEROTTO HAD KILLED ALL who might challenge his authority in Fermo or who might threaten him in the future—no matter if they were boys of ten or twelve, or infants at their mothers' breasts. In addition to Nicolosa's sons, he had also killed her half-brother, Messer Giovanni's infant son by Madonna Montanina. A guard dashed the child's head against the stone portal of the palazzo, and then dropped him to die on the ground.

Dino's family was safe, although his son Giannetto had been taken as a hostage for his father's good behavior. He and other child hostages were being kept in the house of the Paccaroni family, which Liverotto had commandeered for his use. The coup had been expertly planned. All the priors of the city were dead or in prison, dragged from their houses by Liverotto's men even as Messer Giovanni lay bleeding his life out. Liverotto had been building up his guard with a view to this action, recruiting men from the Abruzzi or Lazio, with no allegiance to Fermo. He had been adding to their number for the last six months or so, we had thought simply to protect his own skin.

Among the black thoughts in my mind as I went back through the town, marched between the two guards, was a fear for Lorenzo. He was a son of Giacomo Bongiovanni, one of the men who had been killed along with Messer Giovanni at the feast. Lorenzo was not his heir—he was not even of legitimate birth—and I hoped that this fact might save him, as also the fact that he was a soldier, and a good one, in Liverotto's own ranks.

When I reached Messer Giovanni's palazzo and sought out the youths who had accompanied me to Cesena, I saw that Lorenzo was not with them and asked where he was. They told me the guards had separated him from them when they arrived there and taken him up to one of the high windows giving on to the side street, from which they flung him to the ground. The others had seen this. They were standing in the square still, waiting to be led inside. They told me Lorenzo had been alive after the fall, although he was broken to a pulp. A guard finished him with a lance through his neck.

I sat in a daze among these young men after hearing of Lorenzo's death. I could not encompass this new horror in my mind. My companions spoke of other murders, too. Most, like Lorenzo's, were of the sons and nephews of the men who had died in the first killing, at the feast. You can read of tyrannies in history and know in your mind that these things happen, but nothing can prepare you for the shock of finding yourself amid these atrocities. It is like the difference (I imagine) between reading the *Inferno* of Dante and feeling those dark gates close behind you yourself.

After a while, my new servant came to fetch me and announced that I was invited to dine at Liverotto's table that evening. I could tell from his expression that my stock had risen with him on this account. The youths of my escort looked at me with stricken eyes as I left, and one or two embraced me as if they thought they would not see me again. The same thing had also occurred to me. The more I thought of it, the less probable it seemed that Liverotto would extinguish all who might avenge his initial murders, down to young boys and infants, and yet leave alive Dino, a godson of Messer Giovanni's, and me, a youth raised in his household—both adult men trained in arms. I watched my servant lay out my garments for the evening and wondered whether he was laying out my grave-clothes. He spoke to me once or twice, asking my preferences in matters of dress. I must have looked at him as if he were speaking a strange tongue.

WHEN I REACHED the Euffreducci house, a servant took me upstairs to a room where Liverotto was dressing. Servants were fussing around, lacing his sleeves on, polishing his sword hilt, fetching mirrors and pomanders. A secretary was trying to read him a document about land rights, which he eventually handed him to sign. Liverotto's eyes moved in my direction when I was shown in, but he did not acknowledge my presence by any other means. I could see he was in a foul temper. It was terrible for me to stand there before him, knowing of him what I now knew.

Eventually he said, "You were at your brother's house this afternoon."

"I was," I said, warily, then added, "my lord," which was how the secretary had addressed him.

"I'm sure he told you some fine tales," Liverotto said, curling his lip. When I did not reply, he said, "You can take that look off your face. I honor you, inviting you to my table, when you are *no one*." He was almost shouting. "The least you can do is to show a good countenance."

Spittle flew from his lips as he spoke these last words. He could have me killed at a snap of his fingers. I looked back at him, trying to meet his gaze with a clear eye.

"I am at your command in all things, my lord," I said.

He gave me a hard look, but my docility seemed to pacify him. He turned away towards a mirror a servant was holding up for him and began to examine the line of his beard, turning his head half in profile.

"Valentino," he said eventually, in a more equable tone. "What kind of a table does he keep?"

I DID SUCCEED in showing a good countenance that evening, strange to relate. Fear painted a smile on my face, assisted by wine, of which I drank more than was prudent. I even managed to eat a little, though I have never felt less appetite and feared that each mouthful would stick in my gullet. The meat on my plate looked repellent to me, as if I were being forced to eat something alive.

We dined in a large, high-ceilinged hall, somberly furnished in dark oak. A portrait hung at the head of the table, of Liverotto's long-dead father, looking soldierly and fierce, strangely alive in the candlelight. A lighter patch on the wall beside it showed where another painting must have hung. We had hardly taken our places before it came to me with a sick feeling that this must be the chamber where Liverotto had hosted his murderous feast. Messer Giovanni had dined here, in this same room, smiling down the table with pride at his warrior nephew, unaware that Death was looming at his shoulder as he took his last wine and broke his last bread.

Around the table were seated perhaps twenty guests: middling dignitaries and their wives, with a few wealthy merchants. These were the new men of the city, those who had welcomed the coup, happy to see the great boughs hacked down from above them so they could have their fair share of the light. They looked at me curiously, trying to guess why I was sitting here at Liverotto's table, not lying cold on a slab somewhere like the other men of my household. Their wives scrutinized me too, with an appreciative air, as fanciers of horseflesh might eye a fine colt.

Liverotto had placed me among a group of younger men at the far end of the table, and we spoke principally of my visit to Cesena and of a journey to Ragusa that one of them had recently undertaken. Not a word was said of the happenings in the city, which gave the whole conversation an unreal air. We laughed much that evening, with the strange, sick laughter that comes when the nerves are disordered. After my third glass of wine, I told my table companions the story of Valentino's spectacle featuring the copulating dwarves. This aroused such laughter that those seated at the other end of the table fell silent. Liverotto made me recount it again.

WHEN THIS GRIM repast was over, I felt exhausted, as though I could drop to the ground where I stood. I was making to leave, but a servant drew me back and told me I was to follow him upstairs. He led me to the room with the Ovidian frescoes where Liverotto had received me earlier that day. Two guards followed us up the stairs. When we entered the room, they took hold of me and bound my hands tightly behind my back, then motioned me to sit on a chair.

I knew this was my end. I tried to prepare my soul by repenting of my sins, but I could think of nothing except my death and when and how exactly it would come. One of the guards was in front of me, gazing morosely at the ground, but the other had moved behind me. I felt my shoulders clench. My mouth was dry, and I could not swallow. They would not use a knife in here, I thought—too much blood. They would throttle me with a cord or a wire.

Then Liverotto walked in. He looked at me for a moment half surprised, as though he had forgotten he had ordered me to be brought there.

"Let's go out onto the balcony," he said, after a moment. "I need some air after that stuffy room."

He spoke in a voice so normal I was almost reassured, aside from the sinister detail of my hands being tied. It was not so odd, I should say, for Liverotto to propose going outside for air on a cold January night. He prided himself on the great robustness of his constitution and scorned all niceness about bodily suffering as womanish.

When we were out on the balcony, Liverotto had me sit on the stone parapet, which rose to the level of my thigh. Beside me he placed a lantern he had brought with him, which threw up strong shadows on his face. All my previous fear had returned now. He had me sitting there with my hands tied, where one push from him would send me to my death. I felt the huge black drop of empty air falling away behind me and was tempted for a moment simply to lean back into it and escape him. As though he read this in my face, Liverotto grasped at the neck of my doublet, so my death was no longer for me to decide.

"I did not know you were such an expert dissembler," he said sullenly. "You looked like a bridegroom at his wedding feast this evening, laughing with those youths."

"My lord, I was obeying your instructions. You told me to be of good countenance."

He paused at that, narrowing his eyes, and then went on with more intent.

"You were fond of my uncle?"

"Of course I was," I said, wearily. It was easy to see where this would end.

"And he was fond of *you*. No need to ask about that," Liverotto said in a bitter tone that surprised me. He lifted the lantern with his free hand to illuminate my face better. "So I think you have small reason to love me. You and that brother of yours both."

He was fixing me with his straight eye as though he wished to scrape clean every last content of my skull. His squint eye was in shadow. I had planned what I would say if he confronted me in this way, but I did not know if I could get the words out.

"I do not judge these things with the eyes of common opinion," I began slowly. "I loved and honored Messer Giovanni, but I know you did not act without reason. You saw the way the land lay, and you did what you needed to." I paused, watching his eye. I did not think I had said enough yet. "You are a man of the stamp of Valentino. He said that to me himself."

This was the first lie I had told Liverotto, and I could see from his face that it was a good one. He pressed me on when the duke had uttered this precious thing and what had been his precise words.

Then he looked down at me and said in a surprised tone, "You're cold."

It was true. I could hardly speak, so hard were my teeth chattering. Liverotto reached down for his knife, leaned behind me, and cut through the cords binding my hands.

"Come inside by the fire."

V

WELL, THIS WAS MY GREAT TEST, and I passed it. At the time, I congratulated myself on my cleverness, but it seems to me now that I merely profited from the affection Liverotto bore me, dating from the time of our intimacy. It was on account of this sentiment that he did not wish to kill me, even if his reason rightly told him that he should.

Liverotto kept me up long into that night speaking of the motives for his actions, until my eyes were burning with the smoke from the fire and from lack of sleep. After my speech on the balcony, he had decided I was a kindred spirit, a man to whom he could unburden his mind. As he spoke, I noticed he quoted back to me my phrases about seeing the way the land lay and doing what was needed. Tyrants love such bland language, as it shields them from their iniquity and helps them sleep quietly in their beds.

What Liverotto said that night was what you would expect from a man in his position. You could even say it was true in a way. This was no time for civilian government or for the niceties of politics and justice. These were turbulent times, and no city could escape ruin without a strong man at its helm. The people decried violence, but they did not see it was necessary at times, to prevent greater violence in the future. Did they wish to see Fermo captured by Valentino and put to the sack?

Later, he spoke of Messer Giovanni, saying he had been a fool to marry his daughter to a son of Cardinal Giuliano della Rovere, and he had signed his own death sentence in doing so. Relations were deteriorating now between Pope Alexander and Cardinal Giuliano, despite the French king's mediations.

It would not be long before the pope moved to crush the cardinal and all who stood with him. How would Fermo have fared then, with Raffaele della Rovere strutting around the city as if he owned it, spawning sons at the rate of one a year?

Liverotto paced the room as he spoke, fired up by his own eloquence, while I sat huddled by the fire like a broken old man. At first, whenever he paused, I would interject some murmur of assent. Then I realized it was himself he was seeking to persuade.

AFTER THIS NIGHT, I was in great favor with Liverotto, so much so that I spent a large portion of each day at his side. He kept me with him as a man might keep a trusted servant or a dog, paying me little attention, but needing me there. His goodwill was a relief to me, for my own sake and Dino's, but also a great source of shame. He would often summon me in the morning to ride with him through the city on his way to drill his troops, which was his greatest diversion. We rode in a forest of spears, the tyrant and his minion, the people watching us with sullenness and fear. I kept thinking of the times I had walked these same streets as a boy with Messer Giovanni. He would stop at every corner to greet someone, and men would approach him to recount their troubles and ask him for help. It twisted me inside when I remembered those times and thought I was now riding meekly alongside his murderer. I half expected Messer Giovanni to appear to me in my dreams like the ghosts in Seneca's tragedies, reproaching me with his hollow, dead eyes.

I worked on my dissembling skills in this period of my life as I had once worked at perfecting my Latin. It disgusted me, body and soul, to find myself in Liverotto's company. I felt polluted when I remembered my past dealings with him and repelled at the blood on his hands. My face and voice could not be left to their own devices in his presence; they must be disciplined like soldiers to obey my orders. "Smile," I would command, and my features would resolve themselves into a lying mask of amiability. "Flatter," I would instruct, and my mendacious tongue would find some new way to lick the vanity of my lord.

I was torn in these days, although my fellow citizens believed I had cravenly thrown in my lot with the tyrant. Opponents of the new regime, those few who had escaped Liverotto's purges, were beginning to assemble in the neighboring cities. A half-brother of Lorenzo's was among them, vowing to all who would hear him that he would not rest until he had drunk of Liverotto's blood. I dreamed of joining these men and fighting under their banner. This seemed to me the honorable and virile course, the course worthy of true men of our city—like our ancestors who had torn down Sforza's fortress back in '45.

Yet I could not see how I could do this, in all truth. My nephew was a hostage. Two tiny bodies were already strung rotting from the battlements of the Paccaroni house as a warning to the families of the boys who remained. If I left to join the rebels, Giannetto would be the third, and then Dino would die also, for how could Liverotto trust a man whose son and godfather he had murdered, and whose brother was fighting alongside his foes? If I left, Dino would have to leave with me, sacrificing his son; and he would need to take his family, and Margherita's mother, and her sisters and their children, if he hoped to preserve himself from further reprisals. We would be a caravan of exiles, moving at the pace of the slowest among us, mown down like hay before we had traveled ten miles.

Such was the miserable labyrinth through which my thoughts wandered in these black days. Whatever route I took, my conclusion was the same. I was trapped. My only consolation was the thought of revenge, which I clung to as a martyr to his crucifix. If I could not seek vengeance in the light of the sun, with the rebels, I would seek it in the shadows, employing the arts of subterfuge I was acquiring at so rapid a pace. Each day, Liverotto trusted me more, gulled by my show of devotion. Each day, he was more convinced of my good faith. Tyrants are lonely men, and Liverotto was a novice tyrant, unwilling to embrace fully the consequences of his actions. He wanted to believe he could still command loyalty, having broken every bond of human fellowship himself. He had made himself a monster and half knew it; yet his mind could not help but revolt against this knowledge. There was a seed of opportunity here for a subtle soul. I resolved to make myself the subtlest soul I could.

AFTER PERHAPS three weeks of this misery, Liverotto summoned me to tell me he wished me to accompany a cousin of his to Rome on a diplomatic mission. I was to go as a kind of secretary—or, in truth, as Liverotto's spy, to ensure that this cousin performed his duties in good faith. Our mission was a delicate one: to persuade Pope Alexander to recognize the new regime in Fermo without allowing him to extract more in recompense for this service than Liverotto's stretched finances could afford.

Liverotto's cousin was a man in his forties named Antonio Euffreducci, a lawyer by profession. He was not happy at Liverotto's decision that I should accompany him on this mission: a young man of meager birth, with no surname, even. Liverotto's kinsmen disliked me and were jealous of the favor I enjoyed with him; they called me *il sartino*, which is to say the tailor's boy, and invented tales of my dissolute life. Messer Antonio attempted to persuade Liverotto to appoint his wife's nephew as his secretary in my place, to spare him the indignity of my company. Liverotto tersely informed him he could either choose to take me or be hanged instead from the rafters of his own house.

PERHAPS A WEEK before I was due to set out for Rome, Liverotto conceded me the use of a house near San Martino, so that I was able to move out of the melancholy shell of a house that had been Messer Giovanni's. My new residence had formerly belonged to one of the men who had been murdered in the first days of the regime. It was tainted for me by that history, and I lived there uncomfortably, sleeping little and ill. I took with me the ferret-faced Roman servant I had been allocated when I got back to Fermo—not because he had become congenial to me, but because I did not dare employ a *fermano*. I was so hated in my city that I feared if I did I might be murdered in my bed.

THE DAY BEFORE I left Messer Giovanni's house, a note arrived at my room, brought by Lena, the serving woman with a ruined face who had been my tutor in the pleasures of the flesh when I was a boy. She told me I must destroy this note immediately when I had read it, and I thought at once that it must be from Nicolosa. I opened it when Lena left, leaning with my back against the door. My hands trembled as I tore it open at the seal.

The note had no greeting or signature and was written in such a way that it might pass as an assignation between lovers if intercepted. It said simply that I was to come to the orchard on the following Wednesday at the third hour of the night. The door from the side street would be unlocked. If I could not come to this meeting, I should inform the bearer of the message. This was all.

The instructions were not hard to follow. I knew that Nicolosa had retired to a convent of Clarissans, which stood hard by the church of San Pietro in Campolege, not far from our childhood home. It would not be difficult to find this side entrance, and the quarter was a quiet one. If I were discreet, I would not be observed. The only problem I envisaged was traversing the streets. Liverotto had imposed a curfew, and his guards patrolled at intervals. After some thought, I created a pretext for my night prowling by visiting a whore in the district of the convent a few days before the night of the assignation. I made an arrangement with this woman that I would return on Wednesday, so she could vouch, if necessary, that I was coming to her.

I HAD BEEN thinking of Nicolosa since I heard of her tragedy not only with concern and pity, but also with a kind of awe. It was as though the excess of her suffering had lifted her beyond the usual reach of mortals. I could not imagine how I would speak to her or look her in the face. Nicolosa had lost her father, her infant sons, and her infant brother in the course of a single day (also her husband, if she had somehow come to care for him). I had some fear she might have descended into madness, although I had heard no rumor to that effect.

I reached the convent orchard that night without incident, slinking through the streets wrapped in a cloak, with cloths tied round my boots to silence my footfalls and a hat to hide my light-colored hair. My poor city stood silent, cowering in the darkness behind its shutters. Even in winter, after dark, you could not pass this way normally without crossing men hurrying towards their homes or their pleasures, stamping their feet against the cold and calling out hoarse greetings. Now there was nothing and no one. The taverns were shuttered. A faint glow from behind some windows and the smell of wood smoke from the chimneys were the only signs of life.

THE CONVENT DOOR gave way when I pushed it, and I found myself inside, among the dripping black skeletons of winter trees. Pale clouds veiled the moon, but there was light enough to see. I kept within the shadow of the wall as I looked around for Nicolosa, pulling my cloak up to leave only my eyes uncovered. One window was lit brightly in the great dark bulk of the convent building—brightly enough for it to be clear that the shutters were not closed.

I felt a hand touch mine from behind and started. I could hardly see Nicolosa at first other than as a shadowy shape, although my heart knew her. She was swathed in a great cloak of some kind. Without thought for decorum, I took her in my arms, and we stood for a moment embraced.

As she extricated herself, Nicolosa placed a finger on my lips, and whispered to me to follow her. She led me through the garden, keeping close to the walls, then, taking my hand to urge caution, down a flight of damp, mossy steps and through a door. There was a lantern inside on the floor, but at first I could see nothing of my surroundings. The place was cold as a tomb and smelled very strange: the smell of a cellar, most obviously, damp and closed and musty, but with something else I could not identify behind it, which made my stomach lurch.

"Sorry to bring you here," Nicolosa said, still softly. "It is the only place I know we will not be discovered. They all think it is haunted."

She raised the lantern as she spoke, and I saw ranged behind her, in stacked wire cages, a mountain of white bones. We were in the charnel house of the convent. Every nun who had died here over the last three centuries was desiccating here slowly, jumbled together with her sisters, awaiting the resurrection of the flesh.

"The abbess is a cousin of Liverotto," she continued. "You saw the light in her window. She watches me."

She was shivering, and I took the lantern from her so she could bury her hands in her cloak.

"I am glad you came, Teo."

"Of course I came."

I was trying to avoid the sight of the piled bones behind her. They were sorted, I could see: long bones in one column; in another, skulls staring out accusingly—some tiny, hardly bigger than a fist.

"People are muttering about you because you show yourself a friend to Liverotto, but I know you do it for policy. So he will trust you. So you can destroy him when the time comes."

"God willing," I said fervently.

"You will avenge me. You will avenge us all."

"If I can." I felt nervous before her pleading eyes. "He is guarded like a fortress. He does not take a mouthful of food without having it tasted."

"No matter if it takes time," Nicolosa said, decidedly. "I hear he is sending you to Rome. See my father-in-law while you are there, Cardinal Giuliano. Take counsel from him. He will know what to do. He is a man of great subtlety."

"I do not think he will be there, Nicolosa. They say he is once more at war with the pope, or something close to it."

"Try him. He wrote to me. He told me to contact him at this address if I needed him. Use what is inside to prove you come from me."

She pressed a paper into my hand as she spoke, folded tight. I could feel something inside it, something small and hard and pointed, not much longer than my thumbnail.

"I will try," I said, and we stood for a moment looking at each other in the low, flickering light.

"You must go," Nicolosa said. "I cannot linger. The abbess wanders the corridors and looks into our cells. She will see I am gone."

Nicolosa took the lantern back from me and opened the door, nodding to me to go up the steps, as she locked the door behind her. She extinguished the light before she followed me up, and I reached down to take her hand to guide her up.

We made our way back to the gate without speaking; then I took her once more in my arms, holding her closely. Her loneliness tore at me. I could not bear to leave her here alone in this sinister place.

This time her defenses fell, and she clung to me. I could feel her shoulders convulse and knew she was silently weeping into my cloak.

"My God, Teo," she said finally, in a small, broken voice. "How can I bear this? I pleaded with Liverotto's men to kill me as well, but they wouldn't. I pray to God every day to take me, but he won't."

I held her and stroked her hair but offered her no words of comfort, for what comfort could there be in these circumstances? Eventually, she pulled back from me, wiping her tears with the back of her hand, and waved me away through the gate.

THE JOURNEY TO Rome was uneventful. We went by boat to Pescara and then onwards by horse—four days in all, at a steady pace forced on us by ill weather. Messer Antonio Euffreducci began to treat me less disagreeably after a day or so, when he saw I had the manners of a gentleman, but we had little to say to each other and rode mainly in silence, huddled in waxed leather capes and hoods to keep out the rain. I would more readily have ridden with the soldiers of our escort, but Messer Antonio's nice sense of social distinction would not permit this. I rode with my mind distracted, reliving my interview with Nicolosa again and again in my mind.

When we reached Rome, which I was seeing for the first time, it impressed me as the strangest place I had ever seen. Ruins of great ancient buildings reared out of the ground every time you rounded a street corner, next to hovels like the dwellings of peasants and the elegant new palaces of cardinals. There was no order to the place or its people. You felt that anything might happen here. The streets were crowded with prelates and pilgrims of all nations, speaking in a babble of tongues, while local folk clustered around them attempting to fleece them. There were pigs rooting around in the debris of the street, seemingly half feral. The whores were also feral, leaning down from the windows and screeching invitations, unlacing their bodices to show their breasts, to the delight of our escort. I thought of Cicero and Livy and Horace and thought how strange it was that this was the same city they had described.

It took an extraordinary amount of patience to win ourselves an audience with the pope, even though the ground had been well prepared for us through letters sent on from Fermo. Liverotto's patron in Rome was Cardinal Orsini, a member of the great Roman baronial family and a relative of Liverotto's old mentor Paolo Vitelli. Even to attain an audience with the cardinal was quite an achievement, however, costing long hours waiting in antechambers and numerous bribes to functionaries. Even when we had attained it, this audience only seemed to shift us a few inches closer to the ear of the pope.

THE WORD IN Cardinal Orsini's antechamber was that Cardinal Giuliano della Rovere was no longer in Rome. He had fled before the pope's wrath and was in Liguria, his homeland. This was a bitter disappointment, but I resolved still to try for him at the address he had given Nicolosa. Perhaps he had left some associate there who could get word to him. Perhaps there was some chance of a message in return.

The address was in Parione, a fashionable area near the river: a haunt, I gathered, of high-placed prelates and the better class of courtesan. The note Nicolosa had given me told me to go to this place and ask for a Messer Anselmo. Then I was to hand him the token that had been wrapped in the note to prove my identity. This was a curious thing. It was a cameo of bluish glass, cut with a figure of a Roman goddess, loosely draped—I thought probably Diana. This object had been cut, very cleanly, down the middle, so you only saw half of the figure: the goddess's slender right flank, half-turning; her right arm, resting on a bow; and her hair, piled in elaborate braids.

My chief concern was to find a means to deliver my message without being noted by the men of our escort. I could not trust them. At least one would be a spy, charged by Liverotto to report if I did anything untoward. I found an expedient on my second or third night in the city, when I went on a whoring expedition with some of these comrades after Messer Antonio had retired. Once I was alone with the girl I had chosen for myself, I prevailed on her to deliver the message for me. I gave her money to do this and promised her more once I had proof she had accomplished the task. In case I make myself seem too civil a man, I should also confess that I threatened the poor frightened creature with a knife to persuade her to keep silent. I told her that if she betrayed me, I would seek her out and carve my initials on her face.

A few days later, I returned to this same girl, enduring the mockery of my escort, who thought me a poor creature to plow the same furrow twice when I had the whole of Roman whoredom to explore. She appeared to have delivered my message successfully and handed me a scrap of paper with the oak-tree seal of the della Rovere as proof. I at once threw this into the fire. There was no word on the paper, but Messer Anselmo—or whatever his true name was—had given her a spoken message to pass on to me. This was laconic. I was to wait for a sign.

We eventually won our audience with Pope Alexander, and I had the chance to bend my knee before the man whom many in those days thought the Antichrist in person. Alexander received us in a room in the Vatican palace, in the new series of apartments he had built for himself. It was a room of great splendor, every inch of it adorned in paintings of wondrous brilliance, filled with much curious detail. I felt as if I had stepped into a vast box of jewels.

I had much opportunity to survey these paintings from the corner of my eye as Messer Antonio made his way through the pompous speech he had written. I also cast a discreet glance towards the supreme pontiff, who, to my great surprise, met my eye with a wink. Alexander was a corpulent man with a receding chin and a pendulous lower lip. His hands, which I think he was proud of, for he displayed them without gloves, were the softest and whitest I had ever seen in a man. I had expected him to resemble his son, Duke Valentino, but I could see no shadow of the younger man's looks in him, nor did he have Valentino's air of alertness and mastery. He looked like a harmless, avuncular, well-cushioned prelate—and perhaps therein lay his danger, for this man was a viper, as all knew.

When Messer Antonio had finished, the pope spoke a few bland words of greeting, in strongly accented Latin. Then we passed to the business of the day.

"I do think your master might have let me know in advance about this matter," Alexander opened querulously. "You speak of his arranging things with my son, but Cesare was not pope the last I heard of it. I like to be kept informed about what is happening in my realm."

Messer Antonio was lost for words. Eventually, he said, "I think my lord Oliviero probably felt that Your Holiness ..."

"That I would feel compelled to disapprove of his means. Of course, of course. These are iniquities. But we must work with the grain of the times." He broke off, then resumed briskly, "Your master will appreciate that there's nothing I can say officially at this stage to confirm him as lord of Fermo. But you can tell him informally that I shall not move against him or excommunicate him or anything like that. Cardinal Orsini has already been bending my ear about him. To the point of tedium. No written message."

This was our dismissal, although we were permitted to kiss the pope's silver-slippered foot in homage before leaving. As I approached him, I noticed he was caressing a fat gold ring on his third finger, with some kind of ivory protuberance. He saw my eyes resting on the thing and pulled it off his finger to let me see it, turning it to and fro to catch the light.

"It was made in Valencia, my home town," he said proudly. "Look under the glass. Do you see the fingernail? Saint Casilda of Toledo!"

I murmured appreciation, and Alexander suddenly beamed at me. "Go on, my son. You may kiss it if you like."

I WAS FEELING in need of assistance from Saint Casilda or someone of her ilk by the time the papal audience was over. I had not yet received any sign from Cardinal Giuliano, and there was no further reason for us to remain in Rome now that our business with Alexander was done. I could not think of how I might remedy the situation, but the prospect of returning to Fermo with no word from the cardinal was distressing. I had taken on Nicolosa's view of him as a magus who could conjure our revenge with a flick of his wand.

The night before we were due to leave, I was wandering with some of my escort through the alleys round the quarter they call the Ortaccio, near Campo Marzio, when a veiled woman with a lantern in her hand accosted me and hissed at me to follow her. My comrades jeered at first, then tried to dissuade me from going, alarmed for my safety—but I was desperate for my sign, so I went.

As soon as we had turned the next corner, the woman whispered to me to drop behind her and follow at a distance of a few paces. I trailed her through a labyrinth of narrow, ill-smelling backstreets, my eyes fixed on the frail yellow glow of her lamp. Then she disappeared into a house. I stood in the street, feeling uncertain, until I felt someone tug at my sleeve from behind. It was a boy of perhaps twelve. He indicated with his head that I should follow him and led me round a corner into a street parallel with the previous one. Here we turned into a house through an unlocked door.

All this time, I had been half-thinking that I might finish this escapade with my throat cut, but when I entered the house, the woman lifted her veil and reassured me with a tense smile. She was a plain, keen-eyed creature of perhaps thirty or thirty-five, with yellowish, unhealthy-looking skin. She motioned me into a room to my right and began pulling at a grate in the floor with an iron ring embedded in it. She was having trouble, and I helped her. The boy had been sent to watch at the door. Underneath the grate, when we finally shifted it, there was a tunnel reaching down, with a ladder of metal steps descending into it. The woman prepared a lamp for me, carefully trimming the wick.

"Take off your clothes and leave them here," she said. "Take the clothes on the chest instead. Turn to your left when you get to the bottom—your right as you face the ladder— and go straight ahead, perhaps a quarter of a mile. You'll know when you get there. There should be someone waiting at the other end."

THE TUNNEL WAS wet as I descended the ladder, and a foul smell was coming from below. I could hear the sound of rats scrabbling beneath and what sounded like a fight between two of them, both screaming at full pitch in those eerie mad voices of theirs.

When my feet touched the ground at the bottom of the ladder, I found myself in a kind of corridor of stone, arched at the top, with a channel of liquid running along half the width of it. It was perhaps four arms' breadth wide and as many high. The lamplight threw up strange shadows on the wall. I began to walk along the shelf by the side of the running water, fighting down the fear that was rising inside me. I was increasingly convinced that this was a trap and I would die down here. I had heard the grate heave closed as I got to the bottom of the ladder and the glimmer of light that had been descending from the room above vanished. As I walked, I reached down and touched my dagger to reassure myself that I had a means of killing myself swiftly, at least. I would not have to wait out my death by starvation down here before I was eaten by the rats.

The woman had said a quarter of a mile, but I seemed to have been walking much further in the filthy air before I saw a faint gleam of light ahead, coming from above. Twice rats, perhaps sick ones, stood in my path and I had to kick them out of the way. Once the bones of what looked like a human skeleton lurked in the water, gnawed to whiteness. In another place, I saw something that might be swollen flesh, with rags hanging off it. The smell in that portion of the tunnel was so particularly vile that I almost choked.

When I reached the light, I saw there was another ladder leading upwards, and I seized the rungs and scrambled up like a man chased by demons. I crawled out at the top into a room with bare stone walls, which looked like some kind of scullery, although the shelves were all empty. A dapper young man dressed in a cassock was waiting for me with a jug of water and a basin and what looked like a pile of clothes.

"*Dio mio*," he said with a grimace, as I stumbled towards him. "I was wondering how you'd smell when you got out."

AFTER I HAD washed and changed into a new shirt and doublet, the young priest lit my way along a narrow dark corridor and ushered me into a small room leading off it.

"Wait here," he said, planting a lantern on a desk in the center of the room. Then he disappeared without a word.

The room was a plain one and scantly furnished, with no hangings or paneling. One thing only hung on its walls, a startle-eyed Madonna in the old Greek mode, half-blackened by smoke or age. Wooden crates lined the walls, and in one corner there lay a heap of what looked like rolled tapestries or vestments, with a sailcloth thrown carelessly over them. A fire was dying in the grate, and I went over to see whether I could coax some life back into it. I was stiff with cold from my time underground.

As I was crouching over the fire, the door suddenly opened, and I turned to see Cardinal Giuliano della Rovere. I looked at him for a moment in wonderment and then sank to my knees, bowing my head. I was strangely moved to see him here before me, undaunted, when he was supposed to have fled north in fear of his life. He was just as I remembered him, tall and vigorous, though perhaps a little grayer of hair and bushier of eyebrow. He stood there framed in the doorway for a moment, dressed in a simple black cassock like a country priest.

"Rise, rise, young man," he said airily. "No need for such formality, you know. We are all friends here." Then he added, gesturing around him with a fastidious air, "You can see I am keeping no great state."

THE CARDINAL EXPLAINED to me that what I had just walked along was the ancient Roman sewer, the Cloaca Maxima.

"You'll remember the mention in Livy," he said. I nodded, though as a matter of fact I did not.

"I wish it had not been necessary to inflict it on you," the cardinal said. "But I had no alternative. I am *persona non grata* in this city while Borja holds sway."

This was an affectation of his that I had noted at our first meeting. He always spoke of the pope using only his surname, never calling him Alexander or His Holiness, and he pronounced his name in the Spanish manner, to underline his status as a foreign usurper.

What he said next left me speechless.

"I was sorry to hear about your father. A terrible thing." He looked at my stupefied face. "I assume that Giovanni Fogliani *was* your father, no? Perhaps I trespass on sensitive ground." He paused reflectively, and then continued. "I was surprised he did not acknowledge you, in fact, since he seemed so proud of you—and with good cause. But then I heard that your brother was his godson, which would make it incest of a kind, of course. *Ex damnato coitu.* You could not inherit. You *did* share the same mother as that other youth, the godson? The soldier? I do not recall his name."

I nodded, and he spread his hands eloquently, as if to say *quod erat demonstrandum.*

"Still, it's good that he didn't—acknowledge you, I mean. For your sake. Otherwise you'd be dead with the rest. You'll be wanting to avenge his death, I imagine?"

"Of course, Your Eminence," I said. I found it difficult to get the words out. My mind was reeling from the impact of what he had just said.

"Only natural," he said approvingly. "I ought to feel the same way, I suppose, since Raffaele was my son. Though, in truth, I can't say I ever thought much of him. A half-baked creature. My daughter is twice the man he was."

We had been standing as we spoke, in front of the limping fire. I saw the cardinal glance across at a chair by the desk, and I brought it over for him, a broken-down thing.

."Here's how I suggest you proceed," he said. "Liverotto sent you to Valentino, did he not, at the time of his killings?"

"He did, Your Eminence," I said, startled, wondering how he had come to know of this thing.

"Wait until he sends you to him again, then transfer into Valentino's service. Valentino will not suspect your motives for leaving Liverotto, if you tell him you are Giovanni Fogliani's son." He paused and looked at me with an air of triumph. "What he will not know is that this is a fiction you have cooked up with Liverotto. You will be spying for Liverotto from within Valentino's court."

I looked at him uncomprehendingly. This was supposed to be one of the finest strategists in the College of Cardinals, and he had me risking my life as a spy in order to benefit my greatest enemy.

He saw my disappointment and continued patiently. "Send Liverotto some good information first so he trusts you. Then wait until Liverotto and Valentino fall out. Believe me, it's only a matter of time. Then you have him. You are the main channel of communication between Valentino's camp and Liverotto's. Use it to lure Liverotto into Valentino's sphere, like a fly into the web of a spider." He sketched the outcome of this strategy through a swift gesticulation. "*Et voilà.*"

I could begin to see the contours of his plan now, though there still seemed a risk in this confident assumption that Liverotto and Valentino would become enemies. How could he be so certain of this? And how long would it take? How long would I be condemned to this perilous double life?

"Well, young man," the cardinal said, rising to his feet. "This has all been very pleasant. I mean, setting aside the grievous circumstances of your visit. But you must be eager to get back. Please convey my regards to Madonna Nicolosa. An admirable young woman. And a most attractive one, of course."

He looked at me pointedly as he said this last phrase, and I could feel myself blushing a little.

"Your Eminence," I said, "she will be most happy that I had the good fortune to benefit from your counsel."

The cardinal showed me to the door, one hand resting paternally on my shoulder. The young man who had greeted me earlier was sitting outside on a cassone and leapt assiduously to his feet as we emerged.

"Galeotto will show you out," Cardinal Giuliano said. "Or perhaps I should say *down*, rather. I'm afraid you'll have to endure the Cloaca again."

I bowed to take my leave and was about to follow my escort when the Cardinal said, in a nonchalant tone, "By the way, if you *do* take my advice—about the spying, I mean—I hope you won't mind dropping me the odd crumb of information as well?"

Despite the apparent casualness of the cardinal's parting shot, it seemed that my new career in his service had been carefully planned for. Before he supervised my return to the Cloaca, the young man the cardinal had called Galeotto instructed me in my new profession at some length. I listened half-dazed. I could not tear my mind from the terrible thought the cardinal had placed in it, that Messer Giovanni was my father, and that I was the fruit of a polluted union. Proofs and counterproofs swarmed in my mind, thick as the vapors of the Cloaca, as I tried to concentrate on Galeotto's words.

"Is that all clear?" he said eventually, pushing his chair back.

"Quite clear. I await the receipt of the other half of this." By "this" I meant another cameo split in half, like the one Nicolosa had given me. Galeotto had given me a new one, bearing an image of half of a svelte Apollo leaning on his lyre. "The person who hands it to me will take charge of my messages, which I am to code according to the instructions you gave me. I am to refer to all key personages and places by code names, which my fellow agent will supply."

"Precisely," Galeotto said with an approving smile. "It's all very simple. You'll be coding in your sleep before you know it." Then he added, "Alas, I suppose it is time for your descent *apud inferos*. Here are your clothes."

He pressed my hand in an intimate manner as he handed me the clothes I had arrived in, and I felt awkward as I undressed under his too-observant eye.

"Safe passage," he said warmly, as he handed me a lantern. "I look forward to renewing our acquaintance in happier times."

I battled with the new demons in my mind throughout the whole of my return journey through the Cloaca. My thoughts were so exercised that I was hardly conscious of the foulness of my environs, other than that unremitting, putrefying smell. I entered the sewer convinced that the cardinal's notion that I was Messer Giovanni's son was impossible, an outrage. I emerged from its clammy embrace twenty minutes later half-persuaded of the truth of his claim. I thought of Messer Giovanni's fondness for me and the favor he had always shown me—far greater, in truth, than that he had shown his own nephews and godson. I thought of his violence when he caught me in Nicolosa's chamber that time and threatened me with death if we were found together again. Other things, too, came to my mind, to which I had paid little attention when they happened. I remembered Dino saying to me on the day he saw me after the massacre that he thought Liverotto would have killed me as well.

The worst thing that came back to me as I walked that loathsome gorge was the memory I have recounted to you, of when I was a child and went into my dead mother's room and saw Messer Giovanni weeping over her corpse. I placed this memory in its rightful place in my story, but it was not something that was present to my mind before this time. The whole scene came back to me with great vividness: the strange sound of his sobbing, the light seeping from the room, the door inching open to reveal him. I even felt again the feelings of my childish self, of anger and impotence and fear. When this image came to my mind, I stopped in my tracks in the sewer. I could almost have knelt there amid the rats and given myself over to weeping, like my father in this memory—if my father he was. It was only when a bat flickered close to my face that I came to myself with a shudder and moved on.

CARDINAL GIULIANO's accomplice must have known well from experience how to predict the length of his visitors' sojourns, for she had removed the grate by the time I returned. I scaled the ladder, and she reached down to help pull me up stinking into her room. When I had changed back into my own clothes, the boy led me back through the now silent streets, rubbing his eyes with tiredness, until we emerged near where I had first met my guide.

I took a bed in a hostelry there, rather than try to find my way back to our lodgings alone in the darkness, and lay for a few hours unsleeping, my hand on my dagger for safety, brushing away the lice as they crawled over my face. I left when the first light showed and made my way back to our lodgings, where the men of our escort laughed in relief when they saw me. I hinted at some monstrous night of carnal adventure to satisfy their curiosity, then went to my room and stretched out on my bed, my head spinning. Half an hour later, we set off for home.

VI

I DECIDED ON THE ROAD BACK to Fermo that I would adopt Cardinal Giuliano's advice if the chance came about, even though it was clear he had his own reasons for suggesting it. It was as good as any plan I could think of, and it had the great merit of taking me away from Fermo. The thought of fawning at Liverotto's side was still more loathsome to me now that I thought he was perhaps the murderer of my father and not simply of my benefactor. I had made much progress in the school of guile, but I was not sure I could master myself as completely as this task would require.

I say "perhaps the murderer of my father," and the "perhaps" is important, for I was not fully persuaded of the truth of Cardinal Giuliano's thesis. I had been convinced for a moment in the Cloaca, when I first assembled the evidence in my mind, but this moment soon passed. There was much to make me resist this revelation, and I fought it with all the strength I had. I did not want to believe that I had lived with my father for eleven years of my life without knowing him. I did not want to believe I had abandoned him without a word and would now never see him again. I wanted my mother to be the goddess I remembered her as, not an adulterous trollop who had deceived her husband with her son's wealthy godfather. I did not want to think of her entertaining Messer Giovanni in the bed I used to creep into as a child when I could not sleep at night.

These were the reasons I allowed the most space in my mind, but there was another, more hidden, that was perhaps even stronger. I did not want Nicolosa to be my sister, or my half-sister. I wanted to retain her as my love, at least in my imagination and perhaps more. My hopes of her had sprung anew, like an unruly weed, ever since our meeting in the ossuary of the convent. I had held her twice in my arms then, and she had clung to me. I had been close enough to brush my lips across her hair. This memory haunted me. I had not touched her so since we were children. There was also the fact that she was a widow now, free to marry again if she should ever so choose.

I freely confess to the inappropriateness of these thoughts, when all I should have been feeling was the purest pity for Nicolosa's grief. But this is the tale of myself as I was, not as I might wish I had been—and when did desire ever know rational bounds?

THE FIRST DAYS I was back in Fermo, I was afire to see Nicolosa, expecting a message from her at all hours. When I managed to see Lena, however, she told me that Nicolosa was no longer in Fermo. She was staying with relatives of her mother in a castle near Ancona, some forty miles to the south. This was a blow, though I consoled myself by thinking she would be safer there, far from Liverotto's hands.

I sent a message to Nicolosa through Lena, who was obliged to me, for I had given her money from my army savings to make up her dowry. She rode to Ancona alone, on a mule, an intrepid journey for a woman, even one whose face was no incitement to lust. My message to Nicolosa was cautious, indicating only that I had done what I set out to do, without details. She sent back no message in words, but when Lena returned, she handed me a small piece of cloth in which was wrapped a gold ring with the motif of a coiled serpent on the face.

I looked at this ring for a long time with a strange mixture of emotions. I recognized it immediately as one Messer

Giovanni used to wear on the last finger of his left hand. He said it brought him good fortune. It chilled me to think that it must have been taken from his murdered hand as they were laying him out.

I knew very well why Nicolosa had sent me this relic of her father. She wished to bind me more closely to his memory and hence to my duty of revenge. When I looked at the ring, however, it spoke to me differently. I felt as if it were a message from the dead man himself, confirming to me that he was my father. I could not bring myself to place it on my finger, even though I imagined this was what Nicolosa wanted. After a day or so of living with its troubling presence, I buried it under a fig tree in the garden, telling myself it was a compromising object for me to have in the house.

ALTHOUGH I HAD made my decision easily enough to put Cardinal Giuliano's plan into action, it was less easy to see how I would go about it. I could not stroll into Liverotto's study and propose that he send me as a spy to the duke's court. The idea must come from him. I hoped he would propose at some point sending me as an envoy to Valentino, but this did not seem an imminent prospect. We were still only in late February. Campaigning was in abeyance for the winter months, and little of any moment was going on.

I settled myself to wait, therefore, irksome though it was, and took up my duties in Liverotto's service. This was a time of feverish activity in Fermo, as our new lord had embarked on the task of forging himself an army worthy of his greatness. This would not be some rabble of mercenaries, such as most condottieri were content with, but an army of conscripts plucked from the flower of the youth of Fermo and its territory. They would be trained to the highest standards, equipped with the best artillery, and organized into five companies with their own flag and livery—a thousand men in total, besides his two hundred horse. This is what Liverotto had dreamed of as he sat sweating over his Livy in the schoolroom. This was what he had imagined as we sat on that hill in Pesaro watching Valentino surveying his troops. Now he had the revenues of a well-sized city to play with, together with the confiscated estates of several noble families. He had constituted himself universal heir to Messer Giovanni, leaving Nicolosa with a derisory pension, which she refused.

I was employed in this great project of the army, along with Dino, who was given the command of one of the five companies. My role was to maraud around the surrounding countryside like a bandit, with a squad of a dozen soldiers, looting each village and farmstead we came to of their strongest and most courageous young men. Most of these conscripts came willingly enough, tempted by the prospect of a stipend and the chance to squander it in the inns and brothels of the city. A few were reluctant, and we had to drag them away amid the tears of their mothers and wives. Once or twice, a village opposed our coming, and we were met with hurled stones or men armed with scythes and axes. We would mark this and retreat, leaving the poor fools to savor their victory; then we would return from Fermo with reinforcements and oppress them with great violence, killing all that were not able-bodied and burning their houses and crops.

On one of these recruiting missions, I recruited myself a girl, without really intending to. This is how it came about. As we were leaving some half-starved village in the hills with our conscripts, an emaciated creature in rags appeared on the road before us and demanded we take her with us. She was speaking directly to me, clinging to the bridle of my horse, and my men began to laugh, shouting that they would have her if I had no use for her. Half in a spirit of jest, I lowered my hand to this girl and pulled her up behind me on my horse.

By the time we rode back into Fermo, the jest had worn thin, and I was not at all sure I wanted this strange gift of fate. As my luck had it, it was a market day, and people thronged the streets, so the whole city had a chance to feast its eyes on the strange spectacle we made. I had half a mind to leave the girl on a street corner, but I could not bring myself to do it, when she knew no one in the city. I decided to make the best of it and took her to my house.

When we got there, I had my servant heat water for her to bathe in, and I threw her evil-smelling rags on the fire, sending to Dino's for an old dress of Margherita's. Her hair, which was wild and matted as Medusa's, I cut short, rubbing her scalp with vinegar to free it from lice. When she was clean, I placed a plate of food before her, which she ate with great avidity, cramming it into her mouth with both hands. Another plate followed, no more decorously, and a third. I noticed, as she ate, that she had bruises on her wrists and arms, layered two or three deep, some fading, others fresher. These were from her stepfather, she later told me, a man who beat her when he had been drinking and also used her for his needs.

Agnese was this girl's name. She remained in my house after this and continued to devour her way through the contents of my larder. I tried to teach her the use of a fork, but she never really mastered it and would always resort back to her hands. Her speech was as uncouth as her behavior at table, and you could not say she was particularly refined in her love-making either. These peasants make their acquaintance with the *ars amatoria* by watching beasts couple in the fields.

This uncouthness aside, however, I was not displeased with my new companion. After a few weeks at my table, Agnese lost her gaunt look and emerged as a comely young woman.

Margherita gave her some lessons in housekeeping and taught her how to behave in the streets. The simplest things made this poor creature happy, for she had been used to having nothing. I remember looking in on her once, a few weeks after her arrival, and seeing her gazing at a dress I had just bought for her, a modest garment of blue linen. She was stroking it reverently, with the hushed air of a worshipper contemplating a saint's bones.

I was glad to have Agnese in the house for company, for I had little enough desire to go out at this time. There was no pleasure for me in walking the streets of my city and seeing the loathing in my fellow citizens' eyes. Sometimes I would go to Dino's in the evening, and sometimes Liverotto would summon me to play at chess with him or to listen to his predictions of his army's future glories. Otherwise, I would stay at home and read or write poetry telling of my feelings for Nicolosa—drafts that I scribbled by candlelight to tear up the following day.

Aside from agnese, I made only one new acquaintance at this time who deserves mention in this story. This was a cousin of Dino's and hence perhaps of mine also, a man by the name of Alfonso, a tailor. He was the nephew of my mother's husband, and had been orphaned young, like Dino and me, and brought up by kinsmen of his mother's in Pesaro. He had left that city after its fall to Valentino and had come to Fermo the previous year. Alfonso was a merry, quipping, irreverent fellow, and I liked him at once. Dino and I did him many favors. Most notably, between us, we procured him the contract to supply the uniforms for two of Liverotto's militia companies. This was the making of his business. Within six months of arriving in our city, he had a workshop of eight men, supplemented by an army of pieceworkers around town.

Here is an example of how fate jests with us. I had spent my youth wishing myself a gentleman and cursing Fortune for having made me the son of a tailor. Now that the possibility was in my head that Messer Giovanni was my father, I wanted nothing more than to be a tailor's son again. I would study Dino's and Alfonso's dark, lean faces, so alike in some of their expressions they might have been brothers; then, when I returned home, I would scrutinize my own features in the glass, searching vainly for our common paternal root. The truth was that I did not resemble them at all, although, to my relief, I could see no likeness to Messer Giovanni either. The person I resembled was my mother, as men had been saying ever since I was a child.

As the winter came to an end, I was beginning to feel a keen frustration. I was no closer to my aim of revenge than I had been when I returned from Rome, and I was beginning to doubt whether I would ever attain it through the means Cardinal Giuliano had suggested. Liverotto was tightening his grip on power by the day, and I was actively assisting him by recruiting for his army. Was this what I wanted? I began to meditate wild schemes of how I might assassinate him, trying to think of means to smuggle weapons past his guards.

The spring brought my chance. In May, Liverotto's new army was summoned by the pope to besiege Camerino, around fifty miles from Fermo, to the northeast. The Romagna was now safely in the hands of Valentino, and he and Alexander were beginning to look south. You might have thought this would be a cause of concern for Liverotto, but, instead, the pope's orders were welcome to him, since Camerino was one of the cities where the exiled rebels of Fermo had forgathered. They were sheltered and abetted by the lord of the place, an ancient condottiere by the name of Giulio Cesare Varano,

who had taken against Liverotto after our army quite gratui-
tously sacked a castle of his the previous year.

The campaign against Camerino was a most inglorious
one. It is remembered now, if at all, for a shameful practice
on the part of the heads of the papal armies, and signally
of Liverotto, whose idea it was. Instead of starving out the
inhabitants of the city, as the laws of war demand, they sur-
reptitiously supplied these poor trapped souls with victuals
brought from Fermo, commanding the prices for them you
can imagine—a man's patrimony might procure him a few
pecks of wheat. The papal commissar who had been sent to
oversee the campaign reproached Liverotto for this unholy
trade, justly reckoning that a general who was profiting from
a siege was unlikely to pursue the war with all the vigor he
should. Liverotto flung the accusation back in the commissar's
face, and recriminations continued throughout the campaign.

This is what the world knows of this siege, but there was a
darker truth also, which was revealed to us only in rumors. The
deliveries of food to the city naturally took place in darkness,
to keep them from the eyes of the commissar. Those charged
with the task whispered not only of payments in gold, but of
prisoners being led out and delivered to them, in chains and
with sacks over their heads. It seemed Liverotto was profiting
from his traffic in food to lay his hands on the rebels from
Fermo, afraid they might otherwise slip his grasp in the mayhem that follows the capture of a town.

What happened to these men is not known for certain.
The land around Camerino had been razed before the siege
and there were many burnt-out farmhouses standing in isolation in the hills, remote from all hearing. The rumors were
that the rebels were taken to some such place to be tortured
for the names of their collaborators in Fermo, before they
were killed. I would lie awake at night sometimes, thinking

of these brave men and the horrors they were suffering out there in the darkness. I felt ashamed, for I should have been with them; and instead, here I was, safe in my bed. A rumor circulated later that some of these rebels were buried alive in makeshift coffins in the woods after their torture, crying out vainly for the mercy of death as the lids were hammered down over their eyes.

Two other condottieri took part in the Camerino campaign, alongside Liverotto: Francesco Orsini and Vitellozzo Vitelli. I shall tell you something now of Vitelli, for he has a part to play later in my tale. He was a man of around forty, the lord of Città di Castello, away to the west beyond Perugia, almost in Tuscany. He was the eldest of five brothers, all condottieri of some fame, and one of the most cunning and practiced fighters of his day. Liverotto, who had trained with Vitelli's brother Paolo, greatly revered him. It was a sight to see them together, both vast men, tall and broad, like Mars and Vulcan out for a stroll. Like Duke Valentino, Vitelli had suffered from the French disease, which was returning to haunt him cruelly at the time that I speak of. He did not attempt to hide his scars with a beard, but wore his pitted face clean, as if to proclaim his lack of vanity to the world.

I came to know Vitelli that spring, as he was often with Liverotto; they would even fight one another at times to relieve the tedium of the siege. Vitelli did not lack courtesy and would sometimes address a word or two to me, though I do not believe that he ever learned my name. He had somehow come to hear that I had brought Agnese to the camp with me, and amused himself by figuring me as an overfond young lover, in need of jesting advice on how to treat women if you wanted to keep them in their place.

I felt a secret fellowship with this man, predatory and cruel through his reputation was, for I knew that he too was consumed by a thirst for vengeance. Two years before, when he was fighting alongside his brother Paolo for the republic of Florence, the Florentine commissars had seized them both on a thinly evidenced suspicion of treachery. Vitellozzo had escaped, but Paolo was broken on the rack until he confessed; then he was decapitated and his head grossly paraded as a spectacle to teach the fate that awaited a traitor. Vitelli spoke of his brother's death often, and you could see his face darken with rancor. A forest of stakes ranged before him with a Florentine head stuck on each would barely have been enough to bring his mind peace.

In mid-june, the weather turned fiercely hot, so much so that you might think yourself in Africa, not among our green hills. There were times, even at night, when there was hardly a breath of air to be had. The smells of the camp had risen with the heat, and the place was as rank as a cesspit. I would have reeked just as much myself without the labors of Agnese, who went to the river twice a week at dawn with a pack of women from our camp and returned with my linen pummeled clean. We were plagued by mosquitoes, and itched from head to foot, however sedulously we raided the environs for mint leaves and onions. Tempers were boiling. Our leaders banned card games after a Swiss pikeman was knifed to death in a brawl.

One humid, lethargic evening, Liverotto called me to his quarters and told me he wished to send me as an envoy to Valentino. This was at the height of his battle with the commissar over his illicit supplies to the besieged, and he had just received a furious letter of reproach from the pope. Liverotto feared that this dispute would sour his relationship with

Valentino, and hoped to prevent this by having me regale that shrewd man with a miserable pack of lies.

I said in reply that I would gladly do anything Liverotto commanded, but I asked whether I might make a suggestion: that I use my time at the duke's court to see whether there was anyone, some serving-man or secretary, I might approach to corrupt as a spy. I said I had been thinking much about the danger represented by the pope's seemingly boundless ambition. Nothing could save a man whose territory he coveted; not merit, not loyalty, not trust. Look at the lord of this very city at whose foot we were encamped—had he not fought almost his whole life in the service of the Church? And once Camerino had fallen, what was to say that the pope would not select Fermo as his next prey? A spy in the duke's court, in these circumstances, was not merely desirable; it was a necessity for survival. I was prepared to risk the peril of recruiting one, if Liverotto would supply me with funds.

I spoke all this very finely, if you will forgive me for boasting. I had rehearsed it so often in my head that the arguments came easily, and I could concentrate on the vehemence of my delivery. Liverotto listened gravely, with no expression on his face, looking down at a bowl of cherries that stood before him and turning one slowly on its stalk. When I finished speaking, he said there was matter here to think on, and that he would ponder it and see me again the next morning. I returned to my tent in a rage of nervous anticipation and lay unsleeping for most of the night.

THE GREAT RISK with my plan was that Liverotto would simply accept it exactly as I had proposed it. I prepared myself for this eventuality over the course of the long night, thinking of how I could turn the conversation if he did. Liverotto sent for me around sunrise, and I arrived at his quarters while he was breaking his fast on a dish of salt cod and bread soaked in wine. He greeted me with great cordiality and pressed me to share his repast.

When we had finished eating, Liverotto told me, picking his teeth with a fishbone, that my proposal was good but the method was too risky. There was too much danger that this spy I planned to engage would simply take the money and then betray us to his master, perhaps offering himself as a means through which false information could be conveyed. Safer by far would be if he could place a man of his own, a man of proven loyalty, within the duke's entourage—and who better fitted than I for this task? He would send me to the duke with a request that he permit me to stay on in his army when my mission was completed. I would be there ostensibly to observe the excellence of the duke's military discipline and to convey these lessons back to his trusted ally Liverotto. In fact, I would be there as a spy.

I sat listening to the tyrant of Fermo as he thrashed around in my net like a fine fat trout. When he finished speaking, I sat silently for a while, looking down at the floor like a man who has seen his own doom. Liverotto came over and sat beside me and spoke feelingly of his esteem for my courage and prudence. It was a mark of this regard that he was prepared to entrust me with such a delicate mission.

I ceded quickly to this flattery, for men of Liverotto's sort do not like to waste time in supplication.

"Very well, my lord," I said with a sigh. "The prospect daunts me, I do not deny it. Valentino has the cunning of the devil, and he will show me no more mercy than the devil would if he finds me out. But I will try my best."

Liverotto embraced me warmly and told me that, as a sign of his gratitude, I would have the deeds of the house he had ceded me in Fermo. What was far more precious, he also promised that he would return Dino's son Giannetto to his family's care. I left his presence with a thrill in my heart, which I tried in vain to quell with thoughts of the dangers that lay ahead of me. For the first time since I heard of the massacre at Fermo, I could feel within me the cruel whisperings of hope.

VII

I CONSIGNED AGNESE TO THE TUTELAGE of Dino, asking that he send her back to Fermo to stay with Margherita as soon as he could organize a safe escort for her. I tried to offer him money to cover her expenses, but he brushed the suggestion impatiently aside. He was filled with delight at the news of his son's release and could not stop thanking me. Before I left, he gave me a dagger I knew he prized, which he had looted from a dead Spanish soldier. It was a beautiful, deadly thing, with the thinnest blade you can imagine—a stiletto, a whisper of a knife.

"Remember what I taught you," he said as I admired it. "You need to angle it like *this* if you're coming from below, and like *this* from above."

I smiled at him as he said this and spoke a true thing, that I had forgotten nothing he had ever taught me of the profession of arms.

VALENTINO WAS IN Rome with his father when Liverotto gave me my instructions and I began to plan my journey. The evening before I left, however, Liverotto summoned me in a state of excitement to tell me that I was not to ride west to Rome after all. I was to ride north to Urbino instead. It was eighty miles hence, but on poor and dangerous roads, so I must reckon three days for the journey. He had sent a courier ahead to announce my arrival and to congratulate Duke Valentino on recent events.

These recent events were astonishing. Valentino had taken the great dukedom of Urbino, a place to which no one had even estimated the pope's ambitions extended. He had done so without striking a single blow. He had set off from Rome in great secrecy and collected his forces at Perugia; then he marched to Cagli, twenty miles from Urbino, in a march of such speed that you would think him assisted by demons. Seeing him approach like some great river in flood bearing down on him, Duke Guidobaldo da Montefeltro, whose family had held Urbino for three centuries, quite simply fled from his path.

I stood gaping as Liverotto told me this news. Duke Guidobaldo was an ally of the pope and had fought long for the Church, as had his father, the legendary Duke Federico. Although Guidobaldo was a friend of the lord of Camerino, he had faithfully obeyed the pope's request that he supply artillery for our campaign against the city. He had voluntarily denuded his dukedom of guns to assist Alexander, and Alexander had profited from his defenselessness to expel him from his realm.

Liverotto drew a particular lesson from this news.

"See?" he said when he dismissed me. "He cannot tolerate them anywhere on his lands."

For a moment I could not imagine who "they" were; then I realized he was speaking of the della Rovere family. The deposed Duke Guidobaldo of Urbino was related to Cardinal Giuliano, for one of Guidobaldo's sisters was married to the cardinal's brother. It was likely, moreover, that the son of this union would inherit the dukedom of Urbino from his uncle, for it was no secret that Guidobaldo was impotent, poor wretch—indeed, it was rumored that he was a gelding, inept to lie with his wife, a witch having set a spell on him as a child.

This was Liverotto's vindication, as he saw it. If he had not had the foresight to expunge every last drop of della Rovere blood from the city of Fermo through his killings, we would have risked suffering the fate of Urbino and becoming prey to a foreign tyrant. Instead, through his prudence, we had the patriotic consolation of being tyrannized over by a man of our own soil.

I HAD AN escort of eight men to ride with me to Urbino, so ill famed were the mountainous roads that led to that city. It was pleasant to be moving, after the stasis of the siege, and to be high enough to feel the wind in our hair. I was possessed by somber thoughts on this journey, however. I kept recalling my previous embassy to Valentino and thinking how carefree I had been then, with Lorenzo alongside me, unsuspecting of his fate.

I was lost in some such sad reverie when a sharp-eyed youth from my escort spurred up alongside me to say he thought he had seen a pair of feet in a thicket.

"A pair of feet?" I said, inanely. "What were they doing there?" My comrade shrugged, and I turned back to find out.

I approached the feet, which were quite clear when you were looking for them, with a certain dread, expecting to find some horrible scene of massacre. These mountain stretches were notorious for banditry, and if you were unlucky you could see scenes of carnage at the roadside the equal of anything you might see on a battlefield. Instead, to my relief, we found nothing more fearsome than two living men, bound tightly hand and foot. They had been stripped to their undergarments and their shirts tied tightly round their faces as gags. There were no signs of violence on their person that I could see, apart from some bruises to the arms of one of them, who had perhaps tried to resist his attackers. I told my men to release them and untie their gags, while I watched from the shade of a tree.

I looked curiously at the bandits' victims as my men untied them, wondering what manner of men they were. Strangers to these parts, almost certainly, and men of a certain softness of life. Their naked chests were exposed as my escort untied them, and they did not have a soldierly air to them. One would almost think merchants, but merchants generally had the sense to travel with a decent armed guard to protect them and their wares.

As I was engaged in this musing, the man closest to me was released from his gag.

"God's cunt, *potta di Dio,*" a memorable obscenity, was the first phrase that issued from his mouth.

THIS WAS MY first meeting with the Florentine envoy, Messer Niccolò Machiavelli, and I must say he did not make a favorable impression. My men stood by, a little stunned, as he emptied himself of the wealth of expletives that had been welling up inside him during the time his mouth was stopped. I had spent almost three years in Liverotto's army, and there were oaths here that were new even to me.

Eventually he stopped, looked me up and down, and said, "Thank you for freeing me." His tone now was crisp. "I suppose I can assume they took the horses?"

I nodded my head, swallowing my laughter to leave him some dignity.

"Matteo da Fermo. Envoy of Liverotto Euffreducci, lord of Fermo, to Duke Valentino."

He did not reply with his own name and profession, as would have been courteous, but simply gave me a keen look.

"Liverotto, eh? Interesting figure. I've been following him since his exploits of this winter. What can you tell me of this new army he's putting together? We can speak on the road. I'm headed for Urbino myself."

As WE RODE up to the town, Messer Niccolò filled me in on the circumstances that had led to his falling prey to bandits. He was riding to Urbino from Florence to join the Florentine ambassador there, a man named Francesco Soderini. His employers in the Florentine government, whom he described with many curses, had not supplied him with funds for an escort. He had hired men in Urbania for the final stretch through the mountains, but they fled as soon as the bandits arrived.

I had done my best, within my means, to restore the Florentine envoy and his servant to some form of dignity. We found clothes for them from amidst our baggage and shifted weight from our pack mules so one of the beasts could serve as a mount for the servant. I cleared a horse for Messer Niccolò by having two men of my escort double up on one mount. Despite these efforts, he was much perturbed at the thought of arriving at the city cutting such a poor figure. He made me swear several times I would not reveal the details of the state in which he had been found.

As we approached within a mile or two of the city, we saw a small party of men and women out hunting with falcons. We halted for a moment to watch in admiration as a bird plummeted down, swift as an arrow, taking a heron in a great gawky flurry of wings. After the kill, two of the women broke from the group and rode towards us at a gallop, their hair streaming out behind them. I recognized one as Lucia as soon as I saw the color of her hair. The other was Angelica, as I saw as they came near. They reined in their horses with a flourish before us, and I made them the deepest bow I could from my saddle. They looked glorious, flushed from the exercise and laughing, both wearing green riding habits, Angelica's slashed with scarlet in the sleeves.

"Matteo," Angelica said caressingly, drawing her horse up beside me and looking at me with her whorish flattering eyes. "Welcome! We heard you were coming. You're looking more handsome than ever. Don't you think so, Lucia?" She said this last phrase in a meaning tone, and Lucia blushed.

"You've come from Camerino, I imagine?" Angelica continued. "Is it true what they say about the siege there, that your lord has turned grocer to the enemy?" I laughed, and she made a face. "He sounds such a monster. I think you should stay here with us."

I had been waiting for a chance to introduce Messer Niccolò, who had been staring covetously at the two women ever since they appeared. Angelica glanced haughtily in his direction, and he bowed.

"We'll come up to the city with you," she said. "Won't we, Lucia? I've had enough hunting for today. You're much more interesting."

As we turned towards the walls, she leaned over and hissed in my ear, "Darling Matteo, who's that odd little man?"

WE HAD BEEN allocated lodgings in the lower part of the town and parted company there from Messer Niccolò, who was lodging, rather improbably, in the palace of the bishop of Urbino, as his colleague Soderini was a man of the cloth. Angelica accompanied me up to my room to inspect it, having dispatched Lucia back to the palace in her imperious fashion. I asked when she thought I could get an audience with the duke, telling her I needed to see him alone.

She sighed. "I'll see what I can do. It's not going to be easy, though. He's like a dog with rabies since this business here in Urbino. He can think of nothing except where to sink his fangs next."

It surprised me that Angelica used this disrespectful language of the duke, but then, most things about Angelica surprised me, including her bodily deportment. She was lying on my bed as she spoke, with her arms and legs outspread, supposedly testing its comfort. The effect was distinctly provocative. I asked where she thought the duke would strike next.

"Who knows, with him?" she said, shrugging. "But I'd be worried if I were your little Florentine friend."

She sat up on the bed, having completed her test, and extended a regal hand to me so I could help her to her feet.

"I don't think you have a hope of seeing him tonight, anyway," she said. "He's seeing the Florentines."

I escorted her downstairs and offered to accompany her where she was going, but she shook her head and said she was fine on her own.

"I'll send Lucia down tonight so you won't be lonely, but you'll have to bring her back to the palace before the third hour. They lock the gates then." She smiled at me wickedly over her shoulder as she stepped into the street. "You'd better not get carried away."

THE NEXT DAY and the following one were just as you might imagine: a strange, nervous time of suspension. I was too tense to stay in my room and spent much time walking the streets of the bewildered city, watching its inhabitants come to terms with their fate. There was a fraught air about the place. Since his arrival in the city, Valentino had remained barricaded in the great palace from which the Montefeltro dukes had ruled, so that most of his new subjects had not yet even seen him. Meanwhile, the inns were filling with couriers and ambassadors and envoys, and speculation was feverish about what his next move would be.

As I was passing a tailor's shop on my wanderings in the evening of my first day in Urbino, I heard a voice coming from it that I recognized as that of the Florentine envoy, Machiavelli. He had a distinctive voice, rather high-pitched and deformed by that barbarous Florentine habit of pronouncing "ca" with aspiration as "ha." He was arguing over the price of some shirts, presumably attempting to replenish his wardrobe after the robbery. With the word *camicia* recurring frequently in his speech, along with less salubrious words of the kind he favored, such as *cazzo* and *cacasangue*, he sounded like a devil newly released out of hell.

I was glad of the distraction offered by this altercation and thought I would intervene to assist my new acquaintance. I went into the shop, greeted Messer Niccolò like an old friend, and stood fingering the hilt of my sword and looking down with disdain at the shopkeeper's wares. I had two men with me from my escort, and they loomed behind me in the doorway, almost blocking out the light. Faced with this menacing display, the shopkeeper capitulated on price like a sensible man, and Messer Niccolò had his shirts for less even than he had been offering. As we strolled out into the evening sun, the Florentine scrutinized me from the corner of his eye.

"Quite the knight-errant, eh, Messer Adonis? This is the second time you have rescued me in as many days. The least I can do is offer you a drink."

This was a pleasant hour or so I spent with Messer Niccolò, and it was illuminating also. I had thought him something of a buffoon when we first met, to be frank, but this impression was dissipated as soon as we began to speak of affairs. We sat in the shade in a kind of orchard behind the bishop's palace, with pear trees and cherry trees, drinking cold wine from the cellars of an inn across the way.

The main burden of our conversation, as you might expect, was the duke. What else was there to speak of in those days? He had taken possession of all our minds like a fiend. Messer Niccolò had been given an audience with him the previous night, along with his superior, Soderini. Two hours, he said, but it had seemed much longer, half a lifetime. He had feared they would never get out. The conversation had meandered in circles this whole time. The duke spoke of his goodwill towards Florence and his desire to have the city as his ally; yet when Soderini reciprocated, he began to hint at dark suspicions he held regarding the Florentines' good faith. The cycle ended with his threatening them that, if they chose not to be his friend, they would know what it was to have him as an enemy, a fearful prospect. They replied by protesting their friendship, to which he replied by protesting his, and the cycle began again.

"The cat and the mouse," Messer Niccolò concluded morosely. "The cat and the fucking mouse, precisely, and it will end in the same way. We talk and we talk, and meanwhile the devil alone knows what he is hatching in his head. All we know is that, if he decides to turn against us, we will be in our coffins before we know we have caught cold." He paused. "You know Vitellozzo has taken Arezzo?"

I stared at him in astonishment and shook my head. Vitellozzo Vitelli had left Camerino with his men perhaps a week or ten days before I left for Urbino, but nothing had been said of his destination. I had assumed when I heard of Valentino's march on Urbino that his departure must have been connected with that. But Arezzo! This was a new campaign, a third one, on the doorstep of Florence—indeed, within Florentine territory. Arezzo had belonged to the Florentines this last hundred years, although everyone knew that the Aretines hated them like fire.

"That doesn't look much like friendship," I said, thinking of his account of the duke's speeches.

Messer Niccolò waved his hand wearily. "He had an explanation for it, of course. Nothing to do with him. It was all Vitellozzo's own idea, his personal revenge against Florence. You recall we decapitated his brother?" He looked at me skeptically. "Or perhaps you don't. How old are you, anyway? You look about eighteen. It doesn't matter, you could be ten years old, and you still wouldn't believe this pile of crap about Valentino's condottieri taking things into their own hands. 'Nothing to do with me. I'm just the captain-general of the Church and the pope's son and the ruler of half of Italy.' That's half at the last count. *Madonna lupa!*"

This was the beginning of a stream of imprecations unsuited to the garden of a bishop's palace, which I shall omit.

It may sound from what I have been saying that Messer Niccolò disdained the duke, but this was not true. He had much admiration for him. He saw in him a vastness of ambition and a relentlessness that carried a whiff of the ancient heroes of Rome. I remember he spoke much of the speed of Valentino's march on Urbino, which was like that of some great carnivore leaping on its prey. This would be unthinkable in Florence, which was governed as a republic. Messer Niccolò could go to his superiors and pronounce, "Magnificent Sirs, I think we have the chance to take Urbino if we move this very hour." The reply would come: "Excellent suggestion. We will refer it to the appropriate committee and have an answer for you by Tuesday of next week."

I laughed at this, but said there were those in Fermo who regretted the passing of our councils. Messer Niccolò smiled sympathetically and said that, however much he complained of the present government in Florence, he would not wish to see a change of regime.

"Though it may be coming, if Valentino has his way. He carries the Medici in his baggage-train, he and Vitellozzo."

These Medici were the past lords of Florence, as you know, sent into exile seven or eight years before. I was going to ask the Florentine more about this, but just then, Bishop Soderini emerged from the palace to summon him to a further meeting with the duke. He was a man of around fifty, perhaps twenty years older than his colleague, with a kind, worn face. He looked ragged with exhaustion.

"Wish us luck," Messer Niccolò said as he stood to leave, wistfully glancing around the garden. "Frankly, I'd as soon spend two hours on the rack."

THAT WAS THE last I saw of the Florentine envoy for the moment. He was sent back to his home city the next day to brief his government masters on the progress of negotiations, while Bishop Soderini remained in Urbino on the rack.

The day Messer Niccolò left, I was finally summoned to my audience with the duke, after dinner. I was taken up to the palace by a courtier who came down to my lodgings with a small escort of soldiers. The security on the gates, where I was searched by a posse of grim-faced guards, reminded me of Fermo in the first days of Liverotto's regime.

Duke Valentino received me in a handsome room on the uppermost floor of the palace, hung with tapestries representing scenes of hunting. He greeted me distantly and expressed his apologies for not having been able to see me before.

We spoke about Camerino, and I began to present Liverotto's defense against the accusations the papal commissar had leveled at him. Valentino listened for a minute or so with palpable impatience, then cut in.

"Your master is a liar," he said. "And he thinks I'm a fool. He needs to watch his step, or I will crush him like a worm."

He looked at me loweringly as he said this and sat awaiting my response. I saw my chance and spoke as firmly as I could, meeting his eye.

"Your Excellency, I could wish for nothing more than to assist you in that task."

The duke looked at me keenly for what seemed a very long time; then eventually he said, "Speak."

I spoke, saying words I had long prepared in my head. I explained that I was Messer Giovanni's son and had been brought up in his household, although he had not acknowledged me and my paternity was not known. I said that I wished to avenge his death and, to do so, had persuaded Liverotto to send me to his court as a spy. I had done this out of hatred for Liverotto, but also because of my desire to be of service to the duke and his father. If it pleased him to make use of the expedient I was offering, he could feed Liverotto any information he wished, true or false.

The duke listened attentively to what I was saying, and questioned me afterwards on several points of detail. I could not make any guess at what he was thinking from his expression. After a while, he rose to his feet and made for the door, saying that he would be back shortly and I was to wait. I heard a key turn behind him in the lock.

THE NEXT TWO hours, which I spent locked in this room, waiting, were some of the longest of my life. At first I thought Valentino would be back in a few minutes and spent my time nervously reviewing what I had said to him. After a quarter of an hour or so, I went to the window and looked down through the blackness to the thin lights of the town. A little after that, I heard a church bell toll the hour. I sat down, then stood up, then sat down again. I spent much time inspecting the tapestries. All the while, fear was tightening my stomach at the thought of what this strange imprisonment might mean.

Eventually, I heard the scrape of a key in the door, and the duke stepped into the room, followed by two armed guards leading a civilian between them. The civilian was a bald man aged around fifty who looked faintly familiar to my eyes.

"I'm sorry to have left you here for so long," the duke said. "I was trying to find a fellow citizen of yours, from Fermo, in Urbino. It was harder than I anticipated. We eventually found this one in the town jail."

He nodded towards the bald man as he spoke. Then he began to question him.

"Do you know this young man?"

The bald man nodded eagerly, glad to be of assistance.

"He's one of the orphan boys brought up in the Fogliani house, Your Excellency. The younger one."

"Brought up by Messer Giovanni Fogliani?" The man nodded. "And treated how? Like a servant or like one of the family?"

The man looked at me with small, shrewd eyes, trying to work out what was going on.

"Like one of the family, Your Excellency. If not better. He was always dressed up just so, riding around with Messer Giovanni on his little pony. People used to call him *il princi-pino*, the little prince."

The duke smiled at that.

"And his mother?"

The man smirked in a way that made me want to hit him.

"She was a peach of a woman, Your Excellency. I'm not sure I've ever seen a finer." He paused and then said, with a nod at me. "*He* used to look just the image of her, before his beard began to grow."

"If I told you this youth was the son of Giovanni Fogliani, would you be surprised?" the duke asked.

The man looked astonished. "Why, is he?"

"I'm asking the questions," the duke said patiently. "I asked whether you would be surprised to learn this."

The man grinned nastily at me. "Not really. You know what they say about women, Your Excellency. The only chaste ones are the ones who have never been asked. That one was asked often enough."

There was a silence after this. I looked murderously at him. Then the duke spoke to the guards standing behind the man.

"All right. You can take him back."

"If I might speak, Your Excellency …" I said urgently. The duke signaled that I might, and I said I hoped he would ensure that this man was not freed soon or given the chance to speak to his fellow prisoners. If any rumor of this conversation were to get back to Liverotto, the entire plan of my spying would be spoiled.

The duke smiled and put a hand on my shoulder.

"Don't trouble yourself. I had already thought of that."

He nodded over my shoulder as he spoke, and I turned round. The guards had the prisoner in the corner of the room with a wire round his neck and were on the point of choking his last breath from him. There was a cloth over his mouth. Above it his face was puce and swollen, the eyes almost popping from his head. There was a particular horror in the soundlessness of this thing. I had not heard so much as the faintest scuffle behind me. It is an ugly admission, but I watched the man's brutal, writhing death with satisfaction, so angry had his words about my mother made me feel.

When he was dead and dragged from the room, Duke Valentino turned to me with a smile on his face, the most gracious of lords.

"So they called you *il principino*," he said. "Not so hard to imagine. Matteo Fogliani, welcome to my court."

VIII

THIS WAS THE MANNER in which I transferred to the service of Valentino. The next day, a servant came down from the palace to carry my baggage up from my lodgings in town. I soon learned the ways of the court: how to swagger my way past the guards at the gates, pester the townswomen who served us, and fight with the other courtiers to catch the duke's eye.

I thought much about the strange episode of the duke's interrogation of the bald man. It seemed to me on reflection that his prime motive in staging this spectacle was to bind me to him, my new master, through fear. What he had learned from the man was nothing, only that I had not been lying in the more trivial portions of my story. My principal claim, that I was the son of Messer Giovanni, remained exactly as unproven as before. The purpose of the exercise was clearly not what it seemed, to verify the truth of this matter. It was to impress on me from the outset that I was in the service of a man prepared to kill a fellow human creature for his convenience with as little compunction as he might a rat or a wasp.

YOU WILL HAVE an idea in your mind of the palace of Urbino if you have read that elegant book on the perfect courtier by Count Baldassare Castiglione. Count Baldassare describes the Urbino court four or five years after I was there, when it was back in the hands of its legitimate lords. He figures it as a corner of paradise, filled with well-born ladies and gentlemen, wits and poets, engaging in decorous conversation interspersed with dancing. Needless to say, this was not quite the tenor of life at the Urbino court when I arrived there in the wake of Duke Valentino's army. In place of noble ladies of the Gonzaga and Pio families, we had Roman whores with stilettos in their garters, who could vie with the Florentine envoy in the foulness of their language. In place of gentlemen from the best families in Italy, we had a scrimmage of hungry, lowborn clerks. More than anything else, we had soldiers, camping out in the palace's graciously proportioned rooms, sleeping on piles of fetid straw and pissing in the corridors. Apart from the suite of rooms on the upper floor in which the duke first received me, the rest of the place had the air of a low-grade tavern. The duke even used some of the lower palace rooms for stabling his horses, not a thing of which Count Baldassare would approve.

My employment with the duke was principally military, as Liverotto's cover story for my spying had stipulated. On the first day I was admitted to the court, I was issued one of the crimson and yellow uniforms the duke inflicted on his soldiery. If there is any combination of colors more unflattering for a man to wear, I have yet to discover what it is. I was placed under the command of one of the duke's Spanish captains, who examined my fighting skills with an air of disdain.

We spent most of our time patrolling the wild mountain lands around Urbino where rebels loyal to the deposed Duke Guidobaldo were gathering. These were determined men and well organized, with many trained soldiers among them and stubborn support from the peasants of the region. Every day we would return from our forays with a string of captured rebels, but new men sprang up immediately to replace them. Once they had been tortured for information, the duke ordered our captives' mutilated bodies to be displayed in the main square of Urbino, piled obscenely on the ground as a banquet for the dogs and the flies. In my first days in the palace, I had sometimes asked for a pass to stroll in the town and escape the confinement of the court, but once we started these reprisals against the rebels, I remained thankfully locked behind the gates.

PERHAPS A WEEK after I joined the duke's service, I was in the courtyard playing cards with some French soldiers when a page came with a summons from Angelica. I followed the youth upstairs and along a corridor towards a half-open door from behind which music and laughter could be heard.

The room the page led me into was a vast, high-ceilinged one, decorated with stucco but almost empty of furniture. Sunlight flooded in through the windows, and dust motes floated in the air. At the far end of the room, some of the women of the court were practicing their dance steps together. A lutenist was picking out a tune, his thick shock of black hair bent over his instrument, and a handsome Moorish boy whom these women kept as a kind of plaything was marking out the rhythm on a drum.

Angelica wanted my services as a partner, it seemed, to try out a new dance for which she was devising the steps. She had me walk through a few lines with her and execute some leaps in the style of a galliard, while she trod demurely at my side.

It was a while since I had danced and I was anxious to acquit myself with honor. I did well enough in the event, managing my turns without stumbling and enjoying my proximity to Angelica, who was flushed with the heat and the exercise, in a manner I found quite arousing. At the end, as our audience applauded, she leaned into my side, smiling up at me in that way she had, at the same time seductive and mocking. Behind our backs, out of sight of our watchers, she slipped something into my hand.

I RETURNED TO my room after this episode feeling a mixture of alarm and elation. A love intrigue with the mistress of the most dangerous man in Italy could not seem a good plan from any rational point of view, but my senses were inflamed and my vanity flattered. I must confess that I was by this time half enamored of Angelica, her lascivious mouth haunting my dreams.

When I opened the tightly furled paper Angelica had pushed into my hand, I was dumbfounded for a moment. As I unwrapped it, it became clear to me that there was something inside it, something hard and small and sharp. I released the final twist of paper and saw beneath it a cameo, or a half cameo rather, bearing an image of a lithe young male figure, bisected down his flank. I reached outside the window, where I had secreted under a loose tile the half-cameo Cardinal Giuliano's secretary had given me in Rome. The two fragments glided together in my fingers, and a tousle-haired Apollo gazed up at me, his hand resting insouciantly on his lyre. I stood there staring at this image for a moment like a half-wit, unable to take in what I was seeing. This was something I had not dreamed of in my most colorful imaginings. Angelica was Cardinal Giuliano's spy.

I WOULD NOT BE telling you the truth if I failed to confess that my first reaction to this revelation was one of disappointment. I had vainly fancied that Angelica had written me a love note; now I saw she had quite another aim in mind. My second reaction was to applaud the cunning and diligence of our common master the cardinal. He had a spy in his enemy's bed, and now another in his army. He only needed to suborn the duke's confessor, if he had one, to make his collection complete.

Written on the paper in which the half-cameo had been wrapped, in minuscule handwriting, were instructions for where I was to leave my messages. The place was well chosen: a crevice in the wall of a dark and ill-frequented corridor, which was nevertheless plausible as a route from the men's quarters to the women's, and hence somewhere anyone might pass without attracting suspicion in that loose-living place. The messages were to be in code, using the system the cardinal's secretary had explicated to me. On a day when I left a message, I was to wear a gold or silver chain round my neck to signal it, going the rest of the time unadorned.

Looking back now, it seems to me extraordinary that I allowed myself to drift into this perilous position, serving three masters simultaneously and betraying two of them, Liverotto and Valentino—one, the more dangerous, directly beneath his eyes. Worse, for whom was I risking myself in betraying Valentino? Cardinal Giuliano was a man at the nadir of his fortunes, reduced to watching with impotent fury as the pope destroyed the last remnants of his family's power. His brother, who had ruled in Senigallia, had died that same year, and now his brother-in-law had been ejected from Urbino. His brother's widow clung on by her fingertips in Senigallia, but only because Valentino had been distracted elsewhere.

Why did I risk myself for him? I wish I could claim it was on account of a cool assessment of his chances, such as one might hope to see from an intelligent man. Yet I fear I was mostly led by less rational motives: youthful rashness, an obscure loyalty to Messer Giovanni, who had created this alliance so disastrous to his family—and, I must confess, once I knew of Angelica's involvement, a desire to look good in her eyes.

THE DANGERS involved in my new career as spy were brought home to me a few days after my arrival in the palace, when I awoke at dawn after a night with Lucia to find her meticulously searching through my things. She was kneeling there in the light of the dawn, her head bowed, silently working her way through my trunk, unfolding and refolding linen, feeling for secret compartments, leafing through the pages of books. Watching her from under my lashes, pretending to be asleep, I had a sense this was a discipline in which she was no novice. She was as swift and exact in her movements as a blackbird pecking at a worm.

My first thought when I saw this was that Lucia was acting under the instructions of Angelica, and that this was a routine procedure. It was not difficult to imagine the gathering of information as part of the role of Angelica's squadron of whores. This seemed less probable once Angelica had revealed herself a spy for Cardinal Giuliano, and a more disturbing suspicion then came to me—that the duke himself had instructed Lucia to investigate me and that she was reporting back directly to him.

Fortunately, I was protected against discovery that first time by the excellence of Cardinal Giuliano's provisions. Even if Lucia had found the half cameo in my baggage, it would hardly have looked especially compromising in itself. My codebook for my messages was also innocuous. It consisted simply of an edition of Horace, one of the slim modern volumes Aldus had begun to publish in Venice—a book you could hold in a single hand, almost weightless, a wondrously novel thing at that time. The code was formed by employing as the letters of the alphabet the opening letters of successive lines of the second epistle. If a letter was repeated at the beginning of a line, you simply moved on to the next.

After the incident with the spying, I was wary of Lucia. It was a valuable warning, for she was so sweet to me otherwise that I could easily have fallen into trusting her. Angelica was always teasing Lucia for having lost her heart to me, and I was sometimes almost minded to believe this whorish flattery. When we were together in company, Lucia would always seek me out with her eyes, even when her duties required her to dance with another. When we were alone together, she had many intimate ways of making me feel I was the man of her choice. She was not the only woman of whom I availed myself in that licentious court, but she was the only one for whom I developed a tenderness. I even read her one or two poems of my own composition—the first living soul since Lorenzo with whom I had done such a thing.

AFTER I HAD been in Valentino's service some months, I was reprieved from my military services and employed for a while on an assignment within the palace. I was to help oversee the inventorying and packing of the great library of the dukes of Urbino, which Valentino had decided he would send to Cesena, the capital he had chosen for his state. This was an extraordinary collection, one of the finest in Europe, famed especially for its remarkable manuscripts. Duke Federico, who assembled it, had no time for printed books, thinking it beneath the dignity of a ruler to sully his eyes with volumes a commoner might have on his shelf.

I wandered in that room enraptured, like a child at a fair, picking volumes off the shelves, drawn by the sumptuousness of their bindings. Then there was a moment of wonderment as I opened them and saw the painted worlds within, so delicate and fine that they seemed to have been limned by the brushes of angels, not men. There were many rare works in this library I had heard of only by name—and not always even that—in

Latin and Greek and an alphabet of great mystery I guessed must be Hebrew. Later we had a Jewish merchant come up from the town to catalogue the works in that tongue. I would leaf through these volumes standing at the great eagle lectern where Duke Federico had stood a quarter of a century earlier, thinking sometimes of how desolate that great man's shade must be, watching what had become of his treasures and his palace and his son.

Valentino had stationed guards at the doors of the library, and we who were working with the books were searched thoroughly each time we left the room. Still, he was suspicious that we would find some way to steal these priceless objects and frequently dropped in without warning to check on us and to gloat over the splendors of his loot. I was the best lettered of the men he had set to this task and the only one who had enough Greek to inventory the works in that language. He would always ask me on his visits what manuscripts had surfaced that morning. I would show him the most interesting and rare of them, some of which he would take away with him to read.

Aside from our meetings in the library, I also saw the duke once a week to compose our dispatches to Liverotto. We worked in this manner: he would dictate to me the substance of what he wished to have conveyed, and I would write it up in my own voice and submit it for his approval. He then had it coded and submitted it to my go-between, a youth from Macerata in Liverotto's service who had found a post as an ostler in an inn.

The reports were mainly accurate, since they were intended to establish me as a reliable source of information with a view to future deceptions. The only fabrications and silences seemed directed not at Liverotto himself, but at Vitellozzo Vitelli, to whom the duke knew Liverotto was close. Two weeks after my arrival in Urbino, the duke had met in Pavia with the king of France, an old ally of the Florentines, and had allowed himself to be persuaded to abandon his aggressions in Tuscany. This was a cruel blow to Vitelli, who was forced to retreat just when he thought he had his knife at the Florentines' throat. The rumor in the court was that the wheels of French persuasion had been oiled by a vast sum from the coffers of Florence. Needless to say, this toothsome morsel of intelligence was one that found no place in my reports.

IX

ONE OF THE PLEASURES of my work in the library at Urbino was the chance to renew my acquaintance with Messer Leonardo da Vinci, who had been called from Cesena to Urbino by the duke to review the defenses of the city. Often when I was working in the library, Messer Leonardo would sidle up behind me and surprise me with some fragment of his internal ruminations. "What if you were to take an enormous lens, say the size of that desk?" or, "You would only need some mechanism for breathing under the ocean." He rarely troubled himself with anything as banal as a greeting before regaling me with these thoughts.

Messer Leonardo was allowed a privilege none of the rest of us were permitted, that he might borrow from the library any books that were useful to him in his work. He exploited this freely. At any time, he had perhaps ten or twelve of Duke Federico's manuscripts in his room. I would alert him to any works of a technical character I encountered in my scrutiny. If these were in Greek, he would invite me to his room in the evening to translate portions of them for him, plying me with strange herbal cordials he brewed for himself, which he was convinced extraordinarily nourished the brain. The chief texts on which he had me labor were the *Automata* and *Pneumatics* of Hero of Alexandria, with their descriptions of mechanical wonders operated by steam and water. He would listen to my stumbling translation with a visionary air, as though these things were springing to life before his eyes.

As we became more intimate over the course of these evenings together, Messer Leonardo began to show me inventions of his own, at least as remarkable as anything in

Hero. These were drawn on sheets of paper with the same extraordinary skill I had admired in the portrait he drew of me in Cesena, with annotations in the knotty cryptic handwriting Lucia had told me he summoned a spirit to write. There were inventions of many kinds in his notebooks, but those he pressed on me most were weapons: siege engines, a giant crossbow, a fabulous chariot with scythed wheels, a great armored shell in which men could shield themselves going into battle, a mechanical knight in full armor whose arm rose and fell to the operation of a lever behind. He would show me these wonders in a most jealous manner, snatching the page from before my eyes if I showed too much interest. Only by feigning indifference could I look a little longer, as I managed quite successfully with an ingenious device for throwing siege ladders from walls.

I praised these inventions of Messer Leonardo's with great warmth to their creator, even though some, like the mechanical knight and the armored chariot, seemed to me the products of an overexcited mind. He drank up my praise with the eagerness of a man who feels his genius to be underappreciated.

"*You* can see it," he would say. "A mere infant, a lad of twenty. Why are the rulers of this earth so blind?"

This was his complaint, as I discovered, that Valentino and the other lords he had worked for, instead of embracing these marvelous inventions, wanted only services from him that might be provided by any engineer of talent—strengthening fortifications, consulting on drainage and irrigation, surveying land for projected buildings in their captured towns. He would harp on this theme at great length, sometimes haranguing me fiery-eyed, as if I had come to request a new drain from him myself.

Despite his tenderness on this subject, and the suspicions that came over him when showing me his drawings, our evenings always ended most cordially, generally with earnest recommendations from Messer Leonardo regarding my health. Besides much advice on diet, he counseled me with special zeal against fornication, which he claimed had severely deleterious effects on the male organism, especially in summer. He once even offered to mix me an elixir that would cure me entirely of carnal urges, leaving me freer than the gods. It was an offer I politely declined.

THE TERRITORY of Urbino was increasingly unsettled as we came to the sultry days of late summer. Especially in the remoter reaches of this impossible mountain stronghold, the strength of the rebels was growing by the day. The attempt to keep order in these lands was absorbing a great part of Valentino's forces, and the momentum of his conquests elsewhere was stalled. There was great rejoicing in July when Camerino eventually fell, and the duke rode down with a few score men to take possession of the city. This conquest, however, had taken three months and tied up a good part of the forces at his disposal. This was the achievement of a normal, flesh-and-blood leader, not the bolt from heaven of his taking of Urbino. Meanwhile, the intervention of the French king had put a hold on his ambitions in Tuscany. The remarkable days of June, when it seemed he would run through the heart of Italy like an earthquake, were beginning to seem distant at this point.

This was a bitter moment for the duke, and his mood turned foul and dangerous. He had encountered difficulties before in his conquests, but none to speak of in holding the lands he had taken. He was a man of good policy and sought every way he could to reconcile his conquered lands to his rule. Even Faenza, which had held out for six months the year before under the leadership of its well-loved young lord,

Astorre Manfredi, had now succumbed to him, docile as a lamb. The thought that Urbino, so easy in the taking, might prove impossible to hold was preying on Valentino like a leech. He grew strange in his habits, remaining all day in his room and conducting his business solely during the hours of darkness. No one saw him other than the occasional ambassador, his secretaries, and Angelica. Otherwise, he lived like a recluse.

It was at this difficult time in the duke's fortunes that I first set eyes on his most feared lieutenant, Don Michelotto di Coreglia, or Don Miguel de Corella, to give him his original Spanish name. This was a man of low birth from the pope's hometown of Valencia who had long been a devoted servant of the Borgia family and had accompanied the duke to Pisa when he was studying at the university there. Don Michelotto had resided for the last year in the port of Piombino, where Valentino had appointed him governor, but now, with the new worries that beset him, he wanted this man at his side.

I watched Don Michelotto with keen interest in the days after his arrival in Urbino. He was already quite legendary as the man to whom the duke entrusted the most sensitive and the foulest of his deeds. At the time he came to Urbino, the latest atrocity men were talking of was the murder of Astorre Manfredi, the deposed lord of Faenza. There was much muttering about this cruelty, for Manfredi was a gallant youth, and not yet seventeen years old at the time he met his death. He had been solemnly promised his freedom and personal safety; then he was treacherously imprisoned in the Castel Sant'Angelo. Finally, he was fished out of the Tiber with his throat cut, roped to the body of his half-brother, the only other survivor of the line.

I first saw the reputed perpetrator of this misdeed the evening after his arrival in Urbino, while he was walking with the duke in the courtyard of the palace. The duke had closed off the courtyard for privacy and they were strolling beneath the colonnade. The two were in deep conversation, their heads leaning together, the duke's dark, Don Michelotto's bald and gleaming. Don Michelotto was perspiring copiously and kept bringing a handkerchief to his face as they spoke. There was an air of intimacy between the two men that surprised me. More than master and servant, their bodies spoke the language of friendship. I felt a strange stab of jealousy as I saw them together, as if I secretly wished I could commune with the duke in this same easy manner. I remained watching them until I noticed Don Michelotto glancing up, when I rapidly withdrew myself from view.

AFTER DON MICHELOTTO's arrival, perhaps on his advice, the duke's reprisals against the Urbino rebels became more gruesome. One day, we all had to sit on a wooden grandstand erected in the square and watch as a score of men died with their entrails cut out of their living bodies before they were put to the axe. The stench of this, in August, was revolting, and the cries of the victims almost unbearable. Lucia sat beside me stiff with horror, her hand clamped in mine. This spectacle was for the benefit of the populace of Urbino, to act as a deterrent to them in supporting the rebels. There was a crowd of people watching, presumably coerced, some standing with faces of stone, determinedly evincing no emotion, others wracked with pity and revulsion as they watched. I knew how these men felt. They felt as I had when I heard of Liverotto's torture of our rebels at Camerino. We were not dampening their rancor by this cruelty, but breeding fresh hatred in their hearts, as mosquitoes breed in a swamp.

Not long after the spectacle in the square, Duke Valentino called me to him and notified me that I was to return to

Fermo. He was beginning to hear rumors that a conspiracy against him was fomenting among his condottieri, and he wanted me back in Liverotto's entourage to ascertain whether these murmurings were true. He told me he would take it on himself to devise some plausible fiction to explain my return to Liverotto. All I had to do was to prepare myself to leave Urbino by the end of the week.

Don Michelotto was in the room while I was receiving these instructions, looking intently at me with his narrow liquid dark eyes. He had a disconcerting habit of rubbing his hands together at intervals, as though keeping them primed for his next nefarious deed. I felt he was scrutinizing me with suspicion, trying to gauge whether I was sufficiently surprised when the duke spoke of this conspiracy of the condottieri. I *was* surprised, not having heard any rumor of such a thing, yet I found myself worrying afterwards whether this had been clear from my expression. This is the power of men such as Don Michelotto, as also of a certain breed of confessors, that they make you feel guilty of misdemeanors that have not even entered your mind.

When i told Lucia I was leaving, she looked at me tearfully and begged me to take her with me to Fermo. She could not bear to remain here in Urbino without me. She could not endure the life she was made to lead at the duke's court.

I spoke consolingly to her, saying I would speak to the duke, but without any real intention of doing so. I was not sure I wanted Lucia in Fermo, fond as I had become of her in these last weeks. I already had Agnese in Fermo. She satisfied me well enough, and my house had become her home. Was I to present the poor girl with a rival? Was I to turn sultan and keep a harem?

Besides, even if I wanted Lucia from the depths of my heart, it would be folly for me to think I could have her. I might as well ask the duke for permission to let me depart with the pick of his gold plate or one of Duke Federico's choice manuscripts. To be brutal about the matter, the women of this court were chattels. They had no family to protect them, and their volition meant nothing. This fact had been clear to me from the moment I arrived, and it seemed to me that Lucia also knew it in her heart, however little she wished to accept it. I felt for her and wished I could do something to help her—but it seemed to me that I could no more rescue her than I could turn the stars away from their tracks.

THE DAY BEFORE I was due to leave Urbino, Messer Leonardo invited me to visit his workshop, which was on the outskirts of the city, beyond the walls but within the cordon protected by Valentino's troops. The workshop was a barn, a great soaring wooden building with a series of outhouses around it. There was much activity in the environs, men scurrying between the buildings, carrying planks of wood or crates filled with nails or rope. Outside the main building was a series of cannons, some disassembled into parts, others whole, and the foundation of what looked like a siege engine on a wheeled platform, with levers on it that allowed it to turn.

I admired these sights politely, but Messer Leonardo shook his head and steered me with an air of mystery towards a ramshackle wooden shed. It was mounted on a platform that had axles sticking out, presumably so wheels might be attached. When we reached it, he drew out a key from his pocket and unlocked a padlock that was holding the door. It swung open and we stepped inside.

An extraordinarily vile smell greeted me as the door opened, and I saw that the space before us was crammed with birds' wings in various states of decomposition, some pinned to the walls with notes in Messer Leonardo's bizarre handwriting below them, others spiraling on strings from the ceiling, disposed carefully in order of size. There were wings that looked as though they must have come from a bird no larger than a wren—minuscule traceries of bones, almost as fine as a spider's web. Others were great brutal things like eagles' wings, some with thick clumps of body feathers attached.

Messer Leonardo was looking round in wonderment, reaching out occasionally to stroke a specimen with his forefinger.

"You are acquainted with the tale of Daedalus?"

I swallowed and said I was. This was the true dream of this madman, I realized at this moment. He saw himself soaring through the air like some great pigeon, his hair and beard streaming in the wind.

"God produced no thing more wondrous," he said meditatively, his long fingers probing some foul web of sinews. The smell was beginning to choke me, and I felt desperate to get into the air.

As I was making my excuses to leave, Messer Leonardo leaned towards me conspiratorially.

"Your master, Liverotto. Is he a man of vision?"

I looked at him dubiously and replied that I thought Liverotto had a vision of sorts. He reached into a pocket of his tunic—he always wore these short garments, in outlandish colors—and pulled out a silver-capped tube, made from some thick reed such as you might see in a bagpipe. Through some mechanism I could not see, with a flick of his finger, he ejected a piece of thin paper from the tube, finely rolled. On this paper was drawn one of his inventions, one I had not seen before, of a gun with many barrels, splaying out from a single carriage in the fan-like manner of the wings above our heads.

"Like Hero's device with the multiple arrows," I said, recalling a passage I had translated for him recently.

Messer Leonardo bridled.

"Not at all. I designed this two years ago. Any resemblance is purely a coincidence." He paused, and then continued, almost shyly, "He may have this if he is willing to build it."

"Liverotto?" I said. He nodded eagerly, his eyes searching my face. I looked at the fearsome mechanism of death sketched with such delicacy of line before me on the paper and thought of the damage it could wreak.

"You realize what manner of man he is?" I said, regretting the words as they left my mouth.

"He is a madman. They are all madmen. War is madness. But this is the only language they understand. You must tempt them first with weapons. Then, when they have seen their utility ..."

They might support your greater project. He did not have to complete his sentence. He was looking at me with glittering eyes from amid his forest of rotting wings. In the interest of escaping, I agreed to take the design to Liverotto and reached out a hand for the drawing.

"Not this one," he said sharply, snatching it away. "That's *my* copy. He will have it only when he has promised to build it and paid me an advance." He drew out another tube, identical to the first one, and handed it to me. "I have omitted two vital components from this one. You can tell him when he has his engineers examine it. This is just intended to give him an idea."

When I returned to the palace, I went to Lucia's room, having promised her earlier that I would see her that afternoon. Along the way, I meditated excuses for not having spoken to the duke about her coming with me to Fermo as I had fallaciously assured her I would a few days before.

When I got there, the room was locked from within. I knocked. After a long while, it opened a fraction. Angelica looked out, white-faced.

"Matteo," she whispered. "Don't come in."

I pushed past her and thrust my way into the room. Lucia was lying on the bed, wearing the same yellow silk dress I had seen her in earlier in the day. A white cloth was draped over her face. Between the neckline of the gown and the cloth that covered her chin, her neck stretched, first white like chalk, then lividly bruised and mottled, almost black in places. Running through the middle of this bruising, you could see the mark left by the cord in a clear line, like a purple-black noose.

"The duke did this," I said to Angelica. It was not a question. She nodded. She looked dazed.

"Ordered it done. She asked him this morning whether she could leave with you. I told her not to think of doing such a thing. I begged her. Especially not now, with his mood as it is."

She sat down on the bed as she spoke and took Lucia's dead hand, interlocking her fingers with it as if she was clasping a live hand. It was a simple gesture, but it moved me, and tears came to my eyes.

"Poor Matteo," Angelica said, reaching out her free hand to take mine. Then she said almost accusingly, "She loved you, you know."

I hung my head. I could not speak. Eight hours before, I had been holding this lifeless body in my arms, warm and yielding.

After a while, Angelica spoke, her voice softer than before.

"You shouldn't blame yourself. How could you have helped her? She was not fitted for the life she came to live, that is all."

We remained as we were for a moment; then Angelica rose from the bed.

"Go to your room and lock it and stay there. I'll have some food sent up for you. He's displeased with you. It's best if you aren't seen."

I nodded. I took a step towards the bed before I left, with an obscure feeling that I should not part from Lucia without seeing her face one last time. As I reached out my hand for the cloth, Angelica seized it in both of hers and placed herself between the bed and me.

"*Don't*," she said vehemently. "It's horrible. She wouldn't want you to see her looking like that."

We stood there for a moment like that; then, with my free hand, I pushed Angelica's hair back from her eyes. I could see they were bright with tears.

"Angelica," I said. She looked up at me miserably. "You be careful for yourself."

X

I HAD AN ARMED ESCORT of Valentino's men for most of the journey to Fermo, but they left me some twenty miles outside the city so as not to arouse suspicion. The fiction was that I was returning in fright, having had cause to suspect that my cover as Liverotto's spy was ruined. The agent of Liverotto's I had been using to convey my messages had a post in an inn as an ostler, as I believe I told you. Valentino had sent soldiers to the inn to ask questions about him, and the man, hearing of this, had decided to flee. My story was that I had heard of my accomplice's disappearance, had assumed he had been arrested, and had decided to flee Urbino to save my neck.

I spent some of my time on the road rehearsing my story for Liverotto in my head, but most of it brooding over the fate of Lucia. The image of this poor girl lying throttled on her bed, her face a thing too horrible to look upon, would not leave me. Guilt gnawed at me. I felt I had killed her myself, by not making our case with the duke. If I had asked him whether I could take her with me, he would certainly not have granted my request and would probably have been angered. But he would not have killed me—not while I was of use to him. A spy with a secure place in an enemy's trust is less easy to replace than a girl.

I WAS ON the last stretch before Fermo, riding through a copse of chestnut trees perhaps five miles outside the town, when I suddenly saw armed men appearing in front of me, three of them. I turned and saw more men behind me. I was surrounded and outnumbered, eight to one.

I sat on my horse still as a post, looking at the men before me on the road and calculating my chances. I hoped, if I did not resist, that they would simply take my saddlebags and my horse and leave me trussed at the side of the road like the Florentine envoy. This was assuming they were bandits. In fact, the more I looked at them, the less I was sure of their identity. One, who I thought was the leader, had the air of a gentleman. Even the others looked more like soldiers than thieves.

Eventually the leader stepped forward.

"Matteo da Fermo?"

I nodded, disconcerted.

"I have orders to take you to someone. A friend. You need have no fear, if you come along with us quietly." He paused and held up a black cloth with an apologetic air. "It will be best if you don't see where you are being taken."

I shrugged. It did not seem to me I had a choice whether to go with them or not. One look at their horses was enough to tell me there would be no fleeing from them on my tired mount. I let them blindfold me, and one of the men vaulted up in front of me on my horse and told me to cling to him as he rode. We rode fast, seemingly across country to judge by the roughness of the terrain. Once we forded a stream, and several times we seemed to leap over ditches. It was strange being transported in darkness, and I thought of little in the course of this journey other than how to stay upright on my horse.

After what seemed like an age, we came to a halt. Arms helped me down from the horse and hands led me through a door, still blindfolded. It was hard even to walk straight without the use of my eyes.

When the blindfold was removed, I looked around, dazed. I was in a rough stone room, like the main room of a farmhouse. I could hear birds singing outside but no other sound. One of the men motioned me to a crude wooden bench against one wall, and I sat down. Then the door opened and a young woman of around my age entered the room. She was dressed plainly, in black, but the cloth of her dress looked costly, and she wore a string of pearls at her throat. Her dark hair was artfully coiffed, and she bore herself erect as a queen, her slender white neck like the stem of a flower. She seemed an apparition in this place.

I scrambled to my feet when I saw this lady and gazed at her in bemusement. She was looking at me seriously with her long-lashed dark eyes, but there was the shadow of a smile on her lips.

"I'm sorry to have brought you here in this strange manner, Messere. It was for safety. I have to be careful. My name is Felice della Rovere. I imagine you know who I am."

I DID INDEED know who Madonna Felice della Rovere was. She was the daughter of Cardinal Giuliano. She had not attended her half-brother's wedding to Nicolosa, as an illness prevented her at the last minute, but I remember much speculation among the women of the household about how a lady of this exalted status should be received.

Madonna Felice explained to me that her father had ordered his agents in the Romagna to submit their dispatches initially to her, since she was in this part of the world on a pilgrimage to Loreto. I almost laughed when I heard this, for I remembered that Cardinal Giuliano had claimed to be on exactly the same mission when he stayed at our house and arranged his son's marriage to Nicolosa. When his patron the king of France invaded Italy later that same year, we all wondered whether there had been more covert purpose to his travels. I wondered the same thing about his daughter now. However devout this lady might be, it seemed a strange moment for the daughter of the pope's greatest enemy to be pursuing her spiritual quest in these dangerous lands.

"It's a good thing I happened to be here," Madonna Felice said. "In the last message Angelica sent on to me, you wrote that Valentino had ordered you back to Fermo to look into the rumors of this conspiracy among the condottieri."

I nodded warily, not sure where this was going.

"It is imperative he be kept in the dark." She looked dramatically at me as she said this, to impress on me the importance of her words. "Whatever you learn in Fermo, you must reassure Valentino that the rumors he is hearing are without foundation. Is that understood?"

"And why must I do this, my lady?" I said, bridling at her imperious tone. She looked at me disdainfully, as if I was overstepping my place in asking this. Then she asked what my opinion was of Valentino.

"In truth, my lady," I said, "I begin to think him a monster. He is becoming more tyrannical as he feels less secure in Urbino. It does not serve his cause. He is stirring the rebels like a nest of wasps." I paused. "He is a tyrant also within his own court. The day before I left, he murdered a young woman I was fond of there."

She looked up with interest at my last words. I had told her this with calculation, to avert any suspicion that Valentino had won me to his side, knowing that women always lend special credence to cases where they think love is concerned.

"Well," she said, "if you think him a tyrant, is it not clear why you should deceive him? The Borgias are Spanish bandits who have captured the papacy and are seeking to exploit it to enslave Italy. They must be destroyed for the good of us all."

I found it interesting, this talk of "Italy" and "us all," although I knew it was empty as air. If there was a difference between the good of "us all" and the good of the della Rovere, that distinction was too fine to discern.

"With respect, my lady," I said, "I agreed to spy for your father as a courtesy, because I respect him and because he asked me to. I am not his servant, still less yours. Did he tell you the reason I went to speak with him in Rome and why I am risking my life as a spy, as he advised me?" She nodded reluctantly. "Liverotto murdered my father and enslaved my homeland. I am sworn to destroy him. This is the end I am working for. Now you ask me to lie to Valentino about this conspiracy, in which Liverotto may well be involved and which may be his downfall. You are asking me to protect Liverotto against the one man in Italy who has the power, and now perhaps the motive, to destroy him. How can you ask me this, my lady, in all justice?"

Madonna Felice turned her beautiful dark eyes on me beseechingly. They were her best weapons, and she knew how to use them. She had entirely changed her tone.

"Messer Matteo, I understand your position, believe me. But you must have patience. Once Alexander has fallen, and my father is pope, do you think he will tolerate a man like Liverotto in power for a moment? He will crush these petty tyrants of the lands of Saint Peter the moment he sits on that throne." She paused for effect and then moved on to her peroration. "Help us now. Wait your time. It will come. My father will give you the chance to turn your knife in Liverotto's throat with your own hand if you wish it. I swear to you, if he is not dead within three years, you may have my hand in marriage."

These last words were so unexpected that I laughed. I had thought she would say I might proclaim her a liar in every piazza in the land or some such phrase.

"Does that seem to you so small a thing?" she said haughtily.

"No, my lady," I said. "Quite the contrary. I was just wondering what your father would think of that promise."

She laughed then with me, and said, "It will not come to pass. Liverotto will be rotting in hell long before then. Do not forget that he was the murderer of my brother and my nephews. I have no more cause to love him than you." She paused, then looked up at me most seductively through her lashes. "Although perhaps it would not be such a penance to be wedded to you. Angelica told me you were a handsome man, and she did not lie."

"My lady," I said with a sigh, "I capitulate. What man could deny anything to a woman such as you?"

I said this flirtatiously, in keeping with the tone of her last words, but it was true that I was not in a position to deny her anything. Here I was, I knew not where, in an isolated farmhouse with a band of armed men outside awaiting her orders. She was using her best skills of persuasion on me, out of courtesy or habit, but the result was hardly in doubt.

Still, I was uneasy. Especially since his murder of Lucia, I was not unwilling to work for the downfall of Valentino, as long as it did not compromise the destruction of Liverotto. Madonna Felice's suggestion that these two ends were compatible was as seductive to me as she could have hoped. The sleights of hand in her argument had not escaped me, however. She had forged a seamless causal chain from the downfall of the duke to the death of the pope to her father's election. Yet each of these things was uncertain in itself and the combination of them more uncertain still.

Madonna Felice had me swear to my promise on a crucifix, which I did with a sinking heart; then she had one of her men bring in some bread and roast meat and wine for me to dine on. As I ate, she interrogated me with forensic precision about Valentino's court and the state of disturbance caused to his regime by the Urbino rebels. Then we spoke a little of the politics of the Roman court and the latest outrages of the pope. I was impressed by the acuity of her comments on these things. Behind those girlish long lashes was a sharp and orderly mind. It had seemed extraordinary to me at the beginning of our conversation that the cardinal should allow this young woman such a hand in his affairs, but by the end of our meeting, I could see why he did. Her combination of beauty, intelligence, and, I suspected, a certain ruthlessness made her a valuable weapon in the cardinal's arsenal—perhaps more deadly than many of those that the fertile mind of Messer Leonardo da Vinci had dreamed up.

MY INITIAL RECEPTION back in Fermo was not kind. My Urbino accomplice had arrived back in the city by this time, and Liverotto was angry with me for my cravenness in fleeing when I heard this man was under suspicion without waiting to ascertain his fate. I listened patiently to my master's foul-mouthed rebukes with a mask of contrition on my face.

When Liverotto had vented the worst of his spleen, I presented him with Messer Leonardo's gun design, encased in its cane tube. This proved to be the turning of my fortunes. I made the offering with much flattery, reporting speeches of Messer Leonardo in which he spoke of Liverotto as a man clearly destined for greatness. Liverotto listened with visible pleasure and studied the drawing with the eagerness of a lover contemplating a portrait of his beloved. He was even fascinated by the tube, with its lever and spring mechanism, and kept on playing with it, opening and closing it, while I regaled him with tales of the many other ingenious devices Messer Leonardo could supply.

When I had finished, Liverotto embraced me and invited me to stay to dinner with some visiting dignitaries. He said he would write a letter to Valentino giving some pretext for my departure from his court. His previous ill temper was banished by this evidence of my unexpected genius as an agent. As I left him to change my clothes for dinner, I saw him immediately turn back to Messer Leonardo's sketch.

I WENT TO Dino's the following day to catch up on what had been happening in Fermo in my absence. Liverotto had caused fresh scandal by murdering two wealthy men of the city on his return from Camerino. He had invited them to dinner, fed them guinea fowl stuffed with rat poison, and appropriated their estates to feed the burgeoning costs of his militia. This story helped account for a certain lack of appetite I had observed among Liverotto's dinner guests the evening before.

I had expected to collect Agnese from Dino's house, but Dino told me, to my surprise, that he had married her to a soldier in his company, a man named Giacomino. He said this with a certain embarrassment, and for a moment I was resentful at his high-handedness in disposing of my lover in this way. I was on the point of reproaching him, but then thought better of it. This was a good match for the girl. The husband was a city man, from a decent artisan family, and he had presumably taken her without a dowry. Dino could hardly have been expected to deny her this fair chance simply to preserve her for my ungodly pleasures in the event of my return.

My annoyance vanished, in any case, when Dino told me soon afterwards that Nicolosa was now back in Fermo. She had taken a house on the outskirts of town and was living a retired life, having persuaded Liverotto that she was reconciled to his theft of her inheritance. Margherita had been to visit her a few times, but Dino had not. To avoid gossip, she received only women in her house.

Margherita told me Nicolosa was as well as you could expect and showed me a gown she had embroidered for my third nephew, who was named Matteo after me. He had been born while I was in Urbino. The thought of Nicolosa working on this tender garment, stirring memories of her own murdered infants, made me feel inexpressibly sad. I asked whether there was any possibility of seeing her, feigning that I had something of importance to tell her. Margherita exchanged a glance with Dino that made me feel uncomfortable, but said she would ask Nicolosa when they next met.

ONE TASK THAT pressed on me in my first days in Fermo was to establish a safe means for passing messages to Valentino. These would be worthless, for I had promised as much to Madonna Felice, but a system still needed to be in place.

I entrusted the task of conveying my messages out of Fermo to my cousin Alfonso, the tailor. I asked his help diffidently, warning him that there could be danger in it for him, but he agreed without hesitation. He was a man who knew risk, having fought in the army of the lord of Pesaro for two years before settling to his tailoring trade. This is what we arranged. Each Sunday, Alfonso rode out of town to a smallholding he had bought which was a source of great delight to him. He would leave my useless reports in the hollow of a tree on this farm, from which Valentino's courier would extract them at night.

What did I write? It did not seem prudent to me to deny the existence of the conspiracy, for it was something that was spoken of openly in Fermo, and the rumors that were reaching the duke must by now be sufficient for such a claim to lose me all credit with him. Instead, I spoke of it as something that was talked of, but about which it was impossible to find firm information. I painted Fermo as a maelstrom of rumors and counter-rumors and gave conflicting lists of the possible conspirators' names. I spoke much about Liverotto's concern with secrecy and said that he had not taken me back into his confidence since my return from Urbino.

I prayed to God as I wrote this that Valentino did not have any other source of information in Fermo aside from me. In truth, after my triumph with Messer Leonardo's cannon, I was as much in favor with Liverotto as ever before.

XI

AFTER I HAD BEEN TWO or three weeks in Fermo, Nicolosa sent word to me through Margherita that I could come to her house. She told me I should come in disguise, as she thought she was under observation. I thought it safest to go dressed as a woman, given that Dino had told me Nicolosa did not receive men. I went in a dress I had bought for Agnese, heavily veiled, though not so heavily that I did not need to sacrifice my beard.

Nicolosa smiled when she saw me in this farcical disguise—though with a new, sad smile, not the old smile I remembered so well.

"You make a better-looking woman than many real ones," she said as I released her from my embrace.

This was the first time I had seen her since Cardinal Giuliano had put it into my mind that I might be her brother. I tried to remind myself of this when I was speaking to her, but it did not prevent me from feeling the sense of breathlessness I always felt in her presence.

Nicolosa looked older and thinner than the image of her in my mind, and her hair was now pulled back severely and hidden by a veil. She was still to my mind the image of beauty, however, the thinness of her face even enhancing the lovely shape of her cheekbones. I thought of the beautiful women I had seen since I last saw her—Angelica, Lucia, Madonna Felice—and they all seemed to me nothing at her side.

Nicolosa had received me in a back room of the house, where we could not be observed from the street, and she had given her servants leave for the day so that we could speak freely. I took off my disguise—I was wearing normal dress underneath—and we spoke together for more than an hour. She wanted a full report on my progress against Liverotto, and I told her of my visit to Cardinal Giuliano and my time at Urbino, while she listened to me with her sweet, serious eyes fixed on my face. I made some strategic omissions in the story I told her that now seem to me variously disreputable as I think of them. I did not tell her of Lucia when I was speaking of Urbino, nor of my meeting with Madonna Felice. Most of all, I said nothing of what Cardinal Giuliano had suggested regarding my paternity, even though this was in my mind every moment as I spoke.

When I had finished my story, I rose to leave. We both knew there was danger in protracting my visit. We stood for a moment an arm's breadth apart, looking at one another in silence. My heart was shrinking in misery at the thought of leaving her, with no notion of when I would see her again.

Then Nicolosa reached out and put her hands lightly on my forearms.

"Don't leave, Teo," she whispered.

I looked at her and understood what she was proposing from her expression. A violent shock went through me.

She went on diffidently. "I always thought when I was a little girl that we would marry when we grew up. Do you remember, I used to make you my husband in our games?"

Her eyes were cast down as she spoke. I could see how extraordinary it felt to her to be making this shameless offer to me. I hesitated, thinking of the thing I had not told her, and she pulled back from me sharply and said in a small voice, "Not if you don't want to. I thought …"

I fell on my knees then and buried my face in her skirts, unable to speak. She stood for a moment running her hand through my hair, then knelt beside me and looked into my eyes. A strong golden late-afternoon light shone through the window, lighting up her pale face like a saint in an altarpiece. I took this lovely face in my hands and drew it towards me and kissed her feverishly on her half-parted lips.

WELL, I HAVE shocked you now, reader, and rightly. Up to this point in my story, you have probably thought of me, if not as a good man, at least as a man who has suffered worse from others than he has been guilty of himself. This is the time when your view of me must change. Incest is one of the sins most hateful to God, yet I was willing not only to commit it myself but also to blacken another's soul with it—a woman I had always said I loved. I might say in mitigation that I had no firm evidence of our relationship, which indeed I later came to doubt, for reasons I will tell you. But this is small mitigation. What kind of a man lies with a woman when the suspicion that she is his sister lurks even in the farthest reach of his mind?

I put all this from my thoughts, like the sinful man I was, as my body took its pleasure with Nicolosa. As we lay there afterwards, however, our limbs entwined stickily together in the August heat, guilt descended on me like an axe. A blinding conviction came to me that this was my sister in my arms and that Messer Giovanni was my father. I felt I had been resisting these truths only through the prompting of the devil, or the devil I carried within.

I felt I knew all this now the more clearly because Messer Giovanni had carried this same devil inside him. I suddenly understood him. He had loved my mother as I loved Nicolosa. No scruple could stand in his way. I lay thinking of him lying beside my dead mother on her bed, weeping; then I became aware that, beside me, his daughter was silently weeping into my shoulder.

"What is it, my love?" I asked softly, but Nicolosa shook her head, squeezing my hand to reassure me, and said it was nothing. After that, we were silent for a long time.

IN THE FIRST days after this remarkable event in my life, I staggered round like a drunken man, unable to take in what was happening around me. The poet Petrarca and his followers like to speak of love as an emotion composed of violent simultaneous opposites, such as ecstasy and terror. I had spoken of this often in the verses I had written, but only at this moment did it seem to me true. There can be few joys in life equal to that of discovering that a long and arduous love is reciprocated. Every moment of my life now seemed different, thinking that Nicolosa had loved me all this while. At the same time, it sickened me to think of our ungodly coupling. I could not believe myself capable of such vileness. I tried as hard as I could to convince myself that I had no firm evidence that Messer Giovanni was my father and that my sudden sense of conviction was pure superstition. This persuasion served me well enough during the hours of daylight, but at night the full horror returned.

IT WAS ALMOST a relief, at this tortured time, when Liverotto called me to his house one day and told me to prepare for departure the next morning to an undisclosed location. I was eager to snatch at anything that could distract me for a moment from my thoughts.

We left at dawn, accompanied by a guard of twenty lancers, with a couple of mounted crossbowmen to bring up the rear. Liverotto and I rode in front, with the guards ranked behind us, throwing up clouds of white dust on the road. We rode west, through fields where peasants were harvesting their grapes under the sun of early October, which was still hot that year. Liverotto was in good spirits and amused himself by harassing any unaccompanied women we chanced upon on the road. One he seized at knifepoint and hoisted up onto his horse, unlacing her bodice as he rode, so the poor creature was half naked. He kept her for the night at an inn that we stayed at, charging me to pay her for her services the next day.

We were two days on the road, riding west towards Perugia. On the afternoon of the second day, when we had left that city behind us, a glint of water met our eyes, and I saw what I knew must be the great lake of Trasimeno, where Hannibal once butchered the armies of the Romans. The day was a glorious one, and the land looked beautiful and rich and peaceful, the occasional burned or ruined farmstead the only sign of the violence of the times. We skirted the lake for a while along a road lined with vineyards, cutting ourselves bunches of grapes to refresh ourselves under the resentful eyes of the peasants; then we turned inland towards a fine modern castle brooding above a village on the crown of a hill.

This castle, it seemed, was our destination. As we approached it, Liverotto sent the head of our escort forward to speak to the guards, who then cranked down the drawbridge to let us in. I had noted as we approached that the castle was flying the curious red and white flag of the Knights Hospitaller, and there were men in the courtyard in the dress of that order. Liverotto called to me to dismount and we followed one of the Hospitallers, in his long black robes, into a fine vestibule hung with tapestries. There, we were given water to wash in and then ushered through to an inner room.

This was a high, vaulted chamber with a magnificent view over the lake. There was a group of men clustered by the window, perhaps five or six, with as many again sitting at a table, some writing. The knot by the window seemed to be in the middle of an argument. All were speaking at the top of their voices, one pounding on the table to keep time with his words. I recognized in the midst of them Liverotto's friend Vitellozzo Vitelli, the scars from his illness more lurid than when I last saw him; also Francesco Orsini, the other condottiere who had participated in the siege of Camerino. My heart quickened at the sight of these men here together. They could only be assembled for one reason. Liverotto roared a greeting above the noise and advanced towards the company, bearing me, seething with speculation, in his wake.

As you will have realized by now, what I am describing is the famous meeting at Magione where the conspiracy against Valentino was sealed. I will remind you of the names of those involved. There were two other condottieri at the meeting besides Vitelli and Francesco Orsini: Paolo Orsini, a cousin of Francesco, and Giampaolo Baglioni, the lord of Perugia. These were bloody-handed men, one and all. If, in some strange tribunal of death, the shades of their victims had been summoned to this castle, they would have filled the hall, the courtyard, and the battlements, packed together like cargo in a hold. Also present at the meeting were Ermes Bentivoglio, a son of the lord of Bologna, and Antonio da Venafro, chief minister to the tyrant of Siena. Later that afternoon, there arrived also Ottaviano Fregoso, nephew of the deposed duke of Urbino, bringing news that his uncle had landed at the port of Senigallia on the mission of recovering his state.

I observed these men's meeting from the end of the table, seated amidst the secretaries and trusted courtiers each lord had brought with him. The interaction among the conspirators was fascinating to watch. Vitelli I judged to be the dominant man among them, although all listened deferentially also when either of the two Orsini spoke. Baglioni was a loudmouth, finding relish in nothing except hearing the sound of his own voice. Liverotto said little. I suspected he was cowed in this company. He was by far the newest and most unproven lord there. Paolo and Francesco Orsini were from a branch of one of the oldest baronial families of Rome, and one was a marquis, the other a duke. The Vitelli had been lords of Città di Castello for almost two hundred years, the Bentivoglio of Bologna for seventy. Even the upstart Baglioni could boast a history of lordship a little longer than Liverotto's nine months.

The best speaker of the meeting was the Sienese representative Antonio da Venafro. He was a law professor, as I later learned: a dapper man of around forty, who spoke in uncannily mellifluous and well-turned sentences. With his long elegant fingers, which had never wielded anything more deadly than a pen, he looked strangely out of place in this meeting of large, brutal, fighting men. So too did Ottaviano Fregoso, who looked like a religious ascetic, with his gaunt cheeks and hollow eyes, and Ermes Bentivoglio, who had all the air of a primped and cosseted young prince.

The motive of these men in conspiring against Valentino was quite simple. It was fear. As Vitelli put it, if they did not move now, the dragon would devour them, one and all. They had watched lord after lord fall prey to the pope's *cupiditas regnandi*, their long service to the Church notwithstanding. They had watched Astorre Manfredi surrender his power by solemn treaty, only to be treacherously murdered in his cell. These were strong arguments for resistance, and my only surprise at the meeting was not to see representatives there of still more lands within the reach of the dragon. Where was Florence? I spent the afternoon half-expecting to see Bishop Soderini's lugubrious visage looking in at the door.

BESIDES SECURING FORMAL agreement that the conspiracy would go ahead, the meeting was also engaged with the difficult issue of who would supply what numbers of troops. This discussion went on interminably and was hotly pursued. I had a sense that each man was attempting to deceive the others about the extent of the resources at his disposal, whether exaggerating them to enhance his importance or diminishing them in order to keep back men and weapons for other uses while pursuing the agreed common war.

There was much skirmishing among the men around the table as these points were being decided, while Venafro waited patiently with his pen poised to inscribe the numbers in a document which all would eventually be willing to sign. It was not difficult to see how the fault lines within the conspiracy would develop if things began to go badly and Valentino tried to divide the participants. Liverotto always sided with Vitelli, the two Orsini inevitably with each other, Baglioni generally with the Orsini, Bentivoglio and Venafro with Vitelli. Of the main protagonists, the most volatile was Paolo Orsini, and I do not say this simply with hindsight. This man's enemies scornfully referred to him as Madonna Paola, and it was true that he had some resemblance to a certain species of matron: high-complexioned, loquacious, domineering, and with a voice that tended, at moments of excitement, to rise to a squawk.

I WAS OBSERVING these details with a purpose. Even as I watched the meeting unfold, I had decided that, on my return to Fermo, I would compose a dispatch to Valentino containing a full account of the discussions there. I was already composing this message in my head while I sat taking notes of the conversation for Liverotto's use. It would include not only what was being said around the table, but also what I thought lay unsaid.

My reasoning was this. After this meeting, to which all the principals had traveled quite openly, the conspiracy could not possibly remain a secret, or even half a secret. Indeed, this was not among the conspirators' intentions any longer. The diet of Magione was a declaration of war. I felt I had satisfied my obligation to Cardinal Giuliano and his daughter in preserving the secret of the conspiracy while it was still hatching and needed the protection of the shadows. Now I could revert to what I saw as my own interest, which I had been reluctantly jeopardizing this last month. If I reported this meeting of the conspirators immediately, I had some chance of winning myself back into Valentino's good graces and dispelling any suspicions my past reports may have inspired. If I did not report it, he would know me to be a traitor, and then God help me if we should ever meet again.

When the meeting was drawing to its tetchy close that evening, with the dark falling and the room already blazing with lamps brought in by servants, a messenger was ushered in straight from the road, his cloak filthy and his face a mask of dust. He was a man of Baglioni's and had ridden from Gubbio that day with the news that the former lord of Camerino, Giulio Cesare Varano, had been killed that morning in the castle at Pergola, by the duke's usual method, strangulation by Don Michelotto. Like Astorre Manfredi, Varano had been assured of his family's safety when he surrendered his city. Six weeks later, he was dead, and his sons were prisoners in the duke's custody and presumably next on the list. As the messenger delivered his news, I looked up the table at the three condottieri who had led the assault on Camerino that summer. Vitelli listened with a grave expression and crossed himself, while Liverotto swore and looked shiftily around the table. Francesco Orsini stared coolly over the messenger's shoulder as though he had never heard of Camerino in his life.

No one had the heart to continue wrangling about details of provisioning after hearing this news, and the meeting broke up. As we were leaving the room, Ottaviano Fregoso trapped me in a corner to ask me about the fate of his uncle's great library. Liverotto had earlier been boasting that he had me as a spy at Urbino over the summer, at the heart of the duke's court. I stood unhappily for a moment under Signor Ottaviano's earnest gaze, trying to think of some manner in which to break this news kindly. Then I confessed that when I last saw the library it was vanishing over the hilltops towards Cesena, packed on what looked like an army of mules.

By the time we arrived back in Fermo, I had a plan in my head, that I would ask my cousin Alfonso himself to deliver my report to the duke, to give me the advantage of speed. I offered him money to do this, but he looked at me offended, saying that we were bound by ties of blood and that Dino and I had been the making of him and he was happy to do this in return. This was generous of him, for it was a risky enterprise to make the journey alone, quite apart from the dangers of discovery. Valentino was in Imola, around three days' hard riding to the north. We agreed that Alfonso would tell the guards on the city gates that he was going for a day to his farm in the country and then concoct a story of some sudden sickness that had laid him low so he was unable to return.

There was a risk in all this for me as well, since Alfonso was my kinsman, and he was disappearing so shortly after I had returned from Magione. It would only take some sharp secretary, employed to scrutinize the records of the guards at the gates, to make the connection between these two things. I thought this unlikely, however. This was a period of fierce activity in Fermo, as Liverotto pulled together his army to depart against Valentino. His administrators were all occupied in details of provisioning, in inspecting wagons, and completing inventories of arms. Still, I was on edge from the moment of Alfonso's departure, wondering where he had got to on his journey and nervously imagining the possibilities of discovery. It was a good day for me when I heard a shout beneath my window and saw him grinning up at me from the street. The poor wretch looked haggard enough to have been ill in truth, not merely in the fiction of his story. He told me later he had fasted for three days of his journey to ensure that his appearance bore out his lie.

IT HAD BEEN agreed at Magione that Liverotto's contribution to the conspirators' forces would amount to two hundred cavalrymen and five hundred infantry. I groaned internally when I heard him agreeing to this. The infantry amounted to around half of Liverotto's total forces, but the cavalry to his complete numbers. No man in Fermo who had ever been trained to fight on a horse would be spared conscription to this army. That meant I was going to war.

A few nights before we left to march north, I had another tryst with Nicolosa, again going to her house under the disguise of a woman. I had sent a message to her after I returned from Magione, this time asking Lena to deliver it. There was no reply at first, and I feared that Nicolosa would shun me through guilt at our transgression. Eventually, however, she summoned me, and, with many precautions, I went.

When I had first written my note to Nicolosa, I had been meditating a confession of what I had so culpably kept a secret from her the first time. I would kneel before her and confess to her and suffer her righteous anger and that would be an end to our sin. By the time I saw her, however, this godly resolution had receded in my mind. Given the dangers of the campaign I was embarking on, it seemed to me quite probable that this would be our last meeting on earth, and I had no appetite to spend it in misery and contrition. In all honesty, I am a coward, as many men are, where the speaking of hard truths is concerned. Underlying this motive was an itch of the senses, which made me wish to possess once again this woman I had desired for so long. The prospect of war and death inclines men to Venus, and I was no exception to this rule.

Perhaps Nicolosa was possessed by this same itch, for, in truth, I had barely entered her house when we fell to kissing, and the rest very soon followed. She did not weep afterwards this time, though she did when I was leaving, as did I. We spoke for long hours that evening, between intervals of dalliance, mainly not of the cruel present, but of our memories of our adolescence. These we pieced together raptly, knowing now of the secret thread of love that had bound us together all this time. There was a strange comfort in speaking of those innocent times, across the barrier of horror that divided us from them. We even laughed at times, something I had not imagined we would ever do so freely again.

Nicolosa told me that, after Messer Giovanni had forbidden us to see each other alone, she would go sometimes in the afternoon to the house of a friend, where they would spy from an upper window as we youths practiced our military exercises. I said I thought it was a wonder her love had survived this experience, since I was such a poor swordsman at the time. She ought to have favored Dino. She laughed and said these were not things that mattered to women as much as men liked to believe.

When I returned home after this evening with Nicolosa, I sat out on my balcony for a long time in darkness, wrapped in a cloak, listening to the patrols of Liverotto's soldiers passing below on the streets and looking up at the cold distant stars. Guilt was beginning to rack me, as it had after the first time, but the pain was mingled with much sweetness. I kept thinking of the words Nicolosa had spoken to me and her face as she had spoken them, engraving both things on my mind. The more I thought of the sweetness of my love and its evil, the more impossible my situation appeared. It seemed to me almost that I *must* die on this coming campaign, for I could not imagine how my life could go on. I felt I could not live without this love now that I had it, yet I could not enjoy it without becoming a monster. Only by reminding myself that I might soon be beyond this dilemma, bleeding out my life in a ditch somewhere, could I find a strange peace in my mind.

ONE FURTHER SURPRISE was in store for me before I left Fermo. The day before we left the city, I was coming out of Alfonso's shop, where I had gone to wish him farewell, when I saw Agnese emerging from a church opposite. She was looking most attractive, as I have learned since is often the case with former lovers who are now in another man's hands.

I had seen Agnese twice on the street since I had been back in Fermo, but she had been in company and had greeted me distantly. This time she was alone, and she answered my greeting with an intimate, almost mischievous, smile. I made a move to cross the road to speak to her, but she made a gesture to deter me and turned to walk away. As she did, she stood for a moment in profile to me and smoothed down her dress quite deliberately in a manner that made clear that she was with child.

This was disconcerting, and I thought of it much in the course of the day. I saw Dino that evening, and asked him whether he knew of this interesting fact. He laughed and said that it did indeed seem that God had wished to bless Agnese's marriage in a precipitate manner.

"You did well to marry her to Giacomino," I said.

Dino laughed again, shaking his head. "She managed that herself. She's a clever girl." He paused and said more seriously, "I was assuming that you …"

"You were right," I said quickly. "My life is already too complicated."

Dino looked at me with an expression quite difficult to fathom.

"Brother, I can believe that all too well."

XII

WE MARCHED NORTH up the coast and joined near Loreto with the armies of Vitelli and Francesco Orsini. The weather had turned wet and cold as October wore on, and we were churning through mud for most of the march. We rode along in tight order, fearing ambush, since we were nominally in the territories of the enemy, although rumors kept reaching us that Valentino's troops were already in retreat from Urbino, where the rebels had finally prevailed.

The rumors turned out to be true. We caught the duke's retreating forces at a village named Calmazzo, about two days' march from Urbino. They were headed north to Imola to rejoin their leader, who had retreated there, trying to hold his empire in the Romagna together in the face of this unexpected blow. The leaders of the force at Calmazzo were Don Michelotto and another Spaniard, Ugo of Moncada, although we did not know this at the time. There was little intelligence. We heard something from our foreriders of the position of the retreating army, but nothing precise of its composition or strength.

The battle of Calmazzo was the largest pitched battle I experienced in my military career with Liverotto. The forces were around seven thousand on the conspirators' side, eight thousand on that of the duke. Moncada and Don Michelotto had taken a strong position at the top of a hill to await us. There was discussion among the conspirators about whether it was wise to confront the enemy from a position of such weakness, but they eventually decided to do so, perhaps reluctant to retreat from an army in retreat.

I was with Dino at the time the decision was relayed to
him and saw a look of disgust on his face as he heard it, but he
soon set himself to ordering the troops under his command
and speaking to them to steady their resolve. I retreated meanwhile to my cavalry unit, which was positioned to the rear
of the infantry. This was part of the ugliness of our position.
The slopes of the hill on both sides were thickly wooded, and
there was nowhere else we could be deployed except directly
behind our foot soldiers. It was hard to see what role we were
intended to perform other than to stop these poor souls from
running away.

We were smashed. The duke's leaders had their artillery
trained on the slope our infantrymen were attempting to
labor up. They were slaughtered in such numbers that those
behind found it impossible to make their way through the
heaps of the dead. Urged on by their captains, wave after wave,
they died on that slope like sheep driven to the slaughter. The
wind was in our faces, carrying the nauseating smell of blood
down to where we waited below, along with the cries of the
wounded. It seemed as though our army was slowly feeding
itself to a devouring monster, which would not stop while a
single one of us drew breath. Eventually, Valentino's infantry began to descend the hill, armed with the handguns they
called culverins to complete the destruction wreaked by the
main artillery. We watched in trepidation from the rear.

A strange thing happened then. The duke's army started
seething with frenzied motion, as if Valentino's soldiers had
started fighting one another. I could not make sense of it.
It was as if the army had been seized by a sudden collective
madness. A great wild inchoate roaring, mixed with the clash
of metal, filled the air, louder even than the sounds of battle
before.

We learned later what had happened. Five thousand of the Urbino rebels had charged the duke's troops from the woods on the hill. They approached under the cover of the trees, any sound they made drowned out by the clamor of our battle; then they swarmed down like devils among Valentino's troops, sowing chaos. The surprise of their attack was such that they were able to hack their way through the first lines before Valentino's soldiers even understood what was going on.

As the enemy troops faltered under this new assault, our infantry was finally able to break through, clambering beyond the barriers of our dead. The battle turned entirely, in what seemed no more than seconds. For a while, a portion of Valentino's army was surrounded, and it seemed it would be massacred in its entirety, but a core of men managed to fight their way out and escape. This was our cavalry's only involvement in the battle, harrying Valentino's escaping soldiers as they fled in scattered bands through the hills. We were joined in this by parties of the rebels, some no more than farmhands armed with axes and scythes, others impressively well mounted and armed.

I have never enjoyed watching slaughter, unlike some of my colleagues, but there was some cruel pleasure in seeing these rebels enjoy their moment of revenge. The thought kept coming to me of that scene in the piazza at Urbino when we had watched the comrades of these men being disemboweled. We of the conspirators' cavalry tried our best to ensure that surrendered soldiers were taken prisoner, rather than killed on the spot, but this was not always possible given the fury of the rebels. I heard Liverotto cursing viciously that evening about the amount of ransom money that had been squandered in this way.

WHY DID THEY let the duke go, the conspirators, when they had his main army almost broken? When we returned to the camp that evening, we were fully expecting to march on the next day in pursuit of that portion of his troops that had been able to retreat in good order. They had left their injured in the field and so would be traveling at a good speed, but they were still vulnerable to attack and would be demoralized after their shattering defeat. Also, we had taken one of their commanders, Moncada, although Don Michelotto had managed to escape. True, we would have risked ourselves by pressing on into the Romagna, where the duke was presumably rallying new forces. But has there ever been war without risk?

Perhaps this culpable hesitancy was the inevitable result of an army with too many leaders. Certainly, there was much wrangling among the conspirators that evening. Dino told me later that he had been summoned by Liverotto and told to prepare for departure the next morning, then recalled perhaps two hours later to have this order repealed. Vitelli, apparently, was all for pressing on, but the Orsini opposed him, and Baglioni was with them. Liverotto was torn. He was a creature of Vitelli's, yet he was in debt to the Orsini for the work they had done in ingratiating him with the pope after his taking of power in Fermo. He hesitated, and with each hour he hesitated, our prey slipped further out of our hands.

Greed was among the conspirators' problems. The duke had vacated the lands of Urbino in haste, leaving well-provisioned garrisons behind him. These were attractive, easy pickings, especially if the duke of Urbino did not wish them for himself. This was a great weakness of the conspirators, that they were bandits at heart. They considered themselves strategists and generals, but they were as easily distracted as magpies if they caught a glint of silver to the left or the right.

Here is an example of the kind of activity we got up to during the days following Calmazzo, while Valentino's army was limping gratefully back to join him at Imola. Liverotto and Vitelli came to hear that the Spanish garrison of Fossombrone, composed of some forty men, had been given a safe-conduct by the duke of Urbino in return for surrender and was making its way north towards the Romagna with mules laden with four thousand ducats' worth of gold and goods. The two leaders positioned their cavalry, perhaps three hundred of us in total, in the woods at the side of the road that led north, not so far from our old battlefield of Calmazzo. As the ousted garrison passed beneath us, we swooped on it, butchered the men, and sequestered the goods.

This was pure banditry, and it sickens me still to remember it. It was too easy, given the discrepancy in numbers. The day was a foul one, and the road a slick of mud, which was churned with the blood of our victims as we killed them. We left them as they had fallen, in a mangled heap on the road, trampled into something that no longer looked like men.

AT THE END of October, when the conspirators were fat with bounty, Paolo Orsini went to Imola to parley with Valentino. He returned to his companions with an offer of peace, which he counseled them warmly to accept. Liverotto recounted the negotiations to me over dinner in his quarters. He liked to use me as an adviser, or at least an audience, in these matters since the time I accompanied him to Magione.

In return for an end to hostilities, Valentino was proposing that he would guarantee the integrity of the conspirators' territories. This included Bologna, a city he had formerly threatened, but any future aggression against which he now formally renounced. He also promised to disburse five thousand ducats to the conspirators as surety for his goodwill, besides allowing them to keep all they had taken in the course of the late hostilities. This was all. The conspirators would return to the service of the Church and everything would be as before.

"What do you think?" Liverotto asked. "Can he be trusted?"

He had a venison bone in his hand, which he had cracked so he could suck at the marrow, and his beard was slick with grease. The sight was not pretty. He looked like some ogre in an old woman's tale.

I looked at him, calculating. I would have liked nothing more than to advise him to take the offer and trust the duke, for this was clearly his swiftest route to perdition. I had a feeling that he was testing me, however, and I could not risk being caught out. I answered him earnestly in the guise of a well-wisher, saying he should not think of ceding to these approaches of the duke's in any circumstances. There was nothing of substance in these offers, only promises of a kind that Valentino broke by the dozen each day.

When I had finished my speech, Liverotto took the bone from his mouth, finally wiped off his beard, and commended my good sense in the matter. He was minded the same way himself, he said, and so was Vitelli. Their impression was that Orsini had been gulled.

I thought the conversation was drawing to a close at this point, but Liverotto reached for the wine and poured more for us. He could drink wine like water; it had no more effect on his indestructible body than fatigue, heat, or cold.

"I want you to go back there," he said suddenly.

"Back where, my lord?"

"Back to the duke's court. We need intelligence. This time you can pretend to defect." He raised his hand to pre-empt my response. "I know it's dangerous. Do you think I would ask you if I had any alternative? No man in Fermo is dearer to me—not my brother, not my cousins. It must be you. You have a good head, and you are known there."

Liverotto paused to refill his glass and looked over at me, gauging his progress in this persuasion. I looked down at the table, anxious and tight-lipped, my heart cautiously exulting within.

"What would be my reason for defecting?" I said eventually, as though thinking of such a reason might be a difficult task.

Liverotto spread his hands.

"We'll invent something. Perhaps I fucked your sister. Or your mother. Or your wife. Or all three."

He laughed hugely at this, while I summoned a wan smile.

"You'll do it?" Liverotto said eventually. I nodded, like a man with no appetite for speaking. He leaned across the table and clapped me on the shoulder.

"I knew it, Teo. As always, true as steel."

VALENTINO AT THIS time was based at Imola, hardly a day and half's ride from where we found ourselves at the time of this conversation, between Pesaro and Rimini. Since I was purportedly a defector and could hardly be given an escort, I had to ride up there alone.

I set off on this journey wary of bandits, but also prey to a new anxiety concerning the welcome I might meet from the duke. When Liverotto first proposed this mission, it seemed to me as if Cardinal Giuliano's plan was gloriously coming to fruition. He had predicted precisely this: that the duke and Liverotto would become foes and that I, through my spying, would be in a position to deliver Liverotto into his enemy's hand.

I had been so intent on my predictions of revenge that I had hardly pondered the danger I faced in returning to the duke, having deceived him. Yet for the whole month of September I had been feeding him lies, pretending ignorance of the conspiracy even as it brewed all around me like a storm gathering at sea. Had my report on Magione been enough to redeem me? Or had the duke marked me earlier as a traitor, noting my silences? He was no fool to be led by the nose.

The day I set off for Imola was bright, and as I rode up the coast, the water sparkled alongside me like a temptation, making me dream of abandoning my mission and embarking on a boat bound for some distant shore. I rode on dourly, ignoring this lure, keeping my mind on my duty of revenge. After Rimini, I turned inland and rode with a party of merchants I had fortuitously encountered, passing through a land of olive groves and vineyards, the vines now decked in their autumn colors of blood and fire. I parted from this company at Cesena and rode on alone through the plain towards Imola. As its walls loomed before me, they looked to me like the gates of a prison into which I was riding of my own accord.

I took lodgings at the first inn I came to within the gates and sent a boy up to the castle with a note begging an audience with the duke. Half an hour later, the boy returned, telling me he had handed the note to a secretary. Half an hour after this, the door to my room opened, and Don Michelotto da Coreglia walked in.

I felt a moment of pure terror when I saw this man at my door. It was a sight that confirmed my worst fears. I had been sitting on my bed cleaning my boots when he entered the room, not a dignified way for a man to meet his death. I sprang to my feet, gauging in my head as I did so my distance from the window, my only chance of escape. I had estimated the drop to the courtyard when I entered, out of habit. It was not impossible, no more than twelve feet.

"Don Michele," I said, bowing. "You honor me with your presence."

"Messer Matteo," he said distractedly, slightly returning my bow. He was standing in the doorway, rubbing his hands in the sinister way he had and surveying the grimy walls of my room with distaste. I could see two figures in shadow behind him in the corridor. I swallowed, trying not to show my fear.

Don Michelotto stepped forward into the room so that he was no more than an arm's breadth away.

"You have no servant with you?"

He was looking down at the cloth with which I had been cleaning my boots. I shook my head, not trusting myself to speak. Don Michelotto stood looking at me with his head slightly on one side, like a bird deciding which end of the worm to start on. Then, to my great surprise, he smiled.

"Come up to the Rocca. I'm sure we can lodge you in a little more style."

XIII

I WAS INDEED LODGED IN STYLE at the great castle of Imola, in a room of my own, on an ill-frequented corridor near the quarters of the duke. A servant told me the last lord of the town housed a mistress in this chamber, which was hung with faded tapestries portraying scenes of chivalry. It was an equally convenient lodging for a spy.

I settled back well enough into life at the duke's court, assuming my former duties as a crimson-and-saffron-clad warrior. Much reminded me of my time at Urbino, but much was also different and drearier. There was no library to distract me with its beauty and learning and no Messer Leonardo with his fabulous inventions. There were no views from the windows, or none to match those of Urbino, for this was a flat, placid land. There were no summer gardens to walk in, no apricots to pick from the trees.

Above all, there was no Lucia. Her absence was a thorn to me, constantly reminding me of my failings towards her. Many women were at the court who had been at Urbino, and whenever I saw a knot of them together, I kept expecting I would see her glorious red hair in their midst.

Angelica was gone also—or as good as gone, anyway. She was no longer the uncrowned queen of the duke's court, putting men in their place with her witty tongue. She had been displaced in the duke's affections by a pouting minx by the name of Dorotea, who walked round the castle in a grand style with two servants carrying her train. I heard differing rumors of what had become of Angelica: that the duke had passed her to his Spanish captains, who played dice every evening to see who would have her; that she had entered a convent; that she was running a brothel in Forlì; that the duke had given her permission to return to Rome.

I eventually caught sight of Angelica in person, perhaps a week after my arrival in Imola. I was strolling up the main street of the city with Messer Niccolò Machiavelli, whom I had met at the castle the day after my arrival.

"Aha!" was his first greeting. "The turncoat of Fermo. I was wondering when I'd run into *you*."

He was most intrigued by my defection from Liverotto and questioned me on my motives in detail. He told me he thought me canny to transfer into the duke's service, for he judged that he would rout the conspirators like whelps. He told me he had been in Imola over a month, having been sent by the Florentine government at the time of the diet of Magione. Florence had been invited to join the conspiracy, but, knowing Vitelli was at the table, she had fled into the arms of the duke.

I was listening to Messer Niccolò holding forth eloquently on some point of policy when I looked up to see Angelica standing before me. She was dressed in a gray cloak with a black veil, which she had lifted to reveal her fascinating face. To my relief, she looked none the worse for her demotion from court, though she was a little more subdued in her manner than usual. She told me she was glad she had seen me, as she was leaving for Rome the next day. Her mother had been ill and had sent for her, and the duke had granted her permission to go to her side.

After she had told us this, Angelica asked how I was finding the city of Imola and offered some recommendations. She spoke first of a brothel run by a Neapolitan of her acquaintance, who was the son of a bishop. Many French and Spanish officers frequented it, and the owner was someone who knew how to keep his ears open. A man might learn more there in comfort than he could glean in long days eavesdropping at court.

Angelica said this last with a sly glance at Messer Niccolò, who was listening to her on this point most intently; then she proceeded to talk of more inconsequential objects, such as a pawnshop remarkable for its favorable terms and a baker who sold excellent cakes. She looked at me pointedly as she spoke of this baker, in a way that made me take note of her words. When she had finished, she smiled, lowered her veil, pressed my hand, and drifted on her way down the street. Messer Niccolò looked admiringly after her, muttering appreciative obscenities in her wake.

I was curious to see whether there was anything in my suspicion regarding Angelica's recommendation of the baker. One afternoon soon after I spoke to her, I followed her directions and sought out his shop.

Imola was a strange town to ride through at this time, resembling nothing more than an outpost of Babel. Nervous at having lost half his forces at a stroke through the defection of his condottieri, the duke had cast his net wide for replacements. Besides his usual Spaniards, and a consignment of French troops King Louis had dispatched to him, there were men of many nations lured by the prospect of the pope's gold. You saw Swiss and Corsican mercenaries on the streets, and a few strutting, red-faced northerners, English and Germans, who had found their way to Italy as a playground for warfare. There was even a company of Albanian stradiots you could see training with their javelins outside the city walls in the evening, a fine sight. The center of the city bristled with men spoiling for mayhem, and the inns, brothels, and armories churned with their custom. The citizens went warily about their business, eyeing these locusts with mistrust, while their women-folk stayed safely indoors.

The baker's shop was in a pleasant area of the town, near one of the gates, with many good houses and orchards and gardens. It was quieter than the center, though you still encountered parties of jabbering foreign soldiers in the streets. I found the shop without difficulty and paused on my horse to exchange a word with the baker, who was sitting outside taking the sun and watching the world pass, while his apprentices manned the ovens inside. He was a broad-faced man with small, shrewd eyes like currants and an air of self-regard. I could imagine him a tyrant to his wife and his workforce, although he was civil to the point of obsequiousness with me. When I told him that Angelica had recommended his wares, he smiled at me complacently and told me to come back the next morning when there would be goods worthy of my palate on sale.

The short November day was drawing to a close by the time I had finished with the baker, and I decided to turn back on my tracks and return to the Rocca. As I was riding up the street, wondering whether I had been mistaken in reading significance into Angelica's expression, a length of some gauzy black fabric floated down onto my horse's mane from above. I looked up, startled, and saw two faces looking down from a balcony, perhaps a couple of arms' breadth above my head. One was a sweet-faced girl of fifteen or sixteen, the other a young woman of my age, dressed in black. The black-clad woman drew back almost as soon as she met my eye, leaving the girl, who seemed a servant, to reclaim the fallen veil.

I drew my sword and lifted the thing delicately on the flat of it, delivering it into the girl's outstretched hand. She laughed as she took it and I bowed to her before I rode on, hoping her mistress would reappear to thank me. She did not, but when I turned at the end of the street, I saw the two of them watching my tracks.

WHEN I RETURNED to the baker's the next day, he was waiting for me, and handed me a flat cake smelling of cinnamon, with a cross traced on its surface.

"Try this, and tell me it is not the best you have ever tasted," he said loudly, with an oratorical gesture. Leaning towards me, he added in an undertone, "Make sure you're alone when you eat it. And watch out for your teeth."

Both coming and going, I looked up at the balcony from which the black veil had descended the previous day. There was no one to be seen there, but I met the maid at the beginning of the next street, returning from the market with a basket on her arm.

"Be careful of your veil," I said as I passed her. "I hear the wind can be strong in these parts."

She smiled at that, two dimples appearing on her cheeks, and said I seemed a man who knew which way the wind was blowing. I asked her in a meaningful tone to convey my compliments to her mistress, and she laughed and swung gaily back on her path.

I EVISCERATED THE cake that the baker had given me when I got back to my room in the castle. In the midst of it, gleaming dully, was the half cameo Angelica had given me at Urbino, which I had returned to her with the first message I sent.

I stood for a long while looking at this exquisitely wrought object, pressing its sharp point into my thumb until a bright bead of blood blossomed like a ruby. Did I truly wish to risk myself spying for Cardinal Giuliano now, when the consummation of my revenge seemed so near?

I decided to leave my decision to the morning and spent the evening playing cards with a raucous party of German pikemen. I came away with fine winnings, perhaps forty ducats' worth in total. My takings included a fearsome pair of gauntlets with plate at the knuckles and, less usefully, a magnificent gray parrot with beady straw-colored eyes and a dashing streak of red in his tail.

Perhaps this evidence of Fortune's favor was enough to convince me, for I did indeed resume my spying for Cardinal Giuliano. I passed my first message to the baker a few days after this, as we stood exchanging pleasantries outside his shop. Loyalty had a place in my calculation, and also a feeling that the gratitude I had earned to this point from the cardinal would be squandered if I failed him at this juncture, when he was deprived of the services of Angelica and sat chewing his nails in his palace in Savona, waiting to see whether the conspiracy would succeed. I was careful what I wrote to him, for he favored the conspirators, and the conspirators must fail for my end to be achieved. Still, there was much I could tell him without jeopardy, and it seemed wise to keep a foot in both camps while the outcome of events was unsure.

THIS WAS a frustrating time to be a spy, I can tell you. The labyrinth of political intrigue was especially impenetrable at this moment, as the duke sought to cozen his adversaries while building up his forces on the sly. Even Messer Niccolò Machiavelli could make little progress in winnowing truth from rumor, despite the fact that his profession permitted him to spend his days gathering information in all openness. I did not have this luxury and was limited to the few crumbs that came my way in the course of my normal business, supplemented by what I could glean from Messer Niccolò—who, in truth, was not sparing with his readings of events.

The duke's policy with the conspirators was to buy off the most powerful of them, Giovanni Bentivoglio, lord of Bologna, with a separate alliance, while working patiently to conciliate the others, using Paolo Orsini as his go-between. This is easily enough stated—yet what were the intricacies of these things, for those of us who were following events by the day and through a glass darkly, as we must! The treaty with Bologna alone took forty days to negotiate, so little trust did Bentivoglio repose in the duke, who had already once attempted to expel him. Each day of these forty, there was a new rumor to weigh concerning the terms of the treaty and the nature of the guarantees offered. Valentino was pulled on one side by his brother-in-law, the duke of Ferrara, who was linked with the Bentivoglio through old friendship, and on the other by his father, who liked to boast that he would be the first pope who was man enough to bring Bologna to heel. Such was the mood of distrust that no agreement could be reached without external guarantees of observance. Only when the king of France, the government of Florence, and the duke of Ferrara had all accepted to enforce Valentino's compliance could Bentivoglio be persuaded to put his skeptical hand to the page.

Bentivoglio merited this treatment because he was a true lord and well liked by other lords, if not so much by his people. The other conspirators could not command such ceremony, and the duke treated with them together, like a pack of unruly hounds. His policy was to persuade them that their fears had been groundless when they mistrusted his loyalty and thought him a threat. The messages I sent to Liverotto were all intended to reassure them on this point. I portrayed the duke as chastened by the experience of Urbino and newly aware of the limits of his power. He was negotiating from a position of weakness, with his forces much depleted, and potential enemies such as Venice beginning to turn greedy eyes on his lands.

I took this all in dictation from the duke himself, of course, taking notes in a shorthand I had devised for myself as he paced the room speaking. Sometimes I felt almost embarrassed to be describing him so dismissively, even though the words were his, not my own. "He is not the man he was," I wrote on one occasion; "He has the air of a whipped cur," on another. Don Michelotto, who was almost always present on these occasions, laughed copiously when he heard the duke speak of the whipped cur.

MY POLICY IN spying for Cardinal Giuliano was to frequent the street of my collaborator often, so that the neighbors would not especially mark my presence when I came to deliver my messages. When he saw me on the street, the baker would come forward to exchange a few words, his apron looped over his right arm. If I had a message, I would let it fall into the fold of the apron, and he would whisk it aside deftly to extract later in secret. He was sharp, I must say. He marked these exchanges not even by the flicker of an eye.

As cover for these visits, I began to pay court to the attractive widow who had let her veil fall from her balcony that first day. A young soldier with an appetite for women seemed to me a less conspicuous object than one with an appetite for cakes. I was not excessively importunate, for I did not wish to find myself a target of aggression from her menfolk. I merely circled under her windows now and then, calling up compliments and throwing pebbles against the glass, until her maid leaned out of the window and told me to leave. Twice at the beginning, I caught sight of the widow herself, taking the winter sun on the balcony, wrapped in a great dull-black cloak lined with fur. She retreated both times swiftly when she saw me, however, and after these first times she was nowhere to be seen.

The only military duty I undertook in this time was to train a little with my company outside the walls of the city. The training was the usual: a little skirmishing with weapons and much careful drilling of horses, including their habituation to artillery fire, never something at all easy to achieve.

One day when I was retiring from these exercises, I noticed a girl discreetly signaling me from beneath the wall of the city. I immediately recognized the maid of the widow, pink in her cheeks from the cold November air. I felt annoyed, for this almost certainly meant an end to my cover with the baker. If this girl had been sent to plead with me to cease embarrassing her mistress, I knew I would not have the stomach to persist.

I bowed from my horse as I drew near, and the girl looked up at me smilingly and reproached me for having kept her waiting in this sharp weather. There was something flirtatious in her manner, and I extended my hand and said I would be happy to warm her up if she would care to join me on my horse. She laughed at that, with an unexpectedly low, throaty chuckle; then she reached in her pocket and passed up a sealed note into my hand. I tore it open and read it, as the girl watched me keenly. I could feel her bright eyes searching my face.

Well, to make it short, this was a summons from the widow, inviting me to an assignation the following evening. I was to come to the side entrance of her house at a certain hour, approaching it not from the street, but from an alley behind. The note was of few words, written in the laborious hand of someone not accustomed to writing. Still, it was impossible to mistake its amorous intent.

"Well?" said the girl. I looked down at her round childish face, gazing up at me with expectation and a little anxiety.

"Tell your mistress that nothing could give me more pleasure," I said curtly, with many feelings other than pleasure in my heart.

I spent the rest of the day cursing myself as a fool and the widow as a woman of lax virtue. I did not reproach myself for having accepted her invitation now that it had come to this point, for what kind of man would parade himself under a woman's window and then refuse an invitation to her bed? What I regretted was having devised this foolish expedient in the first place, and not having considered the possibility of this outcome. Was I so innocent in the ways of the world? Here I was at a delicate crux in my mission of vengeance, seemingly about to embark on a liaison with a woman of wealth and standing, no doubt equipped with the usual complement of murderous male relatives. The stupidity of the thing dismayed me. It was hardly as though available women were lacking in Imola. They were pouring in through the city gates every day from the surrounding countryside, drawn by the prospect of a city full of loose-pocketed men.

I went to my fate the following evening with an ill grace. The maid met me at the door with a candle, her eyes alive with excitement, and escorted me silently through a corridor and up a flight of stairs to a kind of antechamber, where she left me. A fire burned in the grate, and I stood in front of it thankfully, recovering from the cold of the streets. The room had an air of luxury about it that impressed me despite my mood of truculence. There was a carpet on the floor of some rare Eastern sort, and the hangings on the walls were laced with gold thread and glimmered seductively in the soft light.

After a minute or so, I heard a slight sound behind me. I turned to see the widow standing in a doorway with a lantern in her hand that she set down on a small table. Her hair, which was fair like mine, was flowing over her shoulders, and she was wearing a loose robe with a chemise underneath, such as women like to wear in the house. Her hand crept up to her throat as we stood gazing at one other, and a look of trepidation crossed her face, as if it had suddenly occurred to her that she might have invited a madman into her dwelling.

I bowed to reassure her, and said, "Matteo da Fermo."

"Giulietta," she said simply, and then was silent, twisting a fold of her robe with one hand.

There was a pause; then I remembered my supposed role as ardent suitor. I made my way over to her, reflecting that this was an occasion where actions were preferable to words. Giulietta became more interesting as I got closer and fell within the reach of the perfume she was wearing, which was heady and sweet, like some thick carnal flower. Her eyes looked enormous in the candlelight as she gazed up at me, the pupils great dark glistening pools. She surrendered her hand to me and I kissed it; then, since she offered no resistance, also her wrist and arm and her neck, pushing back her thick hair. Her skin everywhere was plump, soft, and yielding, as opulent as the velvet of her robe.

I was warming to my task by this time and made to kiss her on her mouth, but she pulled away, looking at me amorously. Her timidity seemed to have vanished.

"Perhaps we will be more comfortable in here."

As she spoke, she opened the door behind her, showing a bedchamber extravagantly lit with what looked like two dozen candles. I could see nothing to object to in her proposal whatsoever.

"*Anima mia*," I said. "I shall follow where you lead."

ONCE WE HAD sated ourselves with pleasure on her monstrously large bed, Giulietta told me her life story. She had been orphaned as a child and was brought up by her much older half-brothers, both merchants, who had wedded her when she was fifteen to a business partner of theirs. She had endured this marriage for six years without the blessing of children, until her husband had died the previous winter of an apoplexy. She had been a widow almost a year now, and her brothers were beginning to speak of concocting a new match for her. Such had been her life before she saw me, and Cupid pierced her heart with a fiery arrow (I am reporting here Giulietta's own words).

The mention of the brothers sounded ominous to me, but Giulietta reassured me that they had left that morning for Ancona, where they had gone to inspect a cargo of goods they had shipped from Ragusa. They traded principally in spices and fine fabrics, hence the wealth so conspicuous in the luxury of their dwelling. In their absence, they had left Giulietta under the supervision of an elderly aunt.

"Well, and what of this aunt?" I asked, tracing my hand down the voluptuous line formed by Giulietta's hips. "I trust she is short of sight and hard of hearing?"

"You might say that," Giulietta said with a sly look, leaning forward to kiss me to stifle my questioning. She later confessed to me that she had incapacitated the poor lady by feeding her a sleeping draft in a custard of plums.

WELL, THIS WAS how I began my liaison with the widow of Imola. After my initial misgivings about the affair, I came to relish it greatly, and Giulietta made no secret of her enjoyment of me. I was her plaything and solace after the arid years of her marriage, and she had much to say in praise of my beauty and what it pleased her to term my amorous vigor. She left me in no doubt that she considered her late husband culpably deficient in both these regards. Giulietta was more voracious in her appetite for lovemaking than any woman I had known, I think because she was aware that this interval of pleasure could not last. Her time was precious and she was not going to waste it, especially when she was going to the trouble of drugging her aunt.

When we were not wallowing in our pleasures, we would converse on various subjects. A spy is never truly off-duty, and I found I could harvest material of some value from these colloquies. Giulietta would often complain of the state of her poor home city, host to an army that swelled in size every day like a tumor, insolent in its manners and insatiable in its appetites. Many of her neighbors on the street had soldiers billeted on them, and her brothers had averted this danger to her virtue only by paying quite crippling bribes. People had been happy enough, she told me, when Valentino took the city, for the previous lord had not been well loved by the populace, but now all were beginning to think that to change lords brought no more benefit to a city than it did to an ox to change yokes. I quoted these opinions in my reports to Cardinal Giuliano, knowing this evidence of popular dissatisfaction under the duke would be dear to him until I had something more substantial to put on his plate.

XIV

WHILE I WAS INDULGING myself with Giulietta, the work of the world continued. Towards the end of November, the lord of Bologna finally sealed his hard-fought treaty with the duke. A few days later, Paolo Orsini came to Imola as representative of the other conspirators, to see whether a basis for peace might be found.

The duke prepared prudently for this visit. The day before Orsini's arrival, he moved three of his mercenary companies to a village half a day's march from the city, where they spent two days disconsolately digging irrigation channels under the supervision of Messer Leonardo da Vinci, who had been summoned from Cesena for that purpose. The effect of this evacuation on the city was dramatic. Imola's streets suddenly seemed the streets of a normal small sleepy city. You could stroll into a tavern in the evening and take your place by the fire without fighting your way through a heaving throng ten men deep. When Paolo Orsini rode through the streets with his entourage, he saw nothing to contradict what I had been claiming in my dispatches to Liverotto: that the duke was here licking his wounds like a great beast savaged in a hunt, meagerly supplied with troops and hungry for peace.

The negotiations between Orsini and the duke were conducted in a room in the duke's quarters, not far from my own chamber. During the two days they lasted, I often looked up at the dark window behind which these two men were locked in their battle of guile. I could almost fancy that, if I strained my ears, I might hear the chink of thirty pieces of silver being counted. In the interstices of their official negotiations, I was quite sure Orsini was being bought.

It was not difficult to imagine the means or the rhythms of this corruption. A castle here, a castle there, a quiet sinecure for a slow-witted nephew, a hint of a cardinalate for a sharp one, the canceling of a debt, the shackling of an enemy, a word in the king of France's ear. Valentino would be drawing one of these shiny baubles from his sack every hour or so, showing Orsini just the glint of it to keep his mouth watering. I could imagine him there so easily: stout, slack-faced, stealthy-eyed, his loose lower lip glistening, being wooed by Valentino as assiduously as ever ardent shepherd wooed blushing maid.

THERE WAS NOTHING of all this in my message to Liverotto recording Orsini's visit, of course. I reported only that he had been sequestered with the duke for two days, that the meetings had been secret, and that no reliable news had emerged of their content. The only rumor I deigned to transmit was that a servant had reported hearing the duke's voice raised in anger several times during the meetings, suggesting he was not having things all his own way.

Valentino did not look like a man who was not having things all his own way when he dictated this message to me on the night of Orsini's departure. He seemed in fine spirits, more so than I had seen him since his troubles began that summer with the rebellion in Urbino. Generally when I took his dictation, he treated me with the courtesy that a dog might expect—or less, for Valentino was fond of his hunting dogs. I could consider myself fortunate if he addressed a single word to me, other than the words of his dictated message. He would welcome me with no more than a flicker of his eye and dismiss me with a wave of his hand.

On the night I am speaking of, he was different, quite gracious; he greeted me by name when I entered the room and apologized for disturbing my slumbers. This was the dead of night, I should tell you: a time when normal men sleep and our mysterious lord kept his vigils. A servant had hammered on my door to wake me and I had stumbled along the corridor to the duke's study after throwing some cold water on my face.

When Valentino finished his dictation, I bowed and turned to leave, but he motioned me to stay.

"Liverotto," he said, leaning back in his chair. "You told me he did not trust the last peace I offered."

"He did not, Your Excellency. Neither he nor Vitelli."

"You know him well. You were raised with him. You served him. Teach me how I may win him to my side."

I was thrown for a moment by this unexpected question. I looked at the blackness behind the duke's head, spiked with stars, where a window had been left open for air.

"I can say nothing that Your Excellency's prudence will not already have suggested to you ..."

The duke cut my ceremonies short with a look, and I continued.

"Already to reach out to Liverotto separately from the other conspirators would be a good step, Your Excellency. It will flatter him. He knows he is the least of these men."

Valentino was examining his fingernails by now.

"Anything else?" he said wearily.

"Assure him that His Holiness will confirm him in his lordship of Fermo. It irks him to be a usurper. He knows he did evil in taking the city. He does not utterly lack conscience. He wants your father's blessing to cleanse his hands."

Valentino was looking up now, and I went on, encouraged.

"You might also think to dangle some title before him. Promise him a feud somewhere that carries one with it. He hungers for dignity. That would stroke his vanity beyond all else."

The duke looked at me without speaking, and my words echoed back at me presumptuously in the silence. Who was I to counsel the pope's son about these things? Then I saw a smile begin on his face.

"The butcher of Fermo wants a title," he said, addressing Don Michelotto, who was seated by the fire, cracking walnuts into a silver basin and observing us. "Do you think marquis would do?"

"Not a chance. A man of his stature. Duke at the very least."

I waited until their mirth had subsided before speaking.

"Count would suffice," I said. A sudden bitterness had seized me, hearing them laugh. "Just to show the men he is trampling in Fermo that he is their superior by more than the right of wolf over sheep."

They were both gazing at me now, perhaps struck by the fervor with which I had spoken.

"What do you think of this youth?" the duke said. "Did I not tell you?"

Don Michelotto smiled across at me, reaching out to stir the fire.

"He does not seem entirely a fool."

THIS EPISODE MARKED a change in my relationship with Don Michelotto. He had treated me civilly enough since my arrival in Imola, but now he began to show me favor in a more marked way and to use me occasionally in his service, part as secretary, part as errand boy. I found this development alarming at first, as a man might if a crocodile were to invite him to supper. Little by little, however, I became accustomed to him, and I must say he used me kindly, for a man commonly thought to be Lucifer's spawn. Once or twice, he even summoned me to his room to play cards with him and drink liquors of terrifying potency, distilled at a Benedictine monastery in town.

Don Michelotto took me on because he found me service-able, no doubt: I could write a neat hand and deliver a message without garbling it. I think he perhaps also felt something of a fellowship with me, as a lowborn man in a court with its share of strutting nobles. He was the illegitimate son of a nobleman himself, but he had been raised meagerly and ill, unacknowl-edged by his father. He knew the nobles of the court despised him, even as they feared his power and envied his intimacy with the duke. He despised them in his turn, with the pride of a man who has forged his own fortune. He once told me he thought that servants commonly had a better understand-ing of the crevices of men's minds than their masters, because servants watch their masters while their masters care only for gazing at themselves in the glass.

PERHAPS A WEEK after the departure of Paolo Orsini, I was exercising with my company outside the walls when we heard the bells of the city begin to ring wildly. Our commander looked down at us, alarmed, and said, "Fuck." Then he sent a man off to investigate whether the city had been attacked.

As it transpired, these were bells of celebration, not warn-ing. An envoy had arrived with the news that the conspirators had signed the duke's treaty. The war was officially over, having cost little blood other than that of the poor devils who died at Calmazzo. We were given the remainder of the day free.

I retired to my room at once to code a message for Cardinal Giuliano and rode down to the baker's shop to deliver it. A beefy, prosperous-looking man in a sable coat was standing in front of the doorway to Giulietta's house, holding forth to a small circle of neighbors. The young maid, Maddalena, was on the balcony and made a face at me when she saw me passing. I knew what all this meant. Giulietta had told me her brothers were expected back from Ancona any day.

The streets were already becoming uproarious as I made my way back from the baker's. A German artilleryman had somehow procured himself a bishop's cope and mitre and was delivering obscene sermons in the square. A well-loved whore of the city whose hair was dyed to an odd straw color had been given a sword, and a spry old soldier of perhaps sixty was teaching her to fight with it, as a lewd crowd assembled to watch. I wandered through this jovial mayhem cursing Giulietta's brothers and the winds that had sped them up from Ancona so swiftly. My dangerous pleasures with their sister seemed all the more attractive now they were a thing of the past.

THE CELEBRATIONS FOR the peace were not limited to the streets of Imola. A more exclusive entertainment was held that evening in the castle, to which I had the honor of finding myself invited by virtue of my new friendship with Don Michelotto. The other attendees were mainly leading nobles from the duke's entourage and high-ranking officers in his army. All were his own men, I noticed, chosen from the circles of the faithful. No ambassadors were invited and no dignitaries from the town.

All passed as usual during dinner; then, when the floor was cleared afterwards, a serving man came out and strewed it with chestnuts, while another positioned a silver basin on a stool in one corner of the room. After this, from behind the dais where we were sitting, naked women began to crawl out on all fours, until there were perhaps fifteen of them in the room, scuffling round like dogs on the floor. I recognized some of them, women of the court and a few serving-women, but others must have been whores brought up from the town.

The show consisted of this: the women had to pick up the chestnuts in their teeth and crawl to the basin to drop them in. Their task was made more difficult by a pack of a dozen serving-men and soldiers who were released into the hall just after them, whose task was to catch them and fornicate with them, if they could keep hold of them for long enough to do so. The women's bodies had been covered with some kind of oil to help them to slither away. By the basin stood a court official marking up the number of chestnuts each woman managed to drop in the basin. Another moved round the room inspecting the couplings and recording the performance of the men. I heard at a later time that this entertainment had first been devised at the papal court. Some said that Pope Alexander himself was responsible for inventing it. I do not know whether this was true, but it was certainly a spectacle fit for a pope—though Fra Martin Luther might choose to dissent.

There were no Luthers in the audience that night. I have never seen a sport more uproariously successful. Men were almost crying with laughter, pounding on the tables and yelling support and obscenities. Bets were flying on the outcome. Servants were circulating among us tallying these wagers and they rapidly became competitive. Some men were placing huge sums. A stout, determined woman with thighs like tree-trunks was the initial favorite to win. We watched her slide out like a fat eel from the grip of four or five men before she succumbed to a bull-necked Spaniard, who pumped her heartily to the roar of the crowd. Then there was a slighter girl who writhed around with the speed of a cat. It eventually took three men acting together to bring her down. When the sport was over, the victors were brought up to the duke, the winner among the women wrapped scantily in a tablecloth for decency. Valentino solemnly presented her with a silver chain and pushed her in the direction of Don Michelotto, who bowed his gratitude, passing her back to a servant to take to his room.

I learnt the full details of the duke's treaty with the conspirators in the following days. Valentino had proposed to them that they should rule his lands in Romagna together as a kind of consortium. More than this, once his empire in Italy was secured, he would be content merely with the title of prince, leaving the actuality of rule to them. He colored this offer by speaking of his interests in France, where he possessed the duchy of Valence and a young and reputedly handsome wife, the sister of the king of Navarre. It was difficult to govern his land at a distance and still more so to get an heir; he needed to spend time there in person. By delegating his government in Italy to others, he could hold both of his duchies, whether in title or in name.

It seemed extraordinary at the time, and it seems more so looking back, that the conspirators were prepared to put their signatures to this puerile document. How in the name of all the saints did they persuade themselves that a man with such a hunger for power would carve himself out a kingdom in Italy and then relinquish it to others once it was won? The talk of France lent some credibility to the story, it is true, but a slight one. Why would the pope allow the commander of his forces to absent himself from Italy at this critical moment? And why would Valentino believe that, if he removed himself to France, his lands would still be his when he returned?

I heard later that Vitelli argued bitterly against the peace, but that Paolo and Francesco Orsini wore him down, assisted by the lord of Perugia, Baglioni. Baglioni had entered the peace camp through fear, after hearing that the duke was arming the political exiles of his city against him. The only voices speaking for caution at this juncture were Vitelli and

Liverotto. Vitelli eventually put his pen to the page when Liverotto deserted him and he saw that his case was lost.

NOT LONG AFTER the treaty between the duke and the conspirators was signed, Liverotto came to Imola to consult about the new allies' next task. This was not so strange, since the conspirators were the duke's men once more, but it still seemed extraordinary to watch Liverotto ride through the gates of the Rocca at his recent enemy's side. As during the visit of Paolo Orsini, Valentino took the precaution of emptying the city of his mercenaries. The poor wretches were dispatched once again to the country to trouble the worms with their ditch-digging feats.

The duke treated the lord of Fermo with great honor during his stay and laid on several notable entertainments for him. There was no reprise of the game of the chestnuts, although I imagine Liverotto would have relished it greatly—but there were boar hunts and a horse race and a fight between half-starved mastiffs and bears in a pit by the city gates.

I had a role in one of these entertainments myself, though a rather less sanguinary one than the bear fight. On the morning after Liverotto's arrival, the duke summoned me to the courtyard of the Rocca to be reconciled in public with my former master, as a mark of the new spirit of peace that prevailed. He had ordered a strange little ceremony to mark this event. I knelt before Liverotto and asked his pardon for defecting; then Valentino raised me to my feet, and Liverotto embraced me stiffly, to the onlookers' applause. We both acted our part well. Liverotto looked disdainful and I apprehensive, as though I feared he might renege on this peacemaking and stab me on the spot. After this, we feasted on sturgeon with stewed oysters and a brace of roast peacocks, followed by *biancomangiare* dyed to match the uniforms of the duke's army and Liverotto's, an inspired conciliatory touch.

IN TRUTH, I did not need to be an expert mime to feign nervousness in Liverotto's presence. To see the two masters I was serving and deceiving together in the same town made me uneasy enough in itself. I felt like an adulterer invited to dine with his mistress and her husband, as though a single glance or gesture could find me out. I kept to myself as much as I could while Liverotto was in Imola, although Don Michelotto had me attend some of the events in his retinue. These great men at court need their followers in public as much as they need their fine horses and furs.

The last night of Liverotto's stay was a cold, blustery one, gusts of rain battering away against the shutters. I retired early, but was awoken some hours into the night by a sound at my door. First the handle was tried softly; then, after a moment, there was a slight knock, hardly more than a scraping. I imagined it was a summons from the duke, yet the quietness of the knock was strange, almost sinister. The duke's servants were not so tender with my ears.

As soon as I turned the key in the lock, the door was pushed violently in on me, ramming against my shoulder and throwing me off balance. I had a knife in my hand and seized a buckler that was hanging behind the door. I saw light, as from a lantern; then a voice I knew well hissed my name.

I waited until Liverotto had closed the door behind him, then rounded on him.

"What in God's name are you doing here? This is madness."

Here he was, twenty paces from the duke's quarters, in a castle full of hostile eyes. If I were truly what he thought I was, his spy in an enemy court, this could be my downfall—if he cared about such a thing. Liverotto looked down at my dagger and gave an indulgent half-smile, like a man watching a child wield a wooden sword.

"Calm down," he said. "I needed to speak to you. How else was I going to do it? Stroll up to you for a chat after church?"

LIVEROTTO REMAINED with me for perhaps half an hour, interrogating me on the duke's intentions and on whether I considered him to have signed to the treaty in good faith. This was slippery work, for Liverotto was probing me with his eyes all the while, looking for signs that I had been bought by the duke. I was sitting on the bed beside him, no more than an arm's breadth away, so I could smell the wine on his breath and the fusty odor of the fur he was wearing. His lantern stood before us, flickering, throwing up great black dancing shadows behind us on the wall.

I drew in my speech on the credit I had acquired on previous occasions when I had warned Liverotto against the duke's mendacity and cunning. I told him I was the last man to be gulled by Valentino; I knew his promises were written in sand. This time, however, I thought his word could be relied on. He was a practical man, and expediency was everything with him. He would not seek revenge for its own sake, if there were no advantage in it, whatever his feelings about the conspirators. He needed them as allies and was prepared to put the past behind him if it helped him achieve his ends.

After he had heard me out, Liverotto sighed.

"Let us hope you are right. Otherwise we are all dead."

He was slowly turning his dagger in his hand, making it glint in the light.

"You must be wary, that is all," I said firmly. "I will tell you directly if I see any sign of mischief. You had the wit to see long ago that you needed a spy in his camp. Now you will reap the reward for your foresight."

Liverotto looked at me, still dubious.

"The duke is a man like any other," I said. "Fortune has smiled upon him until now, and we thought him a god, but now she is turning her wheel. You are a greater man than he. Look where you have come from and what you have become. Where would you be now if you were the son of a pope?"

I had him with this flattery, or so I thought from his expression. He was silent for a while. When he spoke, what he said was unexpected.

"I was five years old when my father died, you know. I saw him laid out. He was pierced like a sieve."

I nodded. Everybody knew this story. Liverotto's father had been fighting against Turkish pirates, commanding a ship. They had cut him off from his men and butchered him on the deck before their eyes. His body had more than forty stab wounds.

"I always wanted to make myself a man he would be proud of."

"Well, and have you not? You are a great leader of men and the lord of Fermo, and you are not yet thirty years of age. What father would not be proud of such a son?"

Liverotto frowned at me in the candlelight. His mood seemed strange. I wondered how much wine he had taken that evening.

"Sometimes I wonder," he said.

LIVEROTTO LEFT soon after this. I locked the door behind him, and then collapsed onto my bed in a state of exhaustion. I had barely felt the cold in the room when he was there, such was my tension, but now I was shivering, and my hands were like ice. I settled myself back under the bedcovers and lay there for a while; then I got up and searched out my cloak, which was draped on a cassone. I finally slept for a few miserable hours only when I had heaped the bed high with most of the clothes that I owned.

I went to the duke's quarters as soon as I woke, before informers' reports from the night before would have found their way back to him. I reported to his secretary that I had news for the duke, and later that morning he summoned me to him. I told him very exactly of Liverotto's visit and our discussions, recounting both Liverotto's questioning and the dust I had thrown into his eyes. I even told him of the disparaging way I had spoken of him, Valentino, and of Liverotto's curious moment of self-doubt.

This was a high point of favor for me with the duke. He listened attentively to my story, stopping me a few times to question me on some point of detail. When his scrutiny was over, he commended me warmly and told me this deed alone would have justified the trust he had reposed in me. He fished in a purse on the table as he dismissed me, and I imagined he would hand me a ducat or two as reward for my service. Instead, to my astonishment, he pressed an emerald a third of the size of my thumbnail into my hand.

THE OFFER Liverotto had brought from the conspirators was two-fold. If Valentino wished, they would undertake an attack on Tuscany, with Florence as their main prize. If he was not ready for such a great enterprise in these harsh winter months, they would keep themselves busy by picking off Senigallia, a port on the coast, south of Urbino. This city had been the possession of Cardinal Giuliano's brother Giovanni, a condottiere of some reputation. Giovanni had died the previous year, and his widow held the city now—as much as a woman may be said to hold a city. It was ripe for the plucking, and the wealth they could loot there would keep the troops happy until spring.

I was in the company of Messer Niccolò Machiavelli when the first rumor reached us of these two choices the condottieri were offering. Messer Niccolò later claimed he was quite confident the duke would choose Senigallia; treacherous though everyone knew him to be, he would not abandon his alliance with Florence when it had supported him in his hour of need. I was watching Machiavelli's face when he first heard the news, however, and I do not believe he was so sure as he maintained. He had a small, birdlike head, neat, round, and bright-eyed. His most characteristic expression was of skeptical merriment, as if God had forged the world intentionally to offer him mirth. This was not his expression when he heard of the conspirators' offer to the duke to march on Florence. For a moment, he looked like a pigeon when it glances back over its wing to discover that the shadow above it is truly a hawk.

XV

THE MORALISTS LIKE TO SAY that pride comes before a fall, and perhaps this was true in my case on this occasion. I do not know that I was proud after my survival of Liverotto's visit, but I was certainly relieved, and I had an emerald in my pocket. Perhaps that is sufficient to tempt the fates' revenge.

When I heard that the duke had decided on Senigallia as his next target, I coded a note immediately for Cardinal Giuliano. This was the first news I had heard since I was spying for him that affected his family's interests so closely. As I rode down to the baker's, I was also thinking seriously of whether I should attempt somehow to get a message to the cardinal's sister-in-law, telling her that the condottieri were soon to descend on her city, and she should get out of Senigallia while she still could.

I was in the street of the baker's shop when, suddenly, to my amazement, I heard my name called out in Giulietta's voice. This was so extraordinary a thing, in the light of day with the streets crowded with witnesses, that I must have looked up with the air of Saint Francis when he saw the seraphim hovering above.

Giulietta was leaning over her balcony only an arm's breadth above my head, looking at me with an expression of narrow-eyed fury.

"Traitor!" she exclaimed, loudly enough for the whole neighborhood to hear. "How could you use me so ill? Who do you think you are?"

"What?" I said, floundering, as she continued to spit fire at me. I feared she had taken leave of her senses. I stood frozen in the street for a moment, pinned by her gaze. Then I noticed her eyes flicker sideways, in the direction of the baker's, and suddenly guessed what was going on.

"Let me at least try to explain," I said, in the pleading tone of a lover.

"Very well," she said sulkily. I could see tears in her eyes. She jerked her head towards the alley where the side entrance was. "Come round to the usual door. We'll talk inside."

WHEN I GOT into the house, Giulietta came down to meet me and flung herself into my arms. She was trembling.

"I sent Maddalena to find you," she said, sobbing. "Then, when I saw you coming, I could not think what else to do, to warn you."

I looked at her coldly, putting her away from me.

"What are you talking about, woman?"

"They came today. The duke's men. They questioned Giorgio, down the street, the baker. I thought … I had sometimes seen you …"

"*What* did you think?" I said after a pause, in a scornful tone. There was a fire lit behind me, and I quickly incinerated my message for Cardinal Giuliano as I was speaking. "What is it to me if the duke's men were questioning some shopkeeper on your street?"

Giulietta looked at me levelly and saw my betrayal. She hung her head.

"Perhaps I was wrong. I thought you had some dealing with him. I have seen men going to his door, other men. I thought …"

"You have too much imagination," I said angrily. "You have exposed us for no reason. What will your brothers think when they come to hear of this?"

She wept then, and I stood watching her coolly, this woman who had saved my life. My hands were shaking. If she had not come forward, in two minutes, I would have been at the baker's door, handing him the evidence of my treachery. Giulietta had saved me and had sacrificed her reputation to do so—perhaps even her life, if her brothers chose to avenge this dishonor by blood. It is almost the thing I feel most ashamed of in this history that I gave her such poor thanks for this kindness. I could not acknowledge she had saved me without confessing I was a spy. Instead, I watched her weep without uttering a word of comfort, then eventually walked out of the room.

As Giulietta's words implied, I was not the only spy for whom the baker had served as a conduit. The duke's agents became suspicious of him and investigated him, leaving him in place for a day or so to pick up any spies incautious enough to come his way. He finished on the main piazza of the city, his head stuck on a lance like a pig's, with his eyes gouged out of his face and his nose and ears severed. I do not like to think how much of this mutilation had been inflicted on the poor man before he had been permitted to die.

I lived in trepidation for a few days, anticipating an attack from Giulietta's brothers, but, in the event, they proceeded through the law. I was arrested a few days later, accused of debauching a widow and placed in a prison in the castle. Then I was taken to a judge in the town, who had been appointed by the duke. The case was examined, and I confessed to my guilt.

I shall pass through this part briefly, for it is not something I like to recall. The punishment for this transgression handed down by the judge was twelve strokes with a lash, to be inflicted in public. The duke also demanded restitution of the emerald he had given me a few days before. He had placated Giulietta's brothers by offering a generous dowry to pay for her next husband, with my public castigation thrown in for good measure. I imagine he was not unhappy at the opportunity this case offered to show himself a just and magnanimous ruler, unwilling to tolerate the depredations of cynical men of his court on the populace whose interests he had at heart.

My punishment took place in the main square of the city on a freezing day in early December. Various leading citizens of Imola attended to witness it, as well as the usual curious throng. I was determined, with a young man's pride, not to cry out when the whip hit me, and I succeeded in this, although it took all my powers. The pain was extraordinary and got worse with each stroke, until by the last I could hardly hold back from screaming. When they released my wrists from the ropes I had been tied with, I was trembling from head to foot and could hardly stumble down from the platform. It made me feel sick as I did so to see the whip lying there, the whole length of its five tails drenched in fresh blood.

In a strange way, horrible though it was, I was not unhappy to have this pain visited on me. I felt I deserved it for my betrayal of Giulietta, if not for the offense it was intended to punish. Nonetheless, I cannot say that this was not a humiliation and a cruel one. I crawled back to the castle and spent an evening of the purest agony in my room lying with my flayed skin exposed to the air.

My only comfort was a visit from Machiavelli, who came to express his commiserations, bringing a strange-scented salve he had procured from an apothecary in town and a flask of excellent Tuscan wine. I was moved at this kindness, the more so because I knew this was a man kept cruelly out of pocket by his masters in Florence. The expense of the wine and the salve probably accounted for the greater part of his budget for the week. Messer Niccolò was keen to know about the love affair that had led me to this sad pass, and I recounted it at length for his amusement, emphasizing the lascivious aspects. This was another betrayal of my poor Giulietta, the second she had suffered at my hands.

I REMAINED IN my room for two days after this, waiting for my back to heal sufficiently for me to tolerate wearing clothes. I hardly slept in this time. I could not bear so much as the weight of a sheet on my torn flesh, and it was too cold to sleep without covers, even if I lay on the floor by the fire. I was consumed during this time by a feeling of self-loathing. I thought of the women I had had as my lovers and the disastrous fates I seemed to have brought on them. Lucia had been murdered, Giulietta disgraced, Nicolosa lured into a mortal sin without knowing it. Only Agnese, with her peasant cunning, had survived me intact, and I could hardy take credit for that.

I dreaded returning to the court to meet men's eyes after my disgrace, but the reality was much less ugly than my imaginings. As I skulked round the walls of the courtyard on the first day I emerged, Don Michelotto greeted me with a smile as though nothing had happened. Since all within the court take their cue from the powerful, this signaled my return to the fold. The news had gone round that I had borne my punishment without bleating, which was a thing of some moment in a court made up of soldiers; also, Messer Niccolò had been active in disseminating the details of my affair with Giulietta, with embellishments of the kind you might expect. My reputation rose as a result, and I even became an object of envy in the minds of some courtiers. No thought so inflames men's carnal imagination as that of the rich, bored young widow, hungry for erotic diversion, and the more complicated versions of my legend had me enjoying both mistress and maid. One Spaniard remarked to me that, if even only half of what he had heard reported of my story was true, he thought twelve strokes of the lash a modest price to pay.

XVI

PERHAPS A WEEK AFTER I emerged into the world after my disgrace, the duke departed from Imola with a portion of his forces to proceed to Cesena, fifty miles to the east. This transfer had been spoken of as a prospect for weeks, but the decision was announced suddenly, as was the duke's secretive manner. I first heard of it when a servant came to my room after dinner and told me to be ready for departure the next day.

The thought of this journey filled me with despondency, for my wounds were barely beginning to heal and the thought of sitting on a horse for six hours with a winter cloak on my back was an agonizing prospect. In the end, I volunteered to go on with the foreriders so I could travel at more speed and dress more lightly, though I still arrived at Cesena with my bandages soaked through with blood.

I led a quiet life in this new town. Apart from my physical wounds, I had little appetite for wandering around the city, and the gathering of information had no interest for me without Cardinal Giuliano to supply. When I was not training at arms, I stayed in my room reading or writing letters to Nicolosa in my head. My chief company in this somber life was the splendid gray parrot I had won at cards at the beginning of my sojourn in Imola. I had paid a steward to bring this half-forgotten possession over to Cesena in the first baggage train.

It was during this time that I first began to become attached to this remarkable creature, whom I christened Demosthenes, on account of his eloquence. During our sojourn in Imola, he had dwelled mainly in the kitchens, for I feared he would freeze to death in my room. In Cesena, I kept a fire for him at all hours, careless of expense, and amused myself by feeding nuts to him and teaching him phrases from Cicero and Ovid. He had come to me with no more than the coarse vocabulary of the German soldier who had owned him, a disgrace for so noble a bird.

Two weeks or so after our arrival in Cesena, I received a visit from Machiavelli as I was waking in the morning, perhaps an hour before a late winter dawn. He had a taste for these early calls, I should say, as a man who was astir at all hours. Despite the cynical air he sometimes liked to affect, he was a zealot in the discharge of his profession. You could barely turn a corner without encountering him in a corridor, interrogating some hapless minion or clerk. I am not sure he ever slept, for at night, when there was no one to interrogate, he would compose his reports for his Florentine masters. He also read much, searching in the bowels of ancient history for lessons of use to the present and ruminating on the causes of Italy's decline.

I was crouching by my fire, trying to revive it from its nocturnal slumbers, when Messer Niccolò rapped at my door in his usual peremptory manner. When I opened it, he came in and positioned himself by the fire with his long thin white hands held out towards the flames.

"You'll never be able to guess what has happened," he said. "At Senigallia."

We were all following the siege of that city with great interest. The conspirators' armies had been camped there for two weeks under the leadership of Liverotto, Vitelli, and Paolo and Francesco Orsini. Baglioni, the lord of Perugia, had absented himself and was at home persecuting his subjects instead.

"Well?" I said, having waited for Machiavelli to continue.

"You have to guess," he annoyingly replied.

"The castellan is suing for terms, I imagine. What else is he going to do with three thousand men camped outside his gates?"

"Correct," Messer Niccolò said. "But what do you think is his main condition for surrender?"

"How should I know? He wants to be escorted to the city gates by a phalanx of naked nuns?"

"Unfortunately not. He lacks your imaginative genius." Machiavelli paused impressively. "Listen to this. He has announced he's not prepared to surrender the castle to Liverotto. Or Vitelli. Or either of the Orsinis. Or the whole fucking lot of them together, and their grandmothers. Guess who he has decided he wants to surrender to?"

The truth came to me with a start.

"He wants to surrender to the duke."

THIS WAS extraordinary indeed. We spent the next half hour discussing the implications before my fire, with occasional interjections from my parrot. My first thought—and Messer Niccolò's also, he confessed—was that this was a trick on the part of the conspirators. Either they had signed the peace treaty in bad faith, or they had changed their minds since, like men regretting a decision made while drunk. They wanted to lure Valentino down while they had their armies massed at Senigallia and to finish the work of dragon taming they had started in October and had not had the courage to follow through.

This was one possibility. Another was that it was a trick on the part of Valentino. He had agreed to a clause in the peace treaty that denied him the right to summon the ex-conspirators into his presence together, because they so feared him and his deceptions. Yet in this instance he had an excuse to insinuate himself among them without raising suspicion, since he was obeying a summons that came from outside.

This second hypothesis would require that the castellan of Senigallia be secretly in the pay of Valentino. This was a man of whom we knew little at the time, a Genoese of the name of Andrea Doria—the same fearsome commander who is now so celebrated as admiral of the Emperor's fleet. At the time of which I speak, he was no more than a name to us: a poor wretch of a novice condottiere stuck defending a doomed port city with the help of a few hundred men.

Machiavelli and I stood for a while canvassing the likelihood that Doria was a traitor, a conversation that made me uneasy; I did not like to speak of spying or treachery or double-dealing under the eyes of this shrewd, watchful man. By good fortune, Demosthenes intervened to rescue me, unleashing a magnificent long string of German oaths in a manner that left Machiavelli quite captivated. He would not rest until he had enriched the poor beast's stock of obscenities with a choice phrase or two of his own.

VALENTINO ASSEMBLED his army within days to march south towards Senigallia. The weather was brilliant, though punishingly cold, with a bright winter sun glinting off the sea and making the frost on the ground sparkle like diamonds. I almost enjoyed the ride, though the scars on my back were still giving me pain.

We paused in our march at Fano, a city around fifteen miles north of Senigallia, not so near that the conspirators would take fright. Here Valentino conducted negotiations with his allies regarding his arrival in Senigallia. Vitelli and Liverotto sent envoys, laying out a plan whereby they would withdraw from the city with Liverotto's army the day before

Valentino marched in, leaving a core of men under trusted lieutenants to prevent Doria's garrison from escaping. Vitelli's forces were already stationed at some distance from Senigallia, in a ring of castles in the hills perhaps five miles away. There was only room for one army on the plain.

The duke rejected this proposal with scorn, in a tirade that he delivered in the presence of his whole court in the castle at Fano. I had never heard Valentino deliver a speech of this length before, and I must say he spoke well and looked magnificent in his anger. The envoys stood cowed before him, like frightened children being scolded. Liverotto's envoy was his disagreeable cousin Antonio, my companion on the mission to Rome the previous winter. He had greeted me disdainfully when he saw me, and I took pleasure in watching him quail before the duke.

The thrust of Valentino's speech was that it was impossible to conduct his affairs with his allies when such mistrust prevailed among them. The ink was still fresh on their peace treaty, and already they trusted him so little that they planned to flee his presence as if he were a wolf coming into the sheepfold. He had forgiven them their betrayal and offered them terms when many men in his position would have given no quarter. What more did they want from him? Had any of them cause to complain of his dealings with them in the past?

THIS SPEECH was the duke's public response, but he knew that platitudes about trust would not be sufficient to carry his point, however fiercely delivered. More secret negotiations were needed, and this is where I had a role.

On the night of the ambassadors' visit, Valentino called me to his chamber and dictated a message for me to convey to Liverotto. In it, I told my former master that I had surmised that Valentino had an undeclared motive in wishing to assemble all his forces in Senigallia. After the capture of the city, he was minded to move swiftly on Tuscany, while the Florentines were off their guard. I presented this merely as conjecture, but reported certain facts that appeared to support it. Arrangements were being made for the provisioning of the army far beyond what was needed for the brief march to Senigallia. An envoy of the exiled Medici lords of Florence had arrived in Cesena, purportedly to negotiate a sale of antiquities to the duke.

I gave much thought to the best way to deliver this message to give an appropriate impression of secrecy and danger. I was a spy in a hostile court, in constant fear of discovery. I could hardly stroll up coolly to a foreign ambassador's door. In the end, I decided to scale down the inner wall of the castle on a rope and knock on Messer Antonio's window when he had retired for the night. I cleared this plan with Don Michelotto, who took charge of securing the rope for me himself.

When I reported the success of this mission to the duke the next day, he looked sardonically at me and asked whether I had learned these tricks of scaling walls in my career seducing widows. I was abashed by this mention of my disgrace, but then he commended me more seriously, and told me he would not forget this service.

"Return here at the hour of vespers," he said. "You will learn of my gratitude then."

I SPENT the whole day in a state of anxiety, waiting for the call to vespers with an eagerness that would do credit to the most devout novice. Around midday, I watched from the battlements as the convoy of the conspirators' envoys began to wind its way southwards from the gates. I thought of the councils the conspirators would hold that evening to chew over the duke's public and private messages. I imagined them steaming in their furs by the fire in some cold purloined palace, fearful, greedy, rash, calculating in turn.

The more I thought of the message I had conveyed to Liverotto, the more it seemed to me a masterstroke on the part of the duke. The shrewdest of the conspirators was Vitelli, yet his shrewdness was more than matched by his ancient loathing for Florence. The prospect of a march on Tuscany, with the full forces of his own army, Liverotto's, the duke's, and those of the Orsini was so fat a bait I did not think he would be able to resist. With the Orsini cousins already in the duke's pocket, any chance of resistance at this point could only come from Liverotto. Had the duke already bought him with promises? Would he have the prudence to stand against the rest?

WHEN VESPERS finally tolled, I almost had to fight my way to the duke's rooms through the crowded corridors of the castle. The place was filled with officers and functionaries completing preparations for the march to Senigallia the next day.

A servant opened the door to me. The first person I saw inside was a fox-faced Romagnol condottiere named Dionigi Naldi, one of the duke's most trusted lieutenants. He was speaking to Don Michelotto and paused to stare at me when I entered the room. I could see why when I looked around. The company, aside from me, was a distinguished one, the core of the army's leadership, and noblemen all, aside from Don Michelotto. I stood uncomfortably by the wall, ticking off names in my head, wondering whether I had come to the right place.

Valentino strode into the room not long after I entered and nodded to Don Michelotto, who began to address us. What he was going to say was a matter of high secrecy. The following day, the nine of us present in the room were to ride to Senigallia in the duke's immediate party. After the conspirators had come out to meet us, we were to act as their escort of honor, accompanying them back to Valentino's lodgings in town. Each conspirator would have his own escort. We should keep them apart, though without giving cause for suspicion. We must converse with them urbanely as we rode with them, to calm any fears they might have.

"You could ask, for example, whether the ladies of Senigallia are looking forward to our arrival."

Don Michelotto accompanied this phrase with an obscene gesture, and everyone laughed.

Once he had finished this preamble, Don Michelotto read out the names of each of the conspirators, and the names of the men in the room who would serve as their escorts. Two were allocated to Paolo Orsini, two to Francesco Orsini, two to Vitellozzo Vitelli. Then Don Michelotto announced that he himself would escort Liverotto, together with Messers Dionigi Naldi and Matteo da Fermo.

He nodded in my direction as he spoke my name, and every man in the room turned his eyes on me.

"This youth is to help with the urbane conversation," Don Michelotto said. "That was never my strength."

The men smiled at this, some still eyeing me curiously; then Don Michelotto led them from the room. The duke held me back as I was following them, and I found myself alone with him.

"Well," he said. "Giovanni Fogliani's son, here is your moment."

On an impulse, I dropped to my knees before him and thanked him fervently for reposing his trust in me. It is never a mistake to use such manners with princes, but the gratitude I was expressing was sincere. This was indeed my moment of revenge, and it was gracious of Valentino to place me so close to the heart of it—even though I knew he was doing this from calculation, knowing I was a man who enjoyed Liverotto's trust.

When I had finished my speech, the duke motioned me to rise.

"Remember this?" he said.

He was holding something out on his gloved palm of pale leather, a small green stone, bright as glass. It was the emerald he had given me in Imola and then confiscated from me over my transgression with Giulietta.

"If you serve me well again tomorrow, you will have it back. You will have earned it."

I bowed low to express my gratitude.

"Watch him," he said. "Anticipate what he is thinking. Be on your guard."

There was a brooding look about him as he spoke these words, and I thought I could see for an instant how fiercely he craved his revenge. Then his face returned to its usual unreadability, and he waved me from the room.

I HARDLY SLEPT that night. I could hardly even breathe, so keen was my nervous anticipation. I stayed down in the hall for a while with the late drinkers and card players; then I thought I should try to sleep so my wits would be sharp for the next day. After that, I lay on my bed for hours watching the moonlight seeping softly through a chink in the shutters, thinking of Liverotto and recollecting the violence he had wreaked on my life. A memory kept returning to me of Fermo on the day of my return after his coup and its silent streets and the horrors they had seen.

I slept briefly at one point and dreamed that I was in a room with Liverotto. He was reaching out with his hand, proffering something, as the duke had the emerald that evening. I leaned very close to it, for at first I could see nothing; then a small black serpent bored up suddenly through a hole in his palm and began slithering up his arm. Liverotto was smiling very strangely, and I knew he had discovered my treachery. I felt a lurching fear that awoke me abruptly. I was sweating, despite the cold, and I think I must have cried out in my sleep. One of the men with whom I was sharing the chamber was cursing at me from the other end of the room.

THE NEXT DAY dawned bright. We left Fano soon after dawn and reached Senigallia while the sun was still high in the sky, though it was already beginning to descend. These were the dregs of the winter, when the days are at their shortest; the next day would be the last of the year.

The city of Senigallia lies on a plain near the sea. Its finest feature is the great new citadel, completed perhaps ten years before the time of which I am speaking. For the rest, it is a walled city, fairly wealthy from its port, but no finer than many you have seen. From the side we were approaching, a river lay before us, with a wide modern bridge and a road leading to the city gates not far beyond. To our left, on the other side of the river, was a settlement outside the walls, and beyond it we could see Liverotto's army drawn up in its ranks. My heart leapt in my breast when I saw the livery of Dino's brigade.

I had been riding behind Don Michelotto, not far from the duke, who was surrounded by his household guard, riding in the center of the army. Half the cavalry were ahead of us along with around a thousand of the infantry. The rest of the army followed behind. When the cavalry at the front reached the bridge, they parted on each side, and the infantry behind them passed through the gap they had left and marched towards the gates. By the time we were at the bridge, Valentino's men had effectively occupied the town.

Three figures came towards us as we crossed the bridge, dressed simply, like merchants going about their business in town. These were the two Orsini and Vitelli. I recognized the figure of Paolo Orsini first, a large man too stout for his mare. They came slowly, with a small entourage behind them, like men of peace. A trumpeter walking before them was the only sign of pomp.

Valentino received his allies with warmth, riding forward to meet them and leaning from his horse to embrace each of them in turn. For a while, we watched them as they parleyed, the duke gesturing gracefully as he spoke. The conspirators were looking subdued. Vitelli had a flinching look about him, as though he could hardly keep upright on his horse. I guessed he was suffering from a recurrence of the French sickness. His face was thin and pale, and you could see fresh scars on his cheeks where the disease was eating into his flesh.

You will have noticed that I did not mention Liverotto along with the other conspirators. This was because he was not with them. He was drilling his troops on the plain beside the city, apparently to honor the arrival of the duke. I saw Valentino exchange a glance with Don Michelotto as he turned to ride into the city with his allies, and he nodded his head very slightly to the left in the direction of Liverotto's troops. As the rest of the party began to make its way towards the city, with the escorts delegated to the Orsini cousins and Vitelli positioned alongside them, Don Michelotto and Messer Dionigi Naldi peeled off. I followed behind at their heels.

As WE CAME closer to Liverotto's army, we could see him there, on the great black steed he liked to ride, reviewing his beloved troops. The army did look a fine sight, to do him justice, glittering with weapons like an ocean in the weak winter sun.

As we approached Liverotto, Don Michelotto turned to Messer Dionigi and me.

"Leave him to me if there's any trouble."

He spoke calmly, as if this was all part of a day's business. He was riding hatless, despite the cold and his baldness, though a leather helmet hung from a strap around his neck.

Liverotto shouted a greeting when we rode up to him, then turned back to his troops on his splendid horse. The sun gleamed on his breastplate, and the gulls wheeled raucously above him. He looked every inch the mountainous warrior: mighty Ajax, bulwark of the Achaeans. I could feel the desire for revenge so hot inside me that I almost feared I could not keep it from my face.

Don Michelotto rode forward and spoke to Liverotto, who frowned, gesturing towards the troops as if to say he was needed here. Don Michelotto spoke again and Liverotto glanced in my direction. I gave him the slightest of nods. He hesitated still and my nerves began to tense. What if he refused to come with us? We were three against seven hundred. I thought of my dream, and the fear I had felt on waking reared up sharply within me again.

Finally Liverotto turned his horse towards us, shouting to the officer nearest him to take charge of the troops while he was gone. We rode towards the gates of the city, with Don Michelotto to the right of Liverotto and Messer Dionigi to the left. I followed behind them with three or four of Liverotto's guards. I asked the one closest to me for news of Dino, and he told me he was well and asked me about life with the duke. In this manner, we entered the city and rode through the streets to a large, noble house in what seemed the main square.

When we arrived at the building and dismounted, Liverotto said he wanted to take his guards inside with him. Don Michelotto spread his hands and said this was no time for suspicion, and that no one was being allowed into the place armed. Liverotto glanced at me again, and I again nodded very slightly, like a man who fears being observed.

The door opened at this point, revealing a man in Valentino's court livery, unarmed, with the air of a steward. Don Michelotto politely gestured to Liverotto to go in, closing the door behind him as he disappeared inside. As soon as the door closed, men began to the stream into the square from the side streets, twenty, thirty, fifty of the duke's soldiers in their yellow and crimson. Don Michelotto turned to Liverotto's guards with a smile.

"Now, gentlemen, give up your arms."

AFTER WHAT SEEMED only a few minutes, the duke emerged from the door and snapped his fingers for a servant to bring a horse for him. He glanced around, his face stiff as a mask, then rode off at a canter with Don Michelotto down the street.

I later learned they had gone to give directions to the troops. Around three thousand men were sent to expunge Vitelli's army, which was occupying a series of castles a few miles away in the hills. The rest of them, aside from the thousand who had entered the town, were given the gratifying task of sacking Liverotto's army on the plain. This was like setting foxes in a hen coop. Liverotto's men were leaderless and outnumbered by around five to one, despite the troops the duke had sent to the castles of Vitelli. They were also ill placed, between the city walls and the river, with the sea blocking escape to one side.

When I heard of this sacking, I rode out of the city to see whether I could do anything to help Dino. The sun was beginning to fall lower now and the shadows were lengthening. There was chaos in Liverotto's camp. As I approached, I could see men swarming over wagons, tearing at the ropes that bound their contents and scrapping over the spoils. The sound of their yelling and cursing mixed with the shrill whinnying of frightened horses, and the pitiful screams of the camp's women as they fell prey to their captors. I thought of Agnese and shuddered, although I knew she would not be with them, married as she now was and with child.

Wisely, Liverotto's army seemed to have put up little resistance. I saw perhaps twenty bodies on the ground, some in the livery of Liverotto's companies, the others probably looters murdered by their own comrades. Some had crows on them already, tearing at their eye sockets, a sight that always makes me feel sick. Perhaps four or five hundred prisoners, mainly infantry by the look of them, had been herded into groups in the custody of Valentino's soldiers, who had lined them up and were stripping them of all they had on them. Their confiscated weapons were already lying in piles. I searched these groups as well as I could in the fading light, but saw no one I recognized from Dino's company. I hoped this meant Dino had succeeded in escaping, which did not seem impossible since he was mounted. The river behind the camp was high, as it was winter, but not too difficult to attempt on a horse.

Eventually, the sight of the humbled men of the army I had once served in, shivering in the few clothes left on their backs, became too melancholy for me. There was nothing I could do to assist them, so I made my way back to the town. In the house to which we had conducted Liverotto, I found a party of Valentino's lesser courtiers playing dice in an antechamber, and joined them to hear what was happening.

These men told me that, as soon as the conspirators had entered the building, the duke ushered them to a secret room, telling them he wished to speak of a thing of high confidence. There they were taken and bound. No one knew precisely where they were now. Some thought they were still in a room in this same building, others that they had been taken to a tower near the citadel. No one doubted they would be killed this same night.

It seemed to me extraordinary how closely the duke's capture of these men had followed the pattern of Liverotto's seizure of Messer Giovanni and his fellow victims at Fermo. What had been the thoughts of Liverotto when he saw himself fall into a trap that he, of all men, should have known?

I felt a need to be alone as I meditated on this, and I walked out into the bleak winter courtyard of the house, where a youth in a jerkin was methodically cutting a pile of logs into firewood with an axe. I watched the inexorable rhythm of his falling arm like a man in a trance, imagining the instant when my enemy knew he had been taken. What was he feeling now, alone with his conscience, knowing that these were his last hours on earth?

VALENTINO PRESUMABLY hoped that, by letting his men sack Liverotto's army, he could provide a safe outlet for their energies. If this was his calculation, it was a poor one. Their sacking had given them a taste for more sacking, and they began to make their way into the town. This was a mongrel army, quickly raised from all corners of the globe and with the discipline you might consequently expect.

Sounds of violence had begun to intrude from the streets when I returned from the courtyard to the room where Valentino's courtiers were sitting. Soon a Spanish captain of the duke's recruited me to an impromptu platoon set to police the frenzied streets. We did not return to the house until perhaps the fourth hour of the night, when the looting had begun to subside.

When I got back, exhausted, one of the men I had been speaking to earlier told me that Don Michelotto was looking for me. He was off supervising the hanging of looters in the west of the town, but had left word for me to wait for him until he got back. As I was receiving these instructions, the man himself walked in, grim-faced and weary. When he saw me, he nodded slightly and told me to wait. He disappeared into a side room and emerged after a few minutes with two servants carrying lanterns. One of them also carried a bag.

I followed Don Michelotto and the servants in silence through the streets until we came to a squat tower, standing some twenty paces from the high ghostly walls of the citadel, perhaps part of some previous, demolished fort. You could still hear faint sounds of yelling in the distance as the last of the looting was suppressed. The night was a very cold one, brilliant with stars.

When we entered the tower, the servants lit our way along a corridor and then down a spiral staircase, cramped and frigid, with a slime of moss clinging to the stones. We came out in a dark room, where the servants hung up their lanterns on hooks on the walls.

We were in a dungeon, of course, which smelled like every dungeon in the world, of damp and decay and stagnant water and human excrement. Vitelli and Liverotto were there on the floor in manacles, Vitelli in the robe he had worn coming forth to meet us, Liverotto in something black like a cassock that they must have given him when they stripped him of his military attire.

Don Michelotto and I stood there as the servants traversed the room, lighting further lanterns from the wicks of those they had brought. As the light became bright enough for the two men to read our faces, I saw Liverotto's eyes light with hope, seeing me in this dark place, as though I might yet be his guardian angel. I looked at him for the first time with the loathing I felt for him.

"Judas," Liverotto said eventually. He attempted to spit at me, but his spittle fell impotently a yard from my feet.

"That would make you Our Lord, I suppose."

Don Michelotto laughed and reached out to the servant carrying the bag. Liverotto turned to him and began speaking urgently, asking him to give him access to the duke, to say just one thing to him. He was not a traitor. Vitelli had led him astray. He was a young man and inexperienced in the ways of the world, and he had placed his trust in this viper, who had undone him.

Liverotto spoke of Vitelli's iniquities for as long as Don Michelotto would permit him, while Vitelli sat beside him with his head slumped, as though unhearing. Liverotto was gabbling like a man who knows his time is short, his voice sometimes skewing upwards to a strange high-pitched note.

Don Michelotto stared at him without expression and held something out towards me in his hand.

"Do you want to do him?"

I shook my head.

"I'll do Vitelli first then."

He stepped forward and circled round to place himself behind Vitelli. As he did, Vitelli spoke in a breaking voice, asking him whether his death could be delayed until he could have absolution for his sins from the pope. Machiavelli was disgusted when I told him this detail, saying it seemed to him cowardly and abject. He wished this great warrior to die bravely like Seneca or Socrates with a noble last word on his lips. This was well enough, but we are Christians, and I can tell you there is nothing more ugly than to see a man staring at his damnation for eternity. It chilled me to look at Vitelli as he spoke, thinking how soon his soul would stand at the threshold of hell.

This thought affected me so much that I felt an impulse to intervene, to ask compassion for this man, even though I knew it would be useless. Don Michelotto would simply laugh at me, and the thing would go ahead just the same. In any case, by now it was too late. Don Michelotto had his wire round Vitelli's neck, and I must say he made the quickest work of it possible. For a moment he twisted at the wire with great force, until Vitelli's face turned purple with blood; then he jerked his head back sharply towards him, increasing the pressure. I could not see the face after that and was glad of it. After a moment, a convulsion passed through Vitelli's body and he died.

Don Michelotto loosened his wire, wiping it clean of blood on a cloth, and moved towards Liverotto, who was still gibbering away, as if it could do him any good. The smell of death was in the room, which is to say the smell of shit. A servant was seeing to a guttering lamp.

I watched the execution of Liverotto with no shadow of the compassion that had afflicted me watching Vitelli. Perhaps I imagined it, but it seemed to me Don Michelotto slowed down the process this time for my benefit. I had time to summon Liverotto's victims in my imagination to watch his death agony alongside me, a swarm of bitter, savoring ghosts. It is a vile thing to confess, but I felt a pleasure watching his killing akin to the pleasure of eros. Liverotto died hard, his huge body writhing in its manacles like a goaded bull, his limbs furiously jerking and thrashing. By the time he finally subsided into death, still convulsing, I was trembling from head to foot.

When Don Michelotto had concluded, he motioned to one of the servants, who, to my surprise, took soap and a towel from his bag and fetched a pail of water from a corner of the cell. Don Michelotto reached his hands out for the servant to wash, glancing at me ruefully as if this was some weakness on his part.

I had gone over to Liverotto meanwhile. He was lying slumped on his side, and, on an impulse, I kicked his dead face as hard as I could with the metal cap of my boot. It felt good. I wanted to erase him. He was on his back now, and I stamped on his face with my full weight, so I could hear bones crunch under my foot.

I would have continued, but I felt a hand on my shoulder pulling me back.

"The bodies are going out on the piazza," Don Michelotto said. "They have to be recognizable. If it was up to me ..." He shrugged. "Once more if you like, son."

I shook my head, looking down at Liverotto's mangled dead face with a feeling of sickness. I suddenly wanted with all my being to escape from this antechamber to hell.

XVII

WHEN I AWOKE THE MORNING after this memorable night, the light was the gray light of dawn, before sunrise. I felt restless and went up to the battlements to escape the snoring of the men sleeping by my side. It was searingly cold. The men of the night watch were gathered round a brazier trying to warm their hands, breathing great white clouds into the air.

I watched the sun come up over the sparkling sea, trying to avoid the sight of the debris outside the walls where I had watched Liverotto's army being sacked. A few bodies still lay on the ground there, their bones showing through now that the foxes had been at them. I thought of the events of the night before, and they seemed to me like a dream or, better, a nightmare. I remembered the bestiality that had come across me when I desecrated Liverotto's face, and I felt ashamed of what I had become. This was the last day of this strange, atrocious year in my life, which had begun with the massacre in Fermo. I desperately wished for it to be over, so I could be in a new and less terrible age.

There was movement around the citadel as the sun came up, and as I descended the walls I could see the garrison beginning to file warily out from it, their helmets glinting reddish in the morning light. There was shouting at the gates, an officer of the duke's cursing in Spanish, and I wondered what the cause of this altercation was.

I soon learned. By a stratagem, the castellan, Andrea Doria, had succeeded in smuggling the lady of the city and her young son to safety, during the time when the conspirators had been holding the town. Doria himself then absconded, profiting from the chaos following the duke's arrival, leaving a lieutenant to surrender the keep. My heart was gladdened by this news, for the boy was the nephew of my patron Cardinal Giuliano, the fragile hope of his lineage. He was twelve years old at this time. He would not have reached thirteen had he fallen into Valentino's hands.

As I WATCHED the garrison leave the citadel, I saw a thin string of worshippers filing out from an ancient-looking, sparsely adorned chapel beyond it. They shrank past the soldiers looking terrified, and I remembered the brutal sacking the night before. I made my way down to the small church, reckoning it would be empty after mass. I was right. The only people there were two elderly women dressed in black, who would have risen no higher than my elbow had they stood alongside me. There was little chance of that. They turned to stare when I entered, then crossed themselves and scuttled away.

I knelt and thanked God for having seen me safely through the perils of the year and asked forgiveness for the ugliness that had come to stain my soul. I knew I should confess, for I had not been shriven for many months, but my mind revolted from the thought of speaking of my feelings for Nicolosa with some sour-faced priest. I confessed instead to God in my heart, asking Him for strength to sin with her no more. Then I prayed for all those I loved among the dead and the living, placing Dino among the living, as I hoped and trusted he was. I prayed for the souls of Messer Giovanni and Lorenzo with a newly rejoicing heart, for now they were avenged and could bend themselves on the spiritual labors of Purgatory without further distraction from this world.

When I had finished with those I held dear, I prayed for the soul of Vitelli, whose plight had strangely touched me the previous night. Finally, before I rose, I prayed for the black soul of Liverotto—for does not God, in his wisdom, instruct us to love our enemies? This is too much to demand of human nature while those enemies are living; wait until they are dead and you may have some chance. In truth, now that he was no more, now that I had slaked my crueler part watching his death agony, Liverotto seemed to me almost a figure of pathos. I could feel my prayer rising empty as vapor into the cold air, for who could believe he was saved? And even here on earth, what had his brief, noisy, valiant, brutal life won him? He had wanted to be remembered—but who would remember him now, other than with loathing? Who would mourn him? Even as I muttered my wasted words for him, his corpse was being dragged out to the main piazza of Senigallia, there to rot for a few days under the eyes of a bored guard before being thrown to the dogs.

OUR ARMY MARCHED from Senigallia later that same morning, leaving a garrison in the town and a company of men to guard the officers and cavalrymen captured from Liverotto's army. I was not able to ascertain whether Dino was among these captives, who had been locked in a tower on the plain. All these ransomable men were to be taken to the fortress at Fano, where they would be kept until the money for their redemption came in. Liverotto's foot soldiers were less fortunate. Most were taken along with our army as prisoners, wearing chains around their ankles, and assigned to the kind of tasks the lowest infantryman in an army fattened on loot is unwilling to perform.

It was a cruel march we were led on that day. It was easy enough to understand why our restless lord would wish to press his advantage. Vitelli's seat of Città di Castello lay leaderless and open to him, and two of the other conspirators, Baglioni and Pandolfo Petrucci, were still at large in Perugia and Siena. He had lands to seize and blood to spill, and if it meant marching his men through a blinding snow blizzard to take quarters in a town that could barely shelter a third of them, then this was the price that had to be paid. Corinaldo was the name of the place—one of a string of fortified towns that threads across this lawless reach of the Marches. If you visited it in April you might think it a fine place, but on that day in December it looked to me like the guard post to Cocytus, that frozen realm of Hell where Dante places the souls of those who betray bonds of blood.

The day was a bitter one for me and not only because of the brutal cold and the miserable sight of our poor *fermani* prisoners staggering along in chains burdened like pack mules. It was bitter because a truth was coming home to me that I had failed or refused to acknowledge before this time— that I was locked into my service with Valentino even though the reason for my entering into it was no more. In all these months of scheming, I had never looked beyond the fulfillment of my vengeance. It was as if I had imagined I would miraculously find myself back in my former life the moment Liverotto was dead. But how could that be? I had sworn fealty to the duke, and a document bearing my signature and witnessed by a notary was gathering dust in the state chancery at Cesena. Why would the duke release me from this bond simply because my private quest for vendetta was complete?

I was one of a score of soldiers who had been charged on this journey with the task of guarding the remaining two conspirators in the duke's hands, Paolo and Francesco Orsini. There was little guarding needed. The two sat on the mules that carried them slumped and frigid, not speaking to one another, their eyes already dead in their pale, cold-pinched faces. Yesterday they had woken as generals and lords; now they were beasts being led to the slaughter. The rumor was that they were only being preserved alive until the pope had laid hands on Cardinal Orsini and some of the secular heads of the clan. Neither of the men we were accompanying was sympathetic to me, and Paolo was hardly less than repulsive. Still, they were pitiful in their abjection, and my duties as guard contributed to my generally accumulating gloom.

WE WERE TWO nights at Corinaldo. The cavalry and the officers found lodgings in the town, crammed into every inch of space there, even stables and cowsheds. We were lucky. The infantry were stationed in a village a few miles away, sleeping as they could in the icy air, huddled around fires, for the earth was frozen too hard to strike camp. The *fermani* prisoners had the worst of it, poor wretches. Half a dozen perished from the cold as they lay in their chains, their outer garments having been looted on the previous day. They were stripped and left naked for the ravens to feast on; there was no burying them with the earth like a stone.

The duke sent a troop ahead to establish quarters for us at Sassoferrato, and on the third day after our arrival at Corinaldo we moved on there. The following day we marched southwards to a town named Gualdo, in weather that continued to be cruel. There was a delegation awaiting us at Gualdo made up of burghers from Città di Castello, eager to throw themselves into the hands of the duke peaceably before he came and took their city by force. More unexpectedly, also, there were envoys from Perugia, bringing the news that the conspirator Baglioni had fled, abandoning the city with his troops to take refuge in Siena. The tide of Fortune was once more with the duke—although not with his frozen forces, who had sustained themselves on their hellish journey with thoughts of the pickings that awaited them in the cities on which we were marching. To keep their discontent in check,

Valentino was forced to pay his infantry from his own coffers, a most unusual event.

There seemed some hope for me in this propitious turn of events, and I applied to Don Michelotto to press my case with the duke for a period of leave. I said I was anxious for the fate of my property in Fermo since the fall of Liverotto, a motive any man might understand. In reality I was not anxious, for I knew that this property would already be lost to me, so hated was I in Fermo as an intimate of Liverotto's. I wanted to return to see Nicolosa, and to learn what had become of Dino.

By the evening of our second night at Gualdo, I had permission to depart the duke's service until the first day of Lent. On that day, the first of March, I must present myself at Rome or anywhere else that the duke might instruct. I was to pay for this boon by reporting from Fermo on the disposition of the city's new leaders and their state of military preparedness. The duke would send a man to collect the messages from my cousin's farm, as before, or from another location if I wished.

I spent the evening attempting to scrabble together food for the journey, which I estimated at four or five days in this weather. I also procured myself two companions for protection and company—*fermani* I ransomed at great cost from a Spanish captain whose prisoners they were. One was a man named Luca, a brother of Agnese's husband Giacomino, whom I wanted to redeem for her sake and because he was a likeable fellow. The other was a young peasant named Nello whom I had no special cause to ransom at all. He was standing there looking wretched while I bartered for Luca, and before I knew it I had freed him as well. There was something about him that took my fancy, though I could hardly have told you what it was. He was a wiry lad of around sixteen, with a thin pointed face shaped like a triangle and green eyes, the same color as mine.

I HAD BEEN sleeping like a dead man the past few nights, from the fatigue of the march, but the night before we left Gualdo, I was restless. Thoughts of the past and the future were throbbing mercilessly through my head, and I was vexed by the stillness of the men sleeping around me. I extricated myself from the bed and went down to the taproom of the inn where we were lodged, hoping some drinkers would be lurking there to distract me from my thoughts. Instead, there were only a few snoring bodies lying on benches and, scribbling furiously by the fire, Messer Niccolò Machiavelli. He was so intent on his lucubration that he did not notice my presence until I crept over to him and tapped him on the sleeve.

"*Porco Giuda,*" he said, recovering from his shock. "You almost made me knock over my inkwell. You know, this is the third time I have written this same identical letter to Florence. Fucking couriers. God knows whether they'll get it this time."

"What is the hour?" I whispered.

"How should I know? These clowns have been sleeping maybe—I don't know—two hours." He paused. "Are you hungry?"

I suddenly realized I was, very.

"Yes, why?"

For answer, Machiavelli got to his feet, holding the letter he had been writing, glided over to a sleeping figure, and bent over him for a moment, groping around light-fingered in his clothes. Then he beckoned me over to a door at the back of the room and produced with a flourish a large iron key.

WE MADE a fine feast in the kitchen of the inn, of cold meat and pickles from the pantry and wine from a keg standing in a corner. They had even left a fire smoldering in a covered log in the grate that was not too difficult to kindle into life. I had scruples at first about this thieving behavior, but Messer

Niccolò reassured me that the fault lay with the inn's culpable negligence in not taking better care of the key.

We spoke at length of the affairs of the duke. Machiavelli was aflame with admiration for this hero after his remarkable exploit at Senigallia, which he judged worthy to live long in the annals of political deception. He had heard of my part in the taking of the conspirators and made me recount it minutely—also the deaths of Liverotto and Vitelli, of which he wished to hear every detail, some twice.

I do not know whether you have ever had a nocturnal conversation of this kind? Especially if there is wine at hand, they lend themselves easily to intimacy. You are alone with your companion, while the rest of the world snores around you. Things come out that would not in the day. As Messer Niccolò and I spoke of the coup at Senigallia, a desire was growing within me to confide my darkest secret in him, the great matter that had been gnawing away at me as I lay trying to sleep. My mind had begun to shape him as precisely the confidant I needed, a worldly and unshockable man.

When a pause fell in our conversation, I asked Messer Niccolò whether I might confide in him about a most private matter, a moral case concerning a woman.

He looked at me sharply, as if to judge whether I had spoken in jest.

"You've chosen yourself an odd confessor, my son. My friends in Florence would piss themselves laughing at the thought of anyone consulting me on a moral question, least of all having to do with a woman. But go on."

I told Machiavelli the whole story of my love for Nicolosa and my fears that this love was incestuous. I concealed only the identity of the man who had revealed to me that Messer Giovanni was my father, saying that it was an acquaintance of Messer Giovanni's, a banker from Ancona. Machiavelli smiled a little when I mentioned I had disguised myself as a woman to visit Nicolosa, but he looked serious as I told him the meat of the story. It was difficult to speak of. At one point I had to break off and sat gazing into the fire for a moment before I could go on.

When I had finished, I looked at my interlocutor anxiously. I had poured him a glass of wine, and now he swilled it meditatively, holding it up against the light from the fire.

"You wanted my advice?"

I nodded eagerly.

"About what, exactly? It seems clear what you should do. See her, enjoy her, don't think of telling her anything, put this whole incest business out of your mind. Just be sure not to get her with child."

I looked at him in bewilderment, and he resumed patiently.

"Look, if you had asked me whether you should lie with her in the first place, that might have been a different matter. But now the deed is done. You wanted her. You had her. You cannot undo it. So give some thought now to *her*. This is a young woman who has suffered unimaginably. You'd have to look to some particularly lurid Greek myth for a comparison. She has finally managed to salvage some solace for herself, and now you wish to visit this new horror on her. Why? To assuage your conscience?"

This seemed entirely convincing. I gazed at him in astonishment, trying to master this new perspective. Machiavelli was looking at me with an air of faint amusement. Then a keen expression crossed his face, as though something new had occurred to him.

"Besides," he said, "who was it again you said told you Giovanni Fogliani was your father?"

I launched on my lie about the Anconitan banker again, but he waved aside the details.

"Was this a close friend of Fogliani's? An acquaintance?"

"More of an acquaintance," I said, thinking of Cardinal Giuliano.

"So this was not a direct confession of Fogliani's, but merely a surmise on the part of this acquaintance?"

I nodded.

"Well, have you considered the fact that he may have been wrong? There can't have been much of a resemblance between you and Fogliani, I imagine, or the secret could hardly have been kept?"

I shook my head. "He was dark-complexioned, with rather deep-set eyes ..."

Machiavelli waved a dismissive hand again.

"As for the rest of your evidence ... You spoke of seeing Fogliani weeping over your mother's body. Perhaps he loved her, but honorably, knowing she was the mother of his godson. Unlikely, I know, but one reads of such things. And even if he did lie with her, does that necessarily mean that you are his son? Perhaps they only became lovers after you were born, when she was widowed. Perhaps Fogliani favored you as a child simply because you reminded him of her, not because you were his son. You said he had no son of his own?"

I shook my head. I was in ecstasy. Machiavelli's words were pouring over me like balm. This was the first man to whom I had confided my terrible secret, and it was crumbling into dust before my eyes.

"So, what do we have left?" Machiavelli continued, in a lawyerly manner. "He was harsh when he caught you, on the brink of adolescence, with your arm round his precious virgin daughter ... I don't think we need to have recourse to the incest hypothesis in order to explain that one, do we? Let us recall that he later married this same daughter to the son of a cardinal—one of the wealthiest men in Italy, if all that is rumored is true. Was a man like Cardinal della Rovere going to take your Nicolosa as a daughter-in-law if others had supped on her before his son had raised his fork?"

I smiled and shook my head. I could have thrown myself at his feet with gratitude.

"A man can be too scrupulous, you know," he said airily, draining the remainder of his wine. "How do I know what my father really got up to all those nights when he told my mother he was dining with his confraternity? Florence might be littered with secret half-sisters of mine for all I know. Am I going to refrain from fucking any woman in the city under the age of fifty just to be certain I am not guilty of incest?"

"I somehow doubt it," I said, and we both laughed. Then I added, more earnestly, "You have saved my life with this good counsel. I was burning myself up, thinking of it. I could see no way through."

"You're welcome," Machiavelli said. "It's a pleasure to assist in the love dilemmas of the young and well-favored. 'A beautiful woman is throwing herself at me. Should I refuse her out of scruple?' You wait till you're my age, my son."

XVIII

I WEIGHED MACHIAVELLI's arguments on the road back
to Fermo and judged them sound still, even without the
assistance of Bacchus. I had woven a web of supposition
around Cardinal Giuliano's thesis, but I could now see it for
what it was—merely a supposition itself. Indeed, the cardinal's motives were beginning to seem suspect to me, when
I considered how much he had gained by putting into my
head that Messer Giovanni was my father. It was the tale of
my paternity that had given me credibility with Valentino as
a defector, and it was my credibility with Valentino that had
made me valuable to the cardinal as a spy.

We had a good enough journey, though the conditions
were harsh. We spent one entire day kicking our heels at an
inn while a blizzard stormed outside, impossible to penetrate.
At other times, we were forced to take lengthy detours because
the higher routes were all blocked with snow. Our food supplies lasted us only as far as Tolentino, a full two days' ride still
from Fermo. After that, I had to empty my pockets at a cruel
rate to afford us enough sustenance to keep us on the road.

The peasant boy Nello proved a surprisingly entertaining
companion on this arduous journey. I had taken pity on his
youth and innocence when I rescued him in Gualdo, but I
soon saw I had been mistaken in respect of his innocence. He
was crafty instead, a *furbo*, and a good and fast talker, once you
looked past the strange rustic words he used. Nello regaled us
on the journey with tales of the absurdities of peasants, which
extended to amorous relations with their beasts, much to our
amusement. Nello denied at first that he had ever been guilty
of this vice himself, but he eventually confessed to an epi-

sode with a goat. This was his downfall, for Luca and I would pass no sheep pen or cattle byre after this without taking the opportunity to recall his lost love to him. By the end of the journey, we had even elaborated a song on the theme.

In the midst of these childish japes, I continued to ponder the question of my paternity as we inched our frigid way towards Fermo. The more I reflected on the subject, the more I found myself convinced that the cardinal had played me like a fool for his own ends. He had stated almost with conviction that I was Messer Giovanni's son, yet he had offered no evidence for this, for he had none. He had noted Messer Giovanni's fondness for me, this was all: the sole, slender fact around which he had spun his hypothesis. There was nothing more to note, for we resembled one another as a stork might resemble a duck.

Such were my musings by day. At night, lying on a straw mattress in some mean village hostelry, listening to wolves keening from the hills like the souls of the restless dead, new thoughts of Nicolosa filled my mind. Ever since we had become lovers, I had been unable to think of her without guilt descending on me, swift and avid as a flock of harpies. Not one instant had I enjoyed her love simply; it was befouled for me, like a clear spring trampled by cattle. Now I began to see things differently, and what I saw almost dazzled me: that our love was not strange and unclean, but the honest love of a boy and girl, grown into a man and woman. We were guilty of nothing graver than mere fornication; the harpies had no business at my feast. I thought back over our childhood and Nicolosa's marriage and the years I had pined for her in vain. It seemed extraordinary to me that the cruel course of Fortune had delivered this prize into my arms.

WHEN WE REACHED the last village before Fermo, I sent Luca and Nello on with my blessing and put up at an inn, tasking Nello to return and report to me on the state of my reputation in the city. I did not wish to proceed if there was a danger that I would be lynched as soon as I set foot within the walls. I also told him to glean what he could of Dino's fate after Senigallia. The most likely thing—if, by the grace of God, he lived still— was that he was being held at Fano with Liverotto's other captive officers. I had already calculated the likely ransom that would be demanded for him and thought of how the sum might be raised.

I sat nervously in the taproom of the inn as I waited for Nello, trying to distract myself with the volume of Horace's epistles that I had used for the coding of Cardinal Giuliano's letters. I could not concentrate on a word of it. It might have been in Hebrew for all that went in. A few customers entered, travelers bound for the port to embark for Venice or Ragusa, and I threw myself into conversation with them. Then I distracted myself by flirting with a plump serving maid who had come in to attend to the fire.

"Don't you believe a word he says, girl."

It was Dino's voice that I heard behind me suddenly. I turned and was engulfed in his arms so fast I did not even see his face. When I emerged from his embrace, I saw Nello behind him, grinning as though he was personally responsible for my brother's salvation. They had met by chance on the road into Fermo as Dino was riding out to visit his farm.

Dino told me of his escape from Senigallia with his usual concision. He had fled across the river with about twenty other cavalrymen, and they had ridden back by a circuitous route, avoiding the principal roads and foraging as they could for food along the way. When they had arrived back in Fermo, news of Liverotto's death had already reached the city and the reprisals were beginning, directed first at Liverotto's own relatives, and then at those in his pay.

My house had been targeted for looting, as I had expected, but Dino told me that Nicolosa had saved it for me. She stood on the street arguing with the looters, telling them of my role in the downfall of Liverotto. Alfonso then joined her, speaking of the mission he had run for me to Valentino, and together they saw the attackers off. My heart swelled as I heard this tale. The thought of Nicolosa braving the street for me, haranguing the looters like one of the dauntless ancient heroines she used to read of as a girl, filled me with extraordinary sweetness.

I asked how she was, and Dino told me she was well.

"She'll be happy to see you," he said, probing me. I turned to the fire, for I could not trust myself to meet his eye.

"And I her."

I DID A RASH thing when I returned to Fermo. When I had stabled my horse and bathed and changed my clothes, I went straight to Nicolosa's, without warning her of my arrival. It was late afternoon on a gusty, wet day, and the sky was already darkening. There were few people on the streets, and I was able to scramble over the wall into her garden without being observed. I crept round behind the house and looked in at the window of her study, where the shutters were still open a crack. A fire was burning inside, and two candles spilled their soft glow on the table. Nicolosa was sitting reading, her hair loose on her shoulders, wrapped in a great black fur that looked like a bearskin. With her hair down and the gilded light on her concentrating face, she looked miraculously young again, like the girl she had been four years before.

I stood there for a precious moment breathing in the sight of her, fearing to shock her by knocking on the pane. After a moment, she looked towards the window, perhaps sensing my eyes on her face. For a moment she looked frightened; then her look changed to delight as she recognized me, and she jumped up and ran over and threw open the window. This was the first kiss of our new life, through the meager opening of a casement—the first time I had kissed her with a whole and free heart.

Well, I shall not describe any more of this encounter, for I wish to preserve the secrets of my beloved. Nicolosa left me in the garden for a while, staring wistfully through the window at the fire, until she had invented some errand for her servants to take them out of her house. Then she let me in by the back door and I came shivering in, and we stood for a long while there in the corridor wrapped deep in each other's arms. That first evening I do not think we even spoke of Liverotto's death or the revenge we were now free to savor. Nothing mattered to us in those first brief blissful hours except the fact that we were together and alive.

WELL, AS YOU KNOW, bliss cannot endure in this treacherous mortal life, or else we would have no reason to lift our eyes to heaven—but, even so, I was happy in this brief sojourn in Fermo in a manner I had rarely been before. This is not to say that I was so hard of heart as to have forgotten past horrors so quickly. I could not walk a step in Fermo without seeing a street corner on which I used to loiter with Lorenzo watching women go by, or a square where Messer Giovanni used to take me as a boy to hear the *cantastorie* roaring out their tales of war. My happiness was tempered by bitter memories—but it was happiness still: sharp, vivid, unmistakable. I was young and in love and beloved, the weight of guilt and the duty of revenge had been lifted from my shoulders, and I was a free man walking the streets of my own beloved city, bowing my head for the moment to no lord.

I won favor with the citizenry of Fermo by ceding the house Liverotto had given me to a relative of the original owner. Men think highly of such sacrifices, but in fact they are nothing. I did not wish to rest my limbs on dead men's bones, that was all. The family I gave it up to was relieved not to have to fight the case in law and offered me a smaller house near the city walls as a gesture of gratitude. I took this happily enough as my residence, settling there with Nello, whom I had decided to keep on as a companion and servant. He settled well to this new life, rapidly developing a rich acquaintance among the wastrels and loose women of the town.

Before I left my grand house in the center of Fermo, I dug up Messer Giovanni's ring from under a tree in the garden where I had buried it and polished it back to its bright glory. I looked at it a long time, thinking of the man who had worn it so constantly that the gold had rubbed thin. I had hardly mourned him as I should, for it was soon after his death that Cardinal Giuliano had fed me the idea that I might be his son. After that time, the thought of him had been a source only of disquiet to me. Now, as I looked on this relic, a tide of sorrow arose in me, for if he had not been my father by blood, he had in his love for me. I tried to console myself thinking of the vengeance I had wrought for him, but it would not keep the tears from my eyes.

AFTER I HAD been in Fermo for around two weeks, a letter arrived for me from Messer Leonardo da Vinci. It was tied tightly with string, with a seal over the knot, and my name written in a bold hand in ink of a strange purplish hue. Messer Leonardo had supplied the courier who brought it with a caricature he had drawn of me, to ensure that he found the correct recipient. It made me laugh, for although it was marvelously unflattering, the likeness was sufficient for it to be clear that it was a portrait of me.

The letter concerned the many-headed gun whose design Messer Leonardo had entrusted to Liverotto. I knew nothing of the fate of this invention, but it was clear from the letter that its construction was underway at the time of Liverotto's death. I felt almost guilty as I read the message, which begged me plaintively to discover the fate of this engine. Messer Leonardo had struggled long to find a visionary patron for his inventions, and now he would have to struggle again.

I decided I would approach Dino to see whether he knew of the gun, and did so the following Sunday, when he invited me to supper. It was an interesting evening, for Agnese was there with her husband Giacomino and the child I believed to be mine. Dino had offered to be godfather to this boy, who had been christened Alessandro after Giacomino's late father. It was strange to stand and observe from a distance this small shred of humanity who continued my blood. He was much cherished, that was sure. Giacomino was a doting father, his great jovial creased face softening to a most tender expression as he cradled his treasure, who looked tiny in his artilleryman's arms. Agnese gazed on like a happy sphinx in the meantime, lowering her eyes if they ever happened to meet mine.

I managed to get Dino alone after supper to question him about the gun Liverotto had been building. He looked at me diffidently at first, then said we could look at it the following week if I wished. It was in a barn some five miles outside Fermo, not far from where Dino had his farm. We rode out the following Sunday, with an escort of three ex-soldiers from Dino's company who had escaped with him from Senigallia. This was to protect us from possible attacks from Liverottto's family, some of whom had vowed to avenge his death with my blood.

The gun turned out to be in one of the villages that Liverotto had razed the previous year when they opposed his recruiting of troops for his army. I had led the attack myself, as I remembered when I saw the hills rising behind what remained of the village. It was melancholy to be back there, among the charred cottages and stark, blackened trees.

The forge of the village had survived relatively intact, and it was this that Liverotto had adapted as his foundry. Dino told me he had brought down a caster from Milan to oversee the conversion and, more generally, the production of the gun. It had been cast in the foundry, in pieces, and soldered together on location. Then it had been towed into a nearby barn, to await Liverotto's return.

On the door of the barn where the gun stood was the most elaborate padlock I had seen in my life, to which, apparently, only Liverotto had ever had the key. Since the lock was impenetrable, to break into the sanctum Dino had his men take an axe to the door. Within, the sinister hydra lurked, seemingly almost finished. Nine heads branched off from a trunk so thick that it was hard to imagine its being drawn, even by three teams of oxen. Tools lay on the ground near it, as though waiting to be taken up the next morning, yet a cobweb stretched visibly between one barrel and the next.

Dino knelt and looked into the mouths of a few of the cannons, as his men opened a window to let the light in. After a while, he drew back, fed his sword into a cannon mouth, and pulled out a bird's nest with four speckled perfect miniature eggs nestling in it. He smiled with a kind of shyness and fed the nest back with great precision whence it had come.

"Would it have worked?" I asked.

"Not for my money. How would you transport it? And say you did get it to a battlefield ... Remember Tiberti?"

This was a captain of Duke Valentino's who had died at Faenza when a defective artillery piece exploded beside him. We stood contemplating this monster, imagining the holocaust it would cause if it blew.

"I hoped I could use it to kill him," Dino said quietly, his hand dangling almost paternally over one of the creature's nine barrels.

"Liverotto?"

He nodded. "We were going to test it when it was ready. I thought I would have him up here with gunpowder at hand."

Dino's mouth twisted as he said this, and I suddenly felt how shameful it must have been for him to serve Liverotto all this time, tied to this service by fear for his family.

"I always suspected you were planning something, Teo," he said. "From the time we were at Camerino together …"

He did not continue. My brother did not like to speak of anything outside the ordinary. I waited for a moment, then said, "Come on, Dino. Let's leave this wretched thing to the birds."

A MONTH WENT by after my arrival in Fermo so swiftly that I barely registered its passing. Suddenly, it was the seventh day of February. By the first day of March, I was supposed to be kneeling before Duke Valentino in Rome.

Although I could see no way to avoid this immediate summons, I had hopes that I could limit the term of my subsequent service. I approached the bishop of Fermo through a priest who had owed his preferment to Messer Giovanni, to see whether the bishop might be persuaded to speak with certain cardinals of his acquaintance. These I hoped might be persuaded to approach other cardinals, who might eventually win the ear of the pope. My hope was that, with Liverotto dead, I was worth so little to the duke that he would relinquish my service easily enough if requested through the right channels. I longed for my freedom and was happy to labor for it, even if it cost me all I owned in ecclesiastical bribes.

For the month I had been in Fermo, I had been dutifully delivering a message to the duke each week, reporting on events in the city. I rode out each Thursday to my cousin Alfonso's farm with a coded and sealed missive containing nothing of any great interest. These messages I left in a cleft in a chestnut tree, wrapped in a waxed cloth in case of rain.

One day, late in my stay, when I went to deliver my message, I found an alien missive in the cleft in the tree. I could easily have missed it—a rolled-up paper, tied and sealed, wrapped in a cloth similar to that which I used. I first assumed it was from the duke, but when I set myself to deciphering it, using the code we employed, it would not yield up its mystery. Nor was it easy to discover the code though guesswork, for the words had been run together without spaces. I took it home and stared it for a while, annoyed and disconcerted; then I began to count the letters to try to ascertain the vowels.

Halfway through this task, a new idea came to me. I tried the message against the code I used for my messages to Cardinal Giuliano, and it immediately yielded its sense. The message instructed me to wait the following Sunday on a certain road outside town, hidden from passers-by in an abandoned shepherd's hut. I remembered this hut from my boyhood because a macabre tale was associated with it. A lonely shepherd had slain himself there one chill winter, and was found only much later, a rotting corpse hanging from a rope.

I was much puzzled by this missive and the manner of its delivery, which suggested that some agent of the cardinal had been spying on me. That thought troubled me, and I was suspicious also of the cardinal's intent in summoning me in this way. Now that I understood how he had fooled me with his tale of my supposed paternity, I saw him as a fox of whose cunning I must be wary. I did not think of disobeying his summons, however, for my debt of gratitude towards him was too great. Who but he had taught me the path to revenge?

I WENT TO the shepherd's hut the following Sunday directly after mass, still wearing my best garments. It was a cold, windy day, but I did not feel inclined to shelter within a hut where some poor wretched soul had breathed his last. Instead, I shivered behind it in my cloak, finding what shelter I could beneath the branches of a bedraggled pine.

I was half in a reverie when a sound disturbed me, and I looked up to see three men riding across the rough moorland towards me. My hand strayed to my dagger, although how I imagined I would defend myself against three men on horseback I do not know. As they approached, I recognized one of them as the leader of the band who had conducted me blindfolded to Madonna Felice della Rovere the previous summer. He had a melancholy, distinguished face ruined by an ugly scar that ran almost the length of one cheek.

This man smiled affably in salutation as he approached, like an old friend, and spoke some words of apology for keeping me waiting. Then he held out a black strip of cloth for me to bind my eyes, as before. I looked at it resentfully.

"I might have thought they'd trust me by now."

He laughed in reply, as if I had uttered some witticism.

"Trust," he said. "Don't see too much of that these days."

I SHALL NOT bore you with an account of my journey from this point, for the experience was the same as the previous time, only colder. I rode in darkness behind one of the men who had come for me, first through open land, then through a wood, where he had to tell me to duck my head to avoid branches, then up a long ascent to a tract of exposed land where the wind felt like ice. We rode for perhaps an hour in all.

I wondered on the way whether I was being taken to meet Madonna Felice herself or some other agent of her father. I was not sure whether or not I wanted it to be her. I mistrusted this young woman for her manipulative skills, yet I could not deny she was interesting to me. Several times since our meeting, my wayward imagination had conjured her up to me in some mildly erotic guise.

Just like the previous time, I was led into a building still blindfolded and the cloth was removed only when I was inside. The chamber on which I opened my eyes was a gentleman's room, however, very different from the rough farmhouse where I had been deposited after my first blindfold ride. Tapestries carpeted the walls and the room was well furnished, with fine and massive chests in the corners, carved from some dark wood like walnut. A bright fire danced in the grate—a sight that delighted me, as my hands were frozen numb from the ride. Through a window, you could see a row of stark, black, pollarded trees, laced with frost, stoically awaiting the spring.

Standing in front of the fire was Madonna Felice, clad in sober black, as I remembered her, a book trailing from her hand.

I bowed and she smiled at me with a triumphant air.

"Messer Matteo. A pleasure. Did I not tell you when we last met that Liverotto would be dead within the year?"

In fact, she had said three years, but I was in no mood to quibble.

"My lady, I salute your prudence. I trust His Eminence your father is well?"

She nodded.

"I will give you news of him later. Come, warm yourself. Sit."

She gestured to a chair by the fire and sat down herself opposite me, smoothing down her skirts. I held my hands out gratefully towards the flames.

"You are going to rejoin Valentino in Rome next month, I believe?"

I nodded warily, wondering how she had acquired this piece of news.

"My father would be most grateful if you would continue as his …"

She hesitated, and I helped her.

"His spy."

"His most loyal servant," Madonna Felice said earnestly. "Whom he wishes to reward as far as he is able at this time and looks forward one day to rewarding at his true worth."

As she said this, she placed a small leather bag, such as men use for coin, on the table between us. I felt annoyed at this crassness. I had served her father as a free man who shared his interests, not as a mercenary hungry for gold.

"My lady," I said, trying to hide my irritation, "I have great admiration and respect for your father, but I can serve him no longer. You must try to understand my position. My only intent in all this business was to avenge myself on Liverotto. I was happy to help your father when he asked me, and I risked my life to do so. You must know what happened at Imola?" She looked aside, at the flames of the fire, which I took to mean she did. "My life has been governed for a year by this quest for revenge. Now I am free, finally, or will be once I can excuse myself from Valentino's service. I wish to return to my own life now. I want no more of this skulking and fear."

Madonna Felice raised her eyes to me as I spoke these last words, and I held her look steadily, hoping she would see her cause was fruitless and retreat.

Eventually she spoke.

"What did Madonna Nicolosa say when you told her she was your sister?" She traced her finger over a knot in the wood of her chair arm. "Or perhaps you have not yet informed her of this fact?"

There was something insinuating in her look as she said this that filled me with trepidation. I swallowed hard.

"Why do you say Madonna Nicolosa is my sister, my lady? That was merely a supposition of your father's. You have no evidence that it is so."

She was looking at me with a slight smile, as though she knew she had me.

"And you have no evidence that it is not."

We looked at each other for a moment without speaking. Then she said, "If you are so certain it is untrue, you will not worry if I tell her all I know of the matter—or all my father *supposes*. I think she has a right to know. Would you not agree?" She held up a finger to still my protests. "Take a moment to reflect before you speak."

She stood as she said this and walked to the window, as if to allow me more freedom to ponder. I tried to think, though my mind was half paralyzed by the shock of this sudden turn of events. My first notion was to defy her, primed with the confidence I now felt that there was no truth in the story that I was the son of Messer Giovanni. She would tell Nicolosa this tale, and I would deny it and show her through good arguments that it was empty conjecture. It had been devised simply as a means to manipulate me, and make me a stronger instrument in the cardinal's hands.

I had myself almost persuaded, but then certain facts began to trickle into my mind like acid, corroding my courage. Cardinal Giuliano had told me his conjecture about my parentage almost a year ago now, and I had used it in establishing my credentials with the duke. Yet I had said nothing of this to Nicolosa, to whom I had recounted the rest of my story in much detail. I had lain with her when I had the opportunity, despite the fact that this doubt had been put in my mind and I could not disprove it. I might be innocent in point of fact, but I had not acted like an innocent man. I had acted like a scoundrel and a dissolute. Even on my own version of events, I found it difficult to acquit myself—and that was to discount the venom that this witch of a priest's daughter would undoubtedly mix into the brew.

I had my head in my hands when I felt my tormentor's touch on my shoulder, light as a spider.

"Messer Matteo?" she said. "Your answer?"

I raised my head wearily.

"My lady, if your father has half your ruthlessness, he will make an excellent pope."

Madonna Felice laughed. "He will make an excellent pope on all counts. So you will continue to help us?"

I nodded painfully. I could not trust myself to speak.

"Madonna Nicolosa likes you wonderfully well. She could not look me in the eye when I spoke of you."

"You have seen her?" I asked, astonished.

"Why not? She is my sister-in-law. She was kind enough to ride to Matelica to meet me. I asked her to keep it a secret and I see that she did, if she made no word of it even to her lover."

She looked at me slyly as she said this, as though waiting for me to contest that I was Nicolosa's lover, but I did not. I did not have the heart for this lie, for I felt she already knew this fact as well as I.

THE SUN HAD emerged from the clouds as we were speaking and was glancing keenly through the windows, a crisp winter light. Madonna Felice suggested we take a turn in the garden together, and rang a bell for one of her guards, who fetched for her a sumptuous black cloak lined with lynx.

We spoke of neutral things as we strolled among the barren trees. Madonna Felice exerted herself to be charming, now that she had me where she wanted me, smiling up at me and leaning on my arm as we walked. She told me much news of interest. Paolo and Francesco Orsini had been dispatched by Don Michelotto at Castello della Pieve. Cardinal Orsini had perished in prison in Rome—through starvation, the latest rumor went. Madonna Felice recounted these details with a coolness worthy of Messer Niccolò Machiavelli. Even the probable murder of a cardinal by a pope did not make this lady pause in her stride.

When we had conversed for perhaps ten minutes in the weak winter sun, Madonna Felice turned finally to dismiss me. She had brought with her the bag of coin she had offered me before and pressed it into my hand as we stood saying our farewells. I looked down at it with a feeling of resentment, but I did not attempt to return it. It was the price of my servitude, but there seemed no reason to refuse it, since I was now her servant whether I took the money or not.

As I accepted my payment, Madonna Felice's hand strayed up to my head, and we stood for a moment in strange intimacy. Her face was just beneath mine, her cheeks flushed with the cold, her lower lip slightly pushed forward as she concentrated on whatever she was doing with my hair. Many inappropriate feelings rose up in me as she did this. I would have liked nothing more than to do her some amorous violence. Finally she drew back with a burr in her hand that must have clung to my hair as we rode through the wood.

"There!" she said, smiling up at me. "This was marring your otherwise admirable appearance."

I wanted none of her palliation and bowed coldly.

"Do not wish me ill, Messer Matteo," she said in a new tone, almost pleadingly. "I do not torment you for my pleasure. We are both servants of a cause."

I looked sullenly at the ground. *Your cause*, I was thinking. Eventually I said, "I do not wish you ill, my lady."

"You do. But I hope you will not always."

With that she turned away, dismissing me with a wave of her hand.

WELL, THIS MEETING was the end of my happiness. The man with the scarred face and his companions escorted me back to the shepherd's hut in my blindfold, with a new thick bitter darkness in my heart.

I told Nicolosa I must go to Rome for the beginning of my service to ensure my good standing with Valentino, while still claiming that I would endeavor to work with the bishop to ensure my release. My heart was heavy as I told her this, for I knew it was a lie and a prelude to future lies. I would stay in Rome precisely as long as Cardinal Giuliano della Rovere wished it. *That* was the truth, and it was a truth that could never be told.

Nicolosa was very tender with me in the days before my departure, in a manner that stoked my love for her to a new pitch of brightness. I gave much thought to finding a gift that would speak to her of my feelings when I was gone. I had planned to give her my parrot Demosthenes, whom I now had in Fermo, having had him carried down by boat from Cesena.

Sadly, however, after a month as the pet of the garrison there, the poor bird was in no state to be given to an honest woman. His language had never been of the cleanest, but now it was as salt as a barrel of pork.

After much cogitation, I decided instead to have the emerald the duke had given me set as a ring by a goldsmith. This was madness in a man of my slight income, for, had I sold it, this jewel would have kept me for some years.

I gave Nicolosa the ring on the night before I left. She looked at it and then at me in astonishment, and I explained that the duke had given it to me. I told her I wanted her to have it as a keepsake, as it had been a reward to me for my part in bringing Liverotto to justice. It seemed right she should have it, as it was because of her that I had risked myself in this quest for vengeance. I had no courage in myself; all that was good in me stemmed from my desire to do right in her eyes.

Nicolosa's eyes were filled with tears as I finished this speech. She drew the ring on to her slender white finger and held it up for me to see. I turned the stone to catch the light and raised Nicolosa's hand to my lips.

"Constancy," she said. I looked at her quizzically. "Constancy in love. That is what an emerald signifies. They say no one can feel lust when he wears it."

"Is that so?" I said, sliding the ring off her finger and burying my hand deep in her hair, which was loose on her shoulders. "Don't wear it tonight, then. You can start wearing it from tomorrow, when I'm gone."

Nicolosa let me kiss her, then took the ring from my hand and made as if to put it on my finger, which was too large for it.

"Perhaps I should give *you* an emerald, Teo. I suspect that would be a truer test of its force."

BOOK TWO

XIX

I SET OFF FOR ROME before the season of carnival, to ensure that I would be there by Lent, as I was contracted to be. Nello came with me, and my parrot, his cage swathed in fur against the cold; also, to my delight, Dino, who had decided to try his chances in Valentino's service. Dino could have survived for a while serving no one, as he retained some wealth from his past takings, but he was a man who could not live happy in this world for long without the prospect of a fight.

We reached Rome during the last days of carnival, which was an extraordinary moment to encounter the city. You will no doubt have read of Sodom and Gomorrah in the Bible and perhaps wondered what took place in these cities that so aroused the wrath of the Lord. I wondered no longer when I had seen Rome at this time. Valentino's curious entertainments with the copulating dwarves and the chestnut-hunting women found their ideal matrix in this city of excess; yet this was not an entertainment on stage, with a few performers, but rather a whole city, writhing in exuberant venery. After dark, in the narrow, stinking alleyways of this city of Saint Peter, couples rutted with abandon, three or four side by side—men and women, men and boys, men and boys dressed as women. Everyone wore masks. It was as though with this disguise of identity, every inhibition was lost.

The confusion of dress struck me in particular. It was troubling in the extreme. You would find your eye following some seductive female form down a street; then you would see her face as she turned in profile and find yourself wondering. Sometimes it was literally impossible to ascertain whether these creatures were female or male. Aside from these youths dressed as women, a portion of the city's army of whores pounded the streets dressed as men, some gallantly armed with daggers or swords.

I announced myself immediately at Valentino's household, even though I was in Rome a few days earlier than expected. I hoped a room might be offered us. It was clear that to look for lodging in Rome at this season would be like searching for a virgin in the city's heaving streets. Valentino's majordomo, a surly Spaniard, examined my contract and listened as I explained what Dino was doing here. He left us waiting in an antechamber half a day, but eventually Dino, Nello, and I were allocated a room in a remote wing of the Vatican palace, occupied by piles of tattered garments awaiting mending. I was informed that the duke was currently occupied but would give me an audience when his commitments permitted. Meanwhile, we were free to enjoy the pleasures of the city at the risk of our purses and lives.

It was only Nello, of the three of us, who saw fit to profit from this mayhem. He would go out when Dino and I were retiring and return in the morning, pale and wasted, his eyes dazed with the debauchery he had seen. This was a youth who had been raised in the fields, solacing goats, yet he took to the streets of this great city as if he was born to them. Rome at carnival was the fulfillment of his dreams.

One day towards the end of the festival, Dino and I went to watch one of the bullfights that the pope laid on each year in the square before Saint Peter's to entertain the populace. We went with a knot of Spanish soldiers, ensuring ourselves the dubious privilege of a place in the front line of spectators. Twice during the fight, blood sprayed our faces when a beast was slaughtered an arm's length away. The pope watched the event from a balcony of the palace in a magnificent scarlet cape, leaping to his feet to shout encouragement at moments of particular excitement. For part of the spectacle, Valentino sat with him, dressed in black and looking scornful and withdrawn. Valentino had a reputation as a bullfighter himself, and the crowd roared for him to take to the ring, as he had in past years. He would not indulge them, consenting only to hand a bag of silver to the victor of the day as he knelt on the blood-drenched sawdust at the end of the show.

ONCE ROME'S ORGY of the flesh was over, and Lent safely in place, Valentino received me in his quarters. He was distant and distracted, but cordial enough, especially when I told him of Dino's presence in Rome. He said he was aware of my brother's reputation and would be happy to offer him a commission in his forces. He should report to Don Michelotto that same day.

The duke had just returned to Rome at this time after a month spent fighting the forces of the Orsini, who were rebelling against the pope after the murder of their leaders. It was proving a stiff challenge, as they had been joined by some of the other great Roman baronial families, with whom their relations were usually venomous in the extreme. Valentino's brother Gioffrè was officially conducting this war, but Valentino had been summoned by his father to assist him. People said he was sulking because his father had dragged him back to Rome when he wished to be attending to his own lands in the Romagna. The two had quarreled, apparently, and the pope had threatened him with excommunication if he disobeyed.

As I have told you, I had been diligently supplying Valentino with reports during the time that I had sojourned in Fermo. Their interest was scarce: essentially, I listed the city's new rulers and described the military forces on which they could draw. The duke interrogated me a little on the subject and then dismissed me, telling me to await further orders. I had a sense that the city of Fermo was not at the heart of his attention. He yawned during our brief conversation three times.

MADONNA FELICE had told me that her father's collaborator would reveal himself to me by the usual method. I was in no hurry to watch for this contact, but it came soon enough, perhaps a week into Lent. I was dining in the Vatican, among the lower ranks of courtiers, where the meat gets more gristly and the wine gets more acid, when I felt a bony grip descend on my shoulder. I turned to see a tall, gaunt man behind me, who gestured towards the high table. There I saw Don Michelotto looking down at me with his crooked smile, a welcome sight in my current meager state.

I rose to accompany the tall man, who I gathered had been sent down to the outer darkness to fetch me to greet my old patron. As we walked up to the high table together, he grasped my hand discreetly and pressed into it a small sharp object, disguising this contact in the folds of his robe. I guessed at once that this must be a half-cameo such as Cardinal Giuliano habitually issued to his flock. I investigated it when I was alone later that evening and saw that it bore the image of a Pan-like, horned figure. I tried it against a broken cameo Madonna Felice had given me at our last meeting, and the two halves fused neatly together, revealing an image of a satyr dragging a nymph by the hair.

I was impressed when I learned of the caliber of my associate, who was a Spaniard named Diego. If the test of a good palace spy is his closeness to his subject, Cardinal Giuliano could hardly have done better than this. Diego was one of

Pope Alexander's most intimate servants, entrusted with such tasks as assisting him in dressing, tasting his food for poison, and—it was rumored—escorting ladies to his quarters for private pontifical ministrations. He had a unique qualification for this role, of the kind that outweighs all claims of birth, education, and manners. Diego was a mute, quite incapable of utterance, and hence he could not bear tales if he wished.

At first when I heard this, I assumed Diego was a mute from birth, but I later heard that he had lost the power of speech when he was a child. A madman broke into his house and bludgeoned his parents to death with a mace as the boy Diego cowered under a table. A neighbor found him there silent the following day, and from that moment he never spoke again. Diego had arrived at the court three years earlier with a letter of recommendation from a Spanish bishop recounting this pitiful tale. He had been employed first in the kitchens, out of charity; then waiting at table, where he proved himself deft-handed. Finally the pope came to hear of his special talent for silence and plucked him out for his present exalted role.

As soon as he joined the duke's service, Dino was sent to join the forces of Valentino's brother Gioffrè in his war on the Orsini. I was retained in Rome, where my sole tasks were to look the part of a courtier or a soldier as needed and to swell the numbers of Valentino's entourage when he processed around the palace or rode about the city on his amorous adventures. Occasionally he would send us to intimidate a love rival or a creditor or to arrest someone who had met his disfavor. Along with a little drilling and weapon practice, this made up my professional life.

In the time I had free, I explored Rome and viewed its relics and churches and antiquities. By night, I prowled its streets with my colleagues and Nello, indulging in activities unsuited to Lent. I also made a soberer acquaintance, I am glad to report, among the young secretaries who worked in the Curia. These men would cluster after work in the great library of the Vatican, supposedly to study. I found them good company and spent hours there with them talking of literature and their invariably convoluted love affairs. To reach the room we frequented, I had to pass beneath a fresco that showed Cardinal Giuliano as a young man with his uncle, Pope Sixtus. I always averted my eyes from this troubling image in company, as though even glancing towards it might compromise me somehow.

Towards the end of March, when I had been in Rome almost a month, an acquaintance of mine from the library invited me on a visit to the Golden House of Nero. As you will recall, this remarkable site was discovered some two decades before the time of which I am speaking, in a part of the city mainly used for the grazing of beasts. It was difficult of access, as it remains today. The only means to get in was to be lowered down a narrow cleft on a board strung from ropes and then to grope through the underground passageways by candlelight, hoping that no untimely landslip occurred to block the return route.

Perhaps twelve of us assembled that day for the descent, between artists and scholars and clerics. We were led by two youths from the area, who had become adept at guiding visitors on such tours. The visit reminded me of my descent into the Cloaca Maxima to receive my instructions from Cardinal Giuliano. However, where that tunnel had been broad, if malodorous, here the passages were so tight that a man could barely pass through them. A plump, well-dressed young man behind me was laboring through these openings with so much sighing and puffing that I feared he would get stuck at some point. The feeling of being trapped beneath the earth was intense at some moments, even though airshafts had been dug through at points to let visitors breathe. I proceeded cautiously, trying not to panic and imbibing the dank air in shallow breaths.

After being led along what seemed like miles of identical corridors, we finally broke into a great open chamber. The youths who were guiding us held up their lanterns with the expression of bored actors, and a wondrous world was laid bare. You who have seen the *grotteschi* Raffaello subsequently painted in the Vatican and the many decorations of this kind that have followed cannot begin to conceive what impression this painted decoration made on us. We had never seen the like. We breathed it in wonderingly, deep under the earth. Nero had been here, in this same room, with his favorites, looking on these same scenes, fourteen hundred years before.

"Creepy," a voice said in my ear. I mean "in my ear" very literally, a breathy voice whose warmth I could feel lapping on my flesh. I turned and saw the plump young man whose ability to squeeze his way through the narrow corridors had earlier concerned me. He was looking at me with a lascivious interest the low level of light could do nothing to conceal.

"Just imagine," he continued. "Do you remember that business in Suetonius about Nero's marriage with the eunuch Sporus? Hard not to think of it when you're down here, don't you think?" He paused. "Giovanni de' Medici. Cardinal, for my sins." This was accompanied by a quite uncardinal-like giggle. "And whom do I have the pleasure to meet?"

"Matteo da Fermo," I said. "In the service of Duke Valentino." I did not say "Your Eminence." I was completely nonplussed. Frankly, I did not believe for a moment this foppish youth was a cardinal. He was not even wearing clerical dress. He beamed at me, his dark, intelligent eyes fixed on my face.

"Matthaeus Firmanus," he said, speaking in Latin for some reason. "I have a feeling we're going to be friends."

To MY ASTONISHMENT, this eccentric young man did turn out to be precisely who he said he was: a cardinal and the son of the great Lorenzo de' Medici, who had ruled Florence when I was a young boy. As you who are reading well know, Cardinal Giovanni was later destined to become pope, but the most diligent haruspex could not have predicted this then. His father had prevailed on Pope Innocent to make him a cardinal at the age of fourteen, but the family had fallen from power in Florence five years later. He seemed now, at the age of twenty-seven, a curious relic from a previous age.

Despite the great wealth his family had accumulated through their banking activities, Cardinal Giovanni was virtually mendicant by the standards of a cardinal, and he had much to prejudice his chances in Pope Alexander's Rome. He had opposed Alexander at his election, and his mother and sister-in-law were of the Orsini family—a potential death sentence at this time, you might think. He survived this period through his astuteness and feckless charm and the policy he adopted of lying low. He reminded me of Lucius Junius Brutus, who feigned idiocy to survive the tyranny of Tarquinius Superbus. Cardinal Giovanni did not go as far as to feign idiocy, but he feigned innocuous frivolity to perfection. He seemed as soft on the inside as he looked on the outside, with his pink and white skin and manicured hands.

Cardinal Giovanni had taken a great fancy to me and invited me into his circles, which incorporated some of the most learned men in Rome at this time, along with a scattering of courtesans and an ever-renewed stream of sloe-eyed boys of extreme youth. These last constituted the favored erotic prey of most of the cardinal's cronies, although the cardinal himself was more eclectic in his tastes. The boys were of remarkable beauty of feature and did all they could do to enhance their attractions, drawing lines round their eyes with a pencil, staining their lips and cheeks vermilion, and braiding their hair intricately like girls. One in particular remains in my mind, a youth whom the cardinal called Sporus, after the lover of Nero's he had mentioned to me in the Domus Aurea. This boy masqueraded an extreme passion for me and liked to amuse the company with symptoms of his love whenever I entered the room. Sometimes he would swoon away entirely and need to be restored by having smelling salts wafted under his nose.

All this was very strange to me, although I affected to find it normal, as I did not wish to appear provincial. It was the first time I had seen carnal practice between men and boys carried out with such system, as an alternative to women rather than simply a supplement. There was much talk in the cardinal's circle of the writings of Plato, in which the love of boys is extolled as the highest erotic pursuit. Cardinal Giovanni knew these writings as well as any man living; as you will recall, it was in Florence, under his family's patronage, that the great Ficino translated Plato's works.

ONE MORNING a few weeks after my first encounter with Cardinal Giovanni, Duke Valentino summoned me to see him. I obeyed his command anxiously—all the more so since I had left a message with Cardinal Giuliano's contact, the mute Diego, the previous day. The incident with the baker in Imola had given me a sickening sense of the precariousness of my trade. One slip on my part, one slip on the part of my accomplice, and I would find myself in a world of terror from which death would be a longed-for escape.

I found Valentino in a garden behind the palace with his falconer. The whole palace was in a froth of preparation; there was to be a great hunt later that day. The duke greeted me with a wave of his hand and returned to his animated conversation. I stood at some little distance awaiting his attention, trying to calm my nerves by thinking of innocent reasons why he might wish to see me. The sun was warm on my face and the garden delightful, though my mind was too burdened to enjoy it. We were almost at the beginning of April now; the fresh leaves were coming through, the birds singing full throat from the trees.

Finally, the duke interrupted his dealings with the falconer and beckoned me to him. He scrutinized me in silence for a moment.

"They tell me you are frequenting Santa Maria in Domnica." He meant by this Cardinal Giovanni, whose titular church this was.

"Indeed, Your Excellency," I said, wondering what this was about. "The cardinal has been most gracious to me."

"Interesting company you choose to keep. What's his game?"

I was taken aback by this question.

"His game, Your Excellency?"

"He likes to give the air of a man without a thought in his head, but I cannot believe it. He is the son of Lorenzo."

"I do not think the cardinal has a game, Your Excellency," I said. "I think he merely wants a quiet life."

The duke narrowed his eyes.

"Perhaps. Who frequents him?"

I began to list those I had seen at the cardinal's residence, but I could see Valentino's attention begin to wander when he heard them to be mainly intellectuals and other such small fry. He reached down to a hunting dog lying patiently at his feet and began to toy with its ears.

"What are the girls like?" he said when I finished. I had included the courtesans in my listing.

"Difficult to tell apart from the boys, in truth, Your Excellency."

"Madonna," he said, laughing, and shook his head.

At that moment, the falconer returned with the bird Valentino had chosen for the hunt so he could inspect it. It was a magnificent white gyrfalcon in silver-trimmed jesses, which seemed to boast its own servant, a disdainful blond youth in Borgia attire.

I thought myself dismissed and was turning to go, but the duke called me back.

"Keep in with him," he said. "Keep your eyes open. Let me know if you see anything of interest."

I bowed and retreated, thanking God in my heart that this interview had passed so innocuously. I strode back with a smile through the corridors I had crept through so timorously earlier that day.

I thought as I went of the duke's parting instructions and resolved that I would not obey him. I did not trust Cardinal Giovanni precisely, but I had a liking for him, and he had offered me his friendship, as a greater man to a lesser. To betray him would be a despicable thing. I would have to find some scraps of news to throw to the duke, to keep him happy and allay his suspicions. The meat I would keep to myself.

THE WEEK AFTER my conversation with the duke, I saw something at Cardinal Giovanni's that would have made a piquant morsel for him had I been minded to pass it on. There was an evening party at the cardinal's to celebrate the completion of some work of erudition whose title now escapes me; I only remember the author, a thin, twitchy southerner we used to call Merlin, for it was rumored he meddled in sorcery. I was in conversation with Cardinal Giovanni's chief confidant, Messer Bernardo Bibbiena, an amusing and ribald man, later a cardinal, as you will remember. We were speaking of our mutual acquaintance Machiavelli, about whom he was telling me some scurrilous tale.

As we stood there, a familiar face caught my eye, although I could not at first tell where I had seen it. It belonged to a fashionably dressed young man, perhaps the age of our host. He was sitting beside the cardinal, conversing with him in the manner of an intimate, even whispering in his ear at one point.

I was eyeing this man idly, trying to place him in my memory, when a trumpet sounded from the corridor—not an unusual event in this flamboyant household—and the cardinal's handsome Albanian footman Giorgio entered, bearing a silver tray before him in great pomp. I remembered that the cardinal had procured for this evening a dish of pickled flamingo tongues—apparently a great delicacy for the ancients. His reverence for the classical world frequently lured him down such curious paths.

All eyes turned to the cardinal as he reverently lifted a glistening pink sliver on a fork and courteously proffered it to his neighbor. The young man laughed, tilting his head, and at once I knew who he was with certainty, even though he was dressed in secular garb and wearing a beard. It was the young cleric who greeted me when I emerged stinking from the Cloaca to meet Cardinal Giuliano and who had later instructed me in espionage. Galeotto—I even remembered his name.

"Virgin in Heaven, spare me this new torment," Messer Bernardo said beside me. "You realize no one will get out of here alive without tasting one of those wretched things."

Indeed, he had barely finished speaking when Giorgio bore down on us, armed with a small silver dish, a mischievous smile on his face. The cardinal was smiling encouragingly at us, and, as I looked his way, I met the eye of the man at his side. He gave no flicker of recognition, but a moment later, in what I thought was a delicate allusion to our first meeting, he wafted a handkerchief under his nose.

By this time, however, I was barely capable of noticing, for I was absorbed in the difficult task of composing my face while ingesting a mouthful of quite memorable unpleasantness. Here, epicures, is how the legendary dish of pickled flamingo tongue tastes: thick, fishy, tough, caked with cold slime.

XX

I MUST CONFESS SOMETHING HERE. It was not without cause that I answered evasively when Duke Valentino asked me about the courtesans who frequented Cardinal Giovanni's gatherings. I had developed a liking for one girl there and did not wish to acquire him as a rival by piquing his interest in her. Valentino stalked the amorous forests of Rome like a tiger; all we lesser predators shrank from his path.

When I say I had developed a liking for a girl, I do not mean I had transferred my affections. I would not have you think me so light. Nicolosa retained my heart entire, and I missed her cruelly in Rome, both in body and mind, after our brief precious weeks together. Had I been with her in Fermo, I would have been faithful as Lancelot, for she satisfied every part of my being. But Nicolosa was distant, and I was young, and my sap was rising with the spring, and Rome was spreading its bounty before my eyes, inviting me to savor. The soberest hermit would have struggled to resist.

CAMILLA WAS FLORENTINE, like many of those who frequented Cardinal Giovanni's circles. She claimed to be sixteen years old, though I suspect she may have been a little older, for what courtesan does not lie about her age? She had a beautiful face, of a kind that Cardinal Giovanni seemed especially drawn to, to the extent that most of the other courtesans he favored looked like copies of her by a weaker hand. She resembled a figure of Our Lady the cardinal owned, by a delicate Tuscan painter, with a pensive, oval face and blond hair like an angel. From her appearance, you would swear no thought other than the most spiritual had ever passed through her mind. Camilla's other physical virtue was less obvious to the eye, though it was at least as important for her profession. She had an extraordinarily flexible body, well suited to the ambitious coital positions so fashionable in Rome at this time.

I had this young woman with great pleasure on two occasions in a back room in Cardinal Giovanni's residence. This was the most wanton chamber you could imagine, painted with the loves of Jove and furnished with a bed of remarkable capaciousness, hung with long swathes of scarlet and green silk. After the second time, Camilla carelessly mentioned to me that Cardinal Giovanni liked to watch his friends while they engaged in erotic pursuits in this room. A hole had apparently been bored through from his bedchamber to this bower of pleasure for this very end.

This incident put me off my stride, and I resolved to see Camilla henceforth at my own expense, to enjoy the benefit of discretion. I made an assignation to visit her the Sunday following this incident at her mother's house, in a suburb of the city. I went fully armed, with Nello accompanying me, also armed, and with no coin or jewels on me other than a pair of silver earrings I had bought for Camilla. I had heard enough tales in Rome of hapless men being lured to their doom by lust to wish to be cautious on this score.

We were met by Camilla's mother, a woman in her thirties with ill-dyed blond hair and a sour expression. She looked at me shrewdly, assessing my wealth from my horse and dress, and eventually allowed me through to her daughter's room. I left Nello to kick his heels outside the house on guard—or so I thought as I disported myself with Camilla. He later confessed that he had instead paid four *soldi* to have Camilla's mother while he waited, the incontinent young fool.

Camilla put her proposal to me after we had lain together, sitting cross-legged on the bed like a gypsy, looking at me with her heavenly clear light eyes. If I would pay three months' rent for her on a house in a good quarter of Rome and let her have Nello as protection, she would guarantee to return my payment with interest within two months of taking up residence. She would also give me ten percent of her takings in perpetuity. She had everything planned. She would move there with her sister, who was younger than her and a virgin, and with a cousin who was a little older, in her twenties, but a woman of great beauty. She wished to get away from her mother, who was an evil woman, and to have the freedom to exploit herself on her own terms.

I lay back watching Camilla's intent young face as she spoke to me of this partnership, impressed by her shrewdness. It is a commonplace that Florentines have a sharp commercial sense, but I had never fully appreciated the truth of it until then. Camilla played me cleverly, telling me she had two potential investors in Cardinal Giovanni's circle already—men far wealthier than I—but that she was giving me first refusal out of the affection she bore me, of which she spoke with a very pretty tongue. I could see the transparency of her lure, but I still felt its force, and prudence with money has never been one of my virtues. As I watched Camilla speaking on, lovely as Venus, her sheet of blond hair tossed insouciantly over one shoulder, I was already calculating how much money I could piece together if I liquidated the remnants of my takings from my army career.

As IT TURNED OUT, my investment in Camilla was an excellent one, even though it meant that I was profiting from immoral earnings. By sheer chance, I had hit on the secret of good investment, which is to believe in the people involved. You only had to look at Nello to know he was a pimp born, and Camilla proved most gifted at managing the house. She later told me she had sold her sister's virginity to five men in succession, improvising evidence with phials of pigs' blood. All was most propitiously set up. I was able to send a good quantity of custom her way from the men of the court, and Camilla had good contacts herself from her friendship with Cardinal Giovanni. As a figurehead for her enterprise, I ceded her my parrot Demosthenes, who flourished manfully in the new environment to which his vocabulary was so suited. Camilla later also acquired a monkey from a Spanish merchant, a creature trained to perform some astonishingly lewd tricks.

Camilla had already made enough to return my advance on her rent six weeks after she moved in, two weeks before she had promised. We did not celebrate with our acrobatic intimacies of former times, for I was suffering a bout of celibacy at the time, for reasons I will tell you of shortly. We simply drank a glass of good wine as she counted out my money, a triumphant glint in her eye.

Aside from selling girls' bodies, Camilla had improvised herself a lucrative sideline selling stolen and faked antiquities to visitors to Rome. The fakes were of excellent quality. She had them made in Florence, where a half-brother of hers was still living. She claimed some were made by the famous Michelangelo Buonarroti, who was already a sculptor of some renown and a faker of genius. Some years earlier, he had produced an antique sculpture of a sleeping Cupid that had fooled many noted connoisseurs.

Camilla's forgeries were more modest. She specialized in things such as a man might wish to buy after visiting her domain: bronze miniatures figuring satyrs or Priapi, and *spintriae*, those Roman brothel tokens figuring carnal acts that collectors so love. The success of her business was so great that, ten weeks after her house opened, an official of the pope called on her, demanding a cut of twenty-five percent of her takings. Through application to Valentino, I was able to have this reduced to a more manageable ten.

PLAGUING honest businesswomen was not the only method by which the pope sought to keep his finances afloat during this difficult season. He was already stretched by the campaign against the Orsini family, and he had suffered a severe blow in February when Giulio Orsini devastated the alum mines at Tolfa, smashing the machinery and flooding the mines. As you will recall, the papacy has a monopoly on the production of these mines, without which no dyer in Christendom would have mordant for his tinctures, and we would all be wandering this earth drab as lice. This was a substantial part of the papal income, and a reliable one, compared with tithes and benefices, and the sale of dispensations and indulgences. Orsini had done his work diligently; at least six months of production would be lost.

Pope Alexander's response to this crisis was quite diversified, as one would expect from a man of so subtle an intellect. Most straightforwardly, he made himself around a hundred and twenty thousand ducats at one blow by creating nine more cardinals. If you exclude two who bore the name of Borgia and may be assumed to have had their hats out of family sentiment, this came to around seventeen thousand ducats per cardinal, a hard bargain at anyone's price.

Besides creating new cardinals, if one was to believe some of the rumors, the pope also refreshed his coffers by disposing of some of the old. Rumors of this kind especially surrounded the death of the cardinal of Verona, Giovanni Michiel, which took place in April, not long after I first arrived in Rome. Cardinal Michiel was a Venetian nobleman and a good man, people said, notably ascetic in his lifestyle for a cardinal and known for his charity to the poor. He died suddenly, after two days of violent sickness, and, on the night of his death, the pope's servants raided his house and seized what was said to be a hundred and fifty thousand ducats between coin and goods. There was nothing untoward here, strictly, as cardinals' estates are rightfully due to the Church, although few popes enforced this right quite as zealously as Alexander. Nonetheless, the spectacle of a cardinal's residence being ransacked as his body lay cooling was one that left a sour taste in men's mouths.

XXI

WHEN I WAS FIRST IN THE CITY, I exerted myself to trace Angelica, my colleague in spying from my days at Urbino. You may recall that I last encountered her in Imola, at a time when she was returning to Rome. My itch to see this woman was not merely lascivious. I was intrigued by Angelica's intelligence and worldliness and wit, and I wished finally to have a true conversation with her, outside the constraints of the court. I did hope for more also and drew comfort from the fact that Angelica had always expressed great admiration for my looks—but I knew also that, by now, she might well be in the keeping of some new protector, perhaps one hardly less fearsome than the duke.

I inquired about Angelica when I first arrived and discovered that everyone in Rome knew of her. She was legendary. No one could tell me much of her present circumstances, however, except that she was living a retired life in a villa on the Quirinale, and had taken no part in carnival that year. I wrote to her, saying I was in Rome and begging permission to see her. In a few days, a missive came back to me, brought by a disdainful young liveried servant. It was written in an extravagant, looping hand and told me that Angelica craved pardon but was receiving no visitors at this time.

This was in March. In May, shortly after I had helped Camilla establish her house, I received a further missive in Angelica's hand. This was written with less of a flourish, though it was brought by a servant no less polished than the last one. It was a terse message, no more than a single line. "Come now if you wish to see me," it said.

I MADE AN appointment to see Angelica on my first free day and rode to her house in the company of Nello. It turned out to be precisely this—a true, freestanding house in its own garden, a dwelling of some dignity. The aspect of the place contributed to my sense that Angelica might be in the protection of some powerful man, perhaps a cardinal, who liked to keep his business to himself.

The shade of the trees in Angelica's garden looked inviting as we rode towards the gate. The weather was turning warm now and the sun was beginning to flaunt its power, especially at the height of the day. We dismounted and knocked at the door, which was opened to us by a servant, a neatly dressed woman of around fifty. Nello retired to see to the horses, and the woman ushered me into a kind of parlor, with shuttered windows letting in a thin light. A few minutes later, she returned with a dish full of strawberries soaked in sweet wine.

"She has dressed up for you," the maid said in a conspiratorial whisper, slightly opening the shutters to let a shaft of sunlight into the room. "She's been looking forward to your visit so much."

I will not say that I had no foreboding at this point that Angelica might have retreated from the world from necessity, rather than convenience. One evening at Camilla's when we were speaking of her, a man there had said sneeringly, "So the pox got to her, and not before time." The tone of voice of Angelica's servant and the cloistered air of the room into which I had been shown were beginning to give me a sense of disquietude. I sat waiting for Angelica, listening to a caged bird, a finch of some kind, chirping disconsolately in the corner of the room.

When I saw Angelica, it was clear to me at once that Camilla's client had been right in his cruel jibe. It was true what her maid had said, that she had dressed up for me, but dressing up now signified nothing except covering herself as entirely as she could. She was wearing a silk dress the color they call *perso*, the darkest shade of red you can imagine, almost black. She wore over her face a veil of scarlet, and she had gloves the same color on her hands. I almost leapt out of my skin when I saw her. She looked as you might imagine Death to look when she comes for us.

When we had stood contemplating each other for a moment, Angelica spoke, in a voice of disconcerting normality.

"*Carissimo* Matteo, welcome. You will forgive me in the circumstances if I do not kiss you."

"Angelica," I said, but I could not go on.

"Don't be upset," she said tenderly, squeezing my hand with her red-gloved one. "It's God's will—or that's what we are supposed to say, at any rate, isn't it? You forget, everyone has to die, and many of us die young. I was the only one of my sisters who even reached twenty years old."

Angelica's courage strengthened me, and we spoke at some length, in a way I still find remarkable when I recall it. Almost forty years on, I still admire this dauntless woman more almost than anyone I have known. She had summoned me, she told me, because she was planning to kill herself in the next few months, before the disease destroyed her further. As she put it, with her usual trenchancy, she did not wish to outlive her face. I wish now, looking back, that I had done my Christian duty and attempted to persuade her to abandon this sinful resolution. But I was young then and less godly than I should have been and in thrall to Angelica's cleverness and mockery. I took my tune from her and listened as she told me of her admiration for Cleopatra and speculated about where she might lay her hands on an asp.

After this doleful conversation, Angelica asked me for gossip, and I told her about the circles of Cardinal Giovanni and the house of pleasure I had founded with Camilla and our trade in antiquities. Angelica laughed freely at my tales, and at points I almost found I could forget the strangeness of the circumstances and laugh with her. At other times, the thought came to me of what might lie beneath her veil, and I felt my flesh crawl on the back of my neck.

I became conscious of Angelica's voice faltering after a while and had a sense of how much she had exerted herself to speak to me. I rose to go, bowing, with tears in my eyes, knowing we would never meet again on this earth. I had brought her as a gift a small antique bronze of Venus, which I had forgotten to give her in the shock of our meeting. I gave it to her now, and she leaned over to examine it in the slanting light of the window, raising a corner of her veil.

"What a beautiful thing! I suppose this would be one of your friend Camilla's fakes?"

I shook my head. I did not trust myself to speak. Angelica came over to me and planted a muted kiss on my forehead through her blood-colored veil.

"Sit down just one moment, Matteo," she said gently. "There's something I wanted to say to you. I've been putting it off. I can't imagine it will be welcome, but I'm sure you will thank me some day."

I sat, looking at her expectantly, and she perched on a chair opposite, with her gloved hands demurely folded in her lap. There was a pause, as if she were gathering her forces; then she spoke.

"I know the doctors have their own views, but I have come to believe this disease has one cause and one cause only. This goddess, and the acts she inspires in us." She tapped the head of the bronze Venus I had given her, which she was cradling in one hand. "The preachers have been telling us to be chaste for centuries, and we've been laughing and turning a deaf ear to them. Now God has decided to speak to us directly, in a manner we can't ignore. You can't begin to imagine how terrible it is …" Her voice had dropped low. Then she thought better of what she had been planning to say and concluded briskly, with an effort. "You know what they say: *Si non caste, tamen caute.* If you can't be chaste, be careful. You are young, Matteo. You can save yourself." She stood abruptly and held out her hands to me in valediction. "*Basta.* My sermon is at an end. Pray for me sometimes, if you are a praying man."

I RODE AWAY from this meeting with Angelica in a state of distress. The fair spring day around me seemed a mockery, painting life as a garden of delights. It was indeed a garden, filled with flowers and murmuring waters, but a garden infected with snakes. I had a vivid image in my mind of Angelica as she was when I first met her, sharp and brilliant and sure of her powers, a goddess. Now she was something to be hidden away, like the brides they tell of in ghost stories who are worm-eaten corpses behind their veils.

At no time before this had I thought very seriously of the threat posed by Angelica's malady. This was the ill we then called the French disease, or the pox plain and simple. Only recently, with the poem of Fracastoro, has this fancy new term "syphilis" begun to come into vogue. I had known of the disease since I was a boy, of course. You will remember it first surfaced in '95 or '96, after the first French invasion of Naples. At first, we thought it a plague that would pass in a year or a few years, like so many others. By the time I am speaking of here, it was beginning to be apparent that this was a new permanent scourge such as leprosy; also that it was an ailment of great tenacity, returning to afflict many who had thought themselves cured.

There were some from the outset who posited that this new disease was connected with coitus. Its symptoms are first manifest on the organs of sex, and it first erupted among the whore-ridden armies in Naples. As it began to rage throughout Italy in the following years, it was noted that convents were largely exempt. Among the torrent of diverse explications poured forth by the doctors, however, this unpleasant hypothesis was very often drowned out. No one wished to hear the message Angelica had delivered in her sermon. I certainly had no wish to hear it. Yet the memory of her words, issuing from behind that blood-red veil, would not cease to echo in my mind.

THE DREAD ANGELICA had inspired in me was such that, within a few days of our meeting, I resolved to change my ways and curb my taste for the pleasures of the flesh. My new policy would be to abjure congress other than with women to whom I wished to be united in chaste loving devotion. This meant no one other than Nicolosa, who was inconveniently in Fermo. In her absence, I would live as a secular monk.

Having decided this, I felt great calm. I remember well the first evening after my vow, which I spent pleasantly in my room, reading the confessions of Saint Augustine and writing a sonnet of penitence in the manner of Petrarca. Nello now resided at Camilla's, and Dino was absent with the duke's brother's army, so I had the room to myself, and there was no one to mock me for this sudden change of life.

WELL, THE beginnings of these things are always easy, perseverance rather less so. As the days and weeks stretched on, my vow of celibacy began to chafe at me like the hair shirt of a reluctant penitent. It was not the celibacy in itself that irked me, but the fact that there was no end in view. It is one thing to go without carnal release as a result of circumstances, quite another when it is a matter of policy. I was condemned by my own volition to permanent chastity—a hard vow for a twenty-year-old man.

By the beginning of my fourth week of celibacy, I was becoming a monster. I could think of nothing but the pleasures of which I was depriving myself. I had renounced meat and wine, which are said to encourage venery, and now ate with a sobriety worthy of Messer Leonardo da Vinci. Still, I could not pass a serving-woman in the corridor of the Vatican palace without feeling an almost irresistible urge to drag her into a corner and perpetrate some outrage on her. I slept poorly at night. I woke in the morning horribly erect. My moral character was deteriorating by the day.

You may perhaps remember that, when we were in Urbino the previous summer, Messer Leonardo offered me a potion that would cure me of the lusts of the flesh. This recollection came back to me now, and such was my desperation that I sent a letter to him by courier begging him to share with me the recipe of this cure. Messer Leonardo was in Florence at this time, as I had learned at Cardinal Giovanni's, having been lured into an artistic duel with the young master Michelangelo, whose talents as a painter were apparently as remarkable as his skills as a forger of antiquities. I felt some peace in my cravings once I had dispatched my letter, as I hoped now that a solution was at hand.

ONE DAY DURING this strange period in my life, I was in the Vatican library, scouring herbals for information about anaphrosidiacs, when I looked up to see the figure of Messer Niccolò Machiavelli, standing above me with a dangerous gleam in his eye.

"How very fine to see you," he said in his high, carrying voice. "I have been looking for you all over the palace. People keep telling me about this magnificent brothel you've founded. I insist you induct me into its mysteries without delay."

At the sound of the word "brothel," the eyes of all the readers seated within five benches of me had unanimously swiveled in our direction. I felt too abashed even to question Machiavelli's crude choice of language, so ill fitted to Camilla's refined house. I fixed an appointment with him at the palace gates at the hour of vespers, trying meanwhile unobtrusively to shield from him the herbal I was reading, which was open on some venereal page.

I spent the remainder of the afternoon in a state of despondency, for the prospect of attending Camilla's in my celibate state seemed to me a torment worthy of Tantalus. One of the books I had consulted recommended agnus castus, and I bought an ounce of bitter-tasting dried seeds from an apothecary and swallowed them down in one gulp, cursing everyone I could think of from God downwards for reducing me to this risible state.

CAMILLA'S HOUSE lay in Parione, near the great new palace of Cardinal Riario, and Machiavelli and I made our way down there along the river, elbowing our way through the early evening crowds. We were almost in June now, but the perfume of orange blossom still hung bewitchingly in the air, competing with the baser odors of the streets.

Machiavelli explained that he was in Rome briefly on business of state, conferring with his former ambassadorial colleague, Bishop Francesco Soderini. This man had recently been raised to the cardinalate by the influence of the king of France, no doubt with the assistance of much Florentine gold. We spoke of the affairs of Rome and the court; then

Machiavelli turned the conversation to Cardinal Giovanni, saying he had heard I was frequenting the cardinal's circles. He had known Cardinal Giovanni in his youth, he said, before the Medici were exiled from Florence, and was a particular friend of his younger brother, Giuliano. He could not renew this acquaintance for reasons of political sensitivity but welcomed this chance to hear news of his old friends.

I was suspicious of this line of questioning and responded evasively. I had heard much of Machiavelli in the past few months through the Florentines at Cardinal Giovanni's. I no longer saw him in quite the same light as I did when I knew him before. He was a man on the rise; that much was clear. The Florentines had just elected themselves a kind of doge or head of state, Piero Soderini, who was the brother of Messer Niccolò's patron, Francesco Soderini. Messer Niccolò was a close confidant and minister of this Piero. I had even heard him described as his brain. The man I had first encountered trussed near-naked on a mountain pass near Urbino was becoming a personage of some dignity in Florence. The loathing he attracted from the Florentine exiles in Cardinal Giovanni's circles was eloquent on this score.

For this reason, I was cautious. It was possible that Messer Niccolò was an old friend of the Medici brothers, as he claimed, but it was also possible that he thought me a fool who could be milked for information useful to his Florentine masters. I expatiated much on the colorful side of Cardinal Giovanni's salon, telling him of its exotic culinary experiments and its carnal diversions, but I kept the names of the Florentine exiles I had met there *in pectore*, as they say of the secrets of the pope.

MESSER NICCOLÒ got on famously with Camilla, as I had anticipated when he invited himself to her house. They were compatriots, and Camilla was a great partisan of Florentines, thinking them to possess a genius to which no other nation could aspire. Besides, she was sufficiently informed on the political life of her home city to know that Machiavelli was a man to be cultivated. She exerted herself marvelously to seduce him—in truth, not a particularly difficult task.

I was not surprised, given this, when my guest disappeared upstairs at a certain moment with our hostess. I hardly noticed it, to be honest. To distract myself from my miserable plight as a celibate in a house of pleasure, I had engaged in a wager with a papal protonotary over whether my parrot Demosthenes was capable of reciting the Lord's Prayer without prompting. Things got quite heated when the bird was halfway through, and issues of clarity of enunciation came to the fore.

A voice suddenly spoke in my ear as the parrot was reaching the line *et ne nos inducas in tentationem.*

"*Madonna belva,*" it said. "That woman is a revelation. I think I'm in love. Have you tried this one with her?"

Machiavelli was holding out a *spintria* with a copulating couple most startlingly entwined. I hoped Camilla had given it to him as a souvenir, rather than inveigling him into purchasing a fake.

"I can't say I have," I said, abandoning Demosthenes, who had sadly lapsed into profanity on the verge of his target. "I would have thought it was anatomically impossible."

"It's certainly not for the faint-hearted," Messer Niccolò said with a faraway look in his eye.

Two days after this visit from Messer Niccolò, my response arrived from Messer Leonardo da Vinci. He wrote with great warmth, commending my decision to pursue celibacy, which he said showed remarkable prudence for a man of my years. He regretted that he could not share the secret of his recipe because of its great value, but he was happy to send me a supply of the potion sufficient to last me a year.

I stared down for a moment at the phial Messer Leonardo sent me, which had a curiously wrought metal stopper the shape of a snake. I must act quickly, I knew, for moral resolve has a habit of vanishing if we do not seize it by the horns. There was a jug of water at my hand. I poured a glass of it and measured a few drops of the potion into it, as Messer Leonardo had instructed, turning the water a cloudy yellowish color. A foul, putrefying odor arose from the vessel as I unstopped it, but I did not allow myself to hesitate and quickly drained the thing down.

For a moment I stood there, gazing at my expressionless face in the glass; then a ferocious retching urge seized me. I made to kneel, but before I could, a stream of vomit shot from my mouth with great force, coating the mirror before me and spraying the wall.

It seemed to take an eternity for me to vacate my stomach. When I was finally done, I dropped to my knees, shaking like a leaf. A filthy smell filled the room, and the wall looked revolting, but I was filled with relief that I had survived this experiment. I decided to put a definitive end to my quest for a pharmaceutical solution to my problem. The remainder of the potion I poured into the jakes.

XXII

S ALVATION OFFERED ITSELF to me shortly after this episode from an unexpected quarter. The duke ordered me to Fermo in the company of a party of lawyers and senior courtiers to help conduct negotiations with the leading men of the city for the peaceful capitulation of the town. It was a blow when I first heard of this, that my once proudly free city had escaped Liverotto's tyranny only to fall prey to the duke and his father. But it was folly to imagine that Fermo could escape this outcome, to which Fortune seemed to have condemned all the cities of the Marches, and the thought that this mission would carry me back to Nicolosa was one that smothered all other cares.

We journeyed to Fermo in great style, as representatives of the duke, with an escort of twenty lancers. I was given a horse from the duke's stables finer than any I had ridden: a jet-black gelding bred from a destrier and a racing mare, a delectable blend of power and speed. My clothes were on a par with this, fine cast-offs from the duke's wardrobe, exquisite in their materials and workmanship. I signed these out the day before my departure and spent a pleasant five minutes parading myself in front of the glass, imagining the figure I would make when I rode into my home town. It felt strange to have on my back garments that had been worn by the duke, as if I had assumed some of his mystery with these threads.

WE MET WITH great honor in Fermo. We were lodged in the grand house that had formerly been Liverotto's, where he had once threatened to hurl me from the balcony. It summoned disturbing memories for me, yet it was gratifying for me to return with this new status. I invited my sister-in-law Margherita to visit and watched with pleasure as my little nephews romped raucously up their former lord's stairs.

Such was my new standing in the city that I even received two marriage proposals within a day of arriving in Fermo—though admittedly from men poor in wealth and rich in daughters, hoping to scrimp along with a minimal dowry by stooping to a bridegroom of low birth. I told my prospective fathers-in-law that I was honored by their offers but considered myself too young to marry. They looked at me skeptically, as though suspecting that I was holding out for richer pickings in Rome.

I sent to Nicolosa's house as soon as I arrived in the city, asking to see her, and she replied giving me an assignation and counseling discretion. I climbed in over her garden wall that night, as I had done in the past, forgetting my dignity as ducal representative. After my long weeks of chastity, I was ravenous for love, and the risk of discovery seemed nothing to me compared with the pleasures that lay within.

WE SPENT THE two nights I was in Fermo lying together in Nicolosa's bed above the garden, the window open so that a soft breeze stole in through the window. In the intervals of our lovemaking, we spoke meanderingly of all that had passed since we had last been together. Nicolosa told me of her life in Fermo and I told her a carefully edited version of my life in Rome. I said nothing specific of my prospects of escape from the duke's service, only leaving her to understand that this would take longer than I had envisaged. If she was suspicious of me, she did not let me see it, although Nicolosa was always more subtle than I could gauge in these things.

One development I learned of in this visit was that Nicolosa had succeeded in reclaiming her inheritance from her father, which had been subsumed into Liverotto's treasury during his lifetime. Liverotto had destroyed Messer Giovanni's testament, but the judges had not hesitated in recognizing her as his heir.

Once her rights had been established, Nicolosa had devoted herself to the task of reconstructing her father's bequests, using a draft of his testament that his notary had secretly preserved. I was one of the beneficiaries of this generous act. Messer Giovanni had left three hundred ducats each to Dino and me, as well as the income from a watermill he owned outside Fermo, which he left to us in common. Nicolosa read me the very words of the bequest, so I could hear the affectionate manner in which he spoke of me. He described me as "a youth raised in his household, whom he most consummately loved."

"Nicolosa," I said, moved by this testimony, "keep your money. Your father's will is lost. There is no need for you to track down each beneficiary."

Nicolosa shook her head.

"Nonsense, Teo. How could I live with myself if I did not try to respect his desires?" I could hear her voice thickening with emotion as she spoke. Then she added in a different tone, "Besides, you will need the money if you are going to set up home. I hear you have been inundated with marriage proposals since you arrived back in Fermo."

"It's incredible," I said. "You lead such a retired life, yet you manage to know everyone's business as precisely as if you were out gabbling on the piazza each day."

"Well? Is it not true?"

"That I have had offers, yes. That I considered accepting them for a moment, no."

We looked at each other after that, she half-sunk in shadow, me hovering over her, a breath's distance above her lips. I wanted to say more, that I would consider no offer of marriage because I wished for no one but her as my wife. These words were in my mouth to say, even, but I was deterred by the gulf between us, which was greater than ever now that Nicolosa had won back her inheritance. She was an heiress and a highborn lady and the widow of a cardinal's son, and I was a youth of no birth or name, whose small prospects of wealth were dependent on disreputable means. She could not marry me without bringing shame on herself and I could not woo her without seeming an arrant fortune seeker. I contented myself with saying, "I am yours for as long as you want me"— for that, at least, I was in a position to pledge.

I RETURNED TO Rome from Fermo in a state of exhilaration, my mind filled with sweet memories of my nights with Nicolosa. The negotiations for the handover of the city had gone smoothly, and I had the satisfaction of knowing I had served the duke well. The season was glorious, early June, and I was mounted on a fine horse and had a banker's draft for three hundred ducats in my purse—more money than I had ever imagined I would own.

I even thought I had sorted out the problem of my celibacy, through a new expedient that came to me along the way. I needed a virgin. This was quite obviously the solution, and I was not sure why I had not thought of it before. I would take some young girl and keep her for my exclusive use, as I had Agnese for the few months she was with me. I would move between these two chaste women, the virgin and Nicolosa, until such time that I could return to Fermo for good.

I applied to Camilla for a virgin when I arrived back in the city, stressing that I wanted a real one, not one trumped up through pig's blood. Camilla rolled her eyes when she heard me, in wonderment at the whims of men, but she soon found me a suitable candidate. This was a girl from the neighbor-hood who had been living quite happily until the year before with her mother and her father, who was an ex-soldier and a trader in used goods. Then her father had left, and her mother had plummeted into poverty, as women often do in such cases. They had ended on charity, in the house of a neighbor. There, recently, the girl's mother had died.

Such was the story of the virgin who was presented to me, a tale more pathetic than erotic. I first saw her in person at Camilla's around the middle of June. Francesca was her name. She was a graceful, mannerly little thing, with a fine head of chestnut-colored hair, but she seemed to me far too young and unhappy to be an object of my attentions. I had not asked Camilla her age, but I would not have estimated it as much beyond fourteen. We spoke stiltedly for a while, she hardly lifting her eyes; then I left her a virgin as I had found her, resolving on a policy of charity. I thought I would dower this young orphan and present her to a husband, some respectable young artisan, while remaining myself a prisoner of my lusts.

This was not to be. I met Francesca again the following Sunday, and she was quite different. I imagine that Camilla had been lecturing her on her prospects and duties in the intervening time. She was shy still, but less shy than previously, and she occasionally cast a smiling look in my direction and laughed at some extravagant compliments I made her. I retired with her to a bedchamber after we had eaten, with no thought other than to kiss her and perhaps to induct her into the farthest reaches of Love's kingdom. Needless to say, I did not manifest the discipline required for this, and her virginity was breached that same afternoon.

Francesca did not seem too unhappy at this outcome, and the next time I saw her, I gave her a silver bracelet and pledged under Camilla's skeptical eye that I would take care of her and see she was safe. I found lodgings for my new lover not far from Camilla's, at the house of a glove maker and his wife of whom all in the neighborhood spoke well. I swaggered a little when I went round there, letting it be known that I was a man of the duke's household, in case they were minded to cheat me, but in truth there was no need for such precautions. These were kindly folk and as honest as day; they could have cared for Francesca no better had she been of their own blood.

BY EARLY JULY, the city was beginning to become a furnace of unrelenting heat, and a breeding ground for illness. Half the court seemed to be sick by the beginning of the month, and the other half by the end. Any man of sense at this time would be thinking of retiring to the country, to find some shade and fresh breezes. In Rome, we were preparing for war.

You will recall the details, I am sure. The French and the Spaniards had shared the ill-fated kingdom of Naples for the past two years, since they had wrested it from its legitimate lords. As anyone of sense might have predicted, this solution was not happy, and now the two kingdoms were preparing to go to war. King Louis was storming down with his armies in person from Lombardy, while King Ferdinand had entrusted his forces to Gonzalo de Córdoba—the Great Captain as we later came to call him. Valentino's troops were due to join with those of the French king to march south, in keeping with his long-standing French alliance. Rumors were flying, however: that the duke would abandon the French; that the pope was in talks with the Spanish; that the two of them were whoring themselves to whichever of these powers offered the best chance of support in their own territorial campaigns.

I do not know the truth of these rumors to this day and wonder whether they were put around by Cardinal Giuliano, whose slanders against the pope very often had this burden, that Alexander was a foreigner who would sell Italy like some chattel to other foreigners for his own gain. If the cardinal was indeed initiating these rumors, he must have found my messages quite tedious, for I spoke of little else at this time. I sent these messages via Diego, the Spanish mute of whom I told you, leaving them in a corridor close to the pope's private chambers, where Diego worked most of the day. A crucifix hung in this corridor, an ugly wooden thing given to the pope by some visiting German princeling. It was behind this monstrosity that I would tuck my folded message, in a small crevice Diego had made in the wall.

One thing spoke for the truth of the tales of the duke's incipient treachery, aside from the fact that treachery ran deep in his blood and his father's. This was that King Louis's alliance with Florence was frustrating his plans for a Tuscan campaign. You will recall that the summer before, having positioned Vitellozzo Vitelli in Arezzo, on the threshold of Florence, he had been forced by the French to pull back and relinquish his gains. A change of alliance on his part, from the French to the Spanish, would leave Tuscany open for conquest. It was not difficult to see how the thing would play out. If the Spanish won in Naples with assistance from Valentino, they would be only too pleased to return the favor. The duke would storm Florence with Spanish auxiliaries and finally plant his colors in the city of the Arno, as he had been thirsting to do since the previous year.

MY SUSPICIONS on this front were compounded one evening when the duke called me to his quarters and asked me to deliver a message to Cardinal Giovanni. This was quite out of the ordinary; in three months since he had been receiving my desultory reports on the cardinal's gatherings, he had never asked me to act as go-between in this way.

I went a little early to the cardinal's residence, at a time when I thought I would find him without company. I half imagined I would catch him curling his hair or engaged in immodest acts with his footman. Instead, in a manner most fitting for a prelate, he was closeted in his study, reading a Greek manuscript of the orations of Saint Gregory of Nazianus. The only hint of frivolity was a pile of saffron cakes, a favorite dish of his, at his side.

The cardinal received my delivery with no obvious surprise, wafting his hand towards the cakes to invite me to partake of them.

"Dear Cesare," he said fondly, when he had finished reading. "I well remember when he first became a cardinal. He looked so dashing in his scarlet. If I might trouble you to pass me that knife?"

I sat in silence while he sharpened his nib and penned his response to the duke. The room was cleverly angled so it did not take the sun; it was cool here almost, despite the brutal heat outside. An ethereal perfume hung in the air—like jasmine, but diluted to the ghostliest of essences. I noticed the cardinal was writing fluently, without obvious pauses for reflection, as though he was already sure in his mind of what he would say.

Eventually, he sealed the note.

"Here," he said gaily. "*Redde Caesari*," which is to say, "render unto Caesar." He rose graciously to see me to the door, where he studied me for a moment, his head on one side.

"I knew it," he said. "You really are turning out to be a remarkably useful young man."

IN THE DAYS that followed, I meditated much on the significance of this episode, including some of my conjectures in a message to Cardinal Giuliano. There was a great deal about it to excite wonder. The previous year, when Valentino had Vitelli move on Tuscany, he did so with the Medici as allies, hoping to use their supporters in Florence to facilitate his taking of the city. But that was when he was in league with the Orsini, who were allies and kin of the Medici and wished to see them restored to power. Things were quite different now. The pope had spent the last six months slaughtering every member of the Orsini family on whom he could manage to lay his hands and snaffling up their castles and estates by the dozen. Yet here was the pope's son cheerfully renewing his acquaintance with Cardinal Giovanni, whose mother had been an Orsini. The cardinal, for his part, seemed quite happy to bury the memory of the kinsmen he had lost.

In attempting to probe the truth of these matters, I was more than usually assiduous in my attendance at Cardinal Giovanni's. This diligence was quite useless, however. If the cardinal was playing dangerous games with the duke, plotting the recapture of his home city, nothing in his demeanor indicated this. He was as cherubically serene as ever. The talk of his salon was not of the impending war, as it was everywhere else in Rome, but of the latest elegant editions from Aldus in Venice, of the gossip from Florence concerning the rivalry of Leonardo and Michelangelo, of the remarkable discoveries of ancient manuscripts by Annius of Viterbo, which, even then, some believed to be fakes. I sometimes looked across the room at my host's beaming visage, attempting to guess what was passing through his mind. I might as well have been gazing at the smooth features of his favorite statue of Apollo for all I could ever discern.

WITH THE approach of the Neapolitan war, our military exercises had taken on a new rhythm and intensity. We were up each day before dawn to drill and practice our skill with weapons before the sun became too hot to bear, and we returned to these exertions in the evening. Sometimes, if our captain believed we were in need of toughening up, we did not even have respite in the middle of the day. Dino was back in Rome and had been given charge of a company, a great honor since he was so new to this army. I would happily have served with him, but the duke would not have it; I continued under my dislikeable Spanish captain instead.

Sunday was the sole day of the week we were free from these labors. I would go with Dino to Camilla's, where her girls would also be resting from their exertions of the week. We would eat in her garden under the shade of two fig trees, and Camilla's sister Sabina would sing for us, with Camilla picking away languorously at her lute. Dino and Nello would withdraw with some girl after this, and I would go back with Francesca to the glove maker's house, where I would spend the remainder of the afternoon rolling around with her on her bed and fitfully sleeping. Then, late at night, after a supper we shared with her landlords, I would make my way back to the palace, hastening to arrive before the curfew, so I could present myself for duty the next day.

One punishingly hot Sunday at the beginning of August, I found myself lingering in Camilla's garden after the rest of the company had retired. I wished to be alone. I felt listless and melancholy, and not only on account of the heat. A shock had come to me that morning, which was no less a shock for the fact that it was entirely expected. An unctuous little Neapolitan canon had sidled up to me after mass to regale me with the gossip that Angelica was dead.

I do not know to this day whether Angelica took her own life or fell to the sickness that was scything down Romans that summer like grass. The man who told me of her death assumed she was a victim of the sickness, telling me she had been buried in haste in a closed coffin in Sant'Angelo in Pescheria, supposedly at the expense of the duke. He did not seem to know she had been suffering from the French disease, nor was there mention of it in a scabrous Latin epitaph that began to circulate round the palace that morning, recounting Angelica's arrival in the Underworld and her lascivious welcome by its gods.

I was haunted by memories of Angelica all that day—not of the strange ghoul she had been at our last meeting, but of how she had been formerly. For some reason, one image in particular kept returning to me, of a time we danced together in Urbino, just before she revealed herself as Cardinal Giuliano's spy. Angelica was wearing a loose white gown that day, with something silver at her throat, her hair falling free like a nymph's in a painting. If I closed my eyes, I could see her marking time at my side, light-footed and supple as a reed.

I was lost in this memory when I suddenly looked up to see Camilla standing before me. I started a little. She had her arms crossed and was wearing a mannish brimmed cap to protect her fair skin from the sun. She liked to indulge in such eccentricities of dress when she was off-duty and not trying to seduce.

"Francesca went home, Teo," she said softly. "We did not want to disturb you. She said she would wait for you there."

I stirred myself and said I would go there to find her, but Camilla shook her head.

"Not yet. There's someone to see you inside."

CAMILLA WOULD not tell me who awaited me but led me to a room at the back of the house that could be entered by a small side door from a little-frequented alley. This was a place she used to accommodate clients who were men of the cloth or otherwise unwilling to be seen stepping up brazenly to the door of her house.

It was dark in the room, as the shutters were closed against the sun, and I could see nothing at first except the shape of a man, lying propped on one elbow on the bed that occupied most of the room. He did not speak at first and I suddenly feared a trap of some kind and reached down for my dagger.

Then a familiar voice said, "I assume that is you, Matteo? I can't see a fucking thing. We need a candle in here."

To my astonishment, the man on the bed was the second chancellor of the republic of Florence, my esteemed friend Messer Niccolò Machiavelli. I opened the shutter a crack and a ray of hot white light sliced into the darkness. Machiavelli had risen from the bed and was regarding me with an expression of amusement, enjoying the spectacle of my surprise.

"Apologies for all this secrecy. I'm not supposed to be here. In Rome, I mean. But I needed to see you. I have a favor to ask."

"What is that?" I said, a little cautiously. There was something in his tone that made me wary.

Before answering, Machiavelli went to the door, which I had closed behind me, and opened it abruptly; then he went to the window and flung open the shutter with equal suddenness, looking outside before pulling it to.

"There are no spy holes into this room?" he asked. "Does Madonna Camilla cater to those who like to watch?"

I shook my head. I was still feeling dazed, torn abruptly from my garden reverie.

"Not here. Only in one of the rooms upstairs."

"*Porco Dio*. Not the one she took me to that time?"

I laughed and said not as far as I knew.

Machiavelli sat on the bed and motioned to me to sit on a cassone opposite. My eyes had adjusted sufficiently to the darkness to see him well enough, though not distinctly. Then he spoke, in a tone I had not heard from him before.

"I have something here with me that I need you to give to your contact in the palace."

My heart leapt violently when he said this. I prayed that he was not saying what I thought he was saying.

"My contact?" I said as coolly as I could. "I do not follow your meaning."

"Yes, you do. The man to whom you pass your messages for Cardinal della Rovere. He goes by the name of Diego, I believe."

I felt sick as I heard these words. My life was absolutely in this man's hands if he knew this. I thought of the dagger at my side and of Dino and Nello upstairs. This was a clerk, not a fighter. He did not even carry a weapon that I knew of. Yet I did not wish to kill him if I could avoid it.

"Don't worry," Machiavelli said. "I am not going to betray your secret. And don't think it would do you any good to kill me, by the way. Others know of this besides me."

I was silent, then said, "Others?" There seemed no point in trying to deny what he had revealed he knew with such precision.

"Only in Florence," he said in a soothing tone. "And only a few. No one with any reason to harm you, as long as you cooperate. Your cover is good. You're in no danger." He paused. "You can trust me. We're friends, are we not?"

"I thought so," I said bitterly, and he laughed.

"Sometimes I forget how young you are. There is nothing personal in this. I do not do it for my own pleasure." He looked at me for a moment with his eyebrows raised. "Well?"

"I am to give something to Diego," I said sullenly.

"Correct," he said, fishing an object from his pocket. "You just need to leave it in the usual place."

I took what he was holding out to me and carefully unwound the cloth in which it was wrapped. It was a ring with something on the face, in relief, though I could not see it in any detail in the darkness. It was large for a ring but not too large to fit into the crevice behind the crucifix.

"That's all?" I said.

"That's absolutely all. And you will not tell a living soul of this transaction, of course—nor a dead one, for that matter. Or we'll expose you to the duke."

Messer Niccolò watched me put the ring in the pocket of my doublet; then he stood and went over to the shutter to let in some light. I sat on the bed staring stolidly at the wall in front of me, wondering how he had come to learn of my spying and what else he might know.

Machiavelli came over and put a hand on my shoulder. His lean face was graver than usual.

"I'm sure you loathe me at this moment," he said. "But you'll be happy at the outcome—you and your master both."

We remained like that for a moment in silence, I wondering what he meant by this last statement. Then he said in a cooler tone, holding me with his eyes, "Your instructions are clear?"

I nodded.

"Just follow them," he said. "Otherwise it won't be pretty." With that he walked out of the room.

I LEFT THE ring for Diego the following day, which was the sixth of August. I remember precisely. We had an arrangement whereby I signaled when I left a message for him. I would draw a mark with chalk at a particular spot on the wall in a passageway leading to the courtyard where the palace servants took the air when they had a break from their labors. Diego would watch for this mark and erase it as he passed.

Before I left the ring, I examined it. The face made me start when I saw it. It was carved in a reddish-brown onyx and showed the portrait of a heavy-featured man in profile. There was lettering around the portrait, minuscule but quite legible. The thing was perhaps two-thirds of the size of a florin.

The image was of the Ferrarese Dominican Girolamo Savonarola, who had preached in Florence with great following in the previous decade. He was famous throughout Italy. I remember seeing a printed copy of one of his sermons when I was a youth in Fermo, which was rubbed almost to illegibility by all the hands it had passed through. Savonarola had attained great power in Florence through his holiness and had thundered from his pulpit against the iniquities of the pope. Then Alexander excommunicated him and the Florentines took fright and hanged him along with two of his acolytes, burning the bodies and dispersing their ashes, as though afraid to let a single atom of them remain.

I stood staring for a long moment at this dead man's profile, wondering what it could mean to be giving this ring to a servant of the pope whom Savonarola had excoriated as the Antichrist. The thing frightened me somewhat. It had a baleful power about it, as if there was something in it of the friar's holy fury, surviving the pulverization of his flesh. It was the kind of ring that has a hidden compartment beneath the face; you could sense it. I wondered whether it held relics of the friar: some fragment of his tunic or a host he had blessed. I had heard of people carrying such things with them as holy relics. Fra Girolamo had died the death of a common criminal, but for many he was a martyr and a saint.

NOTHING HAPPENED whatsoever for a week after I left the ring. Every morning and most evenings I drilled with my company, sweat pouring off my body at each movement. At night, I collapsed exhausted on my bed or wiltingly gambled at cards or dice with my companions, more out of fellowship than desire. One evening when I was free, I rode down to Francesca's, but I was too tired when I got there to do anything but sleep by her side like a man drugged.

On the Saturday night, the pope and Valentino went to dine in the vineyard of Cardinal Adriano Castellesi, one of the richest of the cardinals. He had recently returned from a sojourn in England, where he had been singularly favored by the king. I was on duty that evening and rode up with the pope's party. We of the escort waited through the banquet, playing cards in Cardinal Adriano's fine shaded grounds and drinking wine from his generous cellar. Then we accompanied our masters back to the Vatican, surrounding them in a phalanx armed with blazing torches, a glorious sight.

The next morning the pope was ill, quite seriously, with a raging fever that seemed dangerous in a man of his age. The duke also appeared to be indisposed, for he did not appear in public. Don Michelotto was in charge of his court. News came in the afternoon that Cardinal Adriano, their host of the night before, was also unwell. It seemed likely that this was a severe case of the ague that was ravaging Rome at the time.

The next days were strange indeed. Doctors came to the palace in an uninterrupted train, proposing remedies and squabbling among themselves. You would never have believed there were so many medics in the whole of Italy, let alone Rome.

The wildest rumors of the patients' symptoms were promulgated in the corridors of the palace, in Cardinal Giovanni's salon, at every apothecary's shop and baker's oven and laundry in the city. The hypothesis of ague satisfied no one after the first days. Everyone scented some whiff of foul play. A palace servant told me that, during the first night of his illness, the duke had been in such searing pain that he had plunged into a bath of cold water. He emerged from it with his skin peeling off in strips from his whole body, so he remained a bloody mess of raw flesh.

As THE DOCTORS fought to save these men, and rumor upon rumor ran riot through the city, there was much danger of disorder. At the orders of the duke, who retained his wits despite his bodily decomposition, Don Michelotto organized parties of soldiers to patrol the streets to maintain calm during the day and enforce a new curfew at night. I was placed at the head of one of these patrols, which were allocated extraordinary powers. We had the right, for example, to hang seditionaries directly, without having recourse to the law. I rode through the streets in trepidation, dreading an encounter with a crowd baying for the blood of some supposed villain. The mood in the city was volatile, like that among a family of sons where the father is absent and the mother left in control.

On the afternoon of the second day, I returned to the palace at the end of our patrol, feeling exhausted. It made sense to wear armor, given the potential dangers we faced, but to ride in Rome in August in the heat of the day wearing armor is to experience something like what I imagine lobsters suffer in the pot.

I was dismounting my horse in the main courtyard when Don Michelotto called me over.

"Matteo," he said. He looked shattered and gray-faced, as though he had not slept for days. "I need you and your men."

There were ten of us in my patrol, and he had appropriated what looked like another patrol fresh off the streets, as grimy and exhausted as we were. There were also a few servants, unarmed and carrying sacks. We stripped off our armor, leaving a servant to guard it, then followed him on foot through the corridors of the palace to a part of the building I had never been to, close to the papal apartments. We went through a door, which Don Michelotto locked behind him, trying numerous keys from a large bunch until he found the right one. Then we proceeded into a second room, then a third, where Don Michelotto locked the far door. After that, we returned to the middle room, a spacious chamber with four or five doors leading off it. Don Michelotto went to one of these doors, the grandest among them, and patiently tried each key in turn.

When it became apparent that no key fitted, Don Michelotto hammered on the door, shouting that he would break it down if it were not opened. After a minute or so, he stepped back and called a Spanish name, and a servant stepped forward wielding an axe. As he did so, we could hear a key scraping in the lock from the other side. The door opened a few inches, as though moved by a cautious hand. Don Michelotto kicked it hard and we heard a yelp from behind it. Then we were following him, storming into the room.

There were eight men in the chamber we entered, five armed soldiers, two secretaries, and a cardinal, the last a man of around seventy, who looked as though he had seen the devil and his hordes making their way into his chamber. Don Michelotto drew his knife and advanced on the old man, who stood wordless, swallowing nervously. He raised a gnarled hand as he saw him approaching in a feeble gesture of defiance. I recognized him as Cardinal Casanova, a Spaniard from the pope's hometown and his chamberlain. He had been raised to the cardinalate only in May.

"I want the key, Your Eminence," Don Michelotto said, in a tone of great calm. "Give it to me and no one will be hurt."

"On whose order is this?" the old man said tremulously.

"His Holiness's. Whose do you think? Now give me the key."

The cardinal waited for a long moment before answering, and I watched fearfully, urging him to comply in my mind. I did not wish to see something as unholy as I thought might soon confront me, the murder of this man of God before my eyes. Eventually, the old man drew a key from his pocket and handed it to Don Michelotto with shaking fingers.

"God will punish you for this. You and all your followers. You are stealing what is His, and He will strike you down."

Don Michelotto laughed. Within minutes, we found ourselves in the room behind. An astonishing sight met us there. This was a storeroom, equipped with stone shelves such as you might expect to find in a pantry, harboring cooking irons and sacks of flour. Instead, it was crammed full of silver and gold, mainly in the form of coin, but also some plate. The coin was in bags, of a uniform blue-gray color, but the tops of some of these bags were open and you could see the glitter of the metal within. It looked like some extraordinary wizard's cavern, such as you might read of in romance.

Our task, as became apparent, was to gather this treasure and take it over to the duke's apartment. The servants distributed sacks to the men of our patrols, and they were ordered to fill them with the contents of the bags. First, however, Don Michelotto had them strip naked in the antechamber, so they had no chance of concealing any of this bounty in their garments. One complained of this treatment, and Don Michelotto kicked him to the ground before the cardinal's horrified gaze.

After that, there were no protests. Our naked crew labored meekly away at their task, looking like the damned souls in some mad painter's vision of the Last Judgment. The officer of the other patrol and I paced the room with our hands on our swords, invigilating the poor fellows. Don Michelotto leaned against the wall, cleaning his nails with the point of a stiletto and invigilating us in our turn. No one spoke. The air was thick with the meaty smell of the men's sweating bodies. The only sounds were their grunts as they bent for the bags—that and the seductive, unending rush of pouring coin. You might think yourself Danaë, with Jove cascading down on her. It sounded like a waterfall of gold.

The whole task took almost an hour—a little longer than it should have, since some of our men had to be left outside in the antechamber to ensure that the cardinal's guard made no attempt at resistance. Once the sacks had been loaded and their necks secured tightly, the men were allowed to recover their clothes, and we made our way over to the duke's apartment. Our load was as heavy as if the sacks were filled with stone. We staggered under the weight of them like overladen mules.

After we had deposited the sacks in an anteroom of the duke's apartment, which was crawling with armed men, Don Michelotto dismissed the soldiers and servants, remaining alone with me and the other officer. He bent and cut the string round the neck of a sack, emerging with a handful of silver coin, which he divided between us.

"Thirsty work, eh, lads?" he said, grinning, as if we had been planting an orchard or some other such wholesome pursuit.

WHEN I GOT back to the room I shared with Dino, I ordered our servant to fetch me water to bathe in. This was a boy I had taken on when Nello transferred to Camilla's, a handsome, tousle-haired Roman youth of around eighteen by the name of Masetto.

Masetto returned minutes later with a jug of water, buzzing with news. The pope was dead. He had died some time earlier that day, but the news had been kept secret, even within the palace, presumably until the task I had just been engaged on had been accomplished. The coup was a bold one, and worthy of the duke, who had clearly not lost his wits with his sickness. By the time Christendom became aware it was fatherless, its coffers had already been picked dry.

Masetto and I stood staring at each other in silence for a moment after he told me of Alexander's death. Somehow this felt a shock of great magnitude, even though we had known the pope had been lying on the threshold of death for two days. I was ten years old when Alexander ascended to the papal throne, and Masetto was no more than seven or eight. This pontificate was almost all we could remember. We were suddenly on the brink of a new age.

XXIII

I WENT TO CAMILLA'S THAT EVENING, eager to hear what was being said about the pope's death—although this was a dangerous choice of destination, given my uncertain mood. I was tense and fraught after the past days and would have liked nothing more than to seek solace in carnal oblivion. Instead, true to my plan of celibacy, I remained in the parlor, eating and drinking and gambling—all very fine pleasures, but hardly the same.

Francesca was not in Rome, in case you wonder why I did not go to her. She had departed earlier that week with her landlord and his wife to a farm the wife's brother owned on the Sabine Hills. They had wished Francesca to go with them for her health, having become attached to her, and I did not have the heart to deny her the chance to escape the city's festering summer streets and breathe some clean air.

I left Camilla's in good time for the curfew at the palace. When I got to my feet, a man who had been drinking with me there the last half-hour, an amiable Genoese, stood also and said he would walk with me, as he was going my way.

Once we had emerged onto the street, my companion and I walked in silence for a while, only exclaiming about the heat. When we were on a quiet stretch of street, the Genoese stopped and took me by the shoulder.

"I was sent for you. You are to come with me. I have horses at an inn near here."

I looked at him in astonishment and shook off his hand with a certain violence. He laughed.

"Easy, hothead. Here you are."

He held something out to me and I took it: a half-cameo, the signal of Cardinal Giuliano. I had the man step back four paces while I examined it, leaving me the lantern we had taken from Camilla's for light. I had my own broken cameo in the pocket of my doublet, for it had been impressed on me that I must carry it with me at all times. I brought it edge to edge with the shard that the Genoese had given me, clamping my dagger between my teeth to keep it at hand.

The match was perfect. I sheathed my blade and nodded at the man, who gestured towards a side street. It was not difficult to imagine what this was about. Some agent of the cardinal in Rome, perhaps the mysterious secretary I had seen at Cardinal Giovanni's, must be seeking me to confirm the news that the pope was dead. I only hoped I could avoid the Cloaca this time.

In fact, to my relief, when we had collected our horses, we turned in a direction quite other than that of the house where the entry to the Cloaca was located. After fifteen minutes or so, we were ascending a hill winding up between expensive-looking houses with orchards around them. Fierce-sounding dogs hurled themselves against gates as we passed, but behind them you could hear cicadas, as you could not in the streets of the city. Even the air began to seem purer as we rode.

We stopped at perhaps the fourth or fifth of these houses, and my companion called to a gatekeeper, who swung the gate open, shouting at the dogs to be silent. We rode up an avenue of trees to the main door of the villa and rang on a bell. A servant answered the door and guided me by the light of a lantern up a grand staircase and along a corridor. There he knocked and another servant came to open the door.

The chamber I entered was a strange place. It was lordly in its proportions, a *salone* such as you might see in the palace of a bishop, and there was a cornice of plaster around the ceiling executed with much delicacy and skill. The furnishings were few, however, and mainly draped in cloth, as if to protect them from the sun during a long absence of the owner. Two or three candles miserably lit this whole vast, shadowy space, which smelled of dust. Long doors on the opposite wall gave onto a balcony, from which a merciful breath of air was wafting in.

As I gazed round the room, a door leading off it opened and Madonna Felice della Rovere stepped forward to meet me. She glowed like a jewel in this gloomy setting. She was wearing her usual black, but with a chemise beneath her over-dress of such fine stuff that it seemed to froth like sea foam at her neck and wrists. A pearl necklace circled her neck, as it had the first time I saw her, but this time it was made up of three strands, and gold tracery gleamed among the pearls.

"Is it true that he is dead?" she said, not troubling herself with a greeting. Her eyes glittered.

"Yes, my lady."

She looked at me with triumph and raised her hands in the air, clasped as if in prayer. Then she began to interrogate me on the course of events. I told her of the pope's death and the progress of the duke's illness, and of our looting of the papal treasury. I told her nothing of my passing of the ring to Diego, remembering Machiavelli's warning to me to keep silent and his threat of reprisals if I did not.

Eventually, Madonna Felice released me, saying she had to write a letter. She said she realized the hour of the palace curfew had passed, but I was not to mind, as I could stay here in the house. A servant took me downstairs to a small room with bare walls and an austere bed without a mattress, such as one might imagine occupied by a guard resting between shifts. I curled my lip a little at this poverty of lodging, but, given the lateness of the hour, I had no choice other than to settle to my fate.

I was lying unsleeping on this hard bed, sweating in the airless August night, when I heard the door quietly creaking open. A young woman with a candle entered the room, closing the door silently behind her and crept over to the bedside.

"Messere, my lady wants you upstairs again. There are questions she needs to ask you."

I looked up at her resentfully and asked, "Does it have to be now?" It felt like the middle of the night. The girl looked at me with a haughty air, and then nodded her head, disdaining to squander more words.

I followed this young woman into the corridor, having dressed, and she led me up a back staircase, lighting the way for me with her candle. The house was quite still now, every creak of the stairs whispering complicitly into the silence.

Madonna Felice was in the same room as before, dressed in a loose black silk mantle, with her hair hastily pinned up around her head. The pearls were gone. She looked as though she had been on the point of retiring to bed and then thought better of it. When I arrived, she attacked me anew, this time on the subject of the duke and the strength of his forces. She wanted to know whether he could take Rome into his power and whether there was talk of this in the court and the army. The election of a new pope was supposed to take place within ten days of the death of the old one. Could the duke force this through, whether or not the cardinals of France and England and Germany were able to make their way to Rome by that time?

We spoke for a while of this, I trying to reassure her. The last I had heard, the army of the French king was in Viterbo, no more than fifty miles from Rome. If the duke had any idea of stealing the election through force, this would be sufficient to deter him. In any case, he was too ill to command his troops in person. Don Michelotto was governing for him, and he did not have the same authority as the duke. Madonna Felice seemed at first consoled by this analysis, but then raised new cavils, which I patiently addressed. Her eyes glinted fiercely in the candlelight, no closer to sleep than they had been two hours before.

After this long interrogation, a silence fell between us, which Madonna Felice broke with a change of tone.

"So you are a haunter of houses of ill fame, Messer Matteo. Whoever would have thought it, a mannerly young man like you?"

I looked at her, disconcerted.

"I have money invested in that place. And I dine there sometimes, like tonight. That is all."

She smiled sardonically at that, as if to say she knew better than to believe me, and pulled her mantle more closely around her. I wondered, not for the first time since I had returned to the room, exactly what she was wearing under this gown. Madonna Felice had a provocative manner at times that was difficult to equate with her status as a respectable woman. I had no idea whether, if I were to kiss her, she would welcome my incursion or stamp her foot and call out for her guards.

"Do you hear that?" she said suddenly, tilting her head, and, indeed, the song of a nightingale began to reach us faintly from the balcony. We made our way outside with a candle and listened to that ethereal sound, like some glorious distant message from the gods.

There was a slight breeze in the air, delicious after the heaviness of the day. When the song subsided, Madonna

Felice tossed her head and murmured, "It's been so hot these last nights."

She paused and picked up a great black feathered fan that was lying on the chair on the balcony. She began to fan herself languorously, throwing back her head so I could see her long white throat.

"I was lying awake last night tossing and turning almost until dawn."

This was quite an image to put into my mind. I said without forethought, "I wish I could have been there to assist you, my lady."

Madonna Felice hid her face in her fan for long enough for me to begin regretting this boldness. Then she said, "And how, precisely, would you have assisted me?"

I smiled. She was looking at me now from over her fan.

"I would have sought to entertain you, my lady. To help you pass the long hours of the night."

Madonna Felice lowered her eyes, but not before I had seen the smile in them. I no longer feared she would resist me. A thrill was rising within me at the thought of having this woman who had held me under her thumb for so long. The silence between us went on for a long time; then she put aside her fan.

"I'm sure you can be most entertaining when you try."

THIS SEEMED like an invitation, and I took it greedily. I explored her for a while on the balcony; then we retreated to consummate our lust on her bed, which was in the next room. Madonna Felice was quite pliable to my desires, and I remembered she was a widow, though so young, and hence a woman of experience. I had great pleasure of her; then we lay together naked on the mangled sheets, the hot air of the night barely refreshing our limbs.

"You will tell no one of this," she said eventually. "Or I'll ensure you suffer all the pains of Hell, and some more in addition."

I laughed, annoyed. "I'm not a fool, my lady. I know how to be discreet. Did Endymion tell tales on Diana?"

I could see that Madonna Felice liked this analogy, since it made her a goddess and me a humble shepherd, conveniently fated to sleep whenever she had no use for me. She looked at me from the corner of her eye.

"Maybe he talked in his sleep. Otherwise, how do we know of the story today?"

"Perhaps Diana told the story herself, to teach great ladies they are safe to take their pleasures if they have the sense to choose discreet men as their lovers."

As we engaged in this conversation, I had been touching her breasts with my fingers, which—her breasts, not my fingers—were very perfect, small and chaste and white and exquisitely shaped. At this point, I was once more aroused and we had congress again, more lengthily than the previous time.

This last detail has no relevance to my tale, I must confess. It has nothing to contribute to my story whatsoever. I include it for no reason other than the pleasure of recollecting it, at an age when I count myself favored by the gods if I can satisfy a woman a single time in one night.

NEEDLESS TO SAY, I did not spend the night in the arms of my Diana. After our second amorous joust, I was banished down the servants' stairway to my spartan bedchamber below.

I fell asleep on that hard bed in a witless, happy stupor of the senses, my mind vacant of everything save lewd recollections. I awoke in the quiet dawn groaning as the memory of the previous night began to seep back into my mind. Of all the possible infidelities I could commit, this with her sister-in-law was the one Nicolosa would most hate; I could sense it. I had handed Madonna Felice another weapon to use against me, as if her armory were not already well stocked. I remembered earlier in the evening complacently congratulating myself for mastering my desires at Camilla's. After this commendable achievement, I had yielded to lust with the last woman on this earth I should have so much as looked at—a creature the devil seemed to have crafted with his own busy hands specifically to bring me to grief.

Another truth that forced itself on me in that cruel, contrite dawn was that I had murdered the pope, or been complicit in his murder. Until this point, I had done my best to convince myself that the business with the ring was unconnected with Alexander's illness, but now suddenly I could fool myself no longer. The thing would be clear to a child. There was poison behind the ring, in a secret compartment, and Diego had administered it as soon as he found the occasion—acting on prior instruction, it seemed, for I had passed on no message with the ring. It would not have been too difficult a task for him, I thought, for he was Alexander's food taster and a trusted court servant. He was also a mute, which is to say the last kind of creature a man might expect to carry out such a bold trick.

When I returned to the Vatican, many rumors were circulating concerning Alexander's death. The favored one was that Cardinal Adriano, his host at that fateful dinner, had poisoned the pope and the duke out of fear that otherwise he himself would be killed for his wealth, as many thought had happened to Cardinal Michiel earlier that summer. Another, subtler rumor said that the pope and the duke had indeed intended to kill Cardinal Adriano, but that they had confused the dose or the distribution of the poison and inadvertently poisoned themselves as well.

Such were the darker conjectures, favored by those who love mystery. Less ingenuous men scoffed at these theories as mere flights of fancy, pointing to the fact that the pope's food taster remained hale as a hare. It was an ague, pure and simple, such as had struck a thousand Romans already this summer—why not the pope also? Death has no deference for persons; she strikes the prince in his palace as freely as the peasant at his gate.

As YOU PROBABLY know, it is customary for a pope's body to be displayed after his death to the faithful. Seasoned courtiers in the palace spoke of Pope Innocent's death or even of Pope Sixtus's, almost twenty years earlier, when the clergy of Rome and many laymen and ambassadors had come to pay their respects.

The same custom was observed on this occasion, but the experience was very different. Pope Alexander died in August, when the summer was at its height, and his illness, natural or unnatural, had sinister effects on his body. It was putrefying extremely, even half a day from his death, the flesh darkened and rotting, the body swollen, the tongue huge and black, forcing the mouth open in a manner quite obscene. There was soon nothing of humanity left in this mass of decomposing flesh, whose stench you could smell from all the adjoining rooms.

Don Michelotto, who was effectively running the papal household at this time, had wisely placed on guard in the pope's laying-out chamber men who had no option but to obey him—soldiers of the duke who were in his dungeons for crimes of rape or riot and had been told they could win their freedom through this means. Occasionally he would send someone in to ensure they were doing their job, and one time he chose me.

I went in trepidation to the chamber where the corpse of the pope lay, almost as though I feared he would rise up rotting from his bier to denounce my part in his murder. There were no hordes of the faithful crowding around his body—only the guards, pale and grim-faced, and a few curious souls from the city with cloths held to their mouths, squinting down morbidly at the obscenity on the bed.

I stood there for a few minutes, as I felt duty demanded, then nodded sympathetically to the guards and left. Outside in the corridor, the Venetian ambassador paused to speak to me: an august, acid man of the name of Giustiniano. He was holding a handkerchief delicately to his nose, presumably drenched with some sweet-smelling substance to hold off the smell.

"Young man," he said condescendingly. "How goes the health of the duke?"

His hand hovered near mine, presumably with a coin in it, but I ignored it and answered him coldly and without detail. The Venetians were rubbing their hands at the pope's death, preparing to move on the duke's lands in the Romagna. Looking at this elegantly coiffed man, with his impeccable linen, I saw a vulture waiting to descend.

A few days after my service in the pope's funeral chamber, our army retreated to Nepi, a day's march north of Rome. It was as I had told Madonna Felice. With the army of the French king at Viterbo, it was unthinkable that the duke could continue to occupy Rome as the papal election approached. The Spanish made this even more certain, storming up from Naples themselves to ensure that the French did not have things their own way.

We marched out to Nepi almost in the style of a funeral procession, with the duke at the head of it lying close to death on a litter. Once we had settled ourselves into our camp, perplexed and bored, we amused ourselves playing cards, hunting rabbit and fowl, and pestering any woman rash enough to come our way. Our other amusement was the contests of arms we held with the French troops, in which Dino took a place of honor, to my gratification. In one, he was victorious with the sword against five picked assailants. A French marshal gave him a bag of silver as a prize.

Meanwhile, cardinals were pouring into Rome from all quarters. We heard of the happenings in the city from messengers who rode up each day with the latest news. They first went to the duke's tent and spent an hour or so with him, then came out and distributed selected crumbs to us.

The talk at first was all about the starting favorite, the French candidate, Georges d'Amboise, who was cardinal of Rouen and the king's chief minister. He rode into Rome distributing money right and left like an emperor, and consequently won a hero's acclaim. Roano, as we called him, had the votes of the French cardinals by right and probably thought he could rely also on the Spanish, whose votes were esteemed to be in the gift of the duke. Of the Italian cardinals, he had the Florentines for certain, and might be assumed also to count on Cardinal Giuliano, who had received much support and aid from the French king. To be quite sure of Roano's election, the French released for the conclave another distinguished senior cardinal, Ascanio Sforza, who had been languishing in prison on French territory since his family had been ejected from their dukedom of Milan.

All this looked very well on paper, and Roano was probably already planning his first distribution of cardinals' hats as he rode down in triumphant procession towards Rome. His confidence was premature, however. The Spanish cardinals were not going to vote for a Frenchman when their countries

were at war over Naples, and Cardinal Giuliano, finally seeing his chance, was not going to consign the papacy without
a fight into the hands of a French cardinal who was seventeen
years younger than him. Sforza, too, once the shackles were
off, seemed inclined to explore his own possibilities as a candidate, rather than supporting his former jailors. People also
spoke of a surprise Spanish candidate, Cardinal Carvajal. In
short, the whole thing was a mess.

I FOLLOWED the news of this conclave with great interest,
for my own fate seemed to hang in its balance. If Cardinal
Giuliano were to triumph, I would finally become otiose as a
spy and be at liberty to pursue my own life. When I was free
from duty in Nepi, I sometimes rode out into the countryside
to watch the peasants at their labors and speculate about my
future. It was September now, and the sun was beginning to
soften from the fierceness of August. The grape harvest was
beginning on the south-facing slopes, the vines lushly dripping with fruit.

In the midst of this strange, suspended time, a Sicilian woman
came to our camp offering to tell men's fortunes for money. This
was a curious creature. She was not so very old, perhaps thirty or
thirty-five, yet she did not seem fearful of coming alone into the
company of soldiers—and, indeed, we left her alone, for she had
an uncanny air about her, and no one wished to suffer the evil
eye. She was not ugly, precisely, but she had a tough and weath-
ered look and was one of the tallest women I have ever seen, tall
almost to freakishness. Another oddity about her was the color of
her eyes, one of which was brown and one blue.

Soldiers are the most superstitious men in creation and the
Sicilian witch did a good trade in the few days she was with us.
Her enthusiasts had allocated her a tent, and it was not unusual
to see ten or twelve men standing patiently outside it, waiting

for their future to be read. I was resistant to her lure and scoffed at those who consulted her as gullible fools. I even wrote an epigram in the vernacular deriding her, which circulated widely in the camp. This was folly on my part, because it suggested to my comrades that it would be amusing to get me into the witch's tent, to test whether my skepticism could survive a direct encounter. They persuaded me to this by taunting me that I did not wish to see her because I was afraid of the truths I would hear.

I entered the witch's tent with an ill grace, and a strange smell met my nostrils—vegetal and musky and slightly sweet, presumably a perfume. The woman was sitting hunched behind a table. She looked at me without expression and told me to sit down. The men who had persuaded me to consult with her had already paid her, so there was nothing for me to do but to surrender my hand to her bony, long-fingered, dry one.

She studied the lines on my left hand, and then sat back in her chair.

"I see many secrets."

This took me aback, since there was truth in it, but I did not wish to succumb too easily.

"Everyone has secrets, woman. Tell me something more particular to me."

My adversary looked at me sullenly but complied, bending her head once more over my hand. After a moment, she looked up with an air of triumph.

"You have two children already, even though you are young."

"Close enough, as a guess," I said scornfully. "I have one." I was speaking here of Alessandro, my son with Agnese. It felt strange to acknowledge him aloud as my child, especially to a witch, and I made the sign of the *corna* under the table to protect the poor mite from ill fortune.

The woman shrugged and looked back at me, quite unabashed.

"Perhaps you have two and do not know of it. I am telling you what I see in your lines."

There was a pause and we looked at each other with scarcely concealed hostility.

"So," I said, "what else do you see?"

She gestured at my other hand and held them both for a while, turning them to see the palms in the light, and muttering away to herself. Then she looked at me with a new expression, almost of fear. An answering fear unexpectedly gripped me as I looked at her. I half reached up to cross myself, but forbore.

When she continued to be silent, I got to my feet.

"Well, *brutta strega*? What is it you think you have seen?"

The witch raised herself slowly to her feet opposite me. She was a palm taller than me, a strange and hateful thing in a woman.

"Darkness will come upon you very soon, within a year. When I look at you, I see a dead man."

She shuddered as she said this and shrank back, as though she truly saw a rotting corpse standing before her in its winding sheet. Then she looked away.

"Get out. I do not want you in here."

Now that the witch had come out with this prediction and in such lurid style, I keenly wanted to hear further details of it. An urge came to me to do her some violence, to shake the truth out of her, yet something in me feared to lay a hand on her. Nor did I wish to interrogate her verbally, lest it seem I believed in her follies. I stood for a moment undecided, while the witch whimpered away behind her table. Then I could stand the strangeness of it no longer and barged my way blindly from the tent.

I EMERGED shaken into the camp, trying to compose myself for the interrogation I knew would greet me from my comrades. In the event, I met nothing of the kind. A messenger from Rome had arrived an hour or so earlier and was ensconced with the duke when I entered the witch's tent. Now he was out, and the men of my company were clustered around him like flies around carrion. I approached the group from behind and asked what the news was.

The man in front of me turned and grinned, exposing an execrable set of teeth. "*Habemus papa*," he said in bad Latin, intending to say, "We have a pope."

"Well?" I said. "Della Rovere?" I was shaking as I said this. Everything was happening very suddenly. He shook his head.

"Roano?" I said, my heart plummeting into some dark place. My interlocutor shook his head again, grinning in a superior manner.

"Then who?"

"Guess."

I looked murderously at my informant and might almost have hit him, but the man next to him looked over his shoulder and spoke.

"Piccolomini. Who'd have thought?"

I gaped. This was a Sienese, the nephew of a fine and learned pope, Pius II, but a sickly man and with little of merit to recommend him otherwise. He was quite nakedly a compromise, an unobjectionable puppet to keep the papal throne warm while the true candidates of the election fought it out. The messenger from Rome was speaking, telling of the details of the vote, and the reaction of the Roman people when they heard the announcement. I tried to listen as my mind worked feverishly away, trying to think through the implications of this timid election. At the same time, the witch's predictions, folly and nonsense though I believed them, were echoing darkly in my mind.

XXIV

I F ONE MAN WAS HAPPY at the election of Pope Pius III, as the new pope predictably decided to call himself, it was our master, Duke Valentino. One of Pius's first acts was to confirm the duke in his office as captain-general of the papal troops and as ruler of the duchy of Romagna. Valentino conveniently shared an enemy with the new pope, in the figure of the tyrant of Siena, Pandolfo Petrucci. This Petrucci, as you will remember, was a signatory to the conspiracy against Valentino. Valentino had ejected him from Siena in January, but he had subsequently wormed his way back in.

Our army was allowed back into the city after the election, but it was a far different place from the Rome we had left four weeks earlier. Condottieri of various stripes had established a foothold there and were blustering around as if the city was theirs. Two were sworn enemies of Valentino: Giampaolo Baglioni of Perugia, like Petrucci a survivor of the conspiracy, and his brother-in-law, Bartolomeo d'Alviano, another man who had suffered at the duke's hands and would happy drink his health in a draft of his blood.

These men's troops strutted through the streets of the city, hounding us insolently to show their power, and there was nothing our languishing lord could do to prevent this. Valentino was still transported everywhere on a bier shielded by curtains. No one except Don Michelotto had access to him now. His empire in the Romagna was crumbling. The duke of Urbino was back in his fine palace, and the sole surviving member of the Varano family had limped back to Camerino. Venice was pressing from the north into Rimini and Pesaro. Only Cesena, Imola, and Forlì were holding out.

The duke needed to be in Rome to prepare for the next conclave, which would be soon if the new pope's frailty was anything to go by; yet he also needed to be in Romagna to defend what remained of his lands. A state that has deep-rooted foundations may withstand the incapacity of its ruler, at least for a season. A new state like Valentino's fragile duchy of Romagna, thrown up rapidly through blood and will over the course of a few years, can collapse into dust in as many weeks.

Francesca was back in Rome when I returned, and I went to visit her at the glove maker's as soon as I was able. Our reunion was warm. I clasped her in my arms when I saw her and buried my face for a long time in her nut-brown hair. I was never in love with this girl, as she fell into my hands too easily, and she was too guileless and young to be interesting to me. But I had developed a great fondness for her during our brief time together, and she, I think, also for me.

After we had been reunited in the flesh, Francesca lay looking at me with an anxious expression and told me she had something to tell me. I guessed from her tone before she uttered the words that she was going to tell me that she was with child. As I listened to Francesca stumbling out her revelation, I thought of the fortune-teller at Nepi speaking of my having fathered two children. It chilled me to think of her accuracy on this point, for what did that imply for her prediction of my death?

I must have looked forbidding as I was thinking these thoughts, for, when I turned my attention back to Francesca, she was looking alarmed, as though she was afraid I might throw her out onto the street or deny the paternity of this child.

"Come here, rash girl," I said, winding a strand of her hair round my finger. "Did your mother never warn you of the dangers of mixing with men?"

I reassured her then, brushing away the tears that had sprung in her eyes and told her I would be glad to have a child to succeed me, so some spark of me would live after my death. I did not tell her the fear that was lurking in my heart as I drew her warm young gravid body towards me, that "after my death" might be a time very soon—that I might not even live to see this poor creature born.

SOON AFTER getting back to Rome, I went to Cardinal Giovanni's to learn the gossip of the city. I requested permission first from Don Michelotto; with the political situation as volatile as it was, I did not wish to make a false step. Don Michelotto looked at me probingly, and said he would consult with the duke on the matter. The next day when he saw me, he consented that I go, instructing me only to report back what I heard.

Cardinal Giovanni's rooms were humming extraordinarily with talk of public affairs, a sign to me that we were living an unusual season. Even the cardinal himself had abandoned his usual frivolity to a certain extent. He called me into his study soon after my arrival and questioned me closely on the duke's health and what I knew of his feelings about the candidates for the papacy, by which he meant Roano, della Rovere, Sforza, Carvajal. Like most people in Rome, he was discounting the current pontificate and looking ahead to what would come in its wake.

At the end of our interview, Cardinal Giovanni embraced me and pressed a gift into my hand, a silver medal of the kind that men wear in their hatbands, portraying Jove in the form of an eagle snatching up Ganymede to heaven. The workmanship was very fine, and I had no reason to doubt the cardinal's word when he told me it was a genuine antiquity. We talked of it a little; then the cardinal spoke warmly of his feelings of esteem for me, and his hopes that he would one day be in a position to express this friendship in more concrete terms. What this meant was that he liked the information I had given him and hoped there would soon be more on offer. I replied to him with similar words of compliment, meaning that I would be happy to oblige.

THE NIGHT was clear when I left Cardinal Giovanni's and set off towards the river on my way back to the Vatican. I had no one with me. Usually my servant Masetto would have accompanied me, but he was on leave visiting his family in Frascati, where his mother was ill. I had left early enough to make it back to the palace before the gates closed, and there were still people in the streets in some numbers—mostly men, apart from a few hardy whores.

During my time spying in Imola, I had developed the habit of closely observing all who passed me in the street. As a boy, I had often sauntered along absorbed in my thoughts, but this was a luxury I could no longer afford. I had also become adept at finding pretexts for looking over my shoulder to check whether anyone was following me. Women were invaluable in this. I made myself a dedicated ogler, unable to let a woman walk past me without turning to watch her, be she ever so meager in her charms. When women were scarce on the streets, as now, after dark, I turned my lascivious attention to boys.

Using this precaution, shortly after I left the palace of Cardinal Giovanni, I became aware that someone was following me. He was a tall man dressed in the black habit of a Dominican friar, with a hood falling over his face. I had glimpsed this same man on my way to the cardinal's and had even half-wondered if he was trailing me then. Now I was sure. He was following at perhaps ten yards' distance, a small lantern in his hand, sometimes alone, sometimes absorbed in the crowd.

As I walked on, my neck bristling, I thought nervously about whether I should fear a stiletto in my back from this friar—if friar he was. My main fear was of the Euffreducci, the family of Liverotto, who might still wish to see my blood spilt. Cardinal Giovanni, who was a patron of the Euffreducci through family tradition, had brokered some species of truce for me with the head of the family. But a man may easily enough shake another's hand under the eye of a cardinal in daylight and send an assassin after him under cover of night.

After a few hundred yards, I could tolerate the uncertainty no longer, and turned abruptly into a dark alley on my right. I pulled back into a doorway as soon as I had turned, and waited for the friar to follow in my tracks. He was not quite such a fool as to turn down the alley after me. Instead, he stood hesitating at the entrance to it, peering into the feeble light shed by his lantern, fearing foul play. I lunged at him from the darkness and overpowered him easily, ramming my knee into his groin so he shrieked out in pain. Within seconds, I had him backed against a wall with my knife pressed at his throat.

The friar had dropped his lantern as he fell, but the candle was still guttering within it as it lay on its side. I forced him to his knees so I could right it while keeping my knife at his throat. Then I pulled back his hood, turning his face to the light. What I saw almost made me loose my grip in astonishment. It was Diego, the Spanish mute from the court, my companion in spying for Cardinal Giuliano, and, more recently, my accomplice in eliminating Pope Alexander VI from this earth.

I was mute as Diego himself for a moment; then I said, "Why are you following me? Who are you? *What* are you?"

I shook his head from side to side as I said this, resisting the urge to smash his head against the wall. I was panicking.

"Messer Matteo," Diego said in a hoarse voice, his eyes wide with fear. "For the love of God! I only wanted to talk to you."

I looked at him in horror. He was mute and he was speaking, as clearly as I might speak to you if you were in this room.

"*Dio cane*," I said. I could not say another word. It was as if my horse had turned and begun to talk to me over its shoulder.

Diego crossed himself, muttering at the blasphemy that had escaped me, which was indeed a reprehensible one. Then he said, "We are close to my cell. Come there for a moment. We must talk."

I FOLLOWED the false mute, or false friar, a few streets back on the route by which we had arrived. As I recovered from my shock at his speaking, I realized there was much I wished to know from him, which is why I was content to be led.

My companion turned off the main street and conducted me down an alley, and another, and another, each narrower and more evil smelling than the last. I stumbled after him, my knife in one hand and the lantern in the other, feeling my feet sinking into ordure at each step. The place was practically a sewer. You do not need to go far off the main streets in Rome to find yourself mired in such filth.

Finally, my guide stooped with a key before what looked like an artisan's dwelling and ushered me into a cramped room that, in truth, smelled little better than the street outside. There was a fire burning low in the grate, almost dead, which he bent to stoke. I realized then once and for all that this man was harmless—not a soldier, not an assassin. He bent his neck before me to attend to the fire for a full half minute. I could have slit his throat thrice in that time.

The room we were in was very small, almost a cell, and it was furnished with extreme austerity. A narrow bed stood in the corner of the room, with a chamber pot beneath it that I did not wish to look at too closely. In the other corner of the room, by the fire, there stood a crude pine cassone, with a jug of water and a pewter beaker on top. Above the cassone, a rough-hewn cross hung from a nail in the wall. Beneath it, on the floor, lay a scourge with perhaps ten tails to it, all thickly encrusted with dried blood.

As my antagonist straightened from the fire, I confronted him face-to-face.

"Who are you?"

He looked back at me with a curiosity to match my own.

"Fra Filippo," he said, in an urgent throaty whisper, as though this explained anything at all. It was already clear to me from his accent that this was no Spaniard but a Tuscan, and probably a Florentine. By this time, I was beginning to recognize the truth of the old dictum that the Florentines are the fifth element of the globe, found everywhere on it, along with earth, water, air, and fire.

Fra Filippo was continuing, in a curious, caressing tone.

"Who was it who gave you the ring? Was it *him*?"

I looked into his eyes and saw madness.

"Who do you mean by *him*?"

"Fra Girolamo," he whispered. This was Fra Girolamo Savonarola, the face on the ring, dead these last five years and burned down to dust by the Florentines. I had half-anticipated that Fra Filippo would say this, yet a feeling of fear still shot through me when I heard him say the name, as if this shadowy dead friar was lurking in the room.

Fra Filippo was expecting an answer. I looked at him, trying to find my way into the rhythms of his lunacy.

"No, it was another."

"Fra Domenico, perhaps?"

A faint memory came to me that this was the name of one of Savonarola's companions, who had been executed alongside him.

"Perhaps. It was difficult to see. You could not see his face. He had a hood. And there was a strange light around his face. I could not fathom what I saw."

I paused, out of my depth, but my answer seemed to content Fra Filippo.

"There are many reasons, my son, why the living should not see the faces of the blessed."

I thought I should I press ahead with my advantage.

"Tell me of the beginning of your task. Did your instructions come originally from *him*?"

"They did. It was when I was in prison."

"In prison?"

"Soon after his death. They said I was there for sedition."

"Fra Girolamo spoke to you while you were in prison?"

"He told me I must kill the Antichrist. When the moment was right. He would send me a sign."

"Did you see him with your own eyes?"

"No, brother. It was not given to me. I merely heard his voice."

"And Cardinal della Rovere? Did Fra Girolamo tell you to serve his cause also? "

"No. It was the woman who told me that." His gaze softened as he said this

"The woman?"

"Angelica, they called her. She followed me here, to this place. She is the Woman of the Apocalypse!"

This last phrase was hissed out with great emphasis. I stared at him. There was nothing I could think of to say. The Woman of the Apocalypse was the woman garbed in the sun with the moon under her feet and the crown of twelve stars of whom the evangelist John mystically speaks in *Revelations*. What she might have to do with Angelica was a mystery the deepest theologians would be hard put to parse.

"He is not the Angelic Pope, you know."

Fra Filippo said this sternly, as if I had just boldly put this notion to him. In the lore of the Apocalypse, this was the final pope who would come at the end of time.

"Cardinal della Rovere?"

"Do not mistake it," the friar said. "He will rule, but only in the manner of the Baptist, preparing the way for the Lord."

He leaned forward still closer to me then, until I could smell his breath above the general stench of the room. It had an odor of rotting fish. I almost gagged.

"Cardinal Giuliano della Rovere is of the blessed, but he will not usher in the kingdom of Heaven. He will rule God's kingdom here on earth twelve hundred days and sixty; then Fra Girolamo will descend to earth in his living person to rule until the last day."

"In his living person," I murmured reverently. Fra Filippo's voice had dimmed to something almost inaudible as he pronounced his last words. I knew I would be sick if I did not leave this room soon.

Fra Filippo was eyeing me with a changed air, his rapture seemingly dissolved.

"You are a worldly man, my son. When I was following you, I saw how your eyes strayed after all the boys and women who passed you. But there is time for you to be saved. You must learn how to mortify the flesh. It is your enemy."

He reached, as he spoke, towards the scourge that had been lying on the cassone. I watched his fingers fondling its crusted knots as a man might stroke the head of a favorite dog.

"If you are not ready, my son, I will happily administer it to you myself," he continued, a little too eagerly. "You would not believe how many times, back in my novitiate, we novices helped each other out in this way."

"A thousand thanks, Fra Filippo," I said, edging towards the door. "I have a favorite scourge of my own at home, which was blessed at the shrine of Loreto. I could not bear to use anything else."

My companion nodded understandingly.

"Only make sure that you do."

I nodded my assent and reached for the door handle, desperate to be gone. Fra Filippo gripped me with his bony hand above my elbow and for a moment I feared I was going to have to do him some violence to release myself.

"If Fra Domenico comes to you again, you will tell me?"

"Do not fear, Fra Filippo. You will be the first to know if the Lord chooses me once again as his vessel."

I peeled his fingers from my arm, drew my cloak around my shoulders, and moved out gratefully into the foul-smelling street.

I MADE my way back to the Vatican without incident, squeaking in within the curfew, and lay for a long while pondering the extraordinary tale I had just heard. I had barely had a chance to think as Fra Filippo was speaking, so intently had I been concentrating on keeping in step with his mad logic. Now I attempted to piece the story together. He had been suborned through a trick, presumably orchestrated by Machiavelli, while he was in prison in Florence. He had been convinced of his mission to ensure the death of the Antichrist, which was to say the pope, and the need to masquerade as a mute. This was all clear enough; yet the more I thought of it, the more remarkable it seemed that a man with his faculties intact had succeeded so long in passing as incapable of speech. I had sometimes seen Fra Filippo's fellow servants baiting him, as thoughtless men like to bait the deficient. He remained absolutely silent, however cruel the insults they directed at him. He would probably have remained mute on the rack.

Only Angelica had found him out, with that sharp intelligence of hers, weaving Cardinal Giuliano into the story that Machiavelli had already fixed in the friar's mind. Had she intentionally cast herself as the woman of the Apocalypse, I wondered, or simply followed him to his cell, having seen something that gave her grounds for suspicion, and let his inventive madness do the rest? I felt Angelica's loss keenly as I speculated on this matter, for I would have given much to hear her own version of the story. I could very easily imagine laughing over it with her. I could still hear her laughter in my mind.

XXV

I DID NOT GET TO SLEEP until very late on the night of my encounter with Fra Filippo and was woken a few hours later by a tumult in the corridor outside my room. I put my head out into the corridor, then dragged myself over to a window from which I could look into the courtyard. Soldiers, priests, and courtiers were hastening through with their heads bent. Others were clustered in loud, gesticulating knots in the corners. At first I could understand nothing of what was being said, or rather shouted. Then I grasped it. Our poor interim pope had breathed his last.

I must confess that, when I heard this news, my first impulse was to wonder whether he was poisoned. It is a fundamental urge of human nature to seek conspiracies in all things, especially those having to do with the sudden deaths of popes. Looking back now, however, it seems to me that Pius's death required no more than natural causes to explain it. The ritual of the papal coronation required the poor gout-ridden old man to be on foot for eight hours, clad for much of the time in a fearsome tiara. Then, when he recovered from the experience, it was only to find himself in the thick of a pope's office, which is to say surrounded by wolves. It is possible that he was poisoned, for no pope is without enemies, and Pope Pius had a desperate and bold one in Pandolfo Petrucci. But I prefer to think that God, having selected him as his vicar, then took pity on him and gathered him to heaven before he had a chance to imperil his soul through long exercise of the office of pope.

WITH THE new conclave that Pius's death had occasioned, Rome was suddenly afire once again with partisan scheming. The mood was the more frenzied because the interval between conclaves had been so much shorter than envisaged. After the last election, the worst pessimist among the candidates would have thought he had six months to oil up his supporters and prepare for the next conclave. In fact, Pius's pontificate had lasted the full glory of twenty-six days.

My true master, Cardinal Giuliano della Rovere, shone through almost from the first day of the electoral maneuvers. No one could quite believe his dominance and how rapidly it was achieved. I could believe it less than any man. For eighteen months now, I had been toiling away thanklessly in the service of this beleaguered and ill-omened prelate. Now I discovered to my astonishment that I had picked the right horse all along.

Looking back now, I think his years in exile under Alexander were the making of Cardinal Giuliano. He sat and stewed in his palace in Savona, and meditated on the loss of the '92 election and learned his bitter lessons and applied his bitter rules. I had been a victim of his shrewdness myself, and could imagine very well the way in which he was working on his potential electors. He diagnosed men's desires and weaknesses with a clear eye, and then dug into them relentlessly at their roots.

Among those whom Cardinal Giuliano bought with his promises was Duke Valentino, who was considered to control the votes of the Spanish cardinals. There were ten of these, a significant block within the College, and one Cardinal Giuliano was most eager to have. To secure these votes, the cardinal offered Valentino continuing office in his post as commander of the papal troops and confirmation of his rule in Romagna. The negotiations over this agreement took place over several days, during which the cardinal's ambassadors could frequently be seen scurrying through the back entrance of the Castel Sant'Angelo. The duke had withdrawn to this fortress during the pontificate of his ally Pius, arguing that the presence in Rome of enemy condottieri such as Baglioni and d'Alviano was placing his life under threat.

The result of these negotiations was a formal agreement, signed by the cardinal and the duke, and witnessed by the Spanish cardinals for security. This was a reassuring sight, and all the men of the duke's household took cheer and began to borrow against their expected stipends on the strength of it. I was no different from my fellows, but it is not only hindsight that makes me say that my trust in this outcome was not total—for had not the conspirators walked from their parleys with Valentino with a similar piece of paper in their hand?

THE TIME between the death of one pope and the election of the next is a strange, slightly unhinged period for those living close to it in Rome. I had become accustomed to this strangeness now, with my second interregnum in less than a month. The duke's army was once more banished to a safe distance from the city, as were the rival forces of Baglioni and d'Alviano and the Orsini and Colonna clans. This time I remained behind in the duke's skeleton household in Rome, helping to safeguard his possessions and gathering information to report back to him. The gossip on the election was so intense in the days leading up to it that I was writing to him by courier sometimes three times a day.

One evening during this time, I went down to Camilla's to dine and entered her main room to find Machiavelli ensconced there by the fire. This was not entirely surprising, as most powers in Italy were sending observers to Rome in this delicate period, but the sight of this man was still enough to spoil my appetite for supper. Our last meeting had cruelly revealed the power he held over me, and I had meditated on it since with much bitterness. Must I now tolerate the sight of him sitting at his ease in Camilla's parlor, poking a cuttlebone into my parrot's cage, and leering into his hostess's enticing cleavage as if the place were his own?

I was almost ready to turn on my heel when I saw this unwelcome guest, but Camilla, with her whore's persuasive genius, drew me into their circle. She had seen the coldness with which I greeted her new Florentine friend and did not wish either of us to leave displeased if she could help it. She had fresh reasons for goodwill towards me, as we had recently embarked on a new business venture, buying a pawnbroker's shop a small distance from her house. This was nominally run for us by a Spanish Jew named Messer Isacco, but the purchase money and the bulk of the takings were ours.

In this manner, with assistance from Camilla's emollient graces, I made my peace with Messer Niccolò. He was most solicitous of our friendship. He had even brought along a gift for me, an obscene poem of his own composition, most elegantly copied and bound. Before long, our talk drifted to the topic of the moment, and this conversation so absorbed me that I began to forget my rancor. The Florentines had begun the race as supporters of the French cardinal Roano, the favorite of the previous enclave, but Messer Niccolò now declared himself quite resigned to the victory of Cardinal Giuliano.

"If he keeps a tenth of his promises, Florence should be safe enough with him. That would be ten percent more promises than Alexander was used to observe, but I suppose it's not too much to hope."

Messer Niccolò gave me a sardonic look from the corner of his eye as he spoke of Cardinal Giuliano's likely elevation to the throne of Peter, and I knew he was thinking he had done me a favor in plotting Pope Alexander's demise. This he practically confessed to me in a conversation a few weeks later, when we were alone and able to speak with more candor.

"Admit it," he said. "You are like the virgin who protests when she is ravished, when in fact she was dying to find out what all the fuss was about."

"Meaning? That I was secretly longing to murder the pope, but would not have had the courage without your assistance?"

Messer Niccolò raised his eyebrows and observed me with the dignity befitting the second secretary of the Florentine republic.

"Who said anything about murdering a pope?"

CARDINAL GIULIANO della Rovere was elected pope on the first day of November of the year 1503, in the shortest conclave known to papal history, with the votes of all the cardinals but three. I was playing at *pallacorda* with a colleague when a page told us of this news.

"Shit," my companion said, hurling the ball back across the cord so that it narrowly missed taking my head off. "My money was on Roano. What about you?"

"Mine was on della Rovere," I said, meaning more than he could possibly imagine. "Let me buy you a drink."

I FOUND IT hard to contain myself that day. It seemed to me that I was finally out of the labyrinth into which I had wandered unknowingly when Liverotto wreaked his havoc in Fermo. I had preserved faith with the cardinal at the risk of my life, helping him accomplish his ends, as I simultaneously accomplished mine. Now these ends were achieved. Liverotto was dead, which was what I had craved, and the cardinal was pope, which was what he had longed for. All that was needed now was for the heavens to open and flowers to rain down from the skies.

This was what my heart was singing, but my reason was properly more wary. I would not like you to think me a naïve fool, at least by this time in my life. The duke would not be happy at the thought of my abandoning him at this juncture. He was short of troops. He had sent a contingent of his forces to help the French in Naples, as he was bound to by his alliance with King Louis, and many of the Spanish soldiers in his ranks had defected to join the Spanish army, out of patriotism or greed. He had a force camped near Orvieto under Don Michelotto, but this was nothing like the army it had been. If you excluded his garrisons in those cities of the Romagna that remained faithful, he was down to perhaps a mere thousand men.

Despite this, I was full of hope. I thought I would approach Cardinal Giovanni when a few weeks had passed and ask him to beg the duke as a favor to cede me to his household. I would candidly confess to the cardinal that I was not truly seeking an engagement in his service, but that this was an expedient to regain my freedom. I did not think he would refuse me this help. Nor could I imagine Valentino denying Cardinal Giovanni a trivial favor of this sort if he asked for it. The political situation was a volatile one, with the war between the French and the Spanish still unsettled in Naples and a pope whose true colors had yet to be seen. In these circumstances, no prudent man could afford to squander an ally, and a cardinal was a cardinal and a Medici a Medici. These were my calculations, and very fine ones they were—except that Fortune had quite different plans in store.

THE EVENING after the election I dined at Camilla's, planning to go on afterwards to spend the night with Francesca. I thought I could risk a night away from the palace, as the duke was still absent from Rome. Camilla's was awash with custom, as you would expect at such a time, when half of Christendom had descended on the city for the election. A French cardinal was reputed to have visited the previous evening, fresh from the conclave, taking advantage of its early conclusion. Camilla would neither confirm this rumor nor deny it, deflecting all questions with her most angelic smile.

I dined with Machiavelli, who had become a frequent visitor to the house, his liking for Camilla having burgeoned into a passion of some species. He had a propensity for such ill-judged attachments, I discovered, little fitted to his character as a man of the world. As we discussed the new pope's prospects, I kept noticing his eyes straying towards Camilla, like a well-schooled dog casting a wistful eye towards his master. Occasionally she would come over and gratify him with a word before flitting off to greet some new guest.

After a while, I felt a tug at my sleeve, and a girl named Violante slid in to sit beside me, laying her head on my shoulder. I ignored her and continued to talk with Machiavelli and sup on my excellent venison stew. This girl was a new addition to the household, and she annoyed me, although I could see why Camilla had engaged her. She was attractive in a dark, voluptuous way, with thick, lustrous hair, and had a remarkably pure and clear singing voice. What I disliked about Violante was her ingratiating manner. She always affected a great intimacy with me, although God knows I did nothing to encourage her. This time she was even freer than usual, nestling against me like a lover and searching out my free hand under the table with hers.

Just as I was about to push her away, I suddenly found myself tensing, for something hard was being pressed into the palm of my hand. I recognized the shape of it with a shock, and closed my fingers around it, transferring it into the pocket of my doublet. Machiavelli was in full flow, embarked on a lengthy analysis of what the new pope's election meant for the war between the French and Spanish. I eased my arm round Violante's shoulders as I listened, then let my hand fall lower and begin to unlace the strings of her bodice.

"Don't let me stop you," Machiavelli said, interrupting himself to ogle as Violante's breasts were revealed. I kissed the girl very lewdly, like a man in a hurry.

"If you'll excuse me for a moment," I said. "Don't let them take my plate." Then I rose to retire with Violante upstairs.

WHEN WE were safely behind the door of a bedroom, I took out the object Violante had handed me. As I had suspected, it was a cameo, slit down the middle, of the type I knew only too well. I fished in my doublet for my own under Violante's curious gaze, nervous about what this portentously timed contact from the new pope might mean. I could see at a glance that the images matched, yet I lined them up sedulously, bringing them close to the lantern we had brought with us. This girl's sudden revelation as an agent of Cardinal Giuliano had disconcerted me, and I was feeling edgy, fearing some trick.

Violante had hitched up her dress and was feeling for something she had concealed beneath her chemise. She emerged with a small leather bag, which she held out to me, still warm from where it had lain against her skin. Inside was a paper wrapping tied with many intricate knots and with seals on both sides. I turned away from the girl so she would not see me open it and carefully cut through the string with the point of my dagger. Wrapped in white silk within the paper was a gold chain, set with four rubies alternating with diamonds.

I gazed stunned for a moment at this beautiful object, the reward for my long fidelity. I do not know what I expected to find within the paper, but this bounty was unsought, manna raining from heaven. I remembered Madonna Felice in her hideout near Fermo holding out as a lure that her father would compensate me richly for my services when he became pope, but the prospect of this happening had then seemed so distant that the hope of gain had not lodged in my mind.

Violante had said something I had to ask her to repeat.

"You're to read the description and seal it with your one if it's accurate."

"My one?"

"You know, the cameo thing. Here's some wax if you need it."

The description was written in a minuscule hand on the paper that the chain had been wrapped in. It was very precise, detailing the number of links in the chain and even the facets in each stone. I checked the correspondence of the particulars and sealed the paper as instructed, keeping the chain shielded from Violante's view.

"Thank you," I said eventually, handing Violante a coin, which she pocketed very swiftly. "You handled that cleverly downstairs."

She nodded coolly in reply. She was quite different from her usual wheedling self, almost haughty. I liked her better in this guise and half regretted we were not doing what we were supposed to have gone upstairs to do.

The next thing she said made me forget these light thoughts.

"You're to give your messages to me from now on. Those are your instructions. We can do it this way, or you can hand them to me downstairs if you think that's safe."

I looked at her, thrown. I could hardly understand what she was saying.

"What do you mean, I'm to give my messages to you?"

"For *them*. What do you think?"

I swallowed hard.

"I thought … I did not think they would wish me to continue working for them, now that …"

Violante shrugged, after waiting for me to complete my sentence. "You'll have to take that up with them."

There was a pause, then she said, "We should be going down now."

I nodded. I must have been looking at her like a man who had just heard his death sentence read out. Unexpectedly, she smiled in a comradely manner.

"Remember we're supposed to be lovers now, *bello mio*. You'll have to be a little nicer to me in company."

I tried to force a smile. "Don't worry, you'll be fighting me off." Then I asked, "Was it *her* that you spoke to?"

Violante paused, as if deciding whether it was safe to reply, then nodded warily.

"Tell her this," I said. "I'll continue to serve her, but only for as long as I remain with the duke."

WELL, I COULD say this as firmly as I wished, like a man in control of his destiny, but it was not clear to me at all that I had a choice in the matter. Madonna Felice della Rovere had the same power to destroy me with Nicolosa as she had before, in Fermo, when she forced me to do her bidding. Indeed, she had more, if she cared to use it. She knew of my dealings with Camilla, and she had evidence herself of my faithlessness as a lover. It would be easy enough to paint me with every hue of darkness the most ingenious painter could devise.

I mulled this matter nervously in the days after my meeting with Violante, while I fretted over what to do with the jeweled chain she had given me. I had to carry it with me at all times, stuffed into a long inner pocket in the back of my doublet that Alfonso had stitched for me to conceal my stiletto. I had no strongbox where I could leave it, and I did not dare take it to a dealer, nor even to my banker, for such men talk. Eventually, I took the thing to Messer Isacco, the pawnbroker who ran the shop that I owned with Camilla. I asked him to sell it for me discreetly, promising that if he could find me a price over two hundred ducats, I would give him a quarter of the excess as a fee.

When I returned to the palace from this errand, in no fine spirits, my servant Masetto handed me a message. I assumed it was routine, a note from some creditor, and carelessly tore it open at the seal. Then I recognized the hand and read. I was so struck by wonderment that I stood staring at the paper like a peasant gawping at a paved street on his first trip to town. It was a note from Nicolosa, telling me that she was in Rome to see the new pope's *possesso* and summoning me to an address near Santa Maria della Pace.

PERHAPS YOU will say that it was not such a strange thing that Nicolosa should have come to Rome at this time. It is not often that a woman's former father-in-law accedes to the throne of Saint Peter. What more natural than that she would wish to see him in his glory as pope? Still, the thing left me astonished. I could not equate the idea of Rome with my austere Nicolosa. I felt great delight at the news of her coming but also a certain trepidation—for here was my love in the same city as Madonna Felice, and not a thousand paces from where Camilla plied her trade.

I made my way to the address Nicolosa had given me as soon as I was free, having washed and changed my linen and scented my hair. The house was a good one, a neat, modern villa with a garden behind it, the air not too ill for the center of town. I was shown into a room at the back of the house, where Nicolosa received me. Another guest was there with her, a lady of perhaps thirty, who greeted me with an inquisitive stare.

The two continued their conversation after the interruption of my arrival, and I watched, trying to sate my eyes on my beloved without attracting the suspicion of her guest, who had a busy, sharp, noticing air. Nicolosa was wearing a gown of black taffeta, with sleeves of brocade, and her hair was braided and piled on her head in a most artful manner. It was a bright day for November, and the sun slanting in through the window picked out the threads of silver in her sleeves. I realized to my astonishment that this was the first time I had seen Nicolosa dressed for company since the day of her wedding. I felt almost daunted by her polish. I had lost the habit of consorting with respectable women—or at least in respectable circumstances. It seemed presumptuous of me even to imagine that such a noble creature could be mine.

Nicolosa's guest was reproaching her for having rented a house when she should have come to stay with her kinsmen in Rome. I had gathered at our introduction that this lady was a cousin herself, on Nicolosa's mother's side. Nicolosa excused herself, saying she had not wished to give trouble and that an acquaintance from Fermo had placed this house at her disposal, so that she had felt it would be discourteous not to take it. I listened, eyeing her serene face and wondering whether she was lying, whether she had rented this house so she might receive me at night.

Once she had fended off her cousin's complaints, Nicolosa invited us to take a turn in the garden. A servant brought furs for the ladies, and we stepped out into this pleasant walled space. Nicolosa's cousin, whose name was Madonna Laura, began to speak of the church behind the house and the statue of Our Lady on the facade that had bled miraculously twenty years earlier when a loose-living youth had shied a stone at it one night after losing at cards. She looked sideways at me when she spoke of this gambler and blasphemer, as if suspecting I might be another such man. Then she stooped to examine a plant, and I felt Nicolosa's hand suddenly, warm against mine, folding something into my palm—something hard, wrapped in paper. Immediately afterwards, she bent to join her cousin in her horticultural musings, giving me a chance to spirit the thing away.

I RETURNED that same night, under a moon so full and broad that it might almost as well have been daylight. The streets around the house were quiet, with not so much as a dog abroad, let alone a Virgin-desecrating rogue. I let myself in at the garden door with the key Nicolosa had passed to me as serenely as a paterfamilias returning home from his business of the day. My passage through the house was similarly well fated. The instructions Nicolosa had written on the paper wrapping the key were precise, telling me where the servants slept and which steps on the main staircase might creak. My heart was beating hard as I crept up the stairs, but through desirous anticipation, not fear.

Sometimes we do not know how tired we are on a journey until the day's end, when we stumble down from our horses, nor how thirsty we are until we find ourselves guzzling water straight from the well pail without drawing breath. I did not realize how much I had missed Nicolosa until I held her in my arms that night and breathed in the familiar scent of her skin. She was dressed in a loose white silken robe when I entered her chamber and her hair was a dark cloud around her head, freed from its braids of the day. I went over to her and took her face in my hands and kissed her without a word for a very long time. Then I caught her up and carried her to the bed.

WE TALKED for hours that first night. Although I could not confide in Nicolosa any of the chief cares that pressed on me, it was balm to me even just to hear her speaking. We had extinguished her candle and opened the shutters of the casement to let in the moonlight. Her face looked celestial bathed in this pale silver light, as if an angel had alighted at my side.

Nicolosa was excited to be in Rome and reeled off a list of the ruins and churches she intended to see on her visit. She wished to see Nero's house, which I had described to her in Fermo, and she was disappointed when I told her no respectable woman had seen it, since you had to be lowered down on a rope. She asked me sleepily whether any unrespectable women had seen it, and I told her a little of Rome's courtesans and their boldness. I was braced for her to ask me whether I knew any such women and was preparing a careful answer in my mind in case she did so. By good fortune, however, my beloved was weary from her journey and chose that moment to drift into sleep.

I PUSHED my anxieties from my mind while Nicolosa was in Rome, like a farmer settling down to dine while the wolves prowl his sheepfold. To have her here so unexpectedly, like a gift from God, put me in a kind of ecstasy. I was giddy with excitement during my nights with her, like a child on the morning of a feast-day. I would hardly let the poor woman take her rest without importuning her with declarations of love. I showered her with gifts, also—so many that she laughingly told me to desist lest I finish in prison for debt. She had little inkling of the depth of my pockets. Messer Isacco had sold the gold chain for me, fetching two hundred and thirty ducats, of which I gave him eight for his fee.

My time with Nicolosa was not limited to our nights together. On a few days, when I was free of my duties, we rode out with Madonna Laura and her husband to see the sights of Rome and watch the preparations for the pope's *possesso*. Triumphal arches of wood and paste were being erected all along the processional route—vast constructions ten *braccia* high, painted with simulations of antique sculpture, so that a man might imagine himself back in the Rome of the old emperors. These arches had many people muttering, as also did the name the new pontiff had adopted, which was Julius. Some took this as a reference to Caesar, a controversial model for a pope.

Nicolosa had prepared the ground for me with her cousin by speaking of me as a ward of her father's, much loved by him and hence loved by her also, out of respect for his memory. I was a good-hearted youth, but wayward by nature and corrupted by my time in the duke's service. One reason why she had come to Rome was to exert her influence to guide me back onto the right path.

Madonna Laura took to the project of my reform with great zeal, quickly resolving that I must settle on a career in the church, as the best means of advancement for a young man of no birth and with no taste for a military life. An uncle of hers who was elderly and ailing held a benefice in Calabria that she would press him to bequeath to me. I needed only minor orders to qualify for this office; my ordination could follow in time. Madonna Laura was most warm in her advocacy of the priesthood, speaking much of the benefits of this holy and profitable profession. She seemed quite confident that her uncle would do her the favor of dying as soon as he had left me his heir.

When she was not busy plotting my path to ecclesiastical preferment, Madonna Laura exercised herself in urging Nicolosa to remarry. She was young and would soon have been a widow for two years, quite enough to satisfy God and propriety—yet here she was still in mourning, leading a hermit's life in Fermo, allowing herself to wither on the vine. She owed it to herself and her family to take a new husband, and there would no lack of suitors if she were minded to it. Ten candidates might be listed without a moment of thought who would leap at the chance of Nicolosa's hand.

I rode along morosely when Madonna Laura was on this theme, sometimes falling back with relief on the conversation of her husband, an amiable ex-soldier who had retired after losing half a leg at Fornovo and liked to relive his campaigns. The prospect of Nicolosa's remarriage struck ice into my heart, even though I had no reason to think she was eager to embrace it, any more than I was the ecclesiastical state. I shrank in my own reckoning as I listened to Madonna Laura's litanies of eligible bridegrooms. Who was I beside these virile paragons, with their ancient names and their fine military promise and noble presence, and their ample palaces and country estates?

I WATCHED Pope Julius's *possesso* with Nicolosa and Madonna Laura from a balcony belonging to a friend of Madonna Laura. It was warm enough to sit out in the sun, even though the December air was chill beneath its rays. The women were heaped with furs and servants brought us warm spiced wine and wrapped stones hot from the fire for our feet and hands. I was dressed in a manner that did not disgrace this delicate company, in a black cape lined sumptuously with marten fur. A French nobleman had pawned it at Messer Isacco's shop and I had begged it as a loan, even though it was still within its redemption term. A fear nagged me the whole day that its owner would recognize it from the street and storm up to strip it from my back.

We were well situated for the procession, in a palazzo located directly on the route from Saint Peter's to the Lateran, close to one of the triumphal arches we had seen raised up in the previous days. We watched, kneeling, as the consecrated host passed by under its scarlet baldachin, then sat to observe its motley army of followers: the captains of the *rioni* with their gaudy banners; the Roman barons, bristling with arms, Madonna Laura's husband among them; the cardinals in their crimson; the heads of the curia; the knights of Saint John in their somber black robes. It was a strange, Roman mixture of grandeur and mayhem. Aside from the raucousness of the bystanders, jostling for position in the crowd, two fights broke out within the procession itself during the time it was passing us. Even the sacramental baldachin kept lurching precariously as its bearers fell out of step.

Finally Pope Julius himself rode past, under a canopy like the host, mounted on a magnificent white steed for which he must have scoured half of Italy. He was preceded by servants in livery hurling out handfuls of new-minted coins and a knot of trumpeters valiantly blasting away above the crowd. He was bearing on his head the extraordinary gold tiara he had commissioned for the occasion, not wishing to sully his head with a crown that had touched Pope Alexander's reviled pate. The tiara was a monstrous thing, half an arm's length in height and glittering with jewels, like something you might imagine being worn by some ancient barbarian tyrant. The impression was of a man of inexhaustible wealth, who could laugh Croesus and Midas to scorn. Only later did we discover that our canny new pontiff had not paid out a *soldo* for this magnificence. The tiara was a gift from a Sienese banker friend, Agostino Chigi, who had also funded Julius's extensive campaign of electoral bribery, rightly judging that this was money well invested in pursuit of the prize of becoming the chief banker to the pope.

CARDINAL GIOVANNI hosted a banquet that evening to celebrate the new pope's accession, an extravagant affair featuring a roast swan with its feathers reattached and two rubies replacing its eyes, a strange effect. There was also an oak tree spun from sugar, most beautiful, in allusion to the della Rovere arms. I escorted Camilla there, dressed for caprice in the ancient Greek style, in a draped white tunic that showed her ankles, with a cunningly wrought gold necklace, which she had borrowed from our pawnshop, woven seductively into her blond hair. Cardinal Giovanni was much taken with this costume and composed a Greek epigram on the spot, comparing her to Aphrodite freshly stepped from the waves.

The cardinal was in excellent spirits at this time, for his tide was rising with the new pontificate. He had supported Julius warmly at his election and was now reaping his fruits. His guest of honor that evening was a nephew of Pope Julius, who had been created cardinal that same day, having traversed the clerical *cursus honorum* with a rapidity rarely seen among those not closely related to popes. When I learned of this new cardinal and heard his name, Galeotto della Rovere, I thought immediately of my tutor in espionage, the young man named Galeotto who had greeted me when I emerged from the Cloaca and whom I had subsequently seen at Cardinal Giovanni's wearing a beard and in secular dress. Indeed, he it was: his sallow, humorous face, shaven now as befitted a priest, was one of the first I saw when I stepped into the room.

Cardinal Giovanni called me over to introduce to his guest, speaking in Latin as he often liked to, and effusively praising my beauty, intelligence, and good character.

"The beauty I can judge with my own eyes," Cardinal Galeotto said, somewhat lecherously. "We'll have to see about the rest."

Later in the evening, he found a moment to draw me aside, when the company was distracted by a dance Camilla was treading with one of Cardinal Giovanni's painted boys, to the accompaniment of a harp.

"A pleasure to make your acquaintance, young man," he said. "I hope we will have the opportunity to meet again soon."

He spoke this in a suggestive tone, as if pressing for an assignation, and passed a note into my hand as he turned away to leave. The move was cleverly done, as no one observing us would think this exchange other than amorous—for who would instruct his spy in so open a way? The note was written in code and contained instructions for how I might contact the cardinal secretly, if I needed to, without going through his household. I committed the details to my memory and the note to the fire.

On the last day of Nicolosa's stay in Rome, I went round her house in the afternoon, around the hour of nones. I knew I would see her that night, but I had arranged to see her now also, even with her maid stitching away in the corner so we could not speak freely. Melancholy was already taking possession of my soul at the thought that the next day she would be gone.

I felt a powerful urge to flee as soon as I entered the house, for it was full of servants wearing the della Rovere livery. The notion of feigning a sudden illness ridiculously flashed through my head, but it was too late. The servant who had let me in was returning to fetch me, having announced my arrival. With a sense of doom, I allowed myself to be escorted into the room where Nicolosa was receiving her guest.

Nicolosa and Madonna Felice were sitting by the fire next to a small table on which a lute was lying and some papers. Their dark heads were close when I went in and they seemed to have been laughing about something. It was terrible to see these two women together, knowing the power Madonna Felice held over me. It would hardly have made me more anxious to see Nicolosa comfortably settled by the fire with a snake.

Nicolosa stood as I entered the room and came over to me.

"Let me introduce you to the lady Felice della Rovere, daughter of His Holiness. My countryman Matteo da Fermo."

This was a strange game, but I had no choice but to submit to it. I made Madonna Felice a low bow, and she acknowledged me graciously.

"I have been wishing to meet you, Messer Matteo. I have read some of your verse."

I smiled to acknowledge the compliment. It was even possible that she was telling the truth. I had begun to circulate a little of my poetry, urged to it by Camilla, who wished it to be known for professional reasons that she associated with literary men.

"You must write something for me," Madonna Felice continued. "A song for the lute. My music teacher can set it."

I bowed obsequiously to thank her for this honor and protested my inadequacy for the task. After this we spoke stiltedly of the weather, of the cold turn that morning and the danger of another winter like last year. My mind was working furiously during these innocuous exchanges, wondering whether Violante had delivered her message and what Madonna Felice had made of it. Nicolosa was silent, her eyes moving appraisingly between my face and Madonna Felice's as we spoke.

After longer than I would have wished of this torment, Madonna Felice turned to Nicolosa.

"Well, my dear, this has been quite charming, but I should be leaving."

To my distress, Nicolosa replied solicitously, "Will you not take some refreshment before you go?"

She stood as she said this, as though poised to instruct her servants. Madonna Felice smiled.

"If it would not be too much trouble ..."

The moment Nicolosa was out of the room, she was over at my side, hissing in my face.

"You do not mean to desert us now?"

"No, my lady," I said despairingly, glancing over my shoulder at the door.

"The girl told me ..."

"My lady," I whispered urgently. I think I even seized her by the wrist. "You have nothing to fear. I shall not leave the duke's service without your consent. You have my word on it."

"It will not be long now, I swear."

We were staring into each other's eyes, a hand's breadth apart—to all appearances, two ardent lovers seizing a moment to speak. By some miracle, Madonna Felice succeeded in melting back into her corner by the time Nicolosa entered the room. My heart was beating fast, as though I had escaped from a brush with physical danger. My enemy was the picture of calm.

"I have been importuning your delightful Messer Matteo about the poem I want from him," she said brightly to Nicolosa as she entered. "I have confessed I am the feeblest singer in the world, so he can hope for no glory from it. A madrigal or a *frottola*, what do you think?"

WHEN I RETURNED to see Nicolosa that night, I was submitted to an interrogation on my impressions of her famous sister-in-law. I answered as blandly as I could, my heart sadly vexed at the thought of the deceptions that seemed to cling to me like brambles at each turn of my life. Nicolosa told me

Madonna Felice had seemed determined to meet me, timing her visit to an hour when she had heard I was coming.

"I think she wants you for herself," she said darkly. "All this business about the song, so she has a pretext to summon you to her."

"Nonsense. What would she want with someone like me? She's the pope's daughter. And why would I want her, anyway, when I have you?"

"Because you are a faithless, heartless man, and ambitious to rise," Nicolosa said, narrowing her eyes at me, half mocking, half serious. "And she's attractive, also. Don't pretend you didn't notice. That dress …"

"Nicolosa! I didn't even mark what she wearing." This was true, for I had been too terrified to notice.

Eventually I drew Nicolosa away from the subject by mocking her jealousy; then I amused her by improvising texts for Madonna Felice's lute song, each more ridiculous than the last. Finally, we fell into our amorous pleasures; then Nicolosa slept and I remained in the darkness listening to her breathing beside me, thinking miserably of her departure the next morning and wondering when I would see her again.

XXVI

To explain why I was lingering in Rome, I had told Nicolosa that I could not leave Valentino at this delicate moment without risking his enmity. His mood was volatile with the downturn in his fortunes, and it would be a rash man who would cross him at this time.

There was some truth in this lie, even though my real reason for remaining was the impossibility of escaping my service to the della Rovere. This was a difficult time for the duke and he was nervous and snappish, inclined to take offense at any and all. Pope Julius had lured him into supporting him at his election with the promise that he would be made commander of the papal forces—yet days passed and weeks passed and the pope held his *possesso*, and still the duke was not confirmed in this post. To be seen in this position of weakness weakened him further, for appearance is all in matters of state. His allies began to abandon him, his enemies to disdain him, his admirers to find new figures to admire. Even Machiavelli, who had once thought him the greatest of our Italian rulers, now spoke of him with scorn. He remarked once to me that to watch Valentino in these days was to watch a man slipping little by little into the grave.

When he belatedly recognized the emptiness of the pope's promises, some time in late November, Valentino left Rome with a small entourage for the port of Ostia, intending to sail to join his captains in the Romagna, who were loyally awaiting his commands. This was a rash plan, but, in my view, once he had decided on it, he should have pursued it with the speed and virility he displayed in his taking of Urbino or the coup in Senigallia. This was his best chance: to act and think later, trusting to Fortune and his genius to see him right. Instead, our bold duke was infected with prudence, as if it had been a disease caught along with his sickness in the summer. He got to Ostia, but he did not embark. He waited for a favorable wind and perhaps for favorable omens; he squandered the advantage of the moment and gave the pope time to send agents to arrest him and drag him back a captive to the city. He acted like a remnant of himself.

I REALIZE I have said little of the duke since the time when his illness first struck him. I saw him myself for the first time after his sickness only in October, when he appeared in public to receive the office of captain-general of the papal forces from the short-lived Pope Pius. We of his household were summoned to accompany him and did so with all the dignity we could muster, but the sight of him dismayed us. He looked physically much frailer, almost flinching, like an elderly man, as though he could hardly bear the strength of the light.

As the winter progressed, something of the old duke began to return, in a physical sense, at least. He trained his body for long hours to recover his strength, first in a great room in the Castel Sant'Angelo he had commandeered for this purpose, then in a courtyard beneath the Torre Borgia, where he was confined after his ill-fated flight to Ostia. He was a man whose sense of himself was inseparable from his physical prowess. I once watched him try to make a pass against a wrestling partner and fail, then try it again and again, railing against his weakness and willing himself strength, as though in this bodily mastery lay the secret of his return to the political potency he had once known.

What he was losing now, and could not regain, was his grip on events. For the first time in his life, events were things that happened to him. He was forced to sit by when the pope appointed Guidobaldo da Montefeltro, duke of Urbino, as captain-general of the papal forces, the post that had been promised to him. On the orders of Julius, he even met with Guidobaldo one evening in the Castel Sant'Angelo to pass on his strategic advice. These are reversals of a kind a man usually experiences only in nightmares, before gratefully awakening to find the world as it was. Eighteen months earlier, Valentino had effortlessly driven this same effeminate duke from his lands.

As Valentino lost Fortune's favor, his temper became more uncertain, in a manner I had already witnessed in Urbino when the rebellion rose against him. At that time he had a remedy, in the form of Don Michelotto, whom he had summoned from Piombino to give him courage. Now, Don Michelotto was roaming northern Lazio and Tuscany, trying to hold together some kind of army for him, and Valentino was left to fester in an enemy court alone.

I experienced the duke's temper myself some time shortly after Julius's election, at the time when he was still hoping the pope would respect his promises. One day during this period, he sent me in fury to summon the Venetian ambassador, whom he wished to berate for some incursion of Venetian troops in the Romagna. This was the man I spoke of earlier, Giustiniano, whom I had encountered contemplating the body of Pope Alexander in its foul glory. He was a snake, but a very polished one, in the manner of the Venetians, perhaps the most slippery race of men on this earth. Giustiniano received me civilly, but he laughed when I told him of the duke's summons and excused himself without troubling to devise any pretext. I heard it said later that he had not wished to give the duke countenance by obeying his commands.

I was nervous returning to the duke with the ambassador's message. Earlier in the week, he had beaten a servant for some supposed misdemeanor and broken his nose. When I entered his room at the Castel Sant'Angelo, Valentino was sitting there with his doctors around him, consulting. He was naked from the waist up, and two swollen black leeches were sitting at the base of his neck, supping greedily on his blood. He did not break my nose when I relayed Giustiniano's message, but he looked murderously at me and abused me for having conducted my mission so ill, calling me carrion and a dog. His doctors became alarmed at this agitation in their patient and looked at me darkly as its cause. In the end, in his fury, Valentino tore a leech off his neck and hurled it across the table at me, a thing that still makes me shudder to think of it. I ducked my head to avoid it, and the creature splattered hideously against a tapestry behind me, covering a bucolic scene of shepherds with an explosion of blood.

I was shaking as I left the room, glad to have escaped with my life. The duke's anger was not lasting, however. The following morning, he sent five florins to me by way of apology—carried by the broken-nosed servant, I noted, perhaps to remind me of his continence in restricting himself to verbal abuse. He might be feeling choleric, but he knew that he could not afford to lose the loyalty of the dwindling band of men who remained to him. He had no reason to know that I could no more abandon his service than a prisoner can leave his ball and chain.

My chief solace at this time was Francesca, whom I visited each Sunday and whenever I could during the week. The poor girl was entranced at the idea of her coming maternity and spent her days seeking prognostics about our child from the wise women of the neighborhood. These crones had convinced her that she was bearing a boy, and she would earnestly recount to me the many signs that proved this was the case.

I listened and indulged her—though, in truth, I was hardly inclined to be skeptical, for who, knowing he is to be a father, does not crave for a son?

I wrote a will at this time for the first time in my life, to provide for this unborn son of mine. To my annoyance, I could not shake off the memory of the Sicilian witch who had foretold my death that summer; her words and her fear sometimes came to haunt me if I awoke in the night. I left Francesca a decent dowry if she would marry a man approved by Dino and by the glove maker she lived with, the latter of whom I enjoined to ensure that the boy was well treated in his new household. If the glove maker reported that the child was ill used by his stepfather, then Dino was to take him to Fermo, to bring him up with his own sons. Francesca could go with him, under the protection of Dino, or remain with her husband, as she chose.

I also left money for the boy's education, leaving the choice of his tutor to Messer Bernardo Bibbiena, Cardinal Giovanni's secretary, who was a man of elegant learning and mercifully free from the taste for young boys that characterized so many of the cardinal's friends. I did not wish this son of mine to be unlettered, even though he might be raised in an artisan's household. Secretly, I imagined him endowed with such genius that, with the benefit of letters, he would soar above his rank like an eagle. In this manner I consoled myself for my imminent death, which the drafting of my will seemed to give the status of a fact.

ONE CONSEQUENCE of my master's declining state was that I found myself promoted to the office of ducal pimp. Valentino summoned me one afternoon and asked me to procure Camilla for him and bring her to the Vatican that evening. He said this with great coolness, as if it was part of my habitual duties. I was so surprised that I could only bow, without a word.

I could quite see, on reflection, why the duke might wish to utilize me in his amorous affairs at this stage in his fortunes. He could hardly risk himself in the city at night, even with a guard. There were too many men in Rome who would like to see him dead—including, in some rumors, the pope. Nor could he hope to have much fortune with the kind of noble Roman lady who would have cast a kindly eye on him a few months earlier. He was back now in the realm of whores, or, more politely, of courtesans—a realm in which Camilla, as I could observe with some pride, was now emerging as a sun among stars.

I felt hesitant in communicating this invitation to Camilla, partly because I did not like to see myself in the role of procurer of women, and partly because I did not wish Camilla to be infected with the duke's sickness. I remembered Angelica all too well. Camilla laughed at me when I spoke to her of this danger, saying it was hardly something with which she could afford to concern herself in her profession. In any case, she had heard that this sickness was only conveyed by men freshly infected, and that could hardly be said of the duke.

Camilla told me later that the duke had interrogated her about me in some detail, asking questions about my acquaintances and habits. She said she had told him I was not a whoring man but one who made do with a sole woman, and that I had brought few guests to her house aside from my brother and a few other soldiers of the duke's. These were good answers and cautious, but I still felt uneasy that Camilla had talked of my being faithful to one woman. One woman meant a woman I cared for, and this was a vulnerability not hard to exploit.

THE CHIEF POINT of negotiation between the pope and the duke in this period concerned the handover of the duke's castles in the Romagna. Valentino refused at first to give the countersigns for these; then he conceded and gave them, but his castellans still refused to surrender them, even when he sent his own commissioner along with the pope's men to demand it. The castellan of Cesena, a man named Ramires, invited the commissioner into the castle to negotiate and then hanged him from the battlements, saying that he was a traitor to the duke, and that the duke would not be ordering this surrender if he had not been doing so under duress.

This was an impressive display of loyalty, but, to anyone of a suspicious cast of mind, it also raised the question of whether the duke was sending secret instructions to his castellans, countermanding his official orders. This was something that preoccupied me much at this time, for no piece of information I could convey to the pope would be of greater utility to him. Despite all my efforts, however, I could discover nothing of these secret messages, if indeed the duke were sending them, or of how they were being conveyed.

As I WAS puzzling over this, in late December, the news arrived in Rome of a decisive Spanish victory over the French in the south, on the river Garigliano. This was a victory of great moment, as is clear from this distance—for has not Spain held the kingdom of Naples ever since? It was important news for the duke, since the ascendancy of Spain gave his Spanish friends in the College of Cardinals greater influence with the pope. It would be too much to say that the tide turned for him, but he had something new to grapple onto in the general shipwreck of his hopes.

With the assistance of the Spanish cardinals, Duke Valentino negotiated an agreement with the pope that would allow him safe passage to France and some guarantee of his personal property in Italy once he had secured the surrender of his fortresses in the Romagna. It also—and this was critical—took him out of Rome and the pope's hands until this whole process was complete. He must have suspected that, if he remained there, he would be a dead man as soon as the last castle had ceded. The arrangement he had negotiated was that he would go to the port of Ostia, under the supervision of Cardinal Carvajal, the most senior of the Spanish cardinals. There he would have a ship loaded and ready to depart at any moment. Carvajal would permit him to embark on this vessel once the handover of the castles was complete.

Around fifty of us rode to Ostia with the duke, on a foul day in early March, the roads a mass of churned mud. I count only the duke's entourage when I speak of fifty men, excluding the retinue of Cardinal Carvajal and the armed guard that Carvajal was taking to supplement the papal garrison at the port. Aside from servants and a chaplain, the fifty were mainly soldiers, including Dino, who had recently returned from Naples, where he had been fighting alongside the French army, whose prowess he assessed with great scorn. Also with us was the supposed Spanish mute Diego, whom the duke had kept on after his father's death in a spirit of charity. I eyed him on his mule as we were setting out on our journey and he gave me the look of a secret brother in Christ.

There was much speculation among us about what the duke's plans were. Almost no one gave any faith to the story that he was simply going to his lands in France. Most believed instead that he would head for Naples, where his brother Gioffrè had joined the Spanish army, and where the cardinals of his family had also fled.

We took up residence in the castle at Ostia while the endlessly protracted negotiations over the castles were taking place. The castellans in the Romagna were demanding monetary recompense for their relinquishment of the keeps they were holding. Some of this penalty was due to be paid by Valentino himself, while the rest was to be paid by the pope. Eventually, in April, enticed by this incentive, the castellans of Cesena and Bertinoro surrendered. There remained only Forlì, where the castellan, Gonsalvo de Mirafonte, was demanding fifteen thousand ducats as his price.

IT WAS at this moment that Duke Valentino handed me my great chance. I had been winding myself ever more tightly into his confidence in the last months, as much of the remainder of his retinue had melted away. My offices as go-between with Camilla were a significant factor in this, I suspect. As I have come to learn since, there is nothing like this kind of intimacy to breed trust between great men and their servants, which is why princes often confide more in their gentlemen of the bedchamber than their ministers—often with the most questionable results.

One morning in Ostia around the middle of April, the duke summoned me and asked whether I knew of a man who could be entrusted with a mission of importance, the delivery of a message. He could not send a man from his household. This must be someone with no connection with him.

I knew at once who the addressee of this message must be: the castellan of Forlì, Mirafonte. This was the prey I had been stalking for these last long tiresome months, and it had wandered straight into my hands. I kept all expression from my face and feigned to ponder for a moment, though in truth the name of Nello sprang immediately into my mind. Then I told the duke I knew of a man, an ex-soldier of Liverotto's, now working for Camilla, whose loyalty I commanded for favors I had done him in the past.

Valentino looked at me hard, as if trying to read my heart, then, with a movement so rapid I was hardly aware of it, he was holding a knife at my throat.

"If you betray me over this, I'll cut your heart out. And I'll track down the girl you keep in Rome and tear the child out of her womb and throw it on the fire before her eyes. Is that clear?"

His eyes looked strange as he uttered these threats, and I was afraid for an instant he was going to ram the knife through my throat there and then. I spoke as steadily as I could.

"Your Excellency. When have I ever been anything but loyal?"

He carried on looking at me sinisterly for a moment but then lowered his knife and nodded, taking a small purse of gold from his belt.

"Very well," he said coolly. "Take this. Go to Rome and instruct this man you spoke of to come to Ostia at once. Tell him to take lodgings at the inn called the Phoenix, under a false name. Pay him whatever you think fit and give him money for a good horse."

I LEFT this interview trembling. The duke's threats against my person were something I was accustomed to, but I was shaken by his menaces against Francesca and my unborn son. This was a new horror in my life, and I was not sure I could withstand it. I could not dispel the image from my mind of my living child being thrown like dead meat on the fire.

I thought at first, as I was riding to Rome, that I would simply not pass on my information about the duke's scheming to the pope, even though this offered me my best opportunity yet to escape my double burden of servitude. I would obey the duke, plain and simple, and neglect my role as agent. The pope would never know of this missed opportunity, which could very easily never have come my way.

By the time I was approaching the wretched hovels on the western outskirts of the city, however, I was already beginning to think differently. If I took this chance, I might soon be a free man—perhaps even within the span of a week. If I did not take it, when would another such opportunity come my way? I would remain in the duke's service as he planned some impossible return to his lands in the Romagna, and I would still be risking my life, and Francesca's and my son's, each time I delivered a report to the pope. There was no safe route through for me; I was between Scylla and Charybdis. I must take this risk, chilling as the consequences might be.

I RODE TO CAMILLA's and delivered my message to Nello, who took one look at the gold I was offering and began to pack his things for the journey. He asked nothing of the task I was engaging him for and did not inquire about the level of risk involved. He was young and an adventurous spirit, and money flowed through his hands like water. The possibility of gain was the argument that clinched all.

I assured Camilla I would engage someone else for her protection, and spent the evening tracking down a former soldier of the duke's by the name of Bartolo who had left the army to run an inn off the street called Banchi. He was a great ox of a man, well fitted for what I needed, and, from what I remembered of his habits, I thought he would not be likely to spurn the opportunity to work for a while in a house of loose women. Indeed, he took little persuasion, saying he was always happy to oblige an old comrade-at-arms.

I had composed a letter before I went to the inn, and I had one of the boys who served there take it for me to Cardinal

Galeotto della Rovere, the pope's nephew and Cardinal Giovanni's friend. Cardinal Galeotto was the man to whom I now sent my reports, both in Rome, where I delivered them through Violante at Camilla's, and in Ostia, where I left them in a side chapel in a church for his agent to collect, sliding them behind the base of a candlestick there. This time I could not go through these habitual channels, as my message was urgent and needed an immediate answer. I almost thought of going to Cardinal Galeotto's residence myself but decided against this, in case the duke had sent someone behind me to observe my movements in Rome. Instead, I used the secret directions the cardinal had slipped me at Cardinal Giovanni's on the evening of the roast swan and the sugar oak tree—the first time I had put this system to use.

In my message to the cardinal, I instructed that the pope's agent in Ostia should check for a message from me each day in the chapel, as often as possible without being observed, but morning and evening at the very least. I said I hoped to be able to advise on how to intercept a message from the duke to the castellan of Forlì but that speed of response would be imperative if the messenger were to be caught. I also explained my personal danger and that of Francesca, and I pled with the cardinal that he remove Francesca from her current lodgings to some safe place until the duke was securely under arrest.

I sat for an hour or so at the inn waiting for the messenger boy to return and trying to keep up with Bartolo's formidable consumption of wine. He had agreed to come with me to Camilla's that same night and was pressing me for detail of each girl in the house, his eyes virtually popping from his head. Eventually, the boy returned and handed me a folded paper with the cardinal's seal on it. I opened it and read the single word *placet*, which is as much as to say "very well." I threw the thing into the fire, and Bartolo and I set off for Camilla's through the muddy dark streets.

I DID ONE more thing in Rome that night before sinking gratefully into the bed Camilla had offered me for the night. I went to the pawnshop Camilla and I owned together a few streets away and summoned the shopkeeper, Messer Isacco, down from his bed. Nello had hired an ex-soldier to guard the shop for us at night, a necessary precaution. It was this surly fellow who opened the door to me, and lit candles and began to coax the embers of the fire into life as I waited. Eventually, Messer Isacco came sleepily down the stairs, smoothing his thinning hair back on his head.

I was looking for something quite specific on this visit—a ring I had noticed in a tray of unclaimed pledges a few weeks earlier, when I picked up the marten coat I had worn at the pope's *possesso*. I had the habit of looking idly through this tray when I came into the shop, to see whether there was anything caught my eye. I halted in my sifting when I saw the ring, and almost felt a need to cross myself before I went on.

This ring was small as regards the circumference of the band, perhaps of a size that a woman might wear on her ring finger or a man on his least finger. Mounted on this narrow band was a roundel of some magnitude, bearing a profile of Fra Girolamo Savonarola on its face. It was a cruder portrait, and a cruder object, than the one I had passed to Fra Filippo at the bequest of Machiavelli a few months before, and there seemed no hint of a hidden compartment behind the face of the ring. Still, it had remained in my mind, and recent developments had made me begin to think it might be of use to me. Fra Filippo had killed the Antichrist at the prompting of a ring. Might he be persuaded to kill the Antichrist's son?

I examined the ring and some other objects with feigned casualness, under the long-suffering eyes of Messer Isacco. This man had once recounted to me his family's eviction from Seville in '94, when the Jews had been expelled from all of Spain. Messer Isacco's father had been a great merchant in that city, with a household of ten servants and a mansion in the best quarter of the city. Now his son was reduced to having to drag himself out of bed in the dead of night so I could root through a box of trinkets, pulling a coarse brown wool blanket around his shoulders against the cold and complaining humorously about the aches in his limbs.

"I'll have these," I said eventually, sweeping up four or five objects, in the hope that the ring would not meet with particular notice. I had already explained that I was in town solely for the evening; hence this anomalous visit after dark. Messer Isacco saw me to the door, a weary smile on his face, and I handed him the payment we had agreed on.

"If anyone should ask," I said. "Not that there's any reason why anyone should …"

"I have a remarkably poor memory," Messer Isacco said mildly.

I pressed his hand for a moment, passing him a few *soldi* as I did so, and then made my way into the night.

XXVII

O N THE DUKE'S ORDERS, I took Camilla and her sister down to Ostia for him. He had been making do with the whores of Ostia, but they were not to his taste. A thing that he liked was to have two women at once, and, as he complained to me when making his request for Camilla and Sabina, it was difficult enough to find one decent-looking woman in Ostia, let alone two he could stomach at the same time.

When I got back to Ostia, Valentino kept me much in his company, perhaps wishing to observe me. He had me dine with him and Cardinal Carvajal and some of their retinue on the next two evenings, and he even invited me to play chess with him after dinner, with Camilla and Sabina looking on. I went there intending to play to lose, as I used to with Liverotto, but it turned out that there was no need for such subtlety. The duke was a player of great skill and made short work of me, especially the first time, much to the amusement of the girls.

On the evening of the third day after my arrival back from Rome, the duke gave me a message for Nello. As I had foreseen, he stipulated that it was to be taken to Gonsalvo de Mirafonte, the castellan of Forlì. He instructed me to be careful when I left the castle for the inn, to make sure none of Cardinal Carvajal's men was following me. Nello was to leave the next day before dawn and ride as hard as he could. I was to give him enough money to ensure that he could change horses as often as he needed to in the course of the journey. The payment for his services would double if he could complete the entire trip in a week.

After I had been to the inn and given Nello his instructions, I went to the church where I left my missives for Cardinal Galeotto and left a note informing him that the messenger had departed. It was a well-chosen place for subterfuge, an ancient church with small, high windows, dark and gloomy even in the middle of the day. I remember I had to wait for a long time pretending to pray while an old woman completed her devotions before I could place the message safely. That evening, in the chapel of the castle, I truly did pray, at length, with the godly fervor that afflicts fearful men.

The day after I dispatched Nello with his message, Valentino's official courier was sent to Forlì with a message for Mirafonte, setting out the terms of the surrender of the castle and formally stipulating the sum of fifteen thousand ducats as his payment. Cardinal Carvajal had informally agreed that a favorable response from Mirafonte would be sufficient to ensure Valentino's release.

Much of the week that elapsed before the reply was expected was spent preparing our ship for departure. This was a handsome vessel, a great carrack some Genoese adventurer had built hoping to embark across the ocean, but which he had been forced through lack of funds to deploy closer to home. I helped supervise the provisioning of this monstrous ship and the long process of loading the baggage of some seventy men. Along with the fifty he had brought from Rome, there were others Valentino had been quietly recruiting in Ostia, mostly bandits and desperate men.

This last week in Ostia was very tense. I went about my tasks in a trance, my mind obsessively running over the implications of my betrayal of the duke. If all went to plan, Pope Julius would arrest Nello with the message at Forlì; then, shortly afterwards, he would move on Valentino. With such decisive evidence of the duke's treachery, Julius would have every excuse for breaking their agreement and treating him like the criminal he was.

When the day came that marked a week after Nello's departure, I began to expect the arrival of the pope's arrest party for the duke at each hour. I spent as much of the day as I could on the battlements, looking towards Rome for any sign of troops on the horizon. It was a clear and brilliant day, almost as though the heavens were playing with me. The air was like glass and my young eyes penetrated far and with great precision. Yet, by nightfall, no one had come.

The following day, there was still no sign of any force from Rome, nor of Nello, but Valentino's official courier arrived back towards evening. He brought a clear consent from Mirafonte to the terms of the handover, and Cardinal Carvajal confirmed that the duke might leave when he wished. I hoped he would delay his departure to await Nello's return, for in truth he had no way of knowing whether Mirafonte had safely received his counter-instructions. Yet with a ship at his disposal and a powerful enemy at his back in Rome, I knew the urge to make his escape must be strong.

Naturally, the failure to return of the courier I had been responsible for suggesting put the duke in a vile mood towards me. I do not think he suspected me yet, for he was rational enough to know that a courier may fall prey to illness or bandits or a thousand other dangers of travel without this being his fault, still less than that of the man who recommended him. Nonetheless, I was out of favor from this point and closely observed. The duke had designated two men to watch me, not in any surreptitious manner, but openly, as if he wished me to realize that I was under suspicion and be fearful. It chilled me to see them, for I remembered Senigallia and the men Valentino had placed around the conspirators to escort them to their deaths.

The evening after Nello's failed return, Dino invited me to dine at an inn with some officers who had fought alongside him in Naples. I declined, saying I felt ill—not a hard lie to maintain, for I had been sleeping poorly and was haggard and pale. Dino wished to stay with me or call for a doctor, but I reassured him that all I needed was rest. I wanted, if possible, to keep Dino at arm's length, so that if I fell he would not fall with me. When he said he would call in later to see if I was well, I told him not to trouble himself, as I was taking a sleeping draft and would be dead to the world.

In fact, i hardly slept that night. I lay stiff as a corpse on my bed wondering what had happened to Nello and thinking about Francesca and whether she was safe. When I did finally fall asleep, I dreamed a figure was leaning over me whispering strangely, dressed in a blood-red veil like the one Angelica had worn. I jerked awake in terror. A hand was shaking me, one of the men I was sharing a room with. It was time to wake, he was saying. The duke had given orders that we were to sail.

I would certainly have attempted to run that morning if the duke had not put his minders on my heels. They were waiting outside my room when I left it and watched me like hawks all the way to the ship. The sun was bleeding its red light into the sky as we boarded, and the air was fresh, with a southerly breeze. Bad for France, where we were supposed to be heading; good for Naples, where we were headed in truth.

The sun was already high by the time the porters and infantrymen had loaded the last of the baggage and the horses. We all assembled on deck to hear a mass conducted by Cardinal Carvajal, to assure us a safe voyage; then the cardinal descended to shore, and the sailors began to unfurl the sails and untie the ropes that bound the ship to the quay.

As they were doing so, there was a commotion on the quay-side, where the cardinal's men were gathered. Armed men on horseback were storming towards the water. First there were twenty, then fifty, then eighty or a hundred, cramming the whole quay. An officer wearing papal insignia was speaking furiously with the cardinal, gesturing towards the ship, and men were dismounting and beginning to surge towards us. A gangplank was still standing, connecting the ship to the wharf, down which the cardinal and his priests had just progressed.

On the ship, the duke was speaking urgently with the captain of the ship, who was a Frenchman. The captain cried out to his men and, at the same instant, a cluster of the duke's men seized hold of the ship end of the gangplank and heaved it off its bearings. There were three or four men on it already, papal soldiers. They teetered on it for a moment like acrobats on a rope; then they fell heavily into the sea, throwing up a wild explosion of surf. Others of the duke's men were hacking at the last remaining tie-ropes with axes, and the sailors were hoisting up the anchor as though possessed by demons. I saw the pope's officer looking on in astonishment as the wind filled our sails and we began to move from the shore.

THIS WAS my death sentence and I knew it. The thought came to my mind of the Sicilian witch at Nepi and the strange fear that had struck her as she spoke to me. I knew then that my death was not only imminent, but that it would probably occur in some foul and unconscionable manner of which she had some glimmer in her mind. The duke threw me a black glance as the ship began to sail, and the men who had been allocated to watch me onshore were suddenly at my shoulder. I was led downstairs to the gun deck, where a Spanish captain of the duke's confiscated my sword. Then I was taken to a small dark storeroom in the baggage hold that looked as though it might also be used as a sickroom. There was a strange little bed made up there: a wooden chest with a straw pallet and a grubby wool blanket on top.

It seemed I was going to undergo some kind of execution, down there alone out of earshot, with only crates and trunks around me. At first I thought it would come very soon, and I fell to my knees to think of my sins and seek the grace of God. Then the minutes dragged on and nothing happened, and I realized that my death would not come quickly, for that was not the duke's way. A quick death was a mercy. Why had he left Liverotto and Vitelli to fester together in that dungeon for ten hours, when he could have had them strangled at noon?

I could have lain on that miserable bed and wept when this realization came to me. Instead, I forced myself to look around to see whether I had any chance of saving my life. Dino was my inspiration. I knew he would not succumb to despair until the last drop of blood had run from his veins. I tried each of the trunks to see whether there was something inside that might serve me, but all were locked with chains and padlocks. Nor could I use them to help me climb to the porthole I could see high above me. They were too heavy; I could not shift them an inch. I continued to search feverishly for anything that might serve me for escape or self-defense. All I found was a billet of wood forgotten in a corner behind one chest, and some short lengths of rope, the longest no longer than my arm.

I went round the cell twice, every inch of it, feeling the floor for loose boards, trying to pry nails from the lid of a chest. Then my spirit surrendered. An image came to my mind, of a wasp struggling up the smooth side of a wineglass in which some irritated drinker has trapped it. I was that wasp, fighting vainly for my life when I was already to all purposes dead. All my strength deserted me then. I am not sure I could even tell you how I spent the rest of my day in that hateful cell. All I remember is lying in a wretched stupor, curled on the bed, staring blankly at the floor, like those dead-eyed men you sometimes see being led to the scaffold, seeming not to care whether they live or they die.

My only consolation in this misery was that one weapon remained to me, the stiletto Dino had given me long ago at Camerino. I always carried this hidden, in the inner sleeve down the back of my doublet that Alfonso had made for me so I could carry it unseen. I kept touching its smooth blade like a talisman as I lay brooding on my hard bed, though in truth I could not build too much hope on it. I thought the men who had been watching me in Ostia would most likely be charged with my murder. They had been given the task of guarding me here also: I could see them through the keyhole playing cards outside the door. Both were armed with great brutal daggers, good for hacking as well as thrusting: one a cutlass, the other a *cinquedea*. If I tried to defend myself against these men in a fight, my chances would be as slender as the blade of my knife.

SOME TIME after darkness had fallen, when the only light in the room was the faintest radiance of moonlight, I heard a key cautiously rasping in the lock of the door. I grasped my stiletto and reached for my billet of wood, which I had placed at the end of the bed. The door opened gradually, and a man's hand tentatively appeared, holding out a lamp.

To my astonishment, the man who entered was Diego, or Fra Filippo. I stared at him as if I was seeing an apparition. He swung the door shut behind him and came towards me with a solemn expression on his long, gaunt face.

"Fra Filippo," I whispered. "You here?" It was all I could manage to say.

Fra Filippo carefully set down a tray he was carrying, with a metal flask on it and a plate, covered with a cloth. Then he spoke in his hoarse, urgent voice, placing his mouth close to my ear.

"I saw you taken on the deck this morning. As they took Our Lord in the Garden of Gethsemane. The spirit moved me to discover where you were being held and to have myself charged with bringing food to your captors."

I looked at him with a kind of awe. I could almost believe that God had sent him here for my salvation.

"Fra Filippo," I said, trying to recover myself. "It is not without mystery that the spirit inspired you to come to me."

I was reaching in my pocket as I spoke and drew out the ring with Savonarola's image I had brought with me from Rome. The friar reached for it avidly, but I held it back from him, wanting him first to pay attention to my words.

"He has come to you again?" he whispered. "Fra Domenico?"

I nodded and fixed him with my eyes.

"Fra Filippo," I said, "you must listen and act quickly. I am in great danger. The son of the Antichrist intends to kill me this very evening. It is imperative I be saved, for I am to have a role in the second coming of Fra Girolamo. Unworthy vessel though I am."

"What new wonder is this?" Fra Filippo murmured, leaning forward to place a kiss on my brow. "You had this revelation from Fra Domenico?"

"From his own lips, God be praised," I said fervently. "You must go to my brother Dino and tell him I am in danger. You know who he is?"

Fra Filippo nodded. He was still gazing at me in rapture. Then he said, in an almost accusing tone,

"You look nothing like that Dino, you know. Has it occurred to you that you may be the son of an angel?"

"That is a holy thought and one worthy of you, Fra Filippo," I said. "But there is not a moment to be lost."

"Quite so, my son," Fra Filippo said. He was looking at me pleadingly, and I finally handed him the ring, which he raised with great reverence to his lips. As he left, he gestured at the tray he had been carrying, with a new, sly expression.

"I put powder in your wine. Here, outside the door, so your captors could see me doing it. It is quite harmless."

He nodded beadily twice to impress this on me, and then retreated from the room with a strange gesture of his hand, as if in blessing. As the meaning of his words sank in, I gave thanks to God for breathing such cunning into the holy friar's mind. If the men outside believed I had been drugged on the duke's orders, then they would enter without fear of resistance. Perhaps only one of them would enter, given the closeness of the space. There was a chance for me here if I knew how to exploit it, even if Dino did not arrive in time to help me. I looked around the room, thinking rapidly, my former lethargy completely dispelled.

MY FIRST TASK was simple: to consume the supposedly drugged wine Fra Filippo had brought me. I did so with an appetite that surprised me, wolfing down also three slices of cold beef. Then I dragged a roll of sailcloth over to the chest and positioned it under the blanket to simulate the appearance of a human figure sleeping with its knees drawn up. There was no light that would allow me to judge the effect, but I hoped it would buy me a moment of time.

A new idea had come to me about how I should use the piece of wood I had been planning to employ as a bludgeon. It was a hard wood like yew, and I thought it could serve me as a shield, to take the force of a first blow at least. I strapped it to my left forearm, binding it tight in three places with the scraps of rope I had found. Then I fashioned myself a new weapon of sorts for my left hand from the hat badge that Cardinal Giovanni had given me. This had a sharp silver pin, used to attach it, which I eased outwards until it stood at an angle to the badge. It was hardly the equal of a cutlass, but it had the advantage of stealth, as I could conceal it in the palm of my hand.

I did all this as silently as I could, listening for a sound outside the door, calculating the likelihood at each moment that Fra Filippo had carried his message to Dino. Meanwhile, the great ship was swaying beneath my feet, and I tried to feel its rhythms and move with them. I was no stranger to sailing, having grown up near the sea, and I hoped this would give me an advantage over my assailants. I had noticed one of them lurching like a novice as they accompanied me down the stairs.

When i had finished my preparations, I positioned myself where I would be hidden by the door when it opened. I do not know how long I waited there, although it seemed like an age. Eventually, I heard the key turn in the lock, and saw the door began to open, very cautiously. The man who entered the room had no lamp in his hand, but light from a lantern outside was filtering in through the door. I watched his dark bulk move uncertainly towards the bed and lean over it. I crept up silently behind him to bring myself within striking distance of his bent neck.

Before I could thrust with my stiletto, he whirled round and struck out like lightning. My left arm flew up just in time to take the force of his blow on the wood I had strapped there. Then I plunged my stiletto with all my force into the side of his neck, angling it down to slice into his gullet. He swung wildly with his knife and I evaded the blow and stabbed at his right eye with my hatpin. I was aiming for the center, but caught only the edge; still, it drove straight through the jelly of the eye. He opened his mouth to scream, but he could not. He was choking on the blood gushing up from his severed windpipe. I pulled my stiletto from his neck, twisting it as I did so. A fountain of blood sprayed across the wall.

The second man was in the doorway by now and coming at me over the hemorrhaging body of his comrade. He struck at me, but I parried with my shield arm. Then I cut into his shoulder with the first man's cutlass, which I had seized from his hand when he fell. The blade was shockingly sharp, slicing through his flesh like a silk veil, jarring only when it lodged in the bone. He was mine from this point, for I had weapons in both hands, and he fought without spirit or mastery. I hacked away at him like a butcher until his legs gave way beneath him and he dropped to his knees. Then I wrenched his head back and sawed up through his throat with the cutlass, glad to bring this loathsome task to an end.

ALL OF WHAT I have just told you happened remarkably quickly, as these things do. One moment, I was standing behind the door, tense as a bowstring. The next, my two assailants were lying on the floor, pools of dark blood spreading around them. I was standing above them unscathed, drenched in gore, my heart hammering in my breast as though it was about to explode.

My assailants' lantern had survived the fight, and I carried it down to the end of the hold and tried the handle of the door that led up to the deck. The door was locked, and I went back into the death chamber and searched through my victims' pockets for a key. There was nothing. I searched again, then began to scour the hold with the lantern to see whether they had dropped it somewhere. I soon became aware of the futility of the task.

There was a row of windows on this lower deck, up on high, one with a long wooden ladder leading up to it. It was a narrow thing, no more than a porthole, but perhaps just wide enough for me to squeeze through. I began to climb, though I had to pause twice on the ladder to recover myself. The frenzy that had come upon me while I was fighting had cooled and I was shaking with the shock of the violence, my mind filled with the obscenity of the killings, my nostrils choked with the smell of blood.

When I opened the window, a salt wind hit my face, almost strong enough to throw me off the ladder. I was very close to the water, only a few feet above the waves at their highest extent. The window was wider than I had thought, and I worked my way through it with more ease than I had anticipated. When I was out, I levered myself up gingerly until I was standing, my feet wedged into the window I had climbed through, and my hands clinging on to a metal bar on the shutter of a gun hatch above.

I remained for a few moments in this posture, feeling the swell of the sea and gauging my chances, the cold spray rapidly drenching my clothes. To my left, perhaps an arm's length above my head, was the beginning of the rigging that anchored the main sail, those ropes they call shrouds. I say the distance was an arm's length, and it was no more than that, but the leap was still daunting to me in the darkness, from a standing start, with the sea churning beneath me and the ropes drenched in brine. I waited for the roll of the ship, to feel it, once, twice, thrice. Then I took courage and launched myself over the dark water to grasp onto the beginning of these ropes.

IT WAS extraordinarily fatiguing to inch my way up the shrouds to the point where I was high enough to get a footing on the lower ropes. The muscles of my arms burned excruciatingly with the effort and the nausea I had felt on the ladder in the hold was growing on me as I climbed. When I finally heaved myself over the wet rail of the main deck, I stumbled gratefully to my knees and was sick.

Before this movement of nature was complete, a blow on the back on my neck felled me, and I collapsed forward into the pool of my vomit. Then I felt a violent pain in my side, as something slammed into my ribcage. I tried to reach for the cutlass I had stuffed in my belt, but my assailant was too quick for me. He seized it from my hands, weak and trembling from the climb, and kicked me hard in the side of my head.

When I came to my senses a moment later, Duke Valentino was kneeling over me with the cutlass in his hand. A lantern flickered beside him on the deck.

"You killed them, I suppose, you treacherous little shit," he said, lifting my head and slamming it back against the deck. "I would not have thought you had it in you."

I looked at him stupefied, blackness swimming in the corners of my vision. There was no pain yet from my head, but I could taste blood in my mouth and feel it running down the side of my neck. A muscle above my lip was convulsing. The duke was looking at me with an expression of disgust, as though sickened at the thought that he might have to sully his own hands with my killing. I closed my eyes and spoke desperate words to God.

Then I heard something above me and felt the weight on my arms shift. The duke's body was still above me when I opened my eyes, but his face had gone. His right arm was wrenched back. Someone was gripping him from behind, dragging him back from me. I heard him grunt with the effort. The duke's headless torso was jerking violently, trying to throw his assailant off, like an unbroken stallion under the saddle. A boot lashed out and struck me on the jaw, knocking me backwards as I struggled to my feet.

As I rose, I could see that the duke's attacker had thrown a sack over his head and had him clamped in a headlock. A mail vambrace on his arm was glinting in the moonlight, but his face was in shadow. He dragged the duke towards the bulwark nearest us, like a farmer dragging a struggling calf to slaughter. When he had him there, he smacked his head against a protruding beam, then again and again. After the third time, the body slumped and lay still.

My savior turned to me and the light caught his face, which was drenched with sweat.

Tears of relief were in my eyes.

"Dino," I said.

"Fuck, Teo, I thought you were dead," Dino said. His voice was unsteady. He had a length of rope in his hands, which he began to loop round the duke's wrists. "I couldn't get to you. They locked the door after the mute went down. Your friend the speaking mute. I thought they'd killed you." He looked at me more sharply. "Are you hurt? You're covered with blood."

I shook my head.

"Not mine."

Dino unexpectedly grinned. "That's the way, brother. Tie his feet, can you? "

He was binding a strip of cloth around the duke's mouth as he spoke, having pulled the sack off his head. It was strange to see Valentino's face so helpless and lax. A line of spittle was glistening down his chin.

I fumbled for a moment with the rope Dino threw me, but my fingers were numb with shock and I was good for nothing. Dino took it from me and tied it deftly, then signed to me to follow him towards the other side of the deck. We crept beneath the shadow cast by the forecastle to avoid the attention of the watch.

When we got to the other side of the deck, I could see what Dino's plan was. The smaller of the ship's boats had been in use that day, and by good fortune was still on deck, waiting to be stowed on the gun deck below. As we approached the boat, Dino whistled softly and three men stepped forward from the shadows. One I saw at once was Fra Filippo. The others I could not identify at first, but as we strained to heave the boat up on to the rails to lever it over, I saw in the moonlight that they were Agnese's husband Giacomino and his brother Luca—the only two other *fermani*, apart from Dino and me, among the soldiers who remained with the duke.

ONCE WE HAD got the boat over the rails and lowered it down on its ropes, working intently, there were suddenly lights and voices behind us. Dino hurled himself instantly over the rails, a rope clutched in his hand, shouting at me to follow him. I vaulted over after him, turning in the air so I could enter the water like a diver, headfirst.

The cold was breathtaking when I hit the waves. I went down very deep and had to fight my way up through the blackness, my clothes dragging me down. I struggled free of my cloak, and it lightened me, but my lungs by this time were burning like hellfire. I could keep my mouth closed no longer. Brine began to pour down my throat.

At that moment, I broke through to the surface, coughing and gasping, my eyes stinging. I barely had time to snatch a breath before a dark wave broke over my head and sucked me under again. I fought my way up like a demon this time, knowing I was so close to the air. This time I emerged long enough to look around.

The ship was already a remarkable distance away. Its speed looked uncanny, as though it were flying. The boat lay close by, lurching on the waves, and I could see the head and shoulders of a man clinging to it. I swam over, battling the waves, and saw by the moonlight as I came closer that the man was Dino. He steadied the boat from the other side as I heaved myself up into it; then I helped pull him up in turn. There was a pair of oars lashed to the bottom of the boat and Dino cut them loose with his dagger. Then we looked around in the moonlight for the rest of our crew.

Giacomino and Luca were clearly visible at a small distance. They were together in the water, one supporting the other, struggling to keep their heads above the waves. As we learned when we rescued them, Luca had been seized by a man of the watch before he could leap and had to fight himself free, taking a wound in his shoulder. He was losing blood and could hardly keep himself afloat.

We pulled the two men into the boat and Giacomino took his shirt off and began tearing it into strips to bandage his brother's bleeding shoulder, while Dino and I scoured the dark waves all around us to see if we could catch sight of Fra Filippo. Twice we thought we saw something move and rowed towards it. The first time it was nothing; the second, it was a dead cormorant floating on the waves, half picked to the bone by the fishes. Eventually we gave up hope of finding him. Neither Giacomino nor Luca had seen him leap.

WE TOOK IT in turns to row towards the shore, with the exception of Luca, two of us rowing at a time. When I was resting, I sat in the prow, scrutinizing the horizon for signs of life and thinking of Fra Filippo, who had saved my life that evening and now lay buried deep beneath the waves. The more I thought of his life, the sadder it seemed to me: torn away from his fellow friars and condemned to life as a mute, exploited by cynical men such as Machiavelli and myself, his only comforts his beloved scourge and his poor stinking hovel of a cell. I tried to tell myself his life had been happy, with the special happiness of fanatics, the only men who truly know what they have been placed on this earth for—yet I still felt tears on my face mingling with the salt of the spray as we plowed on laboriously through the waves.

After what seemed an eternity of rowing, a line of bobbing lights appeared before us on the horizon, like fireflies. Giacomino sighted them first, and called over to Dino and me, his voice hoarse with excitement. Fishing boats: a night fleet out from some village on the coast. We rowed towards them and, when we reckoned ourselves within earshot, began to yell as loud as we could to attract their attention. After a minute or two of bellowing into the wind, we heard the faint sound of an answering cry.

IN THIS MANNER we were salvaged from the sea. When they had pulled us up from the boat, the fishermen placed blankets around our shoulders and handed us wineskins filled with water and crude local wine, asking us questions in a rustic parlance we could barely comprehend. We mimicked a ship with our hands and us leaping from the side, and they jabbered away among themselves, looking suspiciously at my shirt and Luca's, still dirty with blood. Giacomino removed Luca's bandages, and we examined the wound, which was an ugly, deep, jagged one, made with a cutlass. Dino stitched it with a bone needle the fishermen brought him and some thick thread of the kind that they use to mend sails. It must have caused Luca devilish pain, yet he barely gave a sign of it, other than to grind his teeth on a salt-soaked handkerchief we had given him to clamp in his mouth.

I must have slept after this, just as I was, sitting propped against a mast. When I woke, the beginning of light could be seen in the sky. I think I woke myself crying out in my sleep. I had dreamed I was back on the ship, in the cabin with the men I had slaughtered. Giacomino and Luca were lying beside me on the deck, asleep under a pile of sailcloth, Luca moaning softly with the pain from his arm.

I could not see Dino at first, but then realized to my amazement that he was down at the other end of the deck, helping the fishermen draw in their flashing, silvery catch, seemingly none the worse physically for our travails of the night. Strength is a language all men speak, and his did us much good with our hosts, as did the knife at his side and his air of knowing how to use it. I had a gold chain round my neck and a couple of rings on my fingers worth more than these men and their fathers and grandfathers and their sons and their grandsons could accumulate in two centuries of hard labor. Yet I had been left to my slumbers undisturbed.

When we reached the land, the sun was rising. The women of the village were lined on the shore to greet their men, carrying baskets of bread for their breakfast. As we drew nearer, they waved and smiled and shouted—pretty girls, some of them, with raven-black hair and dark eyes. I stood looking at this scene half-drugged still with sleep, marveling that I was seeing this day I thought would never dawn for me. I was a new Lazarus, risen from the grave. The simplest things seemed extraordinary to me: the taste of salt on my lips, the breeze lifting my hair.

XXVIII

W E BARTERED WITH THE FISHERMEN after breakfast for a boat to take us north up the coast to
a place where we could find decent horses. They
sailed us to the mouth of the Garigliano River, near where
the great battle between the French and Spanish had been
fought four months earlier. Then we rowed up the river to the
town of Minturno, taking our turn at the oars with the fishermen. It was a melancholy land this, marshy and treacherous-
looking, a sad place for a man to die, as so many had lately.
Cardinal Giovanni's brother had perished here after the battle, I remembered—the one-time lord of Florence, dead in
a swamp.

At Minturno we found horses and salve for Luca's wound,
which was beginning to suppurate. Giacomino resolved to
remain in the town with his brother until he recovered, while
Dino and I proceeded up the old Via Appia to Rome. I persuaded Giacomino to take some coin to cover the expense
of his lodging, but he would take no further reward for his
services or his brother's, reminding me that I had ransomed
Luca from Valentino's army after Senigallia, so that they were
only returning a debt. These were true and decent men, as you
see, and a credit to our homeland. Now that Giacomino had
helped save my life, I felt contrite at the thought that I was the
father of his beloved son and heir.

DINO LEFT ME at the gates of Rome to ride back to Fermo.
I was concerned that he might be in danger from the duke,
for it would not be difficult for Valentino to conjecture his
part in my escape. He laughed when I said this and told me

he would be fine, as the duke would be busy enough dealing with me. This nonchalance was assumed for my benefit, for, as I later learned, when Dino returned to Fermo, he dispatched Margherita and his sons in great secrecy down the coast to Ortona, to stay with a relative of Margherita's mother who lived there.

Dino and I embraced with great feeling as we parted, and Dino enjoined me to be careful. I tried to thank him for saving my life on the ship, but he brushed my words aside with a smile, saying only that, if I wished to thank him, I could beg him a commission in the forces of the pope. On our journey, I had told him the full story of my services to the della Rovere family, so he knew I had some standing in these circles. I told him I did not doubt that Pope Julius would be happy to have him in his army without any begging on my part.

My first stop in Rome was a pawnbroker's, where I pledged a ring to put myself in funds; then a tailor's shop, where I procured myself a new suit of clothes and some linen. I was planning a visit to Cardinal Galeotto, the pope's nephew, and wished to present myself in a respectable state. I kept to areas of the city where I had never been before and rode with my hat crammed down over my eyes to avoid recognition. I also stopped at a barber's shop to have myself shaved clean, for I had worn a beard all the time I lived in Rome. For the duke already to have set an assassin on my tail, he would have had to dispatch a message by a swift courier the moment he arrived in Naples. I hoped I was safe for a day or so at least, but I did not wish to take any risks.

IT SEEMED extraordinary after my long career of espionage simply to march up to Cardinal Galeotto's residence and request an audience, by the light of day and with no subterfuge. The only precaution I took was not to give my name to the servants. I handed them an anonymous note that I had sealed with my ring, borrowing wax at an inn.

The cardinal was very gracious and received me at once. He told me he was delighted to see me alive and had not expected this pleasure. I had been given up for lost when I sailed off with Duke Valentino in circumstances that would have strongly inclined him to suspect me of treachery. Cardinal Galeotto made me recount my escape in great detail, stopping me occasionally to exclaim, "Extraordinary! Extraordinary!" When I finished my account, he pronounced me the Odysseus of my day.

We then spoke of the events at Ostia, and Cardinal Galeotto explained to me the reason for the delay of the arrival of the papal troops to arrest Valentino. Nello had been arrested at Forlì, as I had requested, but only after he emerged from the castle after delivering the duke's letter to the castellan. Rather than the letter itself, the pope had as evidence only the fact that a secret letter had been sent. After this debacle, a day was wasted while a force was assembled to be sent down to Ostia and the pope drafted letters to the kings of France and Spain explaining the reason for the seizure of the duke.

There was no sense of urgency, Cardinal Galeotto explained, because the pope had issued secret instructions to Cardinal Carvajal when he sent him to Ostia that, even if the duke met the terms of his accord, he should not be released until Carvajal had received explicit clearance from the pope. Carvajal had decided to ignore these instructions—either on moral grounds, because of the whiff of foul play they gave off, or because he was a partisan of the Spanish, or even, as some surmised, in the pay of the duke.

I told Cardinal Galeotto of my fears for my safety should the duke hear I was alive, and he said that, of course, I must have a guard during the time I was in Rome. He told me he had acted on my request to place Francesca in hiding, and that he would have a servant escort me to her forthwith. As for payment for my services, he handed me a bag of silver for my immediate needs and said he would place a more substantial sum with a banker. He was sure that the pope would wish to express his gratitude to me also, and he would seek an audience for me in the coming few days. I mentioned Dino's commission, and Cardinal Galeotto took note of his name and said he would convey the request that same day to the captain-general of the pope's forces, Duke Guidobaldo of Urbino. I was tempted to ask whether I might have a title while he was about it, so much favor did I seem to have in this cardinal's eyes.

Well, this was all most satisfactory. I strolled through the gay spring streets with the man who was escorting me to Francesca's new lodging, feeling dazed at this new beginning in my life. The cardinal had lent me a cassock and a priest's hat to aid my disguise, and I felt little fear of detection, although I was half-concerned that some poor soul would fall down with a fit on the street before me and require me to give him the last rites.

I was impressed by the level of security the cardinal had allotted to Francesca. Her new dwelling place, which was on the Esquiline, was surrounded with a high wall topped with metal spikes. We rang a bell at the gate, and a dog began barking behind it savagely. Eventually a guard answered, only letting us through when we showed him a note with the cardinal's seal.

Francesca stared at this unexpected priestly intruder with astonishment for a moment before she realized it was I, her lover, and dissolved into tears. I clasped her to me awkwardly, her vast belly between us; I dare say we made a strange sight.

I stood stroking her hair as she told me through her weeping that she had thought I was dead all this while. It had been a strange, fearful time for her, since the papal soldiers had come one night to escort her here, telling her she would be in danger if she stayed where she was. They could tell her nothing of my whereabouts. Her landlady, the glove maker's wife, had kindly come up here with her, leaving her sister to care for her own children, but the two women had been living here in a state of isolation, seeing only the guards, who supplied them with food.

I STAYED IN that place with Francesca for five days before she went into labor. This was almost two weeks after the birth had been due; she was already a week late when I arrived.

I did little in these days. There was a garden behind the house, with a fountain, and I would sit there talking and playing cards with Francesca and the glove maker's wife, whose name was Maria. After a day or so, I sent one of the guards into the city with money to buy me some books.

One evening during this time, Cardinal Galeotto invited me down to his palazzo for dinner, sending an escort to guard me. When I saw we were dining alone, I had a suspicion he might try to seduce me. Indeed he did, speaking much of my beauty, which he claimed had ignited him from the first moment he saw me emerge from the Cloaca, despite my worse-than-sulfurous smell. When I told him I lay only with women, he sighed and said this was as great a folly as if a man were to say that he lay only with redheads or with those born under a certain astrological conjunction. It was the duty of a good Christian to enjoy the full bounty with which it had pleased the Lord to furnish the world.

Cardinal Galeotto had no news that night of my promised papal audience, but he confirmed that Dino had been offered command of a company in the pope's army. Duke Guidobaldo was eager to have him and had sent to Fermo with his letter of appointment forthwith. The cardinal asked after Francesca as I was leaving and offered his doctor to attend her should she need it. I said the child was due at any moment, and he squeezed my arm sympathetically and told me I must send him word when it was safely in the world.

You sometimes hear people say that childbirth is the equivalent for a woman of war for a man. I realized the truth of this, living with Francesca in these days when she knew that her struggle was approaching and that it might end in her death. I had been in this position often in the hours before a battle. Preachers like to tell us that we may be cut down at any moment and should live each day as if it were our last. I am sure this is true, but I do not believe we can truly feel this, except at these few, particular times.

Francesca had always had a tendency to superstition, like the woman of the people she was, and in these days of her late pregnancy, she was hung around with amulets like a gypsy. She could not lie comfortably because of her bulk and was afflicted with insomnia. I read to her to distract her—foolish books in the vernacular, tales of chivalry and romance.

We were sitting in the garden in the late afternoon when Francesca's contractions began. She had had these before, but this time it was clear they were different and more violent. The glove maker's wife, Maria, confirmed that her labor had begun. Maria took her inside, and I went down into the city for a midwife whose address Maria had given me, saying she had served her well in the birth of her own children. When I returned with this woman, it was around dusk. Maria told me that so far it was going well enough, but there might be another few hours to wait.

I sat with the guards outside playing cards—the evening was a very warm one—and they regaled me with tales of the birth of their own children and the length of their wives' labor. It seemed to me they were competing with each other to concoct the worst tales they could tell. One said his wife had been sixteen hours in the birthing of her first child. I felt a great apprehension all this time and kept going to the house to ask Maria what was happening. After the third or fourth time, she told me quite sharply that she would come out and tell me when there was anything to report.

When perhaps four hours had passed after I had returned with the midwife, a scream pierced the air, astonishingly loud, a scream of agony. This came again and again. I looked at the guards and they looked back at me. One shrugged as if to say this was usual in childbirth. Another looked worried and would not meet my eye. Maria came out soon after this and told me that she was beginning to fear this would be a difficult birth. She looked pale. I asked, foolishly, how Francesca was. Maria said she was being very brave.

I had told Maria before about Cardinal Galeotto's offer of his doctor, and she said she thought it would be a good idea to fetch him at this stage. One of the guards offered to go, but I said I would do it myself. I could not bear any more to sit here listening to Francesca's screams, with nothing to do and no way to help. I rode down into the city and hammered on this man's door, until a servant opened it and let me in. I had a letter of recommendation from the cardinal, which he took up to his master. A few minutes later the doctor came down, a grave man in his fifties with a long, bony face.

WHEN WE RETURNED, we could hear Francesca's screams even before we got through the gate. They were hoarser now and feebler. You could hear her fatigue in the sound. The doctor went through to the bedroom, and I sat in the front room of the house with my head in my hands, feeling great impotency and despair. After a while the doctor came in and sat down beside me.

"It's very bad," he said, gently. "I don't think both the mother and child will live. If you want the child alive, it may be needful to cut it out. I wanted to ask what you would prefer."

I looked at him in horror. "Cut it out?" I said.

He sighed. "This is something only to be done if the woman is dead, or will die." He wiped his hand across his face wearily. "She has lost very much blood."

"Don't kill her," I said. What he was saying seemed an obscenity. He sighed again.

"Very well. But you must go at once for a priest."

I SENT ONE of the guards to look for a priest, as they knew the neighborhood better than I. I went into the garden to try to escape the sounds coming from the bedroom. Between the screams, there was a horrible sound of labored, rasping breathing, which was excruciating to hear. As I stood in the garden, weeping, a nightingale struck up her song, incongruously lovely. I thought of Francesca's pitiful amulets and charms and how little good they had done for her, and I felt a great anger against God and the world. My conversation with the doctor kept haunting my mind, when I had said Francesca should not be killed. I was wondering whether, in saying this, I had killed my own son—whether both would die, instead of one, through my fault.

After what seemed a long while, Maria came out to me, tears streaming down her face, and told me Francesca had died, having received extreme unction from the priest. The doctor had intervened to save the child after this, it seemed perhaps successfully. The creature was breathing and it seemed there was a chance she would live.

This was the first I heard of my daughter, and I must say at the time I hardly cared whether she lived or died. I felt she had killed her mother, and I did not want her. Nor could I forgive her for being a girl, when I had been convinced she was a boy. This seemed a final, cruel trick of fate.

I left Maria in the garden and went in to pay the doctor and contracted with the midwife to see to the cleaning and prepare Francesca's body for burial. I felt hard as a stone as I spoke to them, and angry inside, angry with everyone and everything. I felt as though I had shed the last tear I would ever shed in my life. The priest was still there, conferring with the doctor in the corner, and we arranged a date for Francesca's funeral two days hence. Then the midwife started speaking to me about a wet nurse she had summoned, and I looked at her stupidly. The thought that there was a child in the house, a living child that needed feeding, had not fully penetrated my mind.

WELL, THIS IS a horrible time for me to remember, and I am sure not very pleasant for you to read of. I will deal with the rest more quickly. The next day, when I had slept for a while, Maria persuaded me to see my daughter, who had survived the night and was feeding well. Maria said she was a strong child. I went in to see her with a bad grace, simply in order not to seem unnatural, but when I held my daughter and looked down at her clutching at the air with her tiny, helpless fingers, I felt myself softening towards her. Within a day or so, I had almost forgotten I had ever wished her to be a boy. My desires had reshaped themselves around her miniature form.

On the day of Francesca's funeral, I took Vittoria in to say farewell to her. This was the name I had decided to give to my daughter. I called her Francesca as her second name, but Vittoria as her first, as an augury, because this is what I wished for her—victory in some measure over the miseries of life. I leaned down to touch Vittoria's tiny brow against her mother's dead lips, and made a vow to Francesca that I would be a good father to her.

Francesca looked startlingly young lying there, her face pale and slightly caved in, but otherwise bearing no trace of the agony that she had gone through in her last hours. She was fourteen years old when I first knew her and no more than fifteen when she went to the grave.

XXIX

THE WEEKS FOLLOWING FRANCESCA's funeral were very strange for me. For the first time since I had been drawn into the web of Cardinal Giuliano della Rovere, I was free of my spying duties and could go where I chose. Yet I was less free than I had ever been, for I had a new and help-less creature to care for, and I could not step from my door without fearing a dagger in my back. I longed with all my soul to see Nicolosa, but Fermo was the last place I could risk to be seen.

The gravity of my situation was beginning fully to come home to me, now the misery and solace of Vittoria's birth was behind me. I had betrayed the most vengeful man in Italy, and then humiliated him by escaping my due punishment. I had left him trussed on his ship like a partridge waiting to be roasted—an undignified fate for a duke. There could be no doubt of my fate after these crimes of *laesa maiestas*. It was only a matter of timing. Valentino would not rest until he had seen me struck from the book of the living, and he had resources enough to ensure this was done.

So here I remained, effectively a prisoner in this strange household, half barracks, half nursery. Maria stayed until a few days after the funeral, supervising the plump, shy, cow-eyed wet nurse, whose name was Nuccia, and impressing on her the need to attend to her duties and give no encouragement to the flirtation of the guards. The young woman had brought with her a child of her own, a sturdy, laughing girl of around two, whom she was beginning to wean. I liked this fearless little thing, and would watch her play in the garden while her mother fed my daughter indoors or calmed her wailing.

I wondered whether I would still be alive to see my Vittoria when she came to be that same age.

The first week or so of this life passed easily enough, for I had the guards for company and a pile of books and the garden and my sweet infant. After this time, the sense of imprisonment began to weigh on me more heavily, and I longed for escape; yet my fears had grown greater now I was a father. I went out once or twice at first, to enjoy the pleasure of movement, but every eye that fell on me in the street felt a danger. How many people in Rome knew me by sight?

After these few anxious forays, I resigned myself to my cell and tried to craft some kind of life there. I read for hours on end, sending down to the city every few days for fresh books. I fenced and wrestled with the guards to keep my fighting skills honed, for I feared I might need them at any moment. One of these men, who was of subtler intellect than the others, I began to teach how to play chess.

Before long, my old plague of lust crept upon me—a thing I had been dreading, for I could not see a remedy. The guards had offered to procure me women whenever I chose, but this was something I could not risk, for they would have to be brought to my hiding place. Nor did I dare go into the city, for the places where such diversions might be sought were precisely those where I was best known.

One afternoon, I saw the wet nurse Nuccia looking down from a window while I was wrestling half-naked with a guard in the garden. She withdrew at once when she saw I had seen her, but this incident was enough to prompt me to begin looking at her with a new eye. I could no longer watch my daughter sleeping innocently in her nurse's arms without thinking about what lay under her laxly laced bodice. Even the woman's placid round face became pleasing to me, though it would not turn a single head in the street. I often lay awake in bed at night imagining what I would like to do to her. Once or twice I even rose to go to her room, stopping only at my door.

I resisted these urgings because the thought of debauching my daughter's wet nurse seemed to me something too sordid to contemplate—and, besides, is it not said that an infant imbibes something of a woman's moral character along with her milk? Men search widely and pay good money to secure a wet nurse of proven chastity for their children. Was I to find just such a woman—as I believed I had, through Maria's good offices—only perversely to defile her myself?

PERHAPS THREE WEEKS after I had buried Francesca, one of the guards came through to me while I was sitting in the garden reading, and told me two women had come to the house and asked to see me. The guards had told them there was no one of my name in the place, but they had insisted. They knew the story of Francesca's death and Vittoria's birth, and even the date of my arrival at the house. One was a woman in her forties, who did the talking, the other a veiled woman who would not remove her veil or speak. They would not say what their business with me was.

I went through to the front room of the house in a state of apprehension. The thought that the silent veiled woman might be a man in disguise, an assassin, had come into my mind as soon as the guard mentioned her. It was a good enough ruse, as a way of catching a man off guard, although it would be easy to foil. I had a dagger on me already, and buckled on my sword belt as well as I was going through the hall.

THE TWO WOMEN were dressed like artisans' wives or servants, in clothes that were clean, but worn and of cheap cloth. The veil of the silent woman had none of the shimmering transparency you see in noblewomen's veils. It was a black cloth that was almost opaque. I spoke to her, asking her what she wanted. The other woman replied for her, saying that she merely wished to see me alone for a moment. I asked her to remove her veil, and the other woman moved in front of her and said she could not.

I thought of simply ordering the guards to rip off the woman's veil, but something made me hesitate. A mad thought had come to me that the veiled woman might be Nicolosa, although I could not think of how she could have learned where I was. Besides, it seemed to me now that I had seen these strange women that there could be no danger in indulging their request, just for a moment. If there was a man hidden beneath the veil of the silent woman, he was a slight one and I was armed and alert and had the guards close at hand.

"Very well," I said warily, having weighed all these matters, and been overcome by curiosity and boredom. "Come through, if you must."

The woman removed her veil as soon as we were in the next room, revealing, to my astonishment, the urbane features of Madonna Felice della Rovere. She stood before me, smoothing her hair down, a smile of triumph on her face.

"You truly did not guess?"

"Not for a moment, my lady." I could not help smiling back at her.

"I thought I would come to see how you were, after all your adventures."

I bowed, touched at this solicitude.

"My lady, you are most gracious. You know of my whereabouts from Cardinal Galeotto, I imagine?"

He was her cousin, I remembered. She nodded.

"You need not fear for your secrecy. My companion outside is the most faithful of my servants. I would trust her myself with my life."

Madonna Felice ran her finger along a table as she was speaking, as if to check for dust in this bachelor household.

"I was sorry to hear about the mother of your child."

"Thank you, my lady. It was a cruel blow."

"And the child?"

"She is well, thank the Lord. She is sleeping upstairs."

"May I see her?"

"Naturally, my lady," I said, surprised at this request. "I am honored you should wish to. I should just let the guards know all is well."

When I returned from this task, Madonna Felice had concealed her face once more, and I escorted her out of the room and up the stairs.

Vittoria was sleeping in her cradle in the room that she shared with Nuccia and her daughter. I told Nuccia to leave the room, and she did, carrying her daughter, who stared up open-mouthed at my mysterious faceless visitor. When I had closed the door behind them, Madonna Felice raised her veil and looked down at the child.

"She's lovely. All that hair!"

"She was two weeks late, my lady. They tell me that accounts for it."

"The same color as yours. What's her name?"

"She has not yet been christened, but I intend to call her Vittoria."

"Vittoria," she said pensively. "A good name."

We were silent for a moment, she bending over the cradle; then I asked her how she was enjoying her new life as the pope's daughter.

"I hate it," she said, straightening. "You wouldn't believe how much I miss how things were when I first met you, when I was traveling around pursuing my father's business ..."

"I thought you were on a pilgrimage to Loreto."

She made a face at me.

"It was dangerous, but there was spice in it. Now that he has what he wants, I am expected to sit quietly in a corner with my embroidery until he has arranged a marriage for me with some fat old duke."

I laughed at the vehement way she said this.

"Not all dukes are fat and old, my lady," I said. "Think of Valentino."

She rolled her eyes. "Heaven forbid. But what of you? What do you think to do next?"

I shrugged. "What *can* I do, my lady? I am a prisoner here. I cannot leave the house without fear of meeting my death. If it were not for Vittoria, I would leave and go to some place where I am not known, but I cannot leave her here, without a mother to care for her."

"Come to me," she said. I looked at her and she looked back at me with clear eyes. "I mean it. Bring the child. You will be safe with me. I am living with my mother near Piazza dell'Agone. I will appoint you my secretary. I'll employ guards to watch the house—these same men you have here, if you like."

She seemed to be speaking in all seriousness. Her gaze was almost fervent. I gestured at a cassone in the corner of the room.

"My lady, may it please you to sit?"

We sat on the cassone together, and I took a breath and began.

"My lady, I am honored by this gracious offer. But you know this cannot be. You say I would be safe in your household, but how long before your father comes to be suspicious of my presence there? Or your cousin? You are a young and beautiful woman. If you need a secretary, appoint yourself an ill-favored man of sixty. Otherwise, there will be trouble. You know this as well as I."

Madonna Felice was looking at me rebelliously as I was speaking, as if she was going to argue, but she could hardly quarrel with the truth of what I was saying.

"You want to be with Nicolosa," she said accusingly.

"What does that have to do with anything, my lady?"

"You love her."

"Of course I love her," I said. "She is my life."

I looked her in the eye as I said this, as if to challenge her to say she did not already know this. She looked away; then we sat in silence for quite a long time staring disconsolately ahead of us, as people do in conversations of this kind. After a while, I glanced sideways at her and noticed a tear glistening in the corner of her eye.

This sign of vulnerability moved me, in a woman I had always thought of as proud and manipulative and cold. On an impulse, I took her chin and turned her face to me and kissed her. She kissed me back, and the half-strange, half-familiar taste of her excited me. We remained for a while on the cassone, clinched lasciviously together; then I took her hand and led her unresisting down the corridor into the room where I slept. Nuccia was in the garden and I called down to her on the way to come inside and watch over my child.

WE LAY WITH each other that time with a greater feeling than on the previous occasion—I speak for myself, at least— and remained fondly embraced afterwards. Madonna Felice was delighted, I think, at having secured this lapse from me moments after my declaration of my love for Nicolosa and my wise sermon about how there could be nothing further between us.

After a while, she disentangled herself and began to order her dress.

"I should go."

"I am glad you came here, my lady," I said, catching at her hand. "But we must not ..."

She stood looking at me imperiously.

"Must not what?"

"No matter, my lady."

I rose and prepared myself to accompany her downstairs, bracing myself for the teasing I would have to endure from the guards when she had left. Then she put her hand on my arm. "I have the solution."

I waited for her to proceed. "The solution?"

"We will dissolve this strange household. It should be done anyway, if only for the moral welfare of that poor young woman you have hired as a wet nurse. You may go off and do what you will until it is safe to return. Your daughter may come to me."

I reflected on this surprising proposition. It seemed on the face of it a good idea, but I did not like to think of my daughter in the hands of this scheming woman, who I thought had not abandoned her designs on me.

"You are very kind, my lady, but I ..."

"Was there ever a more insubordinate man?" Madonna Felice interjected, half-laughing, half-annoyed, placing her hand over my mouth. "Your first impulse is always to argue— and yet you know this proposition makes sense if you think about it for a moment. Think of your daughter. She will be much better off with us. She will have experienced women at hand, and the best care an infant can have. And no one will know she is yours, only my mother and I. I will invent some pretext—a poor orphan I have taken in for charity."

I hesitated for a moment, but I could think of no objection to her scheme, or none I could decently voice.

"My lady, you are right," I said, resigned. "It is the best solution and most generous of you."

"Not at all," she said lightly. "I need something to take my mind off my own troubles, and she is a sweet thing. I shall cherish her because she is yours."

This last phrase she said more softly, looking at me with a lingering air. Then she lowered her ugly veil over her face and turned away.

I LEFT ROME after Vittoria's christening, which was conducted with great secrecy by Cardinal Galeotto in the chapel of his palace. The only people present besides the cardinal, my daughter, and I were Madonna Felice and her mother, Madonna Lucrezia, who stood godmother to the child. After the ceremony, I left Vittoria in the hands of these ladies, who carried her off with many exclamations of tenderness. I remained for dinner with Cardinal Galeotto, and then left after dark with an escort for Ostia, whence I took a ship north.

It was a cruel anguish to leave my daughter at this most vulnerable age, when even the strongest child can wake smiling and be carried off by death before nightfall. I could not deceive myself; there was a good chance I would not see her again. I struggled to keep the tears from my eyes as I stood on the ship at dawn, looking back towards the city where her tiny frame rested. I had cut myself a strand of her angel-fine hair to take with me, using the scissors I kept for my nails.

I sailed first to Genova; then I made my way across the north of Italy, traveling under an assumed name. I went to Milan and Brescia and Mantova and Padova and Venice; then, changing identity, to Vienna and to Prague. A man I fell in with in Vienna was planning to travel to Constantinople, and I was within an inch of accompanying him there. This wandering life had seductions for me, when I accustomed myself to it. There was much freedom in it. I did not lack money, for Cardinal Galeotto had procured me bills of exchange to draw on various banks in a series of three or four names.

I SHALL RESIST the temptation to speak of my adventures on these travels, for they do not form part of this story. Also, space presses. As you will have noticed, this notebook, once reaming out profligately ahead of me, is now almost full. A meager ten blank pages remain, and they are not to be wasted, for I still have matters of import to tell.

I kept myself informed of developments with the duke as best I could during my travels. I became adept at deciphering a Neapolitan accent across a room and finding my way unobtrusively into the group containing its owner. The reports I heard were conflicting. Some said that Valentino had received a warm welcome in Naples from the Spanish general Gonzalo de Córdoba, and was now in alliance with this general, plotting a return to his lands. Others reported that the relationship between Valentino and Córdoba was poisonous, and that Córdoba wanted this meddlesome man back in Spain.

I heard the truth in the first week of September, in a tavern near the Rialto in Venice. News flowed through this place like wine through the veins of its regular customers. The landlord had been a sailor and many of the drinkers there were fresh off some ship. You could meet men there from all nations and learn all the affairs of the world. On the evening of which I speak, there were two or three Sardinians from the crew of a merchant ship that had sailed up from Pescara. They boasted first of a narrow escape from a pirate ship that had chased them; then they began to retail the latest from the south.

Valentino, it appeared, had spent his months in Naples plotting a desperate last assault on the Romagna, conscripting any brigand or disaffected soldier he could lay his hands on. Finally, Pope Julius had convinced the king of Spain that it was intolerable for him to offer shelter to this scheming adventurer any longer. Gonzalo de Córdoba arrested the duke on the orders of the king of Spain and held him in Naples until the castellan of Forlì finally surrendered his last remaining stronghold. Now my enemy was on his way to Spain as a prisoner, to be detained at the royal pleasure there.

I MADE MY way down to Rome as soon as I heard this news and took lodgings at an inn, using one of my false names out of caution. The next day I visited Camilla, who wept with joy to see me and paid me my share of her takings for the previous six months. She told me that two men had come looking for me at her house in April, questioning the clients and offering her money if she could tell them of my whereabouts. She had strung them along, telling them I was hiding out in an abandoned farmhouse off the road to Tivoli. Nello ambushed them there with some malefactors of his acquaintance and left them at the side of the road stripped of their clothes and with their throats cut, as if they had been the victims of a bandit attack.

I went to Madonna Felice's house after this and visited my daughter, who had just returned with her nurse from a stay in the country. You could see at once that she had been well cared for; I would wager no child in Rome had such delicate garb. I found Vittoria much improved. Her eyes were alert now and her hands expertly grasping. She was interested in every object in her vision and wanted if possible to have it in her mouth. She was shy of me first, and squirmed back to her nurse's arms when I tried to take her up, but once she had learned my face, she developed a liking for me, and would reach up towards me when she saw me. I became ambitious of her then. I wanted her to reach for me before all others. I wanted to be my daughter's true and sole love.

After i had been in Rome for perhaps a week, Madonna Felice informed me that her father, the pope, had deigned to grant me an audience. He wished to thank me in person for my services to him, being now more at leisure than he had been in the spring. I was honored by this graciousness, but felt also a little wary at what this meeting with the old fox might portend.

When I arrived at the Vatican, a chatty young chaplain led me through a labyrinth of corridors to a door at the back of the palace. This led into a garden. Pope Julius was standing there amid the foliage under a dovecote in a snow-white cassock and *zucchetto* and a scarlet *mozzetta*, feeding a handful of grain to his doves—a most peaceful and edifying sight.

The pope turned when his servant announced me, smiled beatifically in my general direction, and raised a gloved hand to postpone further greetings. Only when he had got through the silver bucket of corn at his side did he allow me to kneel and kiss his hand.

"Let us sit in the shade, my son," he said, indicating a loggia at the side of the garden. Vines meandered up it, hanging luxuriantly with grapes. A pair of doves chastely cooed above.

I had not seen the pope at close quarters since the time of our interview on the night of the Cloaca, two and a half years earlier. He did not seem to have aged since that time, although he had turned sixty the previous year. If anything, he was rejuvenated. Men like Julius breathe power. It is the blood in their veins and the strength in their nerves.

"Well, my son," the pope said when we were seated. "My daughter and nephew have doubtless conveyed my gratitude for your services. Gratitude and admiration. Your escape on the ship … a stirring tale. If I had fifty men of your mettle, Italy would not be in the quagmire she is."

"Your Holiness is too kind."

"And, as a result of your loyalty, you now face these new dangers. My nephew has informed me that you now have to live in hiding. Most regrettable. And your danger has not diminished with Valentino's ejection from Italy. He has a long arm, as I believe the phrase goes."

"Indeed, Your Holiness," I said despondently. I could not deny that this was true. I had been attempting to convince myself that I was no longer in danger with Valentino departed from the shores of Italy and in custody, but there was no reason why this should be the case. A man may pay an assassin from a Spanish prison as well as he can from a Neapolitan army camp, and Valentino did not lack gold or murderous friends

"Something I should warn you of in that connection, indeed," the pope continued. "I shall have to release your old friend Don Michelotto da Coreglia. Part of my agreement with King Ferdinand, you know."

I looked at him in stark dismay. The Florentines had captured Don Michelotto the previous winter, and Julius had been holding him in strict confinement in Rome since May. The possibility had never crossed my mind that he would leave this custody alive.

"No loss to me, I must say. I got nothing from the man. You might as well interrogate a plank of wood." Julius looked at me, and then said briskly, "Don't look so forlorn, my son. I have excogitated a solution to your troubles. You must die."

He smiled triumphantly at this fine piece of logic.

"I must die, Your Holiness?"

"I do not mean in truth, of course. You must *appear* to die, so Valentino will call off the dogs. We can concoct some form of funeral, don't worry, and ensure that the records are in order. Then you merely need to stay well clear of Rome and Fermo and wherever else you are known until the danger from him is over. Valentino will not last forever, you know. He was ever a rash youth. Two years, perhaps three—who knows?"

He reached out for a grape from a bunch hanging over him as he concluded this speech and put it in his mouth.

"Very good. Try one. The soil here is most propitious for vines. Make them struggle and they yield—always works. What do you think of my plan?"

"Your plan is excellent, Your Holiness," I said feelingly. "You offer me salvation, nothing less. Words cannot express my thanks."

I was sincere as I said this. His plan did seem in all truth the solution to my predicament, and I knew he had the power to deliver on his promise. A trusted doctor, a trusted priest, a coffin filled with a vagabond's body; these things would be child's play to a pope.

"Not at all, my son," Julius said. "It is the least I can do after your services for me. Besides, if you wish to express your gratitude, it occurs to me that you might be kind enough to perform a small task for me during the time when you are supposed to be dead. So your time will not be wasted, you know."

THE POPE SPOKE of this idea occurring to him as though he had plucked it from the vine along with his grape, but I do not believe this for a moment. He wanted me as his spy still; he needed me alive for this purpose; his generous offer to masquerade my death was all in function of this. I listened to him speaking on about his plans for me with a feeling of mounting horror. What if Valentino did not die after a year or two, as he so confidently predicted? Was I to remain this man's slave for my whole life?

The pope explained that the task he wished me to perform for him was secret for the present. He could reveal only that it would take me beyond the Alps, a detail he presented beamingly, as if this was a great boon.

"So you see, you will be far from his reach."

"Your Holiness," I said desperately. "I am eager, as ever, to serve you where I can, but I am weary of this life of lying and feigning and danger. I have known nothing else now for more than two years. Perhaps in your great goodness, instead of this new task, you might permit me to undertake a pilgrimage somewhere—to the Holy Land, perhaps? That too would take me far from the reach of Valentino, and it would enable me to do penance for the many sins of which I have been guilty these past years, while in the service of Your Holiness. These are things that weight heavily on my soul."

This was the best I could think of, on the impulse of a moment. Julius was silent for a long moment after I had spoken. I listened to the doves murmuring, silently praying to God to soften his vicar's heart.

"My son," the pope began eventually in a careful tone, measuring each word. "I do not think you have quite grasped the nature of our relationship. I am your spiritual father. We obey our fathers. We do not haggle with them, as we might with our shoemaker, to beat down the price of a pair of boots. Of course, if you wish to spurn my offer to arrange your death and to take your chances with Valentino instead, you are quite free to do so. I do not think I would risk it in your place."

The pope's voice became more clipped as he delivered this speech, and the pupils of his eyes narrowed until they became hostile black pins. It seemed to me I had no choice but to cede, even if I could see my life vanishing down a drain. I thought back to Julius's statement that he had been compelled by King Ferdinand to release Don Michelotto. Was that true? Or had he had decided on this clemency himself, the easier to bend me to his will?

"I will serve Your Holiness as you ask," I said, my heart dying within me. A pure white dove strutted past my ankles as I spoke. I felt an extraordinary urge to kick this venerable symbol of peace.

"Excellent," Julius said, rubbing his hands, his good temper restored. "I knew you would see reason. Galeotto will give you details of your duties at the appropriate time. I am certain you will fulfill this new role with the intelligence and resourcefulness you have shown in your previous missions. I have great confidence in your talents, as you see."

He reached out for a small hand-bell beside him, as if to summon the chaplain to see me out; then he seemed to think better of it. He laid a hand on my shoulder.

"Let me tell you a truth, my son. God often knows a man's vocation better than he does himself. As a boy, I longed for nothing more than to be a soldier. I had no wish to be a churchman when my father and uncle first proposed it. Whereas now ..." He spread his hands at the idyllic scene around him, defying me not to see in it God's will.

"Does God destine some men to be spies, then, Your Holiness?" I said this as bitterly as I dared.

"Of course." Julius nodded earnestly. "What else is the lesson of the story of Judith? Like you, she entered the enemy's camp, armed only with the guile with which God had endowed her. Like you, she struck down the serpent who menaced her land. God has given you, like Judith, great beauty of form. You look as harmless as a dove, in the words of the gospel—yet you possess the wisdom of the serpent, which is to say cunning. You would not be here today if you did not."

I looked at the ground. It was no consolation to me whatever to think that God had expressly crafted me for a life of espionage.

"As for your concern about the sins you have incurred in the service of our mother Church, that is quite legitimate, of course. Let me shrive you."

"Now, Your Holiness?" I said wonderingly.

"What better time? *Hic et nunc.* I have five minutes or so before I must meet with the Spanish ambassador."

He was looking at me expectantly, and I knelt and embarrassedly recounted my sins since my last confession, which, to my shame, was more than two years before. I had killed two men horribly without mercy, the men on the ship; also numerous more while under orders from Liverotto and the duke. I had lied more times than I could count, fornicated with a goodly number of women, attended mass less frequently than I would have wished, and eaten meat on a Friday at least four times that I could remember. The pope absolved me absolutely of the homicides and lies I had incurred in his service and prescribed penances of a not particularly onerous nature for the remainder of my sins.

"Splendid," he concluded, when this curiously accelerated confession was over. "I hope this has put your conscience at rest."

He rose as he was saying this and rang for the chaplain, who arrived with suspicious alacrity, as if he had been hiding behind some arras. As I was bowing my farewell, the pope placed in my hand a very fine medal in gold with a belligerent profile of him on one side and a pastoral scene of a shepherd tending his flock on the other.

Virginia Cox

"Your Holiness ..." I began, but he airily waved aside my thanks, the gesture scattering the doves around him in a graceful flurry of wings.

I followed the garrulous chaplain down the endless corridors of the palace, feeling dazed and numb, like a man who has been assaulted by brigands and left for dead at the side of the road. Even the thought that the pope had just unwittingly absolved me for fornicating with his daughter was not sufficient to put a smile on my face. God had forged the sun to give us light and the fruits of the earth to nourish us, and me, it seemed, as a weapon to place in the hand of this wiliest of his shepherds. Such was my destiny—this was the lesson of this meeting—and it was one I could escape only through death.

XXX

C ARDINAL GALEOTTO WAS IN HIS element arranging my death, his refined intellect worrying away most exquisitely over the details. Did I wish for four plumed black horses pulling my coffin or six? Would four look too few for a valued servant of the pope? Would six be too many for a man of my low birth?

Once the arrangements had been made, I asked for a week in which to settle my affairs, during which I meant to make a brief visit to Fermo. I had to see Nicolosa before news of my death reached her, to tell her it was a fiction so she would not suffer grief at my passing. This I insisted upon, although the cardinal tried to argue that only Dino should be told, as the executor of my will.

I had written Nicolosa a letter at the start of my exile, telling her the whole history of my spying for the della Rovere and explaining that only this duty could have kept me from her side for so long. I told her I had not confided this secret in her because I had been compelled to take a solemn oath of silence, and I had wished also to spare her knowledge of the dangers I was running. In this same letter, I spoke passionately and at length of my love for her, enclosing three sonnets also on this theme.

Cardinal Galeotto offered me an escort once he saw I was determined to go to Fermo, but I refused it, thinking that this would make me too conspicuous. Instead, I traveled alone, merely adopting a few precautions, such as taking a route less direct than the usual and lodging in private rooms rather than inns. One night I even slept out under a hedgerow, though close enough to a village to call for help if in danger. The nights were not yet cold. We were only in September, the meadows still green, the sun still fervent at the height of the day.

When i reached Fermo, I went to my house near the walls, left my baggage, and went at once to Nicolosa's. She greeted me warmly, though we were in the company of a servant so that nothing of import could be said. When we were alone for a moment, I requested a meeting with her that evening. She looked at me diffidently for a moment in silence, and I almost thought she was going to refuse me. Then she consented that I could come to her after the third hour of night, over the wall, as I had been used.

I felt a little fearful of Nicolosa's cold response to my request to meet with her alone. Ever since I had seen her in Rome with her cousin, I had a sense of how keenly her family was pressing her to remarry. I was hoping she would resist this pressure and keep herself for me, now that I had explained in my letter the reasons for my long absence from Fermo. Still, I longed for the chance to persuade her in person, and in a language not composed solely of words.

When i made my way into Nicolosa's house that night, after my usual acrobatics traversing the wall, I found her sitting in her study with a low fire in the grate and a sole candle for light. I embraced her and made to kiss her, but she turned her head away, confirming my forebodings of earlier in the day.

I was nervous after this cool welcome, but I stumbled into an explanation of my forthcoming death and the reasons for it. Nicolosa looked at me intently as I was speaking, with an expression I found difficult to read. When I finished my exposition, I fell on my knees and enjoined her ardently to wait for me this while longer. This was a speech I had been preparing in my mind for a long time, and I embarked on it with conviction, although doubts occasioned by her new manner and her refusal of my kiss were nagging at my heart as I did.

Nicolosa gave me only a moment for my protestations of love; then she put a finger on my lips to silence me and said, almost in a whisper, "Matteo. There is something I need to tell you."

This could be nothing good, from her tone. I fell silent. A dread was coming upon me. Nicolosa eased herself back from the light of the candle, as though she did not wish me to scrutinize her face too closely. I thought she was going to tell me she had agreed to some noble marriage and felt a tumult in my heart already at the thought.

Instead, she said, to my astonishment, "I have decided to take my vows as a nun. I am glad for the chance to tell you in person. I had thought I would tell you by letter, but that seemed cowardly."

She could continue no more and lowered her gaze.

"Nicolosa," I said urgently. "What do you mean, you have decided to take your vows? Who has persuaded you of this?"

"No one has persuaded me," she said, a little haughtily. "It is a decision I have come to."

"And what of me?" I said. "What of my love? What of *our* love?"

She did not reply. She was looking down, avoiding my eye.

"Teo. There is something else I need to tell you." There was another pause, and then she said, more falteringly, "I hardly know how to speak of it."

She was silent for a while longer.

"What is it?" I said.

I made to embrace her, but she pushed me away. We stared at each other for a moment; then she drew a long sigh and spoke.

"There is no kind way to tell you this. Our love cannot be. We must lie together no more." Her eyes were filled with tears. "We are brother and sister. My father was your father. May God forgive us both for what we have done."

I looked at her in horror. I had long forgotten this fear.

"What are you saying, Nicolosa? Who told you of this enormity?"

It could be no one but Madonna Felice, I was thinking. My fists were clenched. Nicolosa looked at me from under her wet lashes.

"He told me himself. Father, I mean, before he died." She wiped her eyes with her handkerchief and paused, as though drawing up her forces. "I will tell you how it came about if you will listen without interrupting. It was at the time when the question of my marriage first came up. I told Father I wished to marry no man but you. I told him if I could not have you I would prefer to be a nun."

My heart leapt extraordinarily, in the midst of my turmoil, to hear this testimony to Nicolosa's love for me. She continued speaking, in a quiet, remembering voice.

"He was very angry, angrier than I had ever seen him before. He would not countenance our marrying; nor did he wish me to become a nun. We argued very bitterly. Eventually he told me I could not marry you because of … the thing that I told you. Then he tried to convince me to take Raffaele, and I agreed in the end, knowing I could not have you."

A hope had seized me as she spoke.

"Perhaps he was lying when he told you what he told you. He could see you could not be convinced by other means."

Nicolosa nodded sadly. "I tried to persuade myself of that same thing. At the time we became lovers, I had convinced myself of it." She paused. "Although, in all truth, I did not care. I was angry with God then, for the horrors He had visited on me. I wanted to defy Him. I did not care if I broke His laws."

She said this passionately, as though for a moment she still felt this same thing.

"That's as may be," I said, clinging to my straw. "But it does not mean you were wrong to suspect your father may have been lying."

"No," Nicolosa said firmly. "What he said was true. I know now."

She was silent for a moment. I thought again of Madonna Felice.

"How do you know? You have some fresh proof?"

Nicolosa looked at me strangely and then said, in a very low voice, "I saw him."

"Saw whom?" The strangeness of her tone was filling me with disquiet.

"My father. Our father."

"In a dream, you mean?"

"It did not seem like a dream. He came and sat at the bottom of my bed. It happened twice. I screamed the first time. That would have woken me, would it not, if I had been dreaming? My maid came in, but she could see nothing. It was only to me that he wished to appear."

"What did he tell you?" I found myself whispering, as she was. A chill had crept on me as she spoke.

"He said nothing, Teo. He is dead. He was not as he was in life." She shuddered at the memory. "He just looked at me. He held up the finger on which he used to wear the ring I sent you after his death."

We were silent after this for a long time. This seemed a message from the dead man that I could not mistake. Darkness was descending in my mind.

"Teo?" Nicolosa said, in a very gentle voice. "I think it is best if you go now. We can speak again tomorrow if you like, during the day."

"Don't make me leave." I could not bear this.

"What do you mean? Of course you must leave. Have you not heard what I have been saying?"

I clung to her. "Just let me stay here in the house with you. I will not lay a finger on you. Do not turn me out of your door. I will kill myself if you do. I will kill us both."

I think this was what I said, though in truth I cannot remember. My mind was in a haze. I felt a great fury against her.

"You must leave this instant," Nicolosa said, pulling free of me and looking at me with wild eyes. She looked frightened and I came to my senses a little.

"Very well," I said bitterly. "But you will regret this."

I turned on my heel and made for the door, without saying another word to her. I felt nothing but anger for Nicolosa at this moment. My hands were throbbing with violence. For nothing I would have choked her to death.

When I got back to my house, I lit a lantern and went out to the stable to saddle my horse. I remember nothing of what was going through my head at this time, only what my outward actions were. I rode through the streets to the gates of the city and bribed the guards to open them so I could go out. I had no plan in my head, except that I wanted to be in movement and far from the city. It seemed a necessity to me in my fevered state.

There was a bright moon in the sky, and I could see clearly without a lantern. I rode on through the night, sometimes spurring my horse on, sometimes going at the pace the beast wished. After a while, I felt a need to be higher and rode up a hill. The road became narrower as I ascended until it was only a track between hedgerows, and then barely that. I passed some dark shapes on my right that seemed like the houses of some mean village, and turned into what seemed a wide meadow. Here I tethered my horse to a tree, lay down on my cloak on the grass, and gazed up into the vast starry blackness of the sky.

I MUST HAVE slept, for the next thing I knew it was light, the pale first light of dawn, before sunrise. There were faces above me. One was old, a brown face scored deeply with wrinkles, like a walnut. Two were young, one the face of a goggle-eyed child who started when I opened my eyes and put his thumb in his mouth. I looked at these faces with no notion of who they were or where I was.

The faces were gone after a while, and I closed my eyes again. Then, after a space of time I cannot gauge, I felt a touch on my elbow. It was the old man again. He was holding something out to me. I gazed at it blankly for a moment. Then I realized it was a rough pewter beaker filled with milk.

This is what I remember as the beginning of my recovery. I raised myself up and drank the milk, which was still warm from the udder, under the old man's impassive gaze. His kindness to a stranger undid me. Here I was, with my expensive garments and my gold chain and my silver-handled dagger, asleep at the side of his field, and this peasant had not seen me as an opportunity for pillage. My fine horse was grazing peacefully alongside me, still tethered where I had left him by the tree. I remembered the times when I was recruiting for Liverotto's army, when I burned villages of this kind and killed old men like this and young boys like his grandson. A great flood of tears arose in me thinking of this, and I wept uncontrollably, not even seeking to check my tears. I wept for what seemed a very long time, until the sun had risen and golden light began to pour across the land.

Finally, I rose and untethered my horse. The peasant was working in the field beneath me with his son, and I rode down and thanked him for the milk. I wished to thank him for curing me of my insanity and gave him a silver coin, which he looked at in amazement, as though he had no idea what to do with such a thing. Then I set off for Fermo, which I found with some difficulty, having no recollection whatsoever of my route.

NICOLOSA GREETED me with relief and some wariness when I went to her house later that morning.

"You were so strange last night, Teo. I was afraid you would do something foolish."

"I did do something foolish," I said, and then told her of what I remembered of my adventures that night. She listened anxiously at first but smiled a little when I spoke of the peasant and the milk. Her eyes were rimmed with pink, as if she not slept.

"You are recovered now?" she asked when I finished. I nodded. Strangely, I was. I felt limpid and calm after my madness, like the sky after a tempest has passed.

"I have been thinking," I said. "There can be nothing between us, that is certain. But do not shut yourself away from the world in a convent. I hate to think of it. There is no need."

I spoke with fervor. A memory had been coming to me all morning of our meeting in the charnel house of the convent of the Clarissans. I had a clear image in my mind of Nicolosa standing there before me, a living woman in the realm of bones.

"Shut myself away from the world?" She smiled, a little scornfully, narrowing her eyes. "Why not rather say 'turn to

God'? In any case, it is not such a penance for a woman to spend her life without men as you men like to think. My stepmother is in that same convent, and a sister of hers, and two cousins of mine. We will rule the roost. And I will have my books and the garden and my prayers."

"May I visit you there?" I said miserably, after a pause.

"Of course," she said. "You are my brother."

This sounded very strange to me. I looked at her, but could not say a word. Finally, I said, "I suppose I should go to my death."

Nicolosa nodded, looking down; then she took my hand and examined it. I tensed to feel her skin against mine.

"You have his ring on."

It was true. I had recouped Messer Giovanni's ring from its hiding place that morning and polished the wretched thing up.

"Don't worry," I said. I half thought to call her sister, but I knew I would choke on the word. "It won't leave my finger from now on."

I turned to go, quite abruptly. Tears were beginning in my eyes that I did not wish Nicolosa to see. I was almost at the door when I turned back and saw her face a mirror of mine in its misery. I stepped back and took her in my arms, and she allowed me to hold her for a moment. Then she pushed me away from her, quite violently. I walked from the room, my heart foundering in pain.

XXXI

O N THE WAY BACK TO ROME, I felt an impulse to confess myself properly, not in the perfunctory manner
I had to the pope. I stopped at a small Benedictine
monastery in the mountains, one of those surprisingly austere
places you still occasionally come across, even in these deca-
dent times. The priest I confessed to was a diligent man and
took his time with me, meting out penance for my sins with
great exactness and some severity. I incurred a further sin of
mendacity by saying I had been two years without absolution,
so I could confess once again the same sins for which Julius
had shriven me with so light a hand.

My journey was a wretched one, such that it grieves me
still to recall it. I rode onwards like a stone, impervious to
the scenes I was passing through; yet within I was not stony.
I felt cut to the core. It seemed to me I was nothing without my love for Nicolosa to sustain me. It had been with me
since my childhood. It had grown up with me, covertly, like a
wild sapling on the edge of a farmer's lands, which is almost
a tree before any have marked it. The prospect of life without
this desire seemed to me as insipid as the saltless bread that
Tuscans so perversely choose to eat.

I felt angry on this journey when I thought of my father
and the poisoned legacy he had left me, along with his three
hundred ducats. I felt angry with myself also, and with the
demons in my mind that had fought so hard to dissuade me
that I could be his son. Nor had these demons entirely ceased
their meddling. For a long stretch of road before I came to
the monastery, I thought about Nicolosa's strange story of
her father's ghostly visit and wondered whether it might be a

fabrication. What if Madonna Felice had told her the tale of our supposed incest for her own purposes, as I had originally imagined? What if Nicolosa had devised this mysterious tale to draw me out and test me, having noted that I did not wear her father's ring?

I was riding into Tivoli, some seven leagues from Rome, when a head caught my eye, impaled on a stake at the side of the road. It was the head of a young bandit, one of a sorry, sightless cluster—some zealous papal governor seeking to reassure wayfarers that crime did not pay in Pope Julius's realm. The head of which I speak was a fresh one, placed there perhaps only that morning; the birds had not been at it yet, though the neck was already swarming with flies. I stopped for a while to look on the boy's handsome, marble face, thinking of the fact that he was probably still breathing when I had risen that day. His expression was curiously tranquil, as you might imagine a martyr. He could not have been older than seventeen or eighteen.

This sight restored some tranquility to me, strangely—more so, in truth, than my confession and shriving. I counted my blessings as I rode on, the first of them being that my head was still resting on its neck. I was young; I was healthy; I had money in my purse. My daughter, who might so easily have been lying in the grave with her mother, was thriving like a young plant in good soil. Nor was Nicolosa herself dead, though she must be dead to my desire. I did not even think that her love for me had withered. Perhaps life in a convent would suit her less than she imagined. Perhaps she would return to the world.

These thoughts cheered me, and I lifted my head and truly looked at the world for the first time on this miserable journey. It was late afternoon, and the light was warm and golden, long shadows beginning to stretch across the ground. I paused on the road and gazed out over the ruins of Hadrian's great villa, tumbling down the hill before me, entangled in greenery. Three white herons were winging their lazy way across this verdure, seeming to take an eternity in their flight. I was a man with a dangerous enemy at my back, tied into a servitude I saw no prospect of escaping—yet I felt my mind as light as a child's in that moment. I thought back over the years since I came into my manhood and the strange dance of death I had been treading all this time. For a moment I could not believe I was still here, living and breathing, the feast of the world spread out beneath my eyes.

I WATCHED MY funeral cortege from the palace by the river where Cardinal Galeotto della Rovere had his residence. Since it is unlikely that you will ever experience this same thing yourself, I will spend a few words describing it, even though this notebook is rapidly coming to its end.

No man can count himself entirely a failure if his funeral procession can boast of a cardinal among its participants. Mine had two, Cardinal Galeotto della Rovere and Cardinal Giovanni de' Medici, each with his well-stocked retinue of adulators following behind. These two weighty souls sat soberly behind my coffin, no doubt exchanging sage observations on the lability of human existence. Cardinal Giovanni was mounted on a white horse, I remember, as if already in training to be pope.

Besides this more august component, much of the remainder of my funeral procession was made up of whores. Camilla led the party, leaning on Nello's arm and, I was touched to see, looking genuinely stricken at my passing. Behind her stood her sister and others of her girls; then the glove maker and his wife with whom Francesca had lodged. Messer Isacco was there, looking dissonant in this Christian company; also various people who find little or no mention in this story—former soldiers of the duke, members of the circle of Cardinal Giovanni, my one-time servant Masetto and his bride. One handsome young couple standing a little apart perplexed me for a moment, until I realized the wife was my former contact at Camilla's, Violante. Camilla had told me that Violante left her establishment soon after my departure for Ostia, having mysteriously accumulated sufficient wealth for a dowry to find herself a husband of her choice.

I was surveying this crowd, with some satisfaction at the turnout, when a figure caught my eye that made my heart turn with astonishment. I only glimpsed him for a moment; then he fell behind somebody's head.

"Diego," I said. Madonna Felice, who was standing at my side, craned down to see down at where I was looking.

"Oh yes," she said, indifferently. "Your contact in the palace. He was with Valentino until he left for Spain; then he came back to Rome. He has become a Dominican friar, they tell me."

I turned away to hide a smile and peered back cautiously at Fra Filippo. He was looking around suspiciously, sniffing the air, perhaps scrutinizing the other mourners for someone who could advise him of the providential significance of my death.

At this moment, Vittoria awoke from her unreliable slumber and immediately began to cry quite piteously. One of her first teeth was coming through, and she was quite indignant at this painful encounter with the tribulations of human existence.

"*Poverina*," Madonna Felice said, reaching her arms out maternally. "Give the poor little orphan to me."

"Orphan!" I said, crossing myself with the hand I had free from holding my daughter. "My lady, not even in jest."

Madonna Felice laughed. "How amusing. I have never thought you a superstitious man. Perhaps watching one's own funeral is enough to bring it on."

"In truth, my lady," I said. "It is partly the funeral and partly the ceremony I know awaits me afterwards."

I gestured as I said this towards the table behind us, where Madonna Felice's mother was standing, Madonna Lucrezia. Lined up on the table before her were a gleaming pair of scissors, a razor, a bowl, and a dark, ominous mixture perhaps intended to blacken my hair.

"You do well to be afraid," Madonna Felice said, cradling my daughter, who had treacherously fallen silent as soon as she took her. "We speak of disguise, but our true intent is to ruin your looks, to make the world a safer place for women."

I glanced at Madonna Lucrezia and she smiled at me indulgently. She was not the most severe of chaperones, in truth—as one might perhaps expect of a lady who had accommodated a cardinal in her youth.

The procession celebrating my death was winding its way down the street, attracting a burgeoning crowd of idlers in its wake. Madonna Felice, who could risk being sighted more easily than I, hung out of the window to watch its last passage around the corner. Then she turned back, gave me a mocking smile, and gestured towards Madonna Lucrezia's instruments.

"That's your death taken care of. *Incipit vita nova.*"

Which is to say, "Here begins your new life."

AFTERWORD

THE POLITICAL NARRATIVE of *The Subtlest Soul* tracks events in central Italy in the first years of the sixteenth century with a reasonably high degree of fidelity. The principal events recounted (Liverotto Euffreducci's coup at Fermo; the conspiracy against Cesare Borgia; Borgia's revenge against the conspirators at Senigallia; the death of Alexander VI; the election of Popes Pius III and Julius II; the downfall of Cesare Borgia) are well documented, and my account here departs little from the historical record.

A major source for these events is Machiavelli, who witnessed and reported on many of them at first hand as a diplomat, and revisited several as a political analyst. Liverotto's coup features in chapter 8 of *The Prince*, and Borgia's revenge against the conspirators and his capitulation to Julius II in chapter 7 of the same work. The Senigallia incident is also the subject of a separate treatise by Machiavelli ("A Description of the Method Used by Duke Valentino in Killing Vitellozzo Vitelli, Oliverotto da Fermo, and Others," available in *The Chief Works and Others*, trans. Allan Gilbert, Durham and London: Duke University Press, 1989). Numerous details in the novel are drawn from these works, as also from Machiavelli's diplomatic letters. I have followed Machiavelli narratives of Liverotto's coup and the showdown at Senigallia even where they differ on points of detail from other contemporary accounts, for the rather postmodern reason that I posit my protagonist Matteo da Fermo as Machiavelli's main source for both events. Similarly, I have followed Machiavelli in his version of Liverotto's name (some modern sources prefer Oliverotto).

My treatment of Liverotto Euffreducci's rise to power and his conduct while in power is obviously conditioned by the point of view of my protagonist Matteo, and so should not be taken as objective. Modern historians of Fermo have attempted to rehabilitate Liverotto's reputation from his traditional image as bloody tyrant, noting that he had some support within the city and proved himself an energetic and far-sighted ruler during his short period in office (see, for example, Francesco Pirani, *Fermo* (Spoleto: Centro Italiano di Studi sull'Alto Medioevo, 2010), 85-86). Despite this revisionism, however, no one disputes the shocking brutality of Liverotto's seizure of power, which led Machiavelli to cite him as his prime modern example of a ruler who gained power by crimes or atrocities *(scelera)* rather than through talent or good fortune.

Although I have respected the main outlines of historical events in constructing the political plot of this novel, I have not attempted to observe strict historical accuracy in every point of detail. My priority throughout has been to craft an enjoyable fiction, true to history in terms of the mentalities and attitudes portrayed, but not necessarily always so faithful to the precise, documented course of events. I have taken particular liberties with the historical record in the early chapters of the novel. Giuliano della Rovere's visit to Fermo in Chapter 1 is invented, as is the embassy to Cesare Borgia on which I have Liverotto send Matteo in Chapter 2 at the time of his coup. Borgia was in Rome, rather than Cesena, in January 1502, and Liverotto seems to have gone to Rome himself to warn him of his planned takeover in Fermo, rather than sending an envoy. Nor would Matteo have encountered Leonardo da Vinci at Cesare Borgia's court at this time, as Leonardo only entered Borgia's service a little later, in August 1502.

There are other points in the novel where I have made adjustments to the historical timeline to serve my fictional ends. I have slightly lengthened the time between the battle of Calmazzo and Borgia's treaty with the conspirators, and compressed events between the election of Julius II and Borgia's departure from Ostia. I have also shaved a few years off Liverotto's life, representing him as born around 1475, rather than 1473, in order to bring his age a little closer to that of my characters Matteo and Dino.

In addition to such deliberate manipulations, I have also freely invented within the interstices of the historical record. A minor case of this is my account in Chapter 6 of Liverotto using his dealings with the besieged citizens during the siege of Camerino to get his hands on the Fermo rebels who had taken refuge in the city. This is pure speculation on my part, although it is true that the ruler of Camerino, Giulio Cesare Varano, had offered shelter to the rebels, and that Liverotto was accused by the papal commissar overseeing the siege of secretly supplying the besieged city with food.

A larger instance of historical invention in the novel is my account of Giuliano della Rovere's spy network. Although it is not at all improbable that a man of della Rovere's wealth and political ambition had some kind of system of informants, all the details given here are purely fictional. Where Felice della Rovere's role as spymaster is concerned, I have profited from the fact that Felice's life prior to the time of her father's accession to the papacy in 1503 is almost entirely undocumented, as Caroline Murphy acknowledges in her 2005 biography, *The Pope's Daughter: The Extraordinary Life of Felice della Rovere* (Oxford: Oxford University Press). The only hint we have of Felice's activities during the Borgia years is supplied by an anecdote in Castiglione's *Book of the Courtier* (3, 49), which tells of her on one occasion traveling by sea to her father's home in Savona and fearing that she is being chased by ships sent by Pope Alexander VI. This intriguing biographical fragment always left me with an image of Felice as something of a female Renaissance James Bond.

Where my representation of the Borgia family is concerned, I have attempted to tread some kind of middle path between the traditional "black legend," on the one hand, and, on the other, modern revisionist scholarship, which tends to dismiss many of the more scurrilous and chilling anecdotes associated with the family as slanders elaborated in the campaign of vilification orchestrated by Julius II after the death of Alexander VI. The notion that the Borgias were responsible for the death of the wealthy Cardinal Michiel in April 1503 is almost certainly an invention of Julius's propaganda machine, and I duly report a rumor to this effect in Chapter 20 purely as rumor. On the other hand, I could not resist giving the status of fact within the novel to one of the most scurrilous episodes of all concerning the Borgias: the extraordinary sex game involving chestnuts that I describe in Chapter 14. The details of this derive from the records of Alexander VI's master of ceremonies, Johannes Burchard, who records this spectacle as having taken place in the papal court on October 30, 1501.

I have taken particular liberties with the historical record where the episode of the death of Alexander VI is concerned (Chapter 22). The severe illness that struck the Pope and his son shortly after dining with Cardinal Castellesi was often attributed by early commentators to poison. A popular theory, mentioned in the novel, is that Alexander and Cesare accidentally poisoned themselves while attempting to murder the enormously wealthy Castellesi, whose estate—like Cardinal Michiel's earlier in the year—would have devolved to the Church after his death. This story is now generally thought to be part of Julius II's edifice of slander. Most modern commentators now attribute the death of Alexander to malaria, which was rife in Rome at the time.

I have here resurrected the murder hypothesis, for the purposes of the fiction of the novel, although I attribute it to political motives—specifically, to Florentine fears of Alexander's territorial ambitions. Although the operative details of the murder plot in the novel (fanatical friars, rings with hidden poison compartments) are obviously fantastical, the political component of the plot is relatively plausible. Florence was within the Borgia sights; the pope's alliance with France had held him back from pursuing aggression in Tuscany in 1502; rumors were circulating in summer 1503 of Alexander's intention to abandon this French alliance for one with Spain. It is also true, as I suggest here, that any Borgia attack on Florence would probably have been conducted in collaboration with the exiled Medici family, who retained the loyalty of an important segment of the Florentine elite.

My description of the salon of Cardinal Giovanni de' Medici is one of the most purely fanciful parts of this novel, although I have drawn on contemporary sources for my portrayal of Giovanni's character and erudition. The future Pope Leo X's joviality and hedonism are well documented, and are memorably captured in his famous—though probably apocryphal—reported quip: "Since God has given us the papacy, let us enjoy it." Leo's sexual proclivities have been much discussed, with many commentators concluding that his principal inclinations were homosexual. Whatever the case, he was certainly more discreet about his tastes than I portray him here, at least during his early career as cardinal, if the historian Francesco Guicciardini could speak of Leo as having a reputation for chastity at the time when he ascended the papal throne.

My representations of the two most famous figures in this novel, Leonardo da Vinci and Niccolò Machiavelli, differ in character. In the case of Leonardo, I have yielded to the temptation of a caricatural representation, emphasizing the personal eccentricities that struck his contemporaries. My representation of Machiavelli aims at a more accurate portrait. Although most modern readers, especially outside Italy, know Machiavelli exclusively through his political writings, where he emerges as relatively sober, a far more witty and outrageous figure is on display in Machiavelli's comedies and in his extraordinary private letters, which deserve to be far better known to general readers. I have tried to capture something of this "other" Machiavelli in my representation of him here.

Moving from the more public and political elements of the novel to its more private, domestic and romantic elements, it probably does not need to be stated that the main character, Matteo da Fermo, is invented, as are his brother Dino and most of the lower-status characters associated with him, both in Fermo and Rome. The Fogliani family are documented, although I have taken a few liberties with the historical record, making Montanina degli Ottoni, Giovanni Fogliani's wife, a second, late marriage, so that Nicolosa Fogliani is her stepdaughter, rather than her daughter, and Giovanni's son Gennaro is a child at the time of the murder, rather than an adolescent, as was the case. Nothing is known of Nicolosa Fogliani's life after the massacre of 1502, in which her husband, sons, brother, and father were killed. It is possible that she entered the convent of Saint Catherine of Siena in Fabriano, where Montanina degli Ottoni is recorded as having ended her days.

Where the sexual mores portrayed in the novel are concerned, my descriptions are broadly accurate. Although the courtesans depicted here, Angelica and Camilla, are invented and do not correspond to particular historical figures, I have drawn on contemporary depictions of figures such as the legendary Imperia, the mistress of Julius II's banker Agostino Chigi, as well as on Pietro Aretino's later satirical dialogues on courtesans, from the 1530s. The term *cortigiana* was just coming into use at the time when this novel is set, to designate a prostitute distinguished by her culture and refined manners, and filling the same social role as the ancient Greek figure of the *hetaera*. Although Venice later became famous for its courtesans, the tradition had its origins in papal Rome (the name "courtesan", *cortigiana*, originally alluded to these women's relationship with the papal court). A good study of the phenomenon of the courtesan in Renaissance Italy, though it is focused on Venice and a later period, is Margaret Rosenthal's *The Honest Courtesan: Veronica Franco, Citizen and Writer in Sixteenth-Century Venice* (Chicago: University of Chicago Press, 1992). Tessa Storey's *Carnal Commerce in Counter-Reformation Rome* (Cambridge: Cambridge University Press, 2008) is useful on the Roman context, though it again focuses on a later, and culturally very different, period.

The representation of male same-sex relationships in the novel draws on contemporary scholarship such as Michael Rocke's excellent *Forbidden Friendships: Homosexuality and Male Culture in Renaissance Florence* (Oxford: Oxford University Press, 1998). While homosexual activity was officially considered a grave sin, and could be punished severely, even by death in some cases, it was widely tolerated in practice and spoken about quite openly, especially in erudite circles where the model of ancient Greek culture was familiar. Especially common as a model and relatively socially accepted was sex between men and adolescent boys, in which the older partner took an active role and the younger a passive. Anything deviating from this model was regarded as more problematic and was more likely to be pursued by the law. Historians of sexuality often argue that the modern notion of sexual identity is inappropriate applied to this historical context, in that many men experienced homosexual activity in their youth without conceiving of themselves as "homosexual" or "bisexual." This is a useful caveat when approaching the period, though literary evidence does give some evidence of the existence of a self-conscious homosexual subculture (Guido Ruggiero, "Marriage, love, sex, and civic morality," in James Grantham Turner, ed., *Sexuality and Gender in Early Modern Europe* (Cambridge: Cambridge University Press, 1993)).

As the novel illustrates, a great and unwelcome novelty in Renaissance Italian sexual culture was syphilis, which was first registered in the 1490s. Initially, the sexually transmitted character of "the French disease" was not widely recognized, and, at the time the novel is set, numerous competing theories of its origins and cure were current. For the early diagnosis history of the disease, in the episode involving Angelica, I have relied on Jon Arrizabalaga, "Medical Responses to the 'French Disease' in Europe at the Turn of the Sixteenth Century," in Kevin Patrick Siena, ed. *Sins of the Flesh: Responding to the French Disease in Early Modern Europe* (Toronto: Centre for Renaissance and Reformation Studies, 2005). A good general history is Jon Arrizabalaga, John Henderson, and Roger French, *The Great Pox: The French Disease in Renaissance Europe* (New Haven: Yale University Press, 1997).

Fermo, where part of this novel is set, is a beautiful city, but it does not retain the medieval aspect so familiar from towns in Umbria and Tuscany. A building frenzy in the sixteenth to eighteenth centuries left the city far more monumental in scale than it would have been at the time when this novel is set. I have relied for my idea of the fifteenth-century topography of the city on Francesco Pirani's useful study of medieval Fermo, cited above. Only one concrete relic of elite domestic architecture survives from this earlier period in Fermo—precisely Palazzo Fogliani, in Largo Fogliani, where the protagonist of this novel was raised.

Made in the USA
Middletown, DE
25 August 2018